KINGDOM OF BEAUTY

THE KINGDOM TALES BOOK ONE

DEBORAH GRACE WHITE

LUMINANT PUBLICATIONS

KINGDOM OF BEAUTY: A RETELLING OF BEAUTY AND THE BEAST

By Deborah Grace White

Kingdom of Beauty:
A Retelling of Beauty and the Beast
The Kingdom Tales Book One

Copyright © 2021 by Deborah Grace White

First edition (v1.2) published in 2021
by Luminant Publications

ISBN: 978-1-925898-67-5

Luminant Publications
PO Box 305
Greenacres, South Australia 5086

http://www.deborahgracewhite.com

Cover Design by Karri Klawiter
Map illustration by Rebecca E. Paavo

For Annabeth
From the very start, full of beauty and full of joy

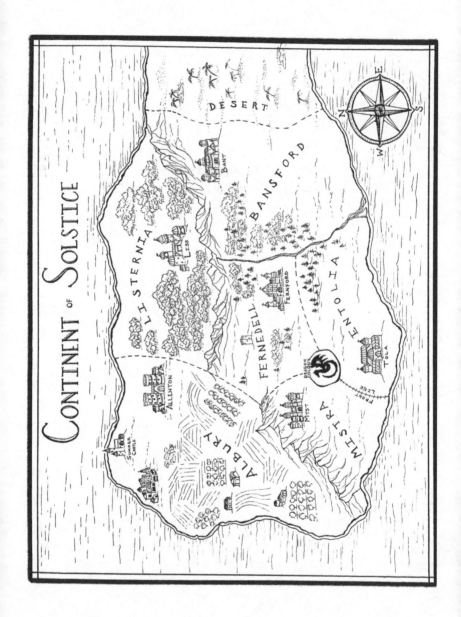

PROLOGUE

The dragon let out an excited huff at the mass growing steadily larger before him. It was land, without a doubt. And not a small island, either. This was a continent.

After two weeks of flight, with hardly a solid place to sleep, Rekavidur was more weary than he'd known a dragon could be. He was beyond glad, not just at the prospect of feeling land beneath his talons again, but to have evidence that his search had been worthwhile.

As he drew closer to the land mass, the beat of his wings faltered in amazement, before picking back up again. It was no longer just the promise of a resting place that excited him. His senses were aflame with his discovery.

He reached out instinctively, eager to share his find with his kin. But his questing communication faded into nothing, and he sagged momentarily on his weary wings. He had forgotten that he was cut off. Perhaps the farsight of an older and more powerful dragon could span that distance, but he was unable to communicate with, or even see, his colony.

Never mind. He had an endless period of time in which to

return to his home and share all that he had seen. They would not be overly curious. It wasn't in the nature of most dragons to explore. That was why he had left, and left alone, after all.

Rekavidur turned his attention back to the land mass, growing ever larger. He may not have anyone to share it with at present, but his own excitement was increasing with the approaching shoreline. The signature of the magic was clear, and stronger than he'd ever felt it outside his own colony. He didn't know the name of this new continent, but one thing he now knew for certain.

He'd found them. Dragons lived here.

CHAPTER ONE

Felicity

"How much for this one?"

"Ah! You have a discerning eye."

The saleswoman's enthusiasm almost made Felicity regret the question. She would have a hard time getting out of buying the trinket now. But it really had caught her fancy.

"That one is extremely rare," the woman gushed. "Wrought from the finest—"

"Not to be rude," said Felicity, cutting off the sales pitch with the hint of a laugh, "but how much?"

The woman didn't seem to be offended, her eyes twinkling as she looked Felicity over. "For you, my dear, two silver coins."

Felicity raised an eyebrow. "Seems steep for a trinket."

The woman smiled. "This is no mere bauble, child. It will help you find what you're looking for."

"Will it?" Felicity smiled indulgently. "How's that?"

"Well," the woman said, spreading out a shapely hand. She obviously hadn't had a life of hard labor compared to many of the merchant women Felicity had met. "It's helped me find you, hasn't it?"

"Very prettily said." Felicity couldn't help the amused smile that curved her lips. There was something endearing about the woman's inability to hide how much she wanted Felicity to buy the item. In her experience, most merchants adopted a disinterested approach when they really wanted to sell something.

She glanced at the trinket, admiring the way the afternoon sunshine reflected softly on its burnished surface.

"Copper, is it?"

"That's right," the merchant woman said comfortably.

Felicity nodded, her attraction to the object fighting with her good sense. The rough metal sphere seemed to serve no purpose but decoration, its twists and curves making it look like a half-untangled knot of rope, and forming no identifiable shape. It wasn't like her to be so drawn to something with no practical purpose. She couldn't afford to be extravagant.

She started to turn away, but again she felt the tug of attraction, and found herself turning back to the object almost against her will. A thought flashed through her mind, and as soon as it occurred to her, she became convinced.

"And it has magic, does it?" she asked, just as casually as she'd inquired about the material. "It's an artifact?"

The merchant stilled, her eyes thoughtful as she searched Felicity's face. "Are you an investigator?"

Felicity snorted. "An investigator? Do I look like an investigator?"

"I don't know," the woman said cautiously. "What do investigators usually look like?"

"Your guess is as good as mine," laughed Felicity. She looked the older woman over in some amusement. "You do realize you're in Albury, don't you? Sure, we tend to be a little suspicious of magic here, ever since the whole 'crown prince banished by a curse' situation. But it's not outlawed. This isn't Bansford."

"Doesn't hurt to be careful," sniffed the woman. She obviously realized that Felicity was waiting expectantly, and she let out her breath in a huff. "Yes, it's an artifact. So you see it's actually a bargain at two silver pieces."

"What does it do?" Felicity asked, turning it over in her hand, liking the feel of its ridges and curves. "You said it would help me find what I'm looking for?"

"That's right," said the merchant eagerly. "It helps the bearer not only to find, but to be found."

"That's...perfect," said Felicity, smiling in satisfaction. "I'll take it."

She handed over the coins, amusement again rising when she noted how the saleswoman was bouncing on the balls of her feet.

"Your delight isn't convincing me that I got it for a bargain," she said. Her tone was reproachful, but her heart wasn't really in it, her eyes twinkling in spite of her words.

"Oh, you did," the woman said brightly. "I'm just pleased to have found a buyer who values the beauty of this particular talisman. I've been traveling around the kingdom for quite some time, and no one's expressed any interest in it before now."

"Well, I have a discerning eye, as you said." Felicity gave her a final smile.

"Indeed you do," the woman said, her twinkling eyes not matching her solemn tone.

Felicity turned the object over in her hand as she walked home. She found it as appealing as ever, but she still felt a little guilty. She had been intending to buy shoes when she hurried out at word of the unexpected arrival of the merchant caravan. She should really have turned immediately for home again when she discovered there was no cobbler among the merchants. But the day was pleasant, and it had been too tempting to stroll through the camp, examining the other wares. She had certainly never intended to spend two silver coins on something that would probably prove useless.

A sudden shadow passed overhead as she made her way out of town, and she glanced up. She stopped for a moment, captured by the rare sight of a dragon wheeling overhead. The beasts weren't common in this part of the kingdom. Apparently they saw them fairly often further south, closer to the border with Mistra, but Felicity had only observed one a handful of times. She would have liked a closer look, but the creature had already passed by, only a glint of yellow and purple visible from this distance.

She looked back down, enjoying the slanting orange light of the late afternoon. The town was pretty at this time of day, although Felicity was finding it more and more difficult to appreciate its quaint charm. The further she traveled from childhood, the less picturesque—and the more confining—the village seemed to become.

Her eyes glazed over as she tried to picture her old home in the capital, Allenton. The haziest memories flitted through her mind every now and then, but she could never hold on to them. Just like the fleeting images of her mother. She supposed it wasn't surprising. She had only been four.

She sighed, her mind drawing up one of the few clear memories, that of her mother reading to her in a library. She could picture the room quite clearly. All those books. She had been far too young to appreciate how much knowledge she had access to. Not like the rusticated corner of the kingdom where her father had banished the family, where the only books were the ones she'd brought with her.

She had reached home, and she shook her head to clear her sudden melancholy. Perhaps one day, when she was settled somewhere more interesting, she would realize the advantages of this rural nowhere, and reflect that once again she hadn't appreciated what was before her until it was gone. The idea seemed more like the moral in a fable than any likely reality, and she chuckled at herself as she pushed open the door.

"Little Felicity, always laughing about something."

Felicity stiffened at the voice, working to keep her features neutral.

"Kurt," she said, turning reluctantly. "Good afternoon."

She nodded tightly to the handsome young man lounging against her kitchen table as if he owned the place. Her gaze slid past him to her brother, shooting him a reproachful look that Ambrose ignored. He never had much patience with her complaints about him bringing his obnoxious friend around so much.

"Fliss." Ambrose nodded a careless greeting, his attention on the crossbow he was mending.

"Good afternoon? It's really closer to evening now, my dear Felicity," Kurt corrected her, a smirk spreading across his face. "Surely you haven't been wandering over the countryside alone?"

Felicity kept her temper with an effort. She hated it when he called her "dear". She had dim memories of her father calling her mother that, and it felt like sacrilege to hear it from Kurt of all people.

"I was walking home, Kurt, hardly wandering over the countryside. And it's not late at all." *And it's no affair of yours,* she added silently.

"If I'd known, I would have been thrilled to see you safely to your charming little cottage," the broad-shouldered villager reproached her.

If the mocking glance Kurt threw around the family home had been intended to embarrass Felicity, it failed. Instead she stifled a snort and fought the urge to roll her eyes. Kurt seemed incapable of having any conversation in which he didn't make at least one veiled reference to the fact that his was the largest house in town. It was tempting, of course, to tell him that he was only too welcome to remove himself from their humble dwelling. But she could hardly kick him out when Ambrose had brought him home.

"She's fine, Kurt," said Ambrose impatiently. He raised his crossbow in one hand. "I'm done, let's go."

"What's the rush, Ambrose?" Kurt said, still wearing his smirk. "Surely I can spare a minute to talk to the prettiest girl in town." He spoke in the tone of one bestowing a prize, his eyes fixed on Felicity with uncomfortable focus. "You are, you know. The prettiest girl in town. I was just telling the baker's daughter that yesterday."

Great, Felicity griped internally, uninterested in having any role in the petty dramas of the village's young people. *Now she'll be selling us stale bread for a fortnight.*

It was such a shame that Kurt was determined to waste his oily compliments where they weren't appreciated, when most of the girls in town would trample their closest friend to have him direct his attention their way. It was a little hard to watch them making such fools of themselves, sometimes. They were like a bunch of clucking chickens, over-awed by the presence of a lone rooster strutting his way through their barnyard.

The thought tickled her fancy, her irritation swallowed up in her ever-ready humor. A chuckle bubbled over before she could stop it.

Kurt narrowed his eyes, looking unimpressed by her reception of his compliment.

"You know," he said, with a hint of reproof. "*I* find it charming, of course, but there are some who think your tendency to laugh at everything is unattractive. They say it's a sign you think you're better than everyone else."

"It is a little rude, Felicity," Ambrose said, shooting an apologetic look at his friend.

Felicity's mirth disappeared instantly. The thought that Ambrose was embarrassed by her behavior toward Kurt, instead of the other way around, was maddening.

"Go ahead, Ambrose," Kurt said, his eyes still on Felicity. "I'll catch up."

Ambrose hesitated for only a moment before obeying, and Felicity's irritation grew. Ambrose's hero-worship of Kurt was even harder to watch than all the rest.

"What do you want, Kurt?" she asked shortly, the moment Ambrose was out of the room.

"I want to help you, of course," said Kurt, his tone self-satisfied.

"How generous," Felicity said flatly.

"Well, I think it is," Kurt agreed simply. "You don't know how to make the most of what you have. You could be the queen of this town. You just need a little polishing. And I can help you with that."

He stepped closer, and Felicity's heart beat unpleasantly quickly. He smelled like leather and sweat, and his nearness made her uncomfortable.

"Thanks for the offer," she said, "but I don't want to be a queen."

He gave a superior smile. "But you *would* like to eat venison four times a week." He didn't phrase it as a question, and his tone was maddeningly smug. "We do, you know." He stepped even closer. "I know for a fact that your father doesn't provide that for you. Not anymore."

Felicity stepped backward, her eyes narrowing at this step over the line.

"I've always considered that a good meal is less about the food and more about the company," she said bitingly.

She didn't give him a chance to respond, turning on her heel and hurrying out of the cottage's back door. Kurt's persistence was becoming a problem, and she wasn't entirely sure how to solve it.

She didn't pause once clear of the house, eager to put some distance between her and Kurt. She picked up her pace as she made her way through a small copse of trees. Glancing back, she let out a sigh of release when she saw that the town was obscured by the thickening trunks.

The copse stretched up the side of a hill, and Felicity's breath was soon coming a little faster. She had done the climb many times, however, and she knew it was worth it. After about twenty minutes, she emerged from the trees, her steps more eager as she covered the final grassy stretch to reach the hill's summit.

She crested the rise, breathing in deeply as she looked out northward. Green, grassy hills stretched out before her, dotted here and there with small clumps of trees. A glint in the distance drew her eyes to the ocean, only a few hours' ride away. She could faintly smell the salt on the breeze that tugged at her copper hair. She reached back, pulling her braid loose and letting her hair dance idly around her. It was too impractical to wear it down when doing housework, but there was something freeing about setting it loose from its restraints when there were no witnesses.

Her thoughts were drawn suddenly to the dragon she'd seen overhead a short time before. For a moment, she allowed herself to imagine what it would be like to be able to just fly away, perhaps even to see the dragon colony to the south east. Not that she was likely to get that privilege. It wasn't located in her kingdom of Albury. The colony's home was nestled at the point where the borders of Fernedell, Mistra, and Entolia met. And even people from those kingdoms didn't generally get a glimpse of the colony itself. Very few humans did, from what she'd heard.

She was still lost in these daydreams when a sudden shadow

was cast over the hill. She glanced up, expecting a cloud, and gasped in shock at the sight of a dark shape descending from the sky. Her loose hair was blown frantically back by an intense, abrupt wind, and then the creature landed right in front of her.

Felicity's mouth fell open in a soundless exclamation. She stumbled back several steps, losing her footing and falling hard on her rear. She sat in the grass, staring up at the beast before her with eyes that felt like they were bulging out of her head.

A dragon. It was an actual, living, close-enough-to-touch, dragon.

It was more than three times her height, every inch of it covered in yellow scales that showed a flash of purple when it moved. It had an enormous reptilian head, with bearded ridges on each side. Its legs were as thick as young trees, and its taloned front feet sat on the ground between its haunches in a posture similar to a cat. Felicity tried not to stare at its talons, which looked like they could spear her through. She swallowed nervously as her eyes traveled from its back all the way down to the end of its tail, following the line of sharp triangular plates that jutted out from its scales. The creature's wings were folded against its back, but it nevertheless looked enormous.

Felicity was still frozen in shock, wondering if she should run or stand her ground. She'd just been telling herself that she wanted to see dragons up close, but she hadn't meant quite this close. She tried to remember all she'd been taught about dragons. It wasn't much.

"Greetings, young maiden," the dragon said, breaking a prolonged silence. It waited, but seeing that Felicity was still too stunned to speak, it continued. "It seems I startled you."

"G-greetings, Mighty Beast," Felicity gasped, pulling herself together. She had some vague memory that formalities were important to dragons. "Please, don't trouble yourself. I'm not injured."

"I wasn't troubled," said the dragon calmly.

In spite of her stupefaction, Felicity's lips twitched slightly. "Well, that's...good."

The dragon tilted its head to one side, studying her with interest. "You appear to be discomposed by my presence. Are dragons not common in this land? Do they not intermingle freely with humans?"

"Well," Felicity managed, pushing herself cautiously to her feet as she struggled to gather her thoughts, "they're not especially common in this kingdom. Their colony is south east of here, between three other kingdoms. Dragons occasionally fly through our skies, but they don't often stop to...to chat," she finished lamely.

The dragon watched her from unblinking orb-like eyes.

"I've never seen a dragon this close before," Felicity went on, feeling the need to fill the unnerving silence. "You're so...huge."

She instantly cringed at the awkward words, but the dragon gave a huff of what seemed to be amusement.

"It is clear that you have little experience with dragons," it said. "I am in fact small for one of my kind."

Felicity shook her head slightly, thinking how overwhelming an even larger dragon would be. She cast around again for her limited knowledge of dragon lore. "That means you're young, right?" she asked cautiously. "Dragons get bigger indefinitely as they age?"

The dragon inclined his head in a silent acknowledgment.

"What is your name, maiden?" he asked, and Felicity flushed as she again remembered the importance of manners when speaking with a dragon.

"My name is Felicity," she said hurriedly.

The dragon inclined his head again. "And I am Rekavidur." His penetrating eyes were locked on her face. "Are you a power-wielder, Felicity?"

Felicity blinked in confusion. "A power-wielder?"

"A human born with magic in their blood," Rekavidur clarified. "Who has an innate ability to exercise power."

"Oh, you mean enchanters and enchantresses. No, I'm not one of those."

"I see." The dragon examined her in silence for another minute. "Where I come from, they are called power-wielders."

Felicity frowned. "Where you come from? You mean the dragon colony?"

"Naturally I come from a dragon colony," said Rekavidur, sounding like he was on the edge of losing patience with her human obtuseness. "But it is not the one to the south east of here. I come from a different land, many days' flight across the sea."

Felicity's mouth fell open. "A different land? With another dragon colony?"

"Two dragon colonies, actually," the dragon said airily, and Felicity's astonishment grew. "But that is not to the purpose," he continued. He leaned his enormous head forward and gave a sniff, like a dog seeking a scent. "You are sure you're not one of these...enchantresses?"

"Very sure," said Felicity faintly.

The dragon's head was still extended toward her, and he gave another long sniff. "Hm," was all he said, but his eyes were narrowed as they searched her face.

She shifted nervously, completely at a loss for what to say.

"The flavor of the magic in this land is unfamiliar to me," mused Rekavidur. "I must explore more if I am to find answers, I suppose." He withdrew his head, greatly to Felicity's relief. "Do you live near here?" he asked.

Felicity nodded. "My home is in the village just down there," she said, gesturing behind her.

The dragon's gaze followed the direction of her pointing

finger. "And are you familiar with the surrounding area?" he asked.

"Only within a few hours' walk," Felicity confessed. "I haven't left my village since I was a small child."

"I see," said the dragon, sounding faintly disappointed. "Then it is unlikely you will be able to answer my questions regarding the anomaly nearby." He crouched slightly, as if preparing to take off, then paused. "You are absolutely certain you are not an enchantress?"

"Very much so," Felicity assured him.

It was impossible to read the dragon's expression, although it was clear he wasn't entirely satisfied with her answer.

"Good day then, Felicity," he said in his gravelly voice. He gave her a cryptic look. "Perhaps we will meet again."

Felicity barely had time to return the civility before Rekavidur took to the air once more, the wind created by his departure causing her skirt to billow dramatically around her. He disappeared with the impossible speed of his kind, and she stood blinking at the already empty sky.

Had that really just happened? Why had he thought she was an enchantress? She wished the dragon hadn't been in such a rush to leave. She would have liked to ask some of her many questions. But what could she have said? *Don't go, you're the most interesting thing that's ever happened to me!* True, of course, but probably not sufficient to convince the dragon to stick around.

Her mind full of the strange encounter, she hurried back to her house. She had forgotten all about Kurt's unwanted advances, but when she stepped through the back door again, memory came rushing back, and she felt a flash of belated anger. There was no sign of Ambrose, clearly still out with his odious friend, so she made her way to the back room her father used as a simple study.

There was no response to her knock, but that didn't surprise her. She pushed the door open, smiling at the familiar sight of her father staring absently out the little window. The ledgers in front of him were abandoned, the inkwell dry.

"There you are, Father," she said.

"Felicity." He turned from the window, greeting her with a warm, if weary, smile. "I didn't hear you come in."

Of course he didn't. She leaned against the edge of his desk, tapping her foot on the floor. She was full of suppressed energy after her incredible encounter with the dragon. Naturally, her father didn't notice her unusual demeanor. Watching his face, she felt the excitement leak slowly away. Her father wouldn't understand her enthusiasm at having been within talon's reach of a magical and undeniably powerful creature. He would be afraid she'd brought danger on them all through the interaction. If she was going to tell him about it, she'd do better to wait until some time had passed, to convince him no attack was imminent.

So instead, she forced herself to raise a topic she found much more awkward.

"You didn't hear us speaking out there before, Father? Ambrose brought his friend around again. Kurt." She fidgeted with a paperweight. "The one we talked about."

"Did he?" her father asked vaguely. "That's nice."

Felicity sighed, but didn't bother pushing the point. It was no surprise to her that her father had apparently already forgotten her appeal to him about Kurt. It had been an uncomfortable conversation for both of them, and her father had probably put it from his mind as quickly as possible.

"Was it a good market?" he asked. "Did you find some shoes?"

She blinked. She'd forgotten all about the market in the events that followed. "No, I'm afraid not," she replied lightly. "You'll have to make do a little longer."

"That's fine," he said, rifling absently through the papers in front of him. "I don't see what's wrong with them, anyway."

Felicity chuckled. "I'm sure you don't, Father, but shoes aren't supposed to have holes in them, you know."

He shrugged. "They still get me where I need to go."

Felicity shook her head indulgently. "That's because you don't go anywhere. Were you this hopeless when you were a wildly successful merchant, or did you have fully intact shoes back then?"

She had expected him to laugh off her teasing—for all his regrets, he'd never shown much sign of missing the luxuries he could once afford—but instead his face fell.

"I was successful, you know," he said with a sigh. "Perhaps not *wildly* successful, but successful. I wish I still was. I wish I could give you and your brother the kind of life you—"

"None of that, Father," Felicity protested, regretting her light-hearted words. "I was only teasing you. We do fine."

"Ambrose doesn't think so," said her father, smiling slightly. "He wants a new crossbow, and—"

Felicity cut him off with a snort. "I'm sure he does." She shook her head, unimpressed. "If he wants coins for a new crossbow, why doesn't he take up work at one of the farms? I know for a fact that there are at least three looking for laborers. He could work for his living, instead of being lost in dreams." An ungenerous part of her heart wanted to say the same words to her father, but she couldn't bring herself to do it. Unlike Ambrose, he'd already been brought too low by life's blows.

"Oh, well, you know your brother," sighed her father. "I don't think he'll do that." He brightened. "And it's not true that I don't go anywhere, you know. I'm going to the regional market next week. You never know, maybe I'll come back with excellent news."

Felicity hid a groan, trying to keep the impatience from her voice. "Father, do you really think it's wise to go to the expense and effort every time? None of your inquiries have turned up anything, in all these years."

"Of course it's worth it," her father said stubbornly. "When our fleet went down, I thought we'd lost everything. But the report said that one ship made it. That cargo must be somewhere."

"It was a rumor, Father, not a report," Felicity said gently. "And hiring strangers to investigate it hasn't yielded any results."

"Not yet," her father corrected her.

Felicity sighed. "Father, hiring men from a distance, getting them to report to you at the regional market...you must see that you have no way to keep them accountable. Who knows if they're even making inquiries? If you want to look into the matter, I really think you'll have to go to Allenton yourself." She stood up straighter. "Perhaps we could all go."

"Certainly not," said her father, his voice uncharacteristically sharp. "That's three days' journey just to get there. The expense would be too great."

"But you would save money by making the inquiries yourself," Felicity said eagerly, warming to the theme.

"We are not going to Allenton, Felicity." Her father cut her off, his brow dark.

Felicity opened her mouth to protest, but one look at her father's face changed her mind. He was attempting to look stern, but she could see the pain behind his expression.

"I just would love to see our old home," she said quietly. "I wish I could remember it better. I wish I could remember *her* better."

Her father looked up, his face softening but the pain increasing as he reached for her hand.

"I wish you could too," he said. "She was wonderful." He

smiled. "And if you want to know what she looked like, you need only find a looking glass, you know. You're her image."

Felicity was silent. She had heard him say so many times before, but she didn't remind him. He had a faraway look in his eye that told her his mind was elsewhere.

"You're just like her in temperament too, of course," he said, suddenly returning to her. "Always laughing, my tinkling little bell."

She smiled absently at the old nickname. "I was thinking of her today. Remembering, actually. She used to read to me in a library, didn't she? Where was that, exactly?"

"There are several libraries open to the public in Allenton," her father said, his tone decidedly evasive.

Felicity narrowed her eyes as she studied him, but held her peace. There was something hidden behind his words, no doubt about it, but she had learned from experience that asking the question directly was not the best way to get information from him.

"Why did we have to leave?" she asked instead.

"You know the answer to that, Felicity," said her father uncomfortably. "We were already struggling to maintain our home after we lost the fleet. Then your mother died, and I knew we needed a fresh start."

"Yes, I know," said Felicity, trying to speak delicately. "But," she gestured out the workshop's one small window, "...here? Couldn't we have just moved to another district of the capital?"

Her father's brow darkened again. "The capital isn't so wonderful, Felicity. Don't be deceived by the glamour of castles and nobles and such. King Justus never cared about his people. We're better off far away from the royals and their like."

Felicity raised an eyebrow. "King Justus has been dead for ten years, Father."

Her father shrugged. "And what makes you think Prince

Justin is any better? Would an enchantress have put him under a curse if he was?"

"I suppose not," Felicity acknowledged. "But I still wish we could've stayed in Allenton." She sighed. "It's been fourteen years, and I still feel out of place here."

"Nonsense," said her father vaguely, his attention back on his ledgers. "We blend in just fine."

Felicity was silent, her expression unusually serious as she studied her father's profile. Was he really so oblivious? More likely he just shied away from facing an uncomfortable truth, as was his way. He wasn't exactly one to keep a sharp eye on his surroundings.

"Oh, I almost forgot!" she said suddenly. "I didn't find shoes, but I did get you something else." She dug the artifact out of a pocket, holding it up. "One of the merchants was selling it. She was a little strange, but I don't think she was lying to me." Felicity lowered her voice slightly. "She claims it has magic. She said it will help you to find things, and to be found."

Her father had been looking at the object with interest, but at her explanation, his gaze passed to her, his expression becoming unimpressed. "Fliss," he said, in a long-suffering tone. "I'm not a lost child, always wandering off."

"True," she agreed with a twinkle. "You're not a child."

He looked like he might protest further, but she slipped it into his hand before he could speak, pressing a light kiss to the top of his head for good measure.

"Carry it when you go to the market, Father? Just to humor me?"

He sighed, but he took hold of it, and his expression was indulgent as he looked up at her. "For you, my dear, anything." He studied it in silence for a moment. "It is beautifully made, isn't it? And there's something about it...a weight. I've never actually handled an artifact before."

"Nor have I," Felicity said, leaning her elbows on top of a high-backed chair. "I thought it was beautiful, as well. I kept coming back to it." She grimaced. "I'm afraid it was quite expensive. But I'll make up the shortfall over the next few weeks." She sent him an apologetic look. "We might just have to have more beans and less meat for a while."

"Oh certainly, whatever you think," her father said vaguely, slipping the artifact into his pocket and returning to his papers. "I have no doubt you'll manage beautifully—you always do."

Felicity regarded him in silence for a moment, before releasing a sigh she couldn't quite keep in. No matter what she'd said to Kurt, she couldn't deny that the idea of meat every day of the week was appealing.

"Yes, Father, I'll manage."

CHAPTER TWO

Justin

J ustin prowled down the corridor, his robe swirling with his agitated stride.

"Disbanding the royal guard? What was he thinking?" he growled to no one in particular.

A pointedly cleared throat made him bite back a sigh. He hadn't realized Stewart was so close, or he wouldn't have spoken his disgruntled thoughts aloud. The middle aged servant had known him all his life. He showed none of the hesitation most of Justin's staff seemed to feel about offering an opinion when their master was in a black mood.

"I imagine, Your Highness," Stewart said, with a hint of reproach, "that your uncle was thinking it was hard to justify the expense of a fully staffed royal guard when there have been no royals to be guarded for...quite some time."

"Two years, four months, and ten days," Justin snapped. He gave a grunt. "Not that anyone's counting."

"Certainly not, Your Highness," said Stewart, with dignity.

"But my uncle is still acting as regent," Justin said, abruptly returning to the topic at hand. "He's basically a royal. Surely he wants the royal guard to protect him?"

"Perhaps he called in his own guards from his estate," Stewart suggested.

"Perhaps." Justin narrowed his eyes. He would have to check it out. It wouldn't be ideal if so. A little suspicious, even.

"If only that blasted mirror allowed communication both ways," he grumbled, for about the twelve hundredth time. "If I'm to be robbed of my voice, it's almost worse to be able to see what's happening in the rest of the kingdom. Sometimes I wish that old hag had never given it to me."

"Your Highness," said Stewart, the reproach more than just hinted now. "May I remind you that it was calling the enchantress such names that got you—and indeed all of us—into this situation in the first place?"

Justin felt a familiar prickle of guilt at the reminder that all his dependents were suffering with him. He pushed it down ruthlessly, knowing he couldn't afford to let it get a foothold. He drew a breath, remembering what his father had taught him. He was a prince—who should be a king by now—and it wasn't his job to carry the burdens of servants.

Besides, most days he felt like he was an inch from drowning in his own problems. In his more honest moments, he had to admit to himself that he was terrified that if he took on even the tiniest bit of his companions' grief and frustration as well, he wouldn't be able to stay afloat.

"Were you looking for me?" he growled curtly, feeling the need to cover his moment of vulnerability, however internal it had been.

Stewart cleared his throat, and Justin looked at him apprehensively. It was never a good sign when Stewart opened his communication with a throat clearing. Either another scold or some bad news was coming.

"Yes, Your Highness, I was." The servant's voice was carefully flat. "The head gardener has just given me his daily report on the rose garden."

Justin came to an abrupt stop, his brow lowering as he turned to his companion. "And?" he pressed, the sound more growl than voice now.

Stewart coughed delicately. "I am happy to report that no more blooms have perished, Your Highness."

Justin wasn't fooled. "But?" he prompted.

Stewart sighed. "But there are now at least a dozen roses dropping petals. The gardener said that the garden beds are littered with them."

"He didn't remove them, did he?" Justin snapped, his expression growing stormy.

"Of course not, Your Highness," Stewart responded, his offense clear at the suggestion that anyone in his domain would dare to step outside their instructions. "He is aware of your orders that no one is to touch the rose garden."

Justin nodded, hoping he looked regal rather than relieved. "Thank you Stewart, you are dismissed."

He turned away, but his peripheral vision—much better, incidentally, than it had been in his human form—told him that Stewart was still lingering.

"What is it?" he asked, his eyes narrowing again.

"If I may be so bold, Your Highness," Stewart said, his posture stiff. "Autumn is upon us. I would imagine that the regional market will be taking place any day now. It's only about two hours' ride away...if it's still held in its usual location, that is."

Justin's eyes had narrowed almost to slits by the end of this seemingly innocuous speech.

"And?"

Stewart cleared his throat again. "And, Your Highness, some of the other servants and I wondered if you had considered making another attempt to leave the estate. It is a rare opportunity to find so many people in one place, and so close by. Perhaps you might encounter someone who—"

"No," Justin growled. He glared at the man, trying to ignore the many layers of discomfort swirling through him at the suggestion. Quite apart from everything else, the fact that Stewart was willing to admit to having been gossiping with the lower servants was an indication of just how dire he considered the situation to be. "You know what happens if I leave the estate."

"Yes, Your Highness," said Stewart uncomfortably. "And naturally I hesitate to suggest any course that would be painful for you, but since you are the only one who the curse doesn't actually restrain from leaving, you could perhaps—"

"It's not the pain I'm worried about," Justin cut him off, waving a clawed hand dismissively. "It's the effect on the rose garden."

Stewart sighed. "It is a risk, I realize, Your Highness. But it would only be a matter of hours...perhaps the losses would be worth the possibility that you might encounter—"

"No," said Justin again, his voice curt. "Last time I was gone only fifteen minutes, and ten roses wilted. If I was outside the boundary for hours, it might be enough to doom us all. I won't take that risk. Not for some regional market full of peasants."

Stewart bowed stiffly. He didn't speak a word, but his disappointment was clear in his posture as he made his stately way down the corridor.

Justin watched him go, his face impassive. Inside, his mind was in turmoil. Could the servants be right? Was there even the slimmest possibility that there could be someone at the regional market who could break this blasted curse?

It seemed incredibly unlikely. And although he hadn't admitted as much to Stewart—incapacitated as he was, the last thing he could afford was to appear weak in front of his servants —the pain *was* a significant factor. His servants knew that it hurt him physically to be outside the castle's estate, but they had no concept of the full extent of it.

It wasn't that he shrank from pain, not with such high stakes. But for all it had been almost a year ago, he remembered with distinct clarity the last time he'd attempted to venture from the estate surrounding the Summer Castle. It was true that he'd returned to find ten roses had withered on their stems, the cost of his attempt to flee his prison. But that was only one of the reasons he hadn't repeated the attempt.

The other was the pain. It had begun the moment he'd left the gates, and had intensified with every step he'd taken. He'd barely lasted the fifteen minutes, and by the end of that time he'd been in agony, hardly able to crawl back inside the boundary. It was hard to imagine that he could ride for two hours to a market while still retaining the ability to move.

And what would be the point? Even if he did manage to make contact with anyone, they weren't going to stop for conversation with the terrifying monster he'd become. All he'd achieve would be to clear out the market, most likely.

He ground his teeth, humiliation mixing with his anger. He was the rightful king of what *had* been one of the most prosperous kingdoms in Solstice. And this was what he was reduced to. He turned, his robe once more billowing out behind him.

One thing was certain. If he ever got his hands on that enchantress, she would regret ever knocking on the door of his castle.

CHAPTER THREE

Felicity

"Father, Ambrose, you forgot the food I packed for you." Felicity hurried across the grass, waving for the wagon to stop. The neighbor who was allowing her father and brother to ride to the market with him pulled his nag up with a long-suffering sigh.

"You would have missed this long before you made it to the market," Felicity scolded her father, even as she shook her head indulgently. She handed the basket up, a frown creasing her forehead. "Be careful, all right? Stay safe."

"Enough fussing, Fliss, we'll be fine," said Ambrose impatiently.

"Of course we will," said her father, a frown creasing his face. "But are you sure you'll be all right? I don't like the idea of you all on your own."

Felicity barely held in a sigh, her gaze shifting to her brother, who was studiously avoiding her eye. If her father didn't want her to be alone, he had a very obvious solution sitting beside him. Ambrose knew as well as she did that there was absolutely no need for his presence on this expedition. But he was as eager as Felicity to get out of the village, and unlike her, he was willing to keep pushing until he got what he wanted.

"I'll be fine," she said.

Her father looked unconvinced. "I think I should have asked Martha to come stay after all,"

"Nonsense," said Felicity briskly, watching critically as her father stowed the basket at a precarious angle. "We've been over this. I'm eighteen years old—I don't need a minder when you're away anymore. There's no reason for us to pay Martha coins that we could put to much better use elsewhere."

She cast around for a way to get his mind off the topic. The last thing she wanted was for her father to find out the real reason she was determined not to ask Martha to come and stay with her. She had no desire to spend the next three days trying to avoid Martha's overeager son, or getting scolded by Martha for it, as if Felicity was the one attempting to steal clandestine moments. It had been fine when they were children, but somewhere around the time she'd turned sixteen, his behavior had undergone a sudden—and unwelcome—change.

It was around the time Kurt had begun to be smarmy, in fact.

"Did you forget my gift, too?" she said quickly.

"Ah, of course!" her father said, successfully distracted. "I'm supposed to ask you what you'd like me to bring back for you."

She laughed. "No, Father, I meant did you forget to take the gift I got you. I meant to pack it for you, but I couldn't find it in the house."

"That's because I have it here in my pocket," said her father with dignity, patting his threadbare traveling cloak. "I don't forget everything, you know." He smiled encouragingly. "But you haven't told me what you want me to bring back for you."

She laughed again. "I don't need a gift."

"Of course you do," he said jovially. He clicked his fingers. "I

know! You want a rose! You always used to ask me to bring one
back for you, remember?"

"I do remember," said Felicity, amused. "I asked you *one*
time, when I was about ten."

"And did I bring it?" Her father squinted at her.

Felicity couldn't help the laugh that spilled out. "No, dearest
of fathers, you forgot. But it really didn't matter."

"Oh." Her father visibly deflated before straightening up
again. "I'll fix the errors of the past!" he declared brightly. "I'll
bring you the biggest and most beautiful rose in Albury."

Felicity rolled her eyes. "A little late in the season for that,
don't you think, Father?"

"Nonsense," he said cheerfully. "They have everything at the
market, and with any luck I'll have some coin to spend."

Felicity opened her mouth to protest, but closed it again. She
pushed aside her embarrassment at the slightly derisive smile
on the neighbor's face at her father's allusion to his mythical
missing cargo. What right did he have to laugh at them?

"Sounds wonderful, Father," she said, giving him a smile.
What did it matter? He would almost certainly forget before he
even reached the market anyway. Let him enjoy the thought of
bringing her back a beautiful rose for the next half an hour.

"Are we leaving?" Ambrose prompted impatiently, and
Felicity stepped back, waving a final farewell as the nag started
forward.

She watched the wagon until it rounded a bend in the road,
and a rocky mound hid it from sight. She lingered a moment
longer, feeling listless, before turning back to the house.
Glancing up at the cloudless sky, she thought suddenly of her
encounter with the dragon. Where was he now? She wasn't sure
what to make of the incident, and she still hadn't told her father
or Ambrose about it. She couldn't decide how her father would

react, and her brother couldn't be counted on to keep it to himself.

The truth was, as much as she loved them, neither of them was a companion she turned to when she wanted to confide something. In fact, no one in the village fit that description.

An involuntary sigh escaped her as she entered the house. There must be something, *somewhere*, else for her. Ambrose would leave home if the opportunity presented itself, she was sure, but the last thing she wanted to do was abandon her father. She shuddered to think the state he'd get into if left to take care of himself—she could still remember the chaos of their lives in their early years in the village, before she was old enough to take the reins of the household.

She had hoped that with enough time, he might be ready to emerge from the isolation that he had fled to in his grief over losing his wife. But his determination to stay sequestered didn't seem to be lessening with the passing years. She was starting to fear that if she didn't want to abandon him, she might be stuck in this town forever.

FELICITY WHISTLED CHEERFULLY to herself as she kneaded the dough. Puffs of flour floated around her, catching the slanting light of late afternoon.

Rap rap rap.

She looked up, a smile lighting her face. They were back earlier than she expected. They'd only been gone three days.

She wiped her hands on her apron, pushing an errant strand of hair behind her ear. A small sigh escaped her as she made her way to the front door. As pleased as she was to have her father and brother home, the timing of the interruption was unfortunate. If she didn't get her task done soon, the dough wouldn't have sufficient time to rise before the day's warmth fled.

Her smile of welcome disappeared the moment she opened the door, to be met with a most unwelcome sight.

"Kurt," she said flatly. "What are you doing here?"

"Felicity." Kurt gave a grating chuckle that didn't in any way soften the irritation that had sprung to his eyes at her greeting. "That's not a very polite way to welcome a guest."

He made a move, as if to stride forward, but Felicity shifted in the doorway, blocking the way.

"I didn't realize I was expecting a guest," she said, unimpressed. "Ambrose isn't here." She had hoped that her brother's absence would at least spare her the unwelcome company of his friend.

"I know," said Kurt. "That's why I came. To check on you."

Felicity narrowed her eyes. "I'm just in the middle of making bread, Kurt, so it's not really a good time for entertaining."

"So I see," said Kurt comfortably, his eyes drawn to something on her cheek. Uninvited, he reached out to rub off what must have been a spot of flour.

Felicity could only assume he had intended the gesture to be romantic, but his thumb was rough and the touch unpleasant. She drew back, trying to communicate with her scowl just how little she appreciated the invasion of her personal space.

She didn't quite hit the mark.

"Oh, don't worry," Kurt said, smiling in a self-satisfied way. "I like a woman who can bake. It's an important skill." He smirked. "For you, I mean. We buy our bread from the baker, of course."

"Why are you here, Kurt?" Felicity snapped.

"For your protection," Kurt said, leaning against the doorframe in the most obnoxious pose she'd ever seen. "Since you're here all alone."

A shot of amusement lanced through Felicity's annoyance.

He was just so ridiculous, and he didn't even realize it. But the humor disappeared a moment later, when Kurt took advantage of her earlier retreat to push past her into the cottage.

"You should have paid someone to come and stay with you," he said, still smirking slightly. "If coin is the problem, I could have helped you out."

"I don't need or want your coin," said Felicity shortly. "This is no business of yours." She tried to convey only irritation in her tone, but the truth was that Kurt's presence in her home made her acutely uncomfortable.

Kurt had been looking around the room as if he'd been invited to critique its set up, but at her words, he swung his gaze around to her face, stepping forward until he was within an arm's length of her. Felicity's discomfort escalated immediately to unease.

"Of course it's my business," he said, his expression still cocky. "Isn't it my job to keep you safe? As your brother's friend, of course."

"No," said Felicity, hating that her voice sounded breathless. She wanted to respond with only the scorn this man's presumption deserved. But in spite of his talk of safety, her unease was edged with a tiny bit of fear. The maddening thing was that this peacock of a man would no doubt think she was discomposed not because a man she didn't trust or like was in her house, but because she was smitten with him. Like every other fool girl in the village. Nothing she could say was likely to convince him otherwise.

"It's *not* your job," she said, trying valiantly anyway. "It has absolutely nothing to do with you. And I don't appreciate you coming over here uninvited."

"Oh Felicity," chuckled Kurt, stepping closer. "There's no need to play hard to get. You've already won me over."

He moved forward even more. Felicity took a step back,

finding herself against a wall. Her heart beat with unpleasant speed, and she could once again smell leather.

"I already told you," Kurt said, lazily flicking her braid back over her shoulder. "I've decided that you're the prettiest girl in town."

Felicity couldn't quite help the way she cringed away from his casual touch. She was painfully aware of her vulnerability, all alone in the cottage. But her eyes sparked with anger, and she spoke boldly.

"I have no interest in winning you over, Kurt." She stared him down. "I can't stop Ambrose from bringing you here, but I will never be interested in you, and you have no business touching me."

Kurt's eyes narrowed, his face reddening slightly in anger, making it stand out against his ash-blond hair. "You know I enjoy these little games we play, Felicity," he said, leaning closer. "But it's about time you learned where the line is. You're stepping over it a little too often lately."

"That," said Felicity, attempting a lighthearted tone, "is *exactly* what I was going to say to you. How nice to be on the same page."

It took a moment for Kurt to process her words, but when he did, she saw the anger flash across his face. But he made an uncharacteristic effort to master himself, his features smoothing out.

"Very witty," he said, his smile painfully forced. "But your little jokes won't keep you safe here alone, will they?" He rocked back on his heels, his hand going to the hunting knife he wore in his belt. Felicity barely refrained from rolling her eyes. The gesture was vain rather than aggressive—she'd seen him strike that pose many times, usually to great admiration.

"I could stay, of course," he said, a slight smirk lifting one side of his mouth.

"No," said Felicity flatly. "You can't."

Kurt ignored her. "You're obviously too naive to be here all alone, and—"

The creak of an approaching wagon was the most beautiful sound Felicity had ever heard. She was only an arm's length from the door—she had kept the good sense to remain between her uninvited visitor and her escape route—and she had it open in a flash. However awkward the conversation might be, this time she would insist that her father talk to Ambrose about his friend.

But although she saw Ambrose clambering out of the wagon, there was no sign of her father. Ambrose trudged toward the door, and it took only one glance for Felicity to see that something was seriously wrong.

"Ambrose!" she cried. "Where's Father?"

Her brother looked up, startled, and his gaze passed from Felicity to Kurt behind her. He raised an eyebrow, and Felicity gritted her teeth. A glance at Kurt did nothing to improve her mood. He was wearing his usual smirk, clearly happy for Ambrose to draw his own conclusions.

Mentally promising to give Ambrose a piece of her mind later, Felicity pushed the matter from her thoughts.

"Where's Father?" she tried again.

Ambrose swallowed. "He's...he's been...captured. I think."

"Captured?" Felicity repeated, stunned. "What do you mean? By whom? Were there outstanding debts we didn't know about?"

Ambrose didn't immediately answer, pushing past her into the cottage. He glanced at Kurt uncertainly, but the uninvited guest made no move to leave.

"No," said Ambrose hesitantly. He wrung his hands.

Felicity's alarm spiked as she got a good look at him. She'd never seen her brother this unkempt.

"What happened, Ambrose?" she demanded urgently.

"We went to the market," Ambrose said, his voice unsteady. "But the agent Father had hired never showed up."

Felicity held in a sigh. So far, no big surprises.

"I thought that was that, and we'd just wait until the market finished, so we could ride home on the wagon. But Father insisted we leave straight away. He started wandering over the countryside, but he wouldn't tell me where we were going. It wasn't toward home."

Felicity's brows drew further together with every word of the odd tale. She couldn't imagine what her father had been thinking.

"We walked for ages," Ambrose said. "Then we came to a..."

"A what?" Felicity prompted, when her brother paused.

Ambrose grimaced. "A big fancy gate, with a building behind it. It looked almost like a...well, a castle. I think..." he threw another glance at Kurt, "...I think it was the Summer Castle."

"The Summer Castle?" Kurt repeated, sounding amused. "Don't be such a dunce, Ambrose. Everyone knows the Summer Castle is gone. What you saw must have been some nobleman's manor. I'm sure it looked very impressive, but—"

"I know the castle's gone," Ambrose said, glowering at his friend. "But it was there, I'm telling you. I told Father he shouldn't go in, but he was strangely determined. I think he made it through the gates, but—"

"You think?" Felicity cut him off sharply. "You don't know?"

"I didn't go in with him," said Ambrose. "What?" he added uncomfortably, when she scowled at him. "You wouldn't have, either! The place was creepy!"

Felicity just raised an eyebrow, and Ambrose hurried to defend himself.

"I was right not to go in, Fliss. The place is cursed! I think it's haunted by the ghost of the prince or something. The moment Father went through the gates, the whole thing disappeared!

Father included! I don't think he was very far inside, because I could hear him. He started shouting, like he was being attacked or something."

"And even then you didn't go in after him?" Felicity said, aghast.

"I couldn't!" Ambrose protested. "It was gone. The gate, the castle, Father, everything! Just his voice, like an echo, babbling some nonsense about exchanging himself for a person of worth."

"What?" Felicity frowned. "That doesn't make sense."

"I know it doesn't," said Ambrose, shrugging. "But that's what I heard."

"So what did you do?" Felicity demanded. "Surely you looked for him? Surely you *wanted* to find him?"

Ambrose's expression grew angry. "It's easy for you to be brave, safely here in the village," he argued. "If you'd been there, you would have done the same thing I did."

"Which, I take it, was run away without even trying to find Father," she snapped.

Ambrose shrugged, still looking sulky. "It took me hours and hours to find my way back to the market, and I was lucky that our neighbor hadn't left yet, or I would have been stuck there."

"Ambrose, how could you just leave Father there?" Felicity cried.

"I had no choice, Felicity!" Ambrose shouted, the loss of temper betraying how much the whole incident had rattled him. "I'm lucky to be alive!"

Felicity pulled in a shuddering breath, trying to master her emotions. A low chuckle drew her attention to Kurt, and she scowled at his amused expression.

"Quite a tale, Ambrose," said Kurt, and Felicity's frown deepened. It was clear that Kurt thought Ambrose was making things up, although what he thought had really happened to their father, Felicity couldn't guess. She didn't doubt her brother's account. Ambrose was infuriating in many ways, but he wasn't a liar. And he was more shaken than she'd ever seen him.

"Without your father around, you'll be in a bit of a corner, Felicity," said Kurt, unexpectedly turning to her. "It seems you might want my help after all."

His gleeful tone made Felicity want to strangle him, but she restrained herself, instead directing her energy toward shoving fresh supplies into the rucksack Ambrose had just discarded.

"You want to help, Kurt?" she said shortly. "Let us borrow two horses. We all know you're *so* well off, surely you have a couple to spare."

Kurt raised his eyebrows, looking genuinely confused. "Horses?"

"Yes," said Felicity impatiently. "It will take us a week to get there on foot."

"We can't go after him, Felicity," protested Ambrose. "I tell you, the place disappeared. He's been taken by the curse—he's gone!"

"Don't be ridiculous," said Felicity briskly. "You said it your-self, you could still hear him speaking. If we look for him, surely we'll find him."

"I'm not going looking for him," said Ambrose, setting his shoulders. "I don't want to die in some haunted castle."

"Fine," Felicity snapped. "I'll go by myself. Where will I find the place?"

"This is madness," Ambrose protested. "I'm not telling you where to find it."

Felicity drew in another deep breath, willing herself to remain calm. "No matter," she said, attempting to keep her tone light. "I know where the market was. I'll find it." She turned to Kurt. "Are you going to lend me a horse, or not?"

"Absolutely not," said Kurt, his tone suggesting the matter was closed. "You're not going."

"Fine," Felicity muttered again.

It was probably for the best—she'd rather not be beholden to him anyway. She rummaged through the cooking jars, finding her stash of emergency coins. For all her brave face, she was trying not to think about what might have happened to her father. Her hands were shaking so much, she couldn't unstop the clay jar, and after a frustrated tussle, she gave up and smashed it. She scooped the coins into her pocket.

"Hopefully that old farm horse is still for sale," she muttered to herself, hoping the coins would be enough.

"You can't take all that," Ambrose protested. "What am I supposed to do? How will I buy food?"

"You'll manage," Felicity said, done with pandering to his selfishness. "You're a grown man."

"Felicity, what are you doing?" Kurt spoke in the condescending tone someone who wasn't very good with children might use on a five year old.

"I'm going after my father," Felicity said, not that she owed him an explanation.

"It will be dark in a couple of hours," said Kurt, clearly losing his patience with her lapse into insanity.

She ignored him, grabbing a tattered traveling cloak and her father's spare hat. She turned to Ambrose. "Last chance, Ambrose. Are you sure you won't come?"

Her brother hesitated for a moment, but she could see in his eyes even before he spoke that his fear had won over other considerations.

"It's a mistake," he insisted.

Felicity sighed, meeting his eyes. "I agree," she said softly, turning for the door.

"Felicity." Kurt's voice had become stern, and he reached out and grabbed her arm as she passed. Irritated, she turned to face him. "I forbid you to go."

For one silent heartbeat Felicity just stared up into Kurt's handsome, arrogant face. Then she burst into a slightly hysterical shout of laughter.

Without a word, she pulled her arm free and strode through the doorway.

CHAPTER FOUR

Justin

"Show me my uncle."

At once, the surface of the mirror shifted, and Justin's scowling, monstrous face disappeared. In its place was the lined brow of a middle aged man with a weary expression.

"Thank you, Dobson," he was saying, running a hand over his face. *"Let us hope the masons are satisfied, and will not attempt a further strike."*

Justin closed his eyes as he groaned aloud. It sounded like his uncle had given in to the demands of the stonemasons. That was almost certainly a mistake. Their wages had been fair, and it was clear they were taking advantage of the crown's weakened position. Could his uncle really not see that? Perhaps he was still on edge from the disaster a few months before, when he had taken too hard a line with that group of woodworkers in their dispute with their employers. But that had been entirely different. Their complaints had actually been reasonable. He shouldn't have been so unyielding on that occasion.

Justin opened his eyes, looking once again at the mirror. His uncle was still speaking.

"Tell the farmers I will see them now."

"Yes Lord Regent. And shall I show them into the audience hall?"

Justin stiffened, but before he could get too angry, his uncle's voice wafted out from the mirror.

"No, Dobson, we've been through this. I'm not the king, and I won't take audiences in the king's audience hall. The public receiving room will be just fine."

Justin narrowed his eyes thoughtfully as his father's steward, who should be *his* steward, and was now—kind of—his uncle's steward, hesitated.

"My Lord Regent, you have been the acting ruler for a decade. No one would think it inappropriate for you to make use of the royal audience hall."

"No one except me," Uncle Cameron corrected. *"And that is enough. I don't wish to discuss it further."*

Justin watched as Dobson withdrew, looking dissatisfied, but knowing better than to press the point. Justin's eyes turned back to his uncle, his mind a confused tangle as he watched the older man sink into thought. After a moment, his uncle shook his head, his eyes becoming clear again. He pushed himself from his chair, giving a weary sigh before schooling his features to an impassive mask.

Justin sat back, putting the mirror down and letting its surface return to simple reflective glass. He drummed his fingers on the tabletop, so used to the sharp click of his claws on the wood he didn't even notice the sound.

As usual, he was left without any clear idea what to make of the mirror's revelations. What was his uncle up to? From everything he could see in the mirror, the state of the kingdom was worsening. His uncle's decisions were driving Albury toward its greatest economic dip in a century, and it was absolutely maddening to see him do the opposite of what Justin would have done, time and time again, and be unable to do a thing about it.

Of course, to be fair, the mysterious disappearance of the crown prince, rumored to have been transformed into a hideous beast by an enchantress, probably wasn't helping Albury's economy either.

Justin sighed, running a clawed hand over his face in a gesture similar to his uncle's, although the face no longer contained any resemblance. With the way things were deteriorating, he was becoming increasingly convinced that his uncle was plotting against him, working to take the crown for good. But despite all the times he'd tried, he'd never managed to catch his uncle in any behavior that would prove his suspicions. If only the mirror allowed him to trawl through actions, past and present. But he knew from extensive experimentation that it only showed what was happening at the specific moment he was using it.

An involuntary growl rose up in his throat as he thought of where the mirror had come from. That enchantress had some nerve to give him a gift, as if he should be grateful to her, after she'd just cursed him. At first he'd refused to use it on principle, but his isolation had soon driven him to come down from that high horse. And he had to admit it had been very revealing these past two years.

Not that he would have needed any help if that cursed enchantress hadn't interfered in his life. It was outrageous that she'd attacked the crown prince of a powerful kingdom. The fact that she'd gotten away with it still made Justin's blood boil.

The memory of that night was imprinted so deeply on his mind, he still dreamed about it more often than not. Last night had been no exception. Without his permission, his mind went back to the scene that had visited him in his sleep.

The unseasonably stormy weather.

The bedraggled woman, claiming she'd traveled all the way from Mistra to seek an audience with him.

Her refusal to wait until he returned to the capital. Her demand that he provide refuge for any magic users who might need to flee the neighboring kingdom of Mistra.

Justin snorted at the memory. As if she had any right to make such a demand. The war between Mistra and Entolia was no affair of his. It wasn't his fault that the war had been going badly for Mistra, and that the magic users feared they would be persecuted if Entolia invaded. It wasn't a burden Albury should have to shoulder.

The enchantress's errand had been pointless anyway, he thought angrily. Entolia hadn't invaded Mistra. The battle lines had set in, and from all he could discover, the war dribbled on still, little more than a border skirmish, a token enmity. And yet, for refusing to help a group of refugees who never existed, Justin was cursed.

He ground his teeth together, causing his fangs to jut out over his bottom lip, as her sanctimonious speech rang in his mind.

Let me repay your hospitality in kind. You have let your crown make you think you are above reproach. See how you fare when your outside reflects what is truly inside. Maybe then you can look beyond your own conceit for long enough to learn to love someone else more than you love yourself. And to have a person of worth look at you and actually like what they see.

Justin had been angry at the audacity of her tirade, but it wasn't until the last sentence, when an unnatural light began to glow around the woman, that it had even occurred to him that she might dare to use magic on him.

If you can't achieve that by the time the last rose in the rose garden dies, you will stay this way forever.

A flash of remembered pain passed through Justin's body,

but it was nothing to the anger and humiliation he felt at the memory of the transformation that had followed. He bitterly regretted that night, but how could he have known?

She had looked so pathetic in every way, weak and tired from her journey, wet and filthy from the weather. How could he have guessed she was a genuinely powerful enchantress—one of the most powerful on the continent, judging by the strength of her curse—rather than one who could just do party tricks?

Well, he wouldn't let himself be fooled by appearances again. And as soon as he threw off this curse, there would be some serious new laws regarding the use of magic. Perhaps the kingdom of Bansford had it right all along—perhaps magic should be outlawed altogether. Magic users from Albury could flee to Mistra, he thought with grim irony. Get out of his kingdom for good. If the enchantress had truly come to him to help the plight of her fellow magic users, she hadn't quite achieved her aim.

"Your Highness?"

Justin turned at the voice, unsurprised to see his steward hovering in the doorway to his study. He was amazed Stewart had left him alone this long. Apparently the servants had calculated that the regional market would be underway right now.

"What is it, Stewart? I hope this isn't about that market. I already told you, it's not worth the risk."

It really wasn't. Even if he made it there, even if he could find "a person of worth" at such an event—unlikely—there was absolutely no possibility that person would "like what they see" when they saw him coming.

"No, Your Highness," Stewart said. "It's not about the market."

Justin shifted in his chair, realizing for the first time that the servant was speaking strangely. He had a look on his face that

Justin had never seen before, some bizarre mix of anxiety and excitement.

"What is it?"

"The gardener just came to me..."

Justin went rigid. Not more flowers lost? Was the magic that had kept the roses in full bloom for two straight years finally starting to fail? But Stewart's next words drove all such thoughts from his head.

"Well, he found someone in the garden. A man. From outside."

Justin was so stunned he couldn't move. He stared at his steward for several frozen seconds.

"From outside? But no one's ever...How did he get in? What was he doing there?"

"How he got in, I couldn't say, Your Highness," said Stewart, and Justin could tell he was holding something back. He narrowed his eyes, and Stewart cleared his throat. "As to what he was doing, well...he, uh...he was cutting a rose."

"*WHAT?!*" Justin was on his feet before the word left his mouth, rage filling him. "He cut a rose? He KILLED one of them? Where is he?!"

He didn't wait for an answer, storming from the room with Stewart hard on his heels.

"He didn't know, Your Highness," Stewart said, his words coming out in a rush. "He thought it was just a rose. He said it's for his daughter, apparently. I'm sure he meant no harm."

Justin ignored his words, his stride furious as he made his way toward the castle's main entrance. His blasted body was attempting to follow some animal instinct and drop to all fours for a faster run. In his anger it was all he could do to keep his mind clear enough to remain in control and stay upright. He was *not* a beast, however much he might look like one.

"Please, Your Highness," Stewart continued, anxiety making

him sound less polished than Justin had ever heard before. "Just stop and think for a moment. Don't do anything rash. As you said, no one from outside has ever entered the estate since we were cursed. Who knows what he might be able to tell us? What help he might be able to give? He won't be any use to you if he's dead!"

That stopped Justin in his tracks. His halt was so sudden, Stewart barreled past him and had to pull himself up.

"Dead?" Justin repeated, the word a growl. "Did you think I was going to call for his execution on the spot?" He glared at the middle aged servant, hoping the expression hid the hurt that was pouring through him at Stewart's words. This man probably knew him better than anyone, and this was his opinion? "Is that the kind of king you think I'll be, Stewart? That I'll execute anyone who does something I don't like? I'm not my father."

"I know you're not, Prince Justin," said Stewart. But although his voice was softer, he still looked anxious.

Justin took a step toward him, his expression menacing. It scared him how much Stewart's words had hurt, and he didn't know any way to bury that feeling other than anger.

"Or did you think I would rip him limb from limb myself? Complete the transformation from man to beast?"

"Of course not, Your Highness," said Stewart. Far from being intimidated by the creature towering over him, the steward was recovering his usual poise. There was a hint of reproach in his tone. "Such an absurd thought never crossed my mind. But if you will allow me to speak plainly—"

"When do you not?" muttered Justin, and Stewart's eyes narrowed slightly, although he continued as if Justin hadn't interrupted.

"—when you lose your temper, you do have a tendency to act...rashly."

"If you bring up my insult to the enchantress again, Stewart, I'm going to rip *you* limb from limb."

Justin could have sworn he saw the ghost of a smile flit across the steward's face, but he didn't wait to hear the man's reply. He turned, continuing his interrupted prowl toward the rose garden.

Thanks to his unwanted extra senses, he could both smell and hear the intruder before he saw him. But when he did round a bend in the cultivated garden, finally bringing the thief into sight, all his rage returned. The full red bloom was still clutched in the man's hand, and this physical reminder of the damage he had wrought was enough to trigger a growl in Justin's throat.

The man, flanked by two of the three guards Justin's staff boasted, whipped his head around at the sound. His eyes widened in unmistakable terror, and his mouth opened in what appeared to be a silent scream.

His reaction set the final seal on Justin's anger. It was painfully reminiscent of the night he had been cursed. He hadn't seen such a look since he had lifted his head from the ground, trying to comprehend the change in his body, and seen his guests, and most of his servants, turn tail and flee before his new form.

Only about twenty of his servants had stayed, and he had no idea why they'd done so. He was certain they must have regretted it as soon as the curse took full effect, and they realized they were physically unable to leave.

"What have you done?!" he yelled, his voice turning to a roar on the last word.

The intruder shrank back from him, his eyes widening even further, if that was possible.

"You...you can speak," he said faintly.

Another growl built in Justin's throat, and he made no

attempt to hold it in. "Yes, I can speak, thief, and I suggest you start speaking if you don't want to find out what else I can do."

The man swallowed hard, his fear making him incoherent. Justin waited with increasing impatience for an answer, his tail flicking involuntarily back and forth.

"Who are you?" he demanded. "Surely that you can answer."

"My name...my name is Gustav," the man finally managed. "I come from a village to the west of here, and I traveled here to attend the regional market."

Stewart gave Justin a pointed look, that said as plainly as words, *what did I tell you?* Justin ignored him. If Stewart thought this man was proving the likelihood of finding "a person of worth" at the market, he must have lost his senses.

"And you couldn't find anything worth stealing at the markets, so you came here?" he asked?

The man's face blanched at Justin's deadly tone. "I'm not here to steal anything! I just...I just picked a flower. It's for my daughter. She—"

"Enough!" Justin cut him off. *Just picked a flower?* This man had no idea what he'd done. "I don't want to hear any more about your fool daughter. How did you get in here?"

"I just...I just walked through the gate," Gustav said, confused and wary. "It wasn't locked. I saw the roses, and I—"

"You just walked through?" Justin's eyes narrowed. "Not likely." He stepped forward, looming over the man. "Who sent you? How many blooms did you destroy before you were found?"

"What?" the man faltered. "No! No, I wasn't sent here. I thought this place was gone...everyone thinks the castle disappeared...I didn't..." His words fell over each other in his panic. "I was just looking for a rose for my daughter, I swear!"

"If I hear one more mention of your daughter," Justin growled, leaning close, "I'm *really* going to lose my temper. I don't believe a word you just said to me, and I *will* discover all your secrets."

All color drained from the intruder's face, and Justin felt a surge of vicious satisfaction. This Gustav was hiding something, no doubt about it.

"Throw him in the dungeons!" he growled. "Perhaps he'll be a little more forthright after a few days in there." The guards sprang into action, but Stewart looked aghast.

"But Your Highness!" he protested.

"Please!" the man shouted. "Please let me go! Don't keep me here! What can I give you in exchange? Anything!"

Justin wheeled around, giving a mirthless laugh. "I'll gladly take an exchange. You think I want a common thief? If you could replace yourself with a person of worth, I would take the exchange in a heartbeat."

"A...what do you mean?" the man said, bewildered. "How can I exchange myself for a person of worth?"

Justin made a derisive noise in his throat, turning away. "You can't," he said dismissively, already regretting speaking his thoughts aloud in his agitation. "You committed the crime, and you will pay the penalty."

He ignored both his steward's reproaches and the intruder's continued pleas, turning in a billow of cloak and stalking away from the castle, to check on the gate.

"Your Highness." Of course Stewart couldn't just let it go. "Surely you don't think he's suspicious?"

"You've said it yourself, Stewart," Justin reminded him. "There's a large market full of people nearby. If he just wandered in here by accident, where are the rest of the hordes? If the castle was suddenly visible to the rest of the kingdom again, don't you think we would be inundated? He must be here by design."

"But, Prince Justin," Stewart said, an edge of scolding to his words. "Look at him! He's a simple peasant. Do you really think he's carrying out some villainous plot?"

Justin flicked his tail, his thoughts dark as he once again turned away. "Don't be deceived by appearances, Stewart."

Justin certainly didn't intend to be. Not this time.

CHAPTER FIVE

Felicity

She would have died rather than admit it, but Felicity was starting to wonder if Ambrose and Kurt had been right. It was possible this rescue attempt had been a mistake.

The ancient horse she had purchased at an unfair price plodded under her, as weary as she was. The night was almost over, and she was cold, hungry, and frightened. She thought she would have arrived by now, but she was still clip clopping through a seemingly endless forest. The road was well maintained, but she was nervous nevertheless. Although the moon was bright, the light filtering through the branches was barely enough for her horse to find the smooth, even path. She couldn't see any distance at all through the trees, and she was trailed by the awful feeling of many eyes watching her.

She held back a shudder, wondering if the road would ever emerge from this forest. And whether she'd be able to find her way from there. She knew the general direction of the market, but that was it. She rubbed a tired hand over her face, dislodging a crusted spot of dough that had still lingered near her ear. Warm as the day had been, the night air was chill, and the cloak she wore didn't keep her from shivering.

But the thought of her father drove her on. It was awful to think of him trapped in a cursed castle, injured or worse. All of a sudden, she felt a curious tug, somewhere near her heart. It wasn't sentiment—it was something more tangible. It tugged at her memory, too, but she couldn't place it. All at once, the trees began to thin, and a few minutes later, the trunks finally disappeared. She breathed a sigh of relief when the forest gave way to an open field, the road winding ahead. But the relief was soon forgotten. She still had no idea where she was going.

"Where are you, Father?" She muttered the words aloud, and felt that tug once again.

The road she was following forked up ahead, and she felt an inexplicable urge to turn left. She obeyed, hoping her senses weren't leading her astray.

After another fifteen minutes of plodding, a faint glimmer made her glance up at the horizon. But it wasn't the approaching dawn that caused her to pull the horse to a stop, a gasp of astonishment on her lips.

She could have sworn there had been nothing but empty fields for miles ahead, but the darkness must have deceived her. Because there in front of her, hardly more than a stone's throw away, loomed an enormous wrought-iron gate. The metal was twisted in a delicate pattern, at odds with the strength of the structure. Stone walls stretched out from the gate on either side, disappearing into the gloom of the pre-dawn.

Felicity nudged the horse forward, swallowing hard as the growing light gave her a good look at what lay on the other side of the gate. A castle loomed up, forbidding in the semi-darkness, and a cold rush passed over Felicity.

She'd found it.

She hadn't thought she'd doubted Ambrose's story. But her amazement at the sight before her made her realize that she hadn't entirely believed him until she saw it with her own eyes.

She'd known that the Summer Castle of Albury's royal family had once stood in this part of the kingdom, of course. But it was lost, as Kurt had said. Everyone knew that. It had disappeared over two years ago, in some kind of magic curse, along with the crown prince. The servants who had fled before it vanished reported that an enchantress had turned Prince Justin into a terrifying monster. Of course, no one could confirm that report. He, like his summer residence, was simply gone.

And yet, what else could this castle be? The rising sun revealed a structure that was too enormous, too intimidating, to be a mere nobleman's manor. Ambrose must have been right. This was undoubtedly the missing Summer Castle.

The inexplicable tug was still there, drawing her toward the castle, but she hesitated. Was she being affected by whatever dark magic had hidden the castle in the first place? Was that why she had felt compelled to come in this direction?

A sudden thought flashed through her mind. If she was feeling some sinister attraction to this place, perhaps her father had felt it too. Perhaps that was why he'd wandered off from the market.

Her heart constricted at the idea of her father being lured into some kind of magic trap. He wouldn't stand a chance—he'd never even think to question any strange compulsion he might feel. Throwing aside her reluctance, she dismounted, testing the small side door that stood next to the large gate. It swung open effortlessly, without even a creak, and she swallowed hard. From the glimpse she could see, the estate beyond was beautiful. But there was an eerie quality about the place that made her reluctant to step inside. She could understand why Ambrose hadn't wanted to enter.

But fear for her father, along with the compulsion that still pulled at her, propelled her through the gate. She was relieved that there was no immediate effect, no sudden attack of dark magic. The place was quiet in the stillness of early dawn, but not silent. A few birds had begun to chirp in the trees lining the broad carriageway that led up to the castle. The sound cheered her. For some reason, she hadn't expected there to be animals in here.

She led her horse behind her on its halter. The animal's relaxed demeanor encouraged her, although it was possible that the horse's senses were too dulled by age to pick up on anything amiss.

As she walked up the broad path, the sheer size of the castle's estate quickly became clear. In addition to the birds, she caught a glimpse of some deer flitting toward the shelter of a copse of trees, perhaps startled by her approach. Maybe they were unused to humans, Felicity thought, as she drew close to the castle without any sign of people.

"Are you in here, Father?" she muttered, mostly to herself.

At the words the tug inside her intensified, and it gave her the courage to approach the castle. She tied the horse up nearby, and it began to graze placidly. She stroked its side, murmuring an apology and a promise to return soon. She didn't know a great deal about horse care—she had a feeling she was supposed to rub it down or something. But her desire to find her father eclipsed everything else.

She hesitated at the castle's large wooden door. Should she knock, or try to sneak in? She decided on the latter. Once again, the door was unlocked, and she slipped in silently.

The sun had properly risen during her walk to the castle, but inside the building it was still dim. She had expected to find dust and cobwebs, a specter leaping from the shadows, that kind of thing. But instead, she was confronted with a broad marble entranceway, beautifully designed and well maintained. Everything was clean, and the banisters that rose up on either side of the large marble staircase glistened in the light slanting through the tall windows. She walked forward into the hall, her footsteps soft on the smooth floor.

A doorway to one side drew her gaze, and she approached it carefully. It seemed to be a large study, and she could see a fire flickering merrily in the fireplace. The sight made her pause. Someone had surely built that fire this very morning. She peered warily around the room, but could see no sign of anyone. She drew her head back, and glanced into the next room over. It was difficult to tell the purpose of this room, because all the furniture was clothed in dust covers.

She hesitated for a moment, but when she looked around the entranceway, she felt that pull, drawing her toward a door positioned immediately behind the staircase. She went through it, and found herself in a stone corridor without windows. She followed the inexplicable feeling for some time, along winding corridors and down two flights of stairs. The polished marble of the entranceway had long since disappeared, and a chill seemed to permeate the gray stone walls. She began to shiver, and not because of the cold. It was becoming increasingly obvious that she was heading toward the castle's dungeon.

Again she considered turning back, but concern for her father drove her on. She descended one final set of narrow stone stairs, the darkness at the bottom alleviated by a torch burning on one wall. Felicity slowed her steps, wondering if there would be some kind of guard. But a sudden whimper propelled her back into motion, a gasp escaping her.

"Father?" she breathed, almost tumbling down the last few steps in her haste. She let out another gasp as she caught sight of the dungeon's only occupant. "Father!"

"Felicity?" her father cried. "Felicity, how did you find me?"

She threw herself to her knees beside the cell, clasping his hands through the bars. Her eyes ran over him in growing concern. He looked weak, and he was filthy. He was kneeling on his tattered cloak, which he'd balled up and seemed to have been using as a pillow. She'd never seen her father so disheveled.

"What happened to you?" she demanded. "I was beside myself when Ambrose came home without you. How did you end up in a dungeon?"

Her father let out a gasp, as if only just remembering where he was. "The castle! The prince! You have to go, Felicity! You can't stay here!"

Felicity made an impatient noise, trying to hide the alarm she felt at her father's rising panic. She gripped his hands more tightly. "As if I would ever leave you here."

"I'm serious, Fliss," her father said, his eyes wide. "I don't want you anywhere near the prince. He's...he's..."

Her father swallowed, seeming unable to continue.

"He's what?" Felicity pressed, frowning.

But her father seemed to have lost all power of speech, his eyes fixed on something over her shoulder.

"*He* is not accustomed to being spoken of in such a manner," said a new voice, as smooth as silk.

Felicity whipped her head around so quickly that something clicked in her neck. Someone was standing at the top of the stairs, but in the dim light of the torch, she couldn't make him out. She could only see the bottom of his billowing cloak.

"I see I have another guest," the newcomer continued. His voice was deep and throaty. It would be a very pleasant sound, actually, if it wasn't so clearly dripping with menace.

"You have a strange way of treating guests," Felicity snapped.

Her father gasped at her boldness, but she ignored him. Her fear for him had quickly turned into anger toward his captor, and it blazed fiery hot.

"What's wrong with you, that you would lock up an old man

simply for getting lost?" Her father made a faint sound of protest at the word "old", but again she ignored him.

"Have you been starving him?" She gestured toward the prisoner. "He looks dead on his feet."

"Just got lost, did he? Wandered by accident into a castle magically concealed from the world for years?" The voice's disdain made Felicity narrow her eyes. What kind of a fool must this man be to think her father was a scheming mastermind?

"Yes," she growled. "Of course."

The man scoffed, but still didn't descend any further into the dungeon. "And it's pure *coincidence* that he immediately began ransacking the rose garden, I suppose."

Felicity blinked, bewildered, and this time it was her father who answered.

"I only picked one! I didn't mean any harm!"

"And who are you?" the voice continued, paying her father no heed. "No doubt you're the daughter who was to receive this stolen gift. Are you here to fulfill the offered exchange? A person of worth in your miserable father's place?"

Felicity bristled at the insult to her father, but before she could retort, she suddenly remembered her father's promise. She drew in a sharp gasp and turned to him, her throat clogging slightly. "You were trying to get me a rose. That's why you came here."

Her father nodded, looking close to tears. The sight was more painful than anything she'd witnessed in a long while. "I know you thought I'd forget, but I didn't. There was no news of the ship, and I couldn't bear to come home to you empty-handed. Only, you were right that it was too late in the season. I searched everywhere through the markets, but no one had any. Then, while I was looking, I felt this strange compulsion to leave the market and head out into the field. I can't explain it, but I was sure I'd find roses here. And I did! In full bloom, even in autumn!"

"Those are *my* roses." The voice was even deeper this time, almost an actual growl.

Felicity turned, glaring up into the darkness at the top of the stairs. "What are you, a child? What harm did he do by picking a flower from your garden?"

"Felicity, no!" Her father's voice came out in a strangled whisper. "Don't—you can't—he's the *prince*!"

Felicity blinked at her father in astonishment, before turning slowly back to face the stairway. "Then he has no excuse for not knowing better," she said.

Her mind was reeling over the fact that the missing Prince Justin had apparently reappeared from oblivion in order to arrest unwary travelers, but she didn't let that show. She was determined to get her father free, whatever it took.

A low growl was all the response she got, but she took his lack of an answer as encouragement.

"I insist that you set my father free, *Your Highness*. He's done nothing wrong."

"Is that so?" the voice—apparently Crown Prince Justin—asked conversationally. "I know I've been...absent...for a while, but I didn't realize that thievery was no longer considered a crime in my kingdom."

"Is picking a rose from your garden really a crime worthy of imprisonment?" Felicity demanded impatiently. "Your Highness," she tacked on hastily, in case it helped.

"Yes," the prince growled, his voice again deep and rumbly. "And a price must be paid."

Felicity stared at the hem of the prince's costly cloak, not sure if she was more angry or bewildered. Was he really so petty as to resent her father's actions that much? It seemed incredible, but his tone was unyielding.

"He will remain here until he has given a more satisfactory answer for his presence on my estate."

"But I've told you the truth!" her father pleaded.

"You can't be serious," Felicity said, at the same time. She was staring into the darkness where the prince's face must be. "You're going to keep him here indefinitely? He'll die!"

Maybe it was an exaggeration, but her fear was real. Her father really did look weak.

"A price must be paid," the prince repeated, sounding bored.

Anger surged up inside Felicity. A life for a rose? What kind of price was that? Clearly her father had been right about the royals. She took a furious step forward. "Then I will pay it. You mentioned an exchange—I'll do it. Let my father go, and I'll stay in his place."

"Felicity," her father protested, aghast. "Absolutely not!"

Felicity ignored him, her gaze fixed on the dark shape on the stairs. The prince was silent, whether from surprise or disinterest she didn't know.

"You will stay?" he repeated at last. "What an intriguing offer. Do you consider yourself a person of worth, then?"

Felicity frowned, confused. "I don't know what you mean by that," she said cautiously. "I can't judge my own worth. But I am all I have to offer. I will stay in his place."

"You won't!" her father repeated, but his voice sounded faint.

The prince made a scoffing noise, but didn't respond to the words. "Guards," he called up the stairs instead. "It seems we won't be interrogating our prisoner this morning after all. I have magnanimously decided to set him free instead."

Two armed guards appeared on the stairs, passing the prince and coming down into the light. They didn't question their orders, just moved purposefully toward the cell.

"You can't stay here, Felicity," her father insisted, reaching for her through the bars. His eyes darted up the stairs. "He'll kill you!"

Felicity gave a brittle laugh. "It will take more than a dungeon to kill me, Father."

"Not the dungeon, *him*," her father hissed.

Felicity frowned at him, trying to understand the terror on his face. The prince responded to the insult with a low growl, and all at once Felicity remembered the rumors about what had happened to the prince. The servants said he'd been turned into a monster before he vanished. But he was standing there, speaking with her, so surely that couldn't be the case. Could it?

"Why don't you join us down here, Your Highness?" she challenged him suspiciously. "Or are you too proud to be among your subjects?"

"Of course," said the prince, his throaty voice so smooth it was almost a purr. "Where are my manners?"

With a swish of his cloak, he descended the remaining stairs, and Felicity's blood ran cold. Her instincts screamed at her to run, but she was frozen to the spot.

"You see?" her father said, in a strangled whisper.

She saw, all right. As terrifying as the sight was, she couldn't pull her eyes away. Prince Justin truly had been turned into a monster.

Or at least, some sort of human-monster mix. He stood upright like a man, and he clearly retained his powers of thought, and his voice. But his features were like an animal's. Or a cross between multiple animals. She couldn't decide if his face was more like a wolf or a lion, and every part of him that she could see was covered in long, thick fur, such a dark brown it was almost black. His hands were like a man's, but much larger and also covered in fur. And they had actual claws.

Felicity's eyes traveled from his feet all the way up his body, her heart beating in a frantic rhythm. He was bigger than he should be, not just in height but in breadth. His shoulders curled inward unnaturally, and his legs bulged against the fabric of his clothes. He looked like he could rip her limb from limb if he chose, and the murderous scowl on his face did nothing to help.

But it was his eyes that most unsettled her. They were startlingly blue, and the intensity of their expression seemed to draw all the air from her lungs. Most startling of all, they were so *human*. It was eerie to see them on the creature before her.

"Well?" Prince Justin said, his tone mocking. "What do you think? Do you like what you see?"

She stared back at him, still locked in the beam of his eyes. Her mind was whirling at a breakneck rate, but she couldn't seem to form any words. At her silence, his expression grew hard, and he turned his attention to the guards.

"Wait." The prince held up one fur-covered, clawed hand, and the guards paused. Prince Justin looked back at Felicity, his eyes narrowing. "Before I let your father out, I want your word that you will stay here as you've promised, until I release you. That you won't leave, won't try to escape."

Felicity swallowed, unable to deny her terror at the prospect of being this creature's prisoner. She opened her mouth, but it was dry, and her thick tongue still couldn't seem to form words.

"An empty offer, then," the prince sneered. "Not that I could have trusted the word of a peasant anyway, I suppose."

His derision shook Felicity out of her stupor, a hot surge of anger passing through her and burning up her terror in its wake.

"I won't leave until I am released," she said, straightening her back proudly. "You have my word."

CHAPTER SIX

Justin

J ustin stared down the young peasant woman before
him, wondering if her word was really worth a thing.

Probably not, but he would still take it. The more he
observed of the man behind the bars, the less he could
believe that he had any significant part to play in a plot against
the crown. There wasn't a strong resemblance between the pair,
but he supposed it was possible the girl could really be his
daughter. Either way, he had a sense that she was more likely to
be a useful source of information than the old man.

Plus, there was no denying that her insolence had inflamed
Justin's pride. Other than her maybe-father, she was the first
person Justin had seen since he was cursed, excluding those
trapped at the estate with him. Her reaction to him had been
incredibly painful, more so than her father's. He had been
unable to help the sardonic question that slipped out—"do you
like what you see?". But he had regretted it when he saw the way
his guards' stoic expressions twitched, betraying that they recognized the wording from the curse. Justin's pride took another hit
at the realization that they probably thought he'd been hoping
this girl would break the curse then and there.

His haughtiness and anger were necessary tools to keep his humiliation from showing. He could not afford to appear weak to this girl.

"Very well," he said curtly. He nodded to his guards. "Remove him, and make sure he leaves the estate."

He gave them a pointed look, not putting the extra meaning into words. His guards would understand that part of his purpose was to see whether the intruder *could* leave, or whether he would now be stuck here like the servants were.

The guards unlocked the cell, but the man didn't emerge.

"No!" he protested instead. "You can't keep her here! Felicity! I won't allow it!"

At a sign from Justin, the guards dragged the old man from the cell, and at once his alarm escalated to panic.

"What is this? What's happening?" His eyes bulged with fear, and he began to thrash wildly. "Where did they go? Felicity!"

Justin raised an eyebrow at the strange reaction, and even the girl looked surprised at the intensity of the man's panic.

"It will be all right, Father," she said, rushing to him and taking his hand. "I'll come home as soon as I can."

Justin scoffed audibly, and she glared at him.

"Why don't you leave with me now?" her father protested, looking almost mad as his eyes darted wildly around the space without seeming to take anything in. "Where's the prince? If we leave quickly, maybe he won't stop you!"

Felicity looked from Justin to the old man, clearly concerned by her father's behavior.

"I've given my word, Father," she said.

Justin gestured to the guards, and they began to pull the former prisoner toward the stairs. He yelped in distress as his hands slipped from the girl's grip. She made no attempt to follow, but she called out after him.

"There's a horse tethered outside! I think he'll know his way back. Ambrose will be at home. And there's food in the saddle bags."

"Felicity!" the old man tried again, but the guards were already at the stairway. "Felicity! You can't stay here! There are things you don't know!"

He broke off as the guards continued to pull him away. Justin could hear his anguished protests all the way up the stairs, but the man's attempts to break free of his captors were weak.

Pathetic.

Justin turned to the girl in front of him, studying her curiously. Her eyes glistened slightly at the departure of her father, but she still stood tall, meeting his gaze with defiance. Peasant though she was, she was worth ten of her father.

"Well, Your Highness?" she asked, in an attempt at nonchalance that wasn't entirely successful. "What next? I've never been locked in a dungeon before. Do I just walk into the cell, or is it important that your guards throw me in there dramatically? I don't mind waiting for them to come back. I've got plenty of time on my hands."

A muscle in Justin's wolf-like jaw twitched, but he kept his expression steely. Any hint of humor would only encourage the girl's impertinence.

"That won't be necessary. I have no intention of locking you into that cell."

"But..." The girl's forehead creased. "I don't understand."

"Your father was of no particular use to me," he said, blithely omitting the fact that he had intended to interrogate the man for information. "He was in prison as a result of his crimes. You, on the other hand, look strong. And you've given me your *word* that you'll stay." He put the slightest sneer on the word, and as he'd known they would, her eyes flashed again. "You're no good to anyone in a dungeon," he continued, pretending he hadn't noticed her anger. "I'm sure my housekeeper will find more than enough work for you. You will earn your bread like anyone else here."

Without another word, he turned, his cloak swirling behind him as he ascended the stairs with his loping, uneven gait. The girl had looked surprised by his declaration, but she made no comment. He wondered whether she was relieved not to be locked up, or resentful about being put to work.

As soon as he reached the top of the stairs, he saw Stewart, hovering in the corridor, his eyes wide. From the way he was glancing between Justin and the darkness at the bottom of the stairs, Justin was guessing he'd been listening in on everything.

"Ah, Stewart, good," he said curtly. "I've let the prisoner go. His daughter has indentured herself in exchange for his freedom." He spoke as if this sequence of events was the most natural thing in the world, and when Stewart opened his mouth to protest, Justin spoke over the top of him. "Tell Mrs. Winters that the girl is waiting in the dungeon for her instructions."

He paused, frowning as he thought of the housekeeper. In spite of her stern facade, she had a tendency to mother people, Justin included.

"And tell Mrs. Winters that the girl is to earn her keep. She looks strong enough. I want her worked hard."

"But Your Highness," Stewart started, his tone a mixture of admonishment and horror.

"That is all," Justin cut him off, beginning to walk away. He paused after a few steps. "Oh, and send the other guard to me in my study."

He didn't pause again, ignoring the spluttering of the steward behind him as he strode away from the dungeon. The castle was well and truly awake now. There were only some twenty servants in the whole place, but clearly news of the commotion had spread, because all of them seemed to be hovering somewhere between the dungeons and the entranceway that led to Justin's study. It was almost like the old days, when there had been so many servants that eyes followed him everywhere he went.

Justin ignored them all, not stopping until he was in his study. He had too much nervous energy to sit in the huge winged armchair he usually favored. Instead he found himself pacing back and forth in front of the crackling fire, his mind going over every detail of the morning's encounter.

In all the time since he'd been cursed, no one from outside had ever entered the estate. And no one but him had been able to leave. Something had changed, and in spite of his disinterested front, he was desperate to find out what, and to figure out how to use it to break free from this nightmare.

A smart knock at the door alerted him to the arrival of the guard.

"Ah, Phillip, good," he said briskly. "Come in."

The guard, a broad-shouldered young man about a year younger than Justin, stepped into the room.

"You sent for me, Your Highness?" Phillip asked respectfully.

"Yes." Justin realized he was still pacing, and stilled his steps with an effort. "Do you know if the others saw the intruder off the property?"

"Yes, Your Highness," Phillip said. "The man, and the horse his daughter left him, were both able to leave the estate. No magic seemed to hinder him, and there was no indication that he experienced physical pain upon leaving."

Justin was silent for a moment, processing this information. He turned shrewd eyes on the young guard. "You believe that the girl is that man's daughter, then?"

"Yes, Your Highness," Phillip said simply. "We all do."

Justin gave a grunt. "Speaking of the girl—"

"Felicity, Your Highness," Phillip interrupted. "Her name is

Felicity. Apparently," he added quickly, noticing Justin's hard stare.

Justin sighed, but he didn't admonish Phillip for the interruption. A couple of years ago he would never have countenanced such casual behavior. But being trapped in isolation together under an apparently unbreakable curse had a way of rendering constant formality a bit ridiculous. No one on the estate had ever given him any reason to doubt their loyalty, and without quite realizing he was doing it, he had gradually given them all a lot more license than he ever would have before.

"Well then, *Felicity* does not have my trust. I want you to follow her."

"Follow her?" Phillip repeated, startled.

"That's right. I want to know everything she does, and if she shows even the smallest hint of trying to leave, I want to be informed immediately."

Phillip blinked.

"Am I understood?" Justin prompted him, when the guard remained silent.

"Yes, Your Highness, it's just that..."

"It's just that what?" Justin made no effort to hide his impatience.

"Well, sire, I don't know how comfortable I feel, following a young woman around like she's a criminal."

Justin stared at the guard in disbelief. "A 'young woman'? She's a peasant girl, Phillip." He shook his head, his expression growing harder. "And I didn't ask if you were comfortable. I've given you your orders. Mrs. Winters is giving the girl her duties, so that's where you'll find her."

"Felicity," Phillip corrected again, his eyes growing slightly wider. "And what do you mean by duties, Your Highness? Surely you don't intend to make her a servant?"

The horror on Phillip's face irked Justin, but it also gave him a faint inkling of the trouble that might be ahead for him. Stewart was one thing, but a junior guard? Perhaps he needed to keep his servants under a tighter rein.

"That will be all, Phillip," Justin said, his words short and clipped.

Phillip hesitated for a moment, as if debating whether to argue. But after a glance at Justin's face, he bowed and withdrew.

Justin paused by his desk, drumming his claws on the smooth wooden surface for a moment. Then, making a sudden decision, he strode from the room, heading for the grand staircase in the entranceway.

Again, there seemed to be an unreasonable number of servants milling about nearby, but no one attempted to speak to him. He reached his private chambers without breaking stride, startling one of the castle's two chambermaids who was in the act of straightening the room. The girl curtsied nervously and withdrew.

As soon as the door was closed behind her, Justin made for the dresser beside his bed. He opened the top drawer and pulled out the mirror.

"Show me the girl," he ordered.

He waited, but his own beastly face still looked back at him. He growled. Even the mirror? Seriously? He focused his mind, trying to pull up the unimportant detail of the girl's name.

"Show me Felicity," he tried again, illogically irritated with the magic artifact.

The surface shifted, and a room came into view. He frowned, taking a moment before he recognized it as the housekeeper's private suite. Why in the world had Mrs. Winters taken the girl there? His outrage grew as he took in the scene. And why was the blasted woman giving the girl tea?

"Thank you," said Felicity, seeming much chirpier than a newly indentured servant to a half-beast master had any right to

be. *"This tea is heavenly. Truth be told, I'm so exhausted, I could almost fall asleep standing up."*

"And no surprise," said Mrs. Winters, in a gruff voice that did nothing to lessen her coddling demeanor. *"Riding all through the night like that! You must be more careful, child. You're lucky you weren't eaten by wolves."*

Felicity had the audacity to laugh. *"I'll try to be more cautious in future,"* she promised with unconvincing meekness. Downing the contents of her cup, she brushed her hands off on her dress and pushed herself to her feet. *"Now,"* she said briskly. *"How does this work? I've never been a servant before, but I'm sure I can get the hang of it. The tea was a pleasant surprise, I must say."*

"Oh nonsense," said Mrs. Winters, a scowl passing briefly across her face. *"None of this servant business."*

"But..." Felicity looked confused, as well she might. *"But the prince definitely said——"*

"Never mind the prince," said Mrs. Winters, and it was Justin's turn to scowl. *"We have one proper resident at this castle, one with nowhere to go, and no guests to entertain. And there are already eighteen of us to care for him. The last thing we need is more servants. I'm having a guest suite prepared for you as we speak."*

Justin growled long and low, although of course no one could hear him. He felt his tail twitch, as it did when he was angry, and annoyance passed through him at the involuntary gesture. He was *not* an animal.

"That's very kind," Felicity said, surprising Justin with her uncertainty. *"But I gave my word, you know. And regardless of what he might think, my word means a great deal to me."*

If he wasn't still so angry with his housekeeper, Justin would have smiled at the disdain in Felicity's voice as she referred to him. She was clearly trying to sound lofty, but she only managed petulant.

"Hm..." Somewhat to Justin's surprise, Mrs. Winters seemed

to be taking Felicity's objection seriously. *"I understand your feelings, my dear. Did you actually promise him to work as a servant?"*

Felicity was silent for a moment, her forehead creased as she thought about it. *"No,"* she said at last. *"I just gave my word that I wouldn't leave until released."*

"Excellent!" The housekeeper brushed one hand against the other, as if dismissing the matter permanently. *"Then I can't see a problem."* She leaned forward, refilling Felicity's cup. *"Well, then. Tell me a little about yourself."*

Justin put the mirror down, grinding his teeth as the image faded. So that's how it was going to be, was it? He rang a bell on the wall, prowling impatiently while he waited for someone to answer the summons. It was a serving man—the only serving man—who eventually came. He looked apprehensive, and only too ready to hurry away again when Justin sent him with a message for the housekeeper.

It took almost twenty minutes for the woman to arrive, and by the time she did, Justin's temper was barely in check.

"Your Highness." She gave a stiff bow. Clearly she was irritated at being interrupted in her attempt to interrogate the girl. "I understand that you wished to see me urgently."

"Mrs. Winters," Justin growled. "Did I or did I not send specific instructions that the intruder was to be put to work immediately?"

"Yes, Your Highness," said Mrs. Winters, meeting his look blandly. "If by 'the intruder' you mean Miss Felicity." The housekeeper may have been advanced in years, but there was a steel in her eyes that belied the apparent frailty of her frame.

"Well then," Justin's voice was soft and dangerous, "perhaps you can explain to me why you would be serving the girl tea instead of starting her on her chores."

Instead of looking chastened, Mrs. Winters raised an

eyebrow, glancing from Justin to the mirror sitting on the table beside him.

"And how would you, as the gentleman you were raised to be, have any idea what the young lady was doing while not in your presence?"

To his intense annoyance, Justin felt a flush rising up his neck. Fortunately his fur-covered form wouldn't show it, but he was still irritated with himself. And with Mrs. Winters for implying that he'd been spying on the girl.

Which he hadn't been, of course. Nothing of the kind.

"I think your memory is at fault if you think my father raised me to be a 'gentleman', Mrs. Winters," he said dryly, neatly side-stepping the accusation. "He raised me to be a king. And a king expects his orders to be obeyed."

His attempt to remind the elderly servant of her place fell far short.

"I remember perfectly what your father raised you to be," Mrs. Winters said tartly, her gaze passing briefly over his form. She gave a reminiscent sigh. "I was thinking of your mother, actually."

"And I was thinking of my orders," Justin cut in unemotion-ally. "And my apparently unreasonable expectation that my own servants will follow them." He was in no mood to get senti-mental about the mother who had died when he was only seven. "If the gi—*Felicity*," he corrected himself, rolling his eyes at Mrs. Winters' stern expression, "is going to stay here, she will work for her keep."

"Her keep?" Mrs. Winters repeated. "She's not exactly staying here by choice, Your Highness."

"Of course she is," he said coolly. "She's the one who gave her word. It was her own foolish decision to offer herself in exchange for her father."

"I'll have you know, Prince Justin," Mrs. Winters had adopted

a scolding tone, "that the rest of us all consider that 'foolish decision' very brave! Miss Felicity is clearly an exceptional young
woman. I will certainly not be putting her to work as a servant."

Justin drew himself up to his full, unnatural height. "Are you
refusing to obey my orders?"

"Only this particular one, Your Highness," said Mrs. Winters
matter-of-factly. She raised that maddening eyebrow again. "I
feel certain you'll forgive the impertinence, and won't throw me
from the estate."

Justin's hunched shoulders drooped, his face dropping into a
scowl that he couldn't quite keep from being petulant. She had
him there, and he knew it as well as she did. With the servants
physically prevented from leaving the estate, there wasn't a
whole lot he could do about any insubordination. It wasn't like
he was going to throw the housekeeper—a grandmotherly
figure who had known him all his life—into the dungeons.

"Of course, you can feel free to assign her duties yourself,
Your Highness," Mrs. Winters said innocently.

Justin sighed, dropping his glare. What was the point? Again,
Mrs. Winters knew she had him beaten. He had absolutely no
idea what kind of duties to give a new servant. Without the
housekeeper's help, turning Felicity into a servant was an impossible task.

"If she's not even going to work to earn her keep, then what
do you propose I do with her?" he demanded. "Surely you don't
want me to throw her back into the dungeon."

Mrs. Winters made a horrified noise in her throat. "I would
think not, Your Highness!" She shook her head indulgently.
"What an idea. I've sent her to the largest guest suite. Do you
realize that the poor thing was traveling all night? She was
exhausted. Stewart and I agree that she should be left to sleep
for most of the day. But we'll send someone to wake her in time
for the evening meal."

Justin shrugged, losing interest in these details. He had accepted that, ruler though he was, he was powerless to force Mrs. Winters to indenture the girl. But that didn't mean he was interested in the minutiae of her schedule. The housekeeper's next words brought his attention back in a hurry, however.

"Shall we say six o'clock for dinner, then? I'll send her to the private dining room, don't you think? She may be a guest, but the formal dining hall is much too large for just the two of you."

"The two of us?" Justin repeated, a dangerous growl to the words. "What are you talking about?"

"I'm talking about dinner," Mrs. Winters said firmly. "Of course Miss Felicity will eat with you from now on."

"No," Justin growled, "she most certainly, absolutely, categorically will not."

CHAPTER SEVEN

Felicity

"His Royal Highness Crown Prince Justin of Albury requests the pleasure of your company at dinner tonight."

"Who does...what?" Felicity said groggily, pushing her hair out of her eyes.

She squinted at the girl standing in the doorway, attempting to clear the sleep from her mind. She cast a glance around the sumptuous room, trying to get her bearings. It seemed it had all been real, then. Not a bizarre and terrifying dream.

She must have slept the day away, because there was an orange tint to the light, and the beams of sun slanting through the windows were angled almost horizontally.

"You're invited to dine with the prince," the girl said, dropping her formal tone and flashing Felicity a grin. "They're even roasting a pig for the occasion."

"What occasion is that?" Felicity asked, still a little dazed.

"Your arrival, of course!" The girl's face was bright with excitement as she advanced into the room. "You're the first visitor we've had from outside since the curse. Except for your father, of course." She grimaced. "And he didn't exactly get to dine with Prince Justin."

A wave of emotion passed over Felicity at the mention of her father, and she fell silent. Where was he now? That nag was slow, but surely it had carried him home by now. Was he still panicking, or had his head cleared since she last saw him? How would he cope without her? It was hard to imagine Ambrose being of much practical use. She thought irrelevantly of her half-finished dough, and sighed. It would be ruined now, of course.

"I've had a hunt for some dresses for you, and there are quite a few options. When the curse hit, the guests all fled, and some of them left very nice dresses behind."

"I don't need a fancy dress," Felicity cut in quickly, the haze of sleep finally falling away. "It's very kind of you, but I don't need any of this attention. I'd rather just keep my head down and get on with my duties."

"Wearing fancy dresses is your main duty," said the girl solemnly, and Felicity couldn't help but laugh.

"All right, enough of this," she scolded, as the girl held a dusky red gown against her for effect. "Who are you, and why did you wake me up to dress me like a doll?"

"Oh, I beg your pardon!" the girl exclaimed. "How rude of me. My name is Viola, and I'm your maid now." She grinned. "It would be more polite to offer you a choice, but we only have two chambermaids left, and we really can't spare them. And the kitchen maids would have no clue about how to do your hair and such. So I'm afraid you're stuck with me."

"Firstly, this is nonsense," said Felicity, smiling in spite of herself at Viola's bubbly manner. "I'm not a fine lady, and prisoners don't get their own maids. Secondly, what do you mean you only have two chambermaids 'left'? What happened to all the others? Did the beast eat them?"

"Of course not!" Viola said, looking so shocked and horrified that Felicity couldn't help going into a peal of laughter.

"Sorry," she said, when her mirth finally subsided. "I couldn't help it. I was only joking. I didn't really think the prince had eaten anyone. I can tell that he's still human, you know, inside."

Viola's features relaxed immediately, her face returning to the cheerful expression that seemed habitual to her. "Well that's a relief!" she said, with more feeling than Felicity felt the occasion called for. "Now," her tone turned businesslike, "the dress."

"You can't be my maid," Felicity protested. "And I can't wear all these fancy clothes. *And*," she added hastily, as Viola showed every sign of cutting her off, "I absolutely can't have dinner with the beast-prince."

"Yes I can, yes you can, and you *certainly* can," Viola said. She frowned. "And I don't think you should call him the beast-prince."

"I don't see why not," said Felicity flippantly. "Having been assured that he doesn't eat people, I now have nothing to fear."

Viola giggled, clearly unable to help herself, but her expression soon became stern again. "I hope you're not going to be difficult, miss. Not when I've gone to such efforts to find you a suitable dress."

Felicity raised an eyebrow, amused. "So that's how it's going to be, is it? Shamelessly trying to make me feel guilty?"

"Shamelessly," Viola agreed, her voice cheerful. "Is it working?"

Felicity sighed. "A little." She smiled at the girl. "Please call me Felicity, by the way."

"If you like," Viola agreed. "Now," she held up the dress again, "this is an excellent color for you." She nodded wisely. "I'm a very good judge of these things. We'd better get moving if we want to have you ready for six o'clock."

"Viola," Felicity protested. "You weren't there, but trust me. I'm *very* certain that Prince Justin did not intend for me to be a guest. Or for me to dine with him."

"Yes, well, Prince Justin didn't intend for a lot of things to happen," Viola said, her tone short. "And yet here we are." She turned beseeching eyes on Felicity. "Please don't be stubborn about it. I know you have reason to be angry with Prince Justin, but if you refuse to eat dinner with him—"

"Oh, I'm not refusing," Felicity interrupted. "Of course I want to eat dinner with him. I just don't think he's going to be happy about it."

"You want to?" Viola said, brightening. "That's excellent!"

"Well, of course I do," Felicity repeated, confused by the intensity of the other girl's sudden jump from dejection to enthusiasm. "I thought I'd be lucky to cross paths with him again in the next month, but this is much better for my purposes."

Viola paused, looking wary. "What purposes are those?"

Felicity stared at her. "Getting out of here, obviously! Since I gave my word that I wouldn't leave until the prince released me, I need to convince him to release me. That will surely be substantially easier if I'm actually, you know, interacting with him."

Viola visibly deflated, and Felicity felt bad. "No offense, of course," she added hastily. "The castle seems lovely, and all that. But I'm more or less a prisoner, you realize." She sighed. "And to tell the truth, I'm not at all sure my father and brother can manage without me."

"Where's your mother?" Viola asked curiously.

"She died when I was a small child," Felicity explained.

"Oh, I'm so sorry!"

Felicity smiled at the look of mortification on Viola's face. "It was a long time ago," she reassured the maid. "It's not something I'm sensitive about."

Viola nodded, but she remained subdued for several minutes, as she helped Felicity into the chosen gown, and began to dress her hair. Felicity submitted willingly to the unprecedented luxury, watching the other girl curiously all the while.

Viola—who Felicity guessed to be no more than a year or two younger than herself—seemed genuinely rattled by Felicity's brief tale. But the loss of a parent wasn't such an uncommon story. She would think Viola must be very sheltered, except that didn't fit with the image of a community gripped by a curse, and forced into serving a beast.

"What's the deal here, anyway?" she asked suddenly, startling Viola enough that the other girl poked her in the ear with a hair pin. "I couldn't get a straight answer out of Mrs. Winters."

Viola remained silent, looking uncomfortable. Felicity guessed the other girl wasn't supposed to talk about it. And as much as she felt for the bubbly young maid's predicament, her curiosity was much stronger.

"Why is the prince half-animal?" she tried again, thinking a more specific question might yield better results.

"He was cursed," Viola said shortly. "By an enchantress." Her voice dropped to a mutter. "The interfering old crone."

Felicity raised an eyebrow, barely holding back her grin, and Viola gave a reluctant giggle.

"I guess she wasn't that old," she conceded generously. "But we like to have a go at her from time to time. It makes us feel better. Phillip comes up with the best insults, which is always so surprising, because normally he's the nicest among us."

"We?" Felicity prodded.

"Oh, us young ones," Viola clarified cheerfully. "There are five of us." She flashed Felicity a grin. "Six, if I count you, I suppose." She paused. "Well, seven if I count the prince, but of course I don't."

"How old is he?" Felicity asked curiously. "It's hard to tell under all the, you know," she waved her hand over her face in a circular motion, "fur."

Viola stifled another giggle. "It is, isn't it? He used to be very handsome, though. He's twenty. He was only a couple of months away from turning eighteen when he got cursed."

"Yes, about that," Felicity pounced on the opening, "why did he get cursed?"

"Oh, that's no big mystery," said Viola breezily. "The enchantress forced her way in here, seeking an audience with him. He refused to help her, and he wasn't very polite about it."

"You shock me," Felicity said dryly, and Viola grinned.

"Well, she had a bit of a tantrum, I guess. Honestly, the punishment far outweighed the crime, but as far as we can tell, she got away without any consequence. Probably because no one knows exactly what she did, or how to recognize her. No one outside, anyway."

"But you're not cursed," Felicity said, frowning. "I mean, I can imagine why Prince Justin was hesitant to show his face after what happened, but why doesn't one of the servants go and get help?"

"Oh, we are cursed," Viola said, her cheerfulness unimpaired. "We're just not..."

"Disfigured?" Felicity offered, and Viola wrinkled her nose.

"Yes, that. Our part in the curse is much less dramatic, thank heavens." She shuddered, presumably at the mental image of herself in a beastlike form. She pulled back, looking at Felicity's reflection in the mirror in front of which she'd seated her life sized doll. She wrestled with a boisterous strand of Felicity's copper hair, giving a satisfied nod before continuing her tale.

"We just can't leave the estate. Magically, I mean. If we try to walk through the gates, we just sort of...can't."

"How awful!" said Felicity, appalled. "How could anyone endure being trapped like that?" To her amazement, Viola laughed outright, pausing her ministrations to wipe the moisture from her eyes.

"Why is that funny?" Felicity asked, a bit miffed.

"Because you've just landed yourself in the exact same situation," grinned Viola. "You can't leave, either, remember?"

"Oh." Felicity slumped slightly as she realized the truth of Viola's words, then straightened her shoulders. "It's different, somehow."

"If you say so," said Viola, still chuckling. She stepped back. "There." Her tone satisfied. "You're a vision."

Felicity looked at herself in the mirror. She had to admit that Viola wasn't wrong. She blinked a few times for good measure, but the 'vision' didn't disappear. She'd never looked like this before. Her hair was no longer in its practical braid, but fell around her in soft, well ordered waves, pulled back from her face by a string of what looked like pearls. She twisted in her seat to see the elegant way the copper tresses cascaded down her back. And the dress was not only finer than anything she'd ever worn, but finer than anything she'd ever seen, at least since leaving the capital. Wealthy travelers didn't come through her village, and even Kurt's family didn't have this kind of gold.

Unbidden, her mind flew to the kinds of oily things Kurt would say if he could see her now. A shudder passed through her.

"Don't you like it?" Viola asked anxiously.

"Of course I do!" Felicity hastened to assure her. "I was thinking about...never mind. Viola, I think *you* must be an enchantress. This transformation is as dramatic as the prince's."

Viola gave the lighthearted giggle that was already becoming familiar.

"Not quite." She beamed. "But I'm glad you like it. It's quite fun actually," she added artlessly. "I was hoping to be a lady's maid one day, but I've never actually had a chance to dress someone like this."

"Well, you're a natural," Felicity declared. "Once the curse is broken and you can leave, I'm sure you'll find a fabulous position with some grand lady." She frowned slightly at Viola's reflection. "The curse can be broken, right?"

"Of course it can," said Viola, although she didn't quite meet Felicity's eye.

"How?" Felicity pressed, but a new voice jumped in before Viola could answer.

"Well done, Viola," said Mrs. Winters from the doorway. "I see our guest is ready in good time." Her approving words didn't quite match the warning look she directed at the young maid. Viola ducked her head, but if anything, she looked relieved by the housekeeper's timely appearance. Felicity pretended not to notice the exchange, but she locked it away for later.

"I'm still not sure this is a good idea," she said, addressing both women. "I'm sure you mean it kindly, but if Prince Justin doesn't want me to dine with him—which I'm certain he doesn't —maybe forcing my company on him will hurt rather than help my cause."

"Your cause?" Mrs. Winters asked, her brow creasing.

"Convincing Prince Justin to release her, so she can return to her home," Viola explained, her tone colorless.

"Ah." Mrs. Winters paused for a moment. "I see. Well, we'll just have to hope he's in a congenial mood."

Felicity looked between her two companions, taking note of their strange demeanor. She decided not to question them on whatever secrets they were hiding, at least not until she had a chance to get her bearings a little more.

"We'd best get you there on time, at any rate," said Mrs. Winters briskly. "It's almost six now."

She turned and swept from the room without further chitchat, and at Viola's encouraging nod, Felicity followed. The light was beginning to fade, but there was still plenty to see by as she and the housekeeper made their way through the broad and well-decorated corridors.

"It must be a job maintaining this big place with so few of you," Felicity commented, pausing momentarily to admire a tapestry.

"We don't keep the whole place functioning," said Mrs. Winters from some distance up the corridor, and Felicity hurried to catch up. "Unnecessary rooms are kept closed, and obviously we don't generally entertain. This way."

Felicity followed her down a flight of stairs, pulling up with an involuntary gasp as she passed a window.

"What a stunning view!" she exclaimed. "Is that the ocean? I didn't realize it was so close!"

Mrs. Winters gave a low chuckle, even as she chivvied Felicity into motion again. "You obviously haven't explored your suite yet."

"What do you mean?" Felicity asked, but Mrs. Winters didn't answer, instead coming to a stop in front of a double door of polished wood.

"This is the private dining hall," she explained, gesturing to the doors. "Are you ready?" She cast an appraising eye over Felicity.

"I'm not sure, to be honest," said Felicity, feeling suddenly nervous.

The housekeeper smiled indulgently, then pulled the double

doors open. "Your Highness," she said grandly. "Your guest, Miss Felicity."

Felicity hesitated, but Mrs. Winters fixed her with a look so stern it sent her hurrying in like a chastened child. She paused just inside the doorway, blinking at the rather incredible sight before her.

The term "private dining hall" had led her to picture a cozy family space, but the room was enormous. The walls were lined with tapestries, a suit of armor even standing guard in one corner. Darkness hadn't yet fallen, but there was a large fire crackling in the fireplace on one side of the room, sending its light dancing across the lush rugs that were laid over the stone floors. A large table of polished wood stretched down the hall, dominating the space.

Actually, no. Felicity's eyes traveled up the table, and she changed her mind. Despite the size of the table, and the general grandness of the room, Prince Justin would have to be said to dominate the space. The thought flashed through her mind that he probably dominated every space he entered, even without the whole beast thing. There was an undeniable presence about him. It must be a feature of being royal.

Felicity was vaguely aware that Mrs. Winters had withdrawn, closing the door behind her. But she still stood frozen just over the threshold for a long moment, taking in the prince's appearance. He had risen at her entrance, rather begrudgingly, she thought, and she had a good view of his embroidered cloak and the gold circlet nestled in the rather alarming tuft of fur between his ears. Her gaze passed slowly from the clawed hand that was drumming on the hilt of a dress sword strapped to his side, to the slightly sulky look in his eyes.

Perhaps it was the emotional turmoil she'd been through over the previous twenty-four hours, but Felicity could feel an almost hysterical edge to the well of humor bubbling up inside her. She tried to hold it in, but she couldn't prevent a single choke of laughter from bursting through.

"I'm sorry," she gasped out, when an icy look descended on his fur-covered face. "I wasn't trying to offend you, Your Highness. It's just that you look like..." She trailed off, already regretting starting the sentence.

The prince kindly finished it for her. "An animal who's been forced into human clothes?"

"Precisely," said Felicity, cheered by his understanding.

Anger flashed through his eyes, and she instantly realized her mistake. She had thought that humor lurked beneath his calm tone, but that had been beyond foolish. After all her father's cutting remarks about royals, she should have realized that Prince Justin would be offended that she was making light of his...situation.

"I'm sorry," she said again, a flush rising up her cheeks. "That really was rude. Your cloak is...very nice."

She was fairly certain she was making bad worse, but she could think of no way to salvage the situation. For a moment the two of them regarded each other in silence, both still standing. She could see the prince's irritation, and it was all she could do to keep her face straight when one of his large furry ears twitched, the movement seeming involuntary. Another laugh threatened to emerge, but she forced it down this time, trying desperately not to look at the offending ear.

She was saved from the awkward moment by the appearance of a stately middle aged man, a younger man following closely. The older man set a bowl of steaming soup down in front of Prince Justin, and the younger one deposited his burden at the only other setting on the table, right beside the prince's seat. He gave Felicity a hesitant smile as he did so, and she returned it warmly. The soup smelled fantastic, making her realize all of a sudden how incredibly hungry she was. The refreshments in Mrs. Winters' room had been many hours before.

"Thank you, Stewart, that will be all," said Prince Justin haughtily. The two men withdrew, the younger casting a curious glance over Felicity before he hurried out the door in his senior's wake.

"Since you're my *guest*," Prince Justin managed to turn the word into an insult, "I suppose you'd better sit down."

CHAPTER EIGHT

Justin

J ustin gestured with a massive arm to the second seat, and the girl hurried toward it. Her gait was awkward, clearly hampered by the bulk of the dress she had presumably been shoved into by his servants.

The thought of people being forced into clothes reignited his irritation over the girl's words about his own attire. He felt a growl building in his throat, but he firmly suppressed it. He had already been feeling ridiculous enough before she laughed at him. The fact that he could be humiliated by the derision of a peasant was a bitter reminder of how low he had sunk. He narrowed his eyes, scrutinizing her with an intensity he hoped she would find intimidating.

"You didn't bring that gown with you," he said, not posing it as a question.

"I should think not," said the girl, the hint of a most unlady-like snort in her voice.

Justin raised his wolflike brow, and the girl explained with unabated cheerfulness.

"I've never even seen fabric this fine before." She chuckled. "Let alone owned a dress like this."

Apparently he had failed to discompose her. Any of the women he'd known before he was cursed would have been completely thrown by a disparagement of either their attire or their rank. This girl seemed utterly unconcerned about either.

"I recognize the gown," he said shortly, keeping his voice impassive. "It belonged to one of the ladies of my court. She and her family were guests here when the curse hit us."

The girl looked surprised, but still quite at ease. Justin pushed on.

"She was the girl my father had selected for me to marry, before his death."

"Oh." The girl blinked. "I, uh...I mean..."

Her stammering was satisfyingly awkward, and Justin allowed himself a small internal smile. He had succeeded in throwing her off balance. He saw the heat rising up her cheeks, and congratulated himself on reminding this infuriating intruder who was in charge.

But apparently his triumph wasn't as internal as he'd thought. The girl had been staring at him, trying and failing to call up a coherent response, but whatever she saw made her pause, her eyes narrowing.

"You just tried to think of the most discomposing thing you could say, didn't you?"

Justin was so startled, it took all his court training to keep his face blank. He wasn't sure what astonished him more—that this peasant girl had seen right to the heart of his admittedly petty attack, or that she had actually called him out on it. And she didn't even seem angry. Her eyes were still narrowed in suspicion, but there was a hint of humor about her lips.

Justin suddenly let out a laugh, the sound surprising himself as much as it seemed to surprise the girl.

"Yes," he acknowledged. "More or less. Did it work?"

"For a moment." The girl grinned unashamedly back at him.

"But then I could see that you were trying to best me." She tilted her head, adding matter-of-factly, "So of course that roused my fighting spirit."

Justin's lips twitched in spite of himself. He hid it with a grunt, already regretting his lapse into informality. "It was true, what I said," he informed her, watching her face for signs of discomfort. But she seemed to have regained her poise—such as it was.

"Well, finders keepers," she said brightly, sniffing hopefully at the soup. She glanced back up at Justin, a cheeky glint in her eye. "Unless you think she's coming back for it?"

Justin kept his face impassive, but inside he was almost smiling. She was bold, he'd give her that. And if he was completely honest with himself, the dress did suit her. He wasn't deceived—he knew she was a simple peasant girl dressed up like a noblewoman, just as he was a beast dressed up like a man. The fact that she had just started on her soup, clearly oblivious to the etiquette that required her to wait until he had begun eating, only highlighted her lack of status.

But that didn't change the truth, that she looked more beautiful in the gown than its original owner ever had. And when she grinned playfully up at him like that, her face was alarmingly attractive. In the dim light of the dungeon, he had noticed only that she was disheveled and impertinent. But now that she was clean and dressed for the occasion, he could see that his uninvited guest—Felicity—had remarkable beauty for a peasant girl.

He sighed, turning his attention to his soup. He was no fool. He understood exactly what his interfering servants were attempting to achieve. But the idea that he could learn to love this girl more than he loved himself was as impossible as her looking at him and liking what she saw. If she could even be considered a person of worth, he thought dryly.

Justin snuck another look, noticing that she was using the

wrong spoon for the soup. He snorted quietly as he picked up his own, correct, spoon. Then he stared at it, realizing how long it had been since he'd had soup. Had his fool of a cook forgotten why he'd commanded that it be dropped from the menu? There was no way he could navigate that spoon between his fangs without making an absolute spectacle of himself. He placed the spoon back down and pushed the soup away from him.

Felicity glanced up, raising an eyebrow the tiniest bit, but not commenting on his gesture. She polished her own soup off with unladylike haste, apparently undeterred by the fact that she was the only one eating.

"What's happening out there?" Justin asked her abruptly, as Stewart reappeared to clear the soup and replace it with more substantial food. Justin eyed the roast fowl with relief. That he could eat.

"What do you mean?" Felicity asked, cocking her head to the side. "Out where?"

Justin waved a paw-like hand impatiently. "In my kingdom. Since I've been...absent."

Felicity had speared some cooked vegetables, but she laid her fork down, looking at him in surprise. "Life's been going on, I suppose. The acting regent still makes all the decisions, same as before." She shrugged. "Times are harder than they were a few years ago. A couple of poor harvests, and an unusual level of conflict between various guilds, from what I've heard." She gave a small sigh. "But we don't hear much in our poky little corner of Albury."

"You don't like your village?" Justin asked without thinking, then chastised himself for betraying interest in her life. She was presumably about to unload some sob story on him, finishing with a demand for his aid. He'd heard it a hundred times before.

But Felicity just shrugged again. "It's not so bad. I know I shouldn't complain, but life is very slow there. I wish we could have stayed in the capital."

"You come from Allenton?" Justin asked, unable to hide his curiosity.

Felicity nodded. "Originally. A long time ago."

A request for details hovered on Justin's tongue, but he pushed it down, returning to the relevant point. "What do they say about my...situation?"

Felicity gave him a considering look before casting her gaze around the room. "Pretty much the truth, actually," she said. "They say you were cursed by an enchantress who...changed your form, and that then you and your Summer Castle just disappeared. No one's seen it or heard from you in over two years. That's the story."

Justin grunted. "So how did you get here?"

Felicity frowned. "I honestly don't know. My brother and my father went to the market, and only my brother returned. He gave this wild tale about a gate appearing and my father passing through it only to disappear." Her expression grew stormy for a moment, and Justin wondered what was going through her head. "Anyway, I came looking for my father, and the gate was there, with the castle beyond it, not hidden at all. I just...opened the door and walked right in."

"I wonder if you can leave," Justin mused aloud.

The girl straightened in her seat. "Are you releasing me?" she asked hopefully.

He raised one furry eyebrow at her, maintaining a haughty silence, and she sighed, her shoulders drooping again.

"I didn't think it would be quite that easy."

"I suppose we'll find out soon enough whether the place is still accessible to the outside, when your father and your brother come looking for you," he said absently, his thoughts on the phenomenon of the unexpected arrivals. His people had checked the situation at the gate thoroughly, and after Felicity's father had left, everything seemed to have returned to exactly how it was before.

Justin glanced up, surprised by the look on his companion's face. She looked suddenly uncomfortable, but he couldn't guess why. And he was too proud to ask her to explain the expression. He should have no interest in her thoughts.

He ate sparingly, only selecting items that he could eat without humiliating himself. But Felicity consumed an incredible amount for such a slight person. Justin couldn't recall ever having a guest who ate so freely, and despite how uncouth she clearly was, it was strangely satisfying. He thought of how the gown's original owner would have reacted to the display, and couldn't quite hold in a smile.

Stewart was laying the final course, consisting primarily of fruit from the estate's orchards, with a few pastries, when Felicity spoke.

"So what's the point in keeping me here? What am I supposed to do?"

Justin made his voice as frigid as he could. "I beg your pardon?"

Stewart shot him a reproving look at the tone, but Justin ignored him. He thought of the girl's eagerness at his comment about her leaving, and his eyes narrowed. She was being pampered like a princess instead of put to work like the peasant she was, and she was complaining?

"Well," she said matter-of-factly, "Mrs. Winters didn't seem to have any work for me to do. I'm not sure why I'm here, really. If you wanted to lock me in the dungeon as punishment, that would sort of make sense, but—"

"I didn't realize your accommodations were so inferior," Justin said, with cold politeness. "If you would prefer to be locked in the dungeons, that can certainly be arranged."

The girl scowled. "I didn't mean that. I'm just not sure why I'm here."

"I was under the impression that you were here because you'd given your word. But of course that wouldn't mean much to you."

Predictably, her eyes flashed at the slight to her honor.

"My word is worth more than yours, *Your Highness*," she snapped. "Or am I wrong in thinking you took an oath when you were crowned, that you would serve the best interests of your kingdom? Getting yourself cursed for bad manners and throwing the kingdom into a state of limbo doesn't quite live up to that promise, does it?"

A shot of cold anger lanced through Justin at her chastisement. As if *he* was to blame for the enchantress's outrageous attack.

"You're forgetting," he said, his voice smooth and deadly. "I was never crowned. I missed my coronation, because my hands were a little tied." He let a guttural growl come out with the last word, slamming one enormous warped hand onto the table in front of him, making the silverware rattle.

If he had hoped to intimidate her, he was disappointed. She raised an unimpressed eyebrow. "No need to lose your temper. *I* didn't curse you."

Justin opened his mouth to retort, but he paused at the sound of a pointedly cleared throat. Glancing behind him, Justin saw that Stewart hadn't left the room after laying the desserts.

"What do you want?" Justin growled at him, and Stewart's look of reproach intensified.

"No need to take it out on your servants, either," Felicity snapped. "I think they've already suffered enough for your sake." She pushed herself to her feet. "Thank you for the meal," she said, in the same angry voice. "I think I'll retire. I've had more than enough of your company."

The impression of outraged dignity was marred by the longing glance she cast toward her untouched dessert. Justin's hot retort died on his lips at her wistful expression, his own lips twitching in spite of himself.

"You are dismissed," he said stiffly, attempting to keep his dignity.

"Your Highness," muttered Stewart, clearing his throat again.

Justin glowered at him, but Stewart just raised his eyebrows expectantly. Their silent battle of wills went on for several seconds, and the girl had almost reached the door. Justin only gave in when he saw Stewart open his mouth, ready to hail Felicity himself.

"Wait," Justin called, already wildly uncomfortable.

Felicity turned inquiringly toward him, and he grimaced. She was making an effort to control her temper, but sparks were still flying from her eyes. Justin gave Stewart a meaningful look, willing the older man to see that it wasn't the moment. But Stewart's face was implacable, and Justin knew the steward's threat was real. If Justin didn't do it, Stewart would. And there was the slimmest chance Stewart was right. After all, the girl didn't seem to be afraid of him. She hadn't even looked at him in disgust, at least not until he'd insulted her word.

Felicity was still looking at him expectantly, and he stood to his feet, gesturing awkwardly to himself. "Do you like what you see?" He forced the words out in a rush, deciding that it was less humiliating to ask her himself than let Stewart do it.

It wasn't.

For several excruciating seconds her face was frozen in blank astonishment. Then her gaze passed from his clawed feet, up the misshapen legs that he'd forced into the largest pants he could find, all the way to his beastly face.

"Is...is that a joke?" Felicity asked carefully, and Justin could sense the mirth bubbling up inside her, barely contained. "I mean...you realize that you're...sort of an animal, right?"

Justin's brow darkened. He let a scowl spread across his face, hoping it masked his humiliation. He should never have let Stewart talk him into any part of this. He could feel the steward deflating behind him, and the man's disappointment only sharpened his embarrassment.

"You are dismissed," he growled again. To his chagrin, he couldn't quite keep the guttural edge from his voice, and he sounded more like an animal than ever.

Felicity, still seeming to struggle with suppressed laughter, bobbed an awkward attempt at a curtsy and fled. Justin slumped back into his seat, every ounce of fight leaking out of him.

"Well," said Stewart hesitantly. "It was worth a try, Your Highness. Maybe if you'd been a little more polite. There's always tomorrow night, of course."

"Out," said Justin, without turning around. Stewart seemed to recognize the tone, because he bowed himself out of the room without further comment.

As soon as he was alone, Justin sprang back to his feet, pacing the room like the caged animal he was. He wasn't sure what infuriated him more, the girl's impertinence, or Stewart's interference.

Or even worse...his own weakness. Because he was honest enough with himself to recognize that he had deflected the girl's question because he had no good answer. If she knew nothing, there was no reason to keep her here. Even more—if she could actually leave, there was every reason to insist that she do so, to send her with a message to his uncle. Not that he could enforce the order. Once she left the estate, he'd be powerless to make her go to Allenton. But that wasn't why he hadn't released her when she asked. Tonight had been the first time in over two years that he hadn't dined alone, and he was embarrassed to realize how desperately he'd craved the company.

His humiliation was complete.

CHAPTER NINE

Felicity

Felicity's eyes opened slowly, her confused gaze struggling to identify her surroundings. Her immediate impressions were that the light was dim, and she was lying on what was surely the most comfortable mattress in the world. Before she could take in anything else, she heard a curtain being drawn, and light flooded the room.

She blinked rapidly, sitting up in the bed. Casting her eyes around the lavish suite, she let out a long breath.

"Still not a dream," she muttered.

A bright chuckle greeted her words, and she turned to see Viola, cheerfully tying back the thick brocaded curtains that had been stretched across the floor to ceiling windows.

"I'm sure it feels like it," the maid said brightly. "Would it be a good dream, or a nightmare?"

Felicity squinted at the other girl, her eyes still adjusting to the light. She tried to weigh the luxury of her new accommodations against the glower on the prince's beastly face at their uncomfortable dinner the night before.

"Still making up my mind," she said, the words half swallowed in an enormous yawn. She frowned at the window. "The sun is so high. How late did I sleep?"

"It's noon," said Viola. "I hope you don't mind me waking you. I thought I'd better not let you sleep all day, or you would have trouble going to sleep tonight."

Felicity grimaced. "Thank you. I was lying awake most of the night, after sleeping all day yesterday. I'd become nocturnal if I didn't have you to rescue me."

Viola grinned. "Happy to help, My Lady."

"None of that," said Felicity sharply. "You know I'm not a lady, and I have no intention of pretending to be something I'm not."

Viola shrugged, an unrepentant sparkle in her eyes. "Just trying it out, seeing how it sounds." Felicity narrowed her eyes, and the maid added quickly, "I won't do it if you don't like it."

Felicity watched her suspiciously for another moment, not trusting the other girl's innocent expression. But Viola just bustled about the room, placing a tray on the bed, and selecting a dress from the wardrobe.

"What's this?" Felicity asked, brightening at the sight of the spread laid out on the tray.

"Your breakfast," said Viola. "I know it's lunch time, but since you only just woke..."

"You bring breakfast to my bed?" Felicity demanded, and Viola grinned.

"Not bad, is it?"

"Not bad at all," agreed Felicity, wasting no time in diving into a boiled egg. "I'm leaning toward good dream. And thank you," she added around a mouthful, belatedly remembering her manners.

Viola chuckled. "If a breakfast tray is enough to make you decide you like it here, you can consider that all the thanks I need."

Felicity regarded the other girl curiously. "You really want me to stay, don't you? Why?"

"Oh, well," Viola looked flustered. "I'm a little starved for company here, you know. The only other girls close to me in age are one of the chambermaids, and one of the kitchen maids, and after two years, we can all do with a bit of a change." She looked up and met Felicity's eye. "And I like you already, Miss Felicity. We all do."

For a moment Felicity wasn't sure what to say. "Well, I'm flattered," she said cautiously. "But I can't stay forever, you know. I need to go home to my father and my brother. Eventually the prince will see reason and let me go."

"Oh, I don't know," said Viola brightly. "His Highness can be very stubborn."

"You sound far too cheerful about that," said Felicity dryly. She downed a cup of tea as quickly as the steaming liquid would allow, and scrambled out of the bed. "Absolutely not," she said, lunging toward Viola as the maid pulled a dress down from the wardrobe. "You'll have to find another victim if you want to play life size dolls. I'm not wearing a ball gown while I explore the castle."

Viola giggled. "Firstly, this is for dinner tonight, not for right now. I may not be a proper lady's maid, but I know better than to put you in evening wear at noon. And secondly, this is *not* a ball gown."

"Are you sure?" Felicity asked, looking doubtfully at the crimson dress with its gold embroidery. "It looks very fancy."

"I'm very sure," Viola said firmly. "Did you say you want to explore the castle?"

"Unless there's something else I'm supposed to be doing," said Felicity hesitantly.

"Not at all," Viola hastened to assure her. "Do you want me

to be your guide? I'm expected to help in the kitchens for a bit, but not for another couple of hours."

Felicity accepted enthusiastically, glad of the company. If only there had been even one girl in her village as friendly as Viola, she wouldn't have felt so lonely for most of her life. To her relief, Viola selected a much simpler and more practical gown for Felicity to wear. She wanted to wear her own, much less costly, gown, but apparently it had been taken to be washed.

"None of our washerwomen stayed," Viola explained, with a gleeful grin. "So one of the chambermaids had to do it. She wasn't too impressed about it."

"Oh dear," said Felicity, feeling guilty, but Viola waved her concern aside.

"Oh, don't worry, she's just sour about everything. She wishes she hadn't stayed, and I suppose I can't blame her for that. But we're all in the same boat—complaining about it constantly doesn't help anything."

While they were speaking, Felicity had been wandering toward the balcony on one side of the room. She'd been about to ask Viola to clarify, but when she caught sight of the view, everything else fled from her mind.

Her sharp gasp startled Viola, and the maid hurried over.

"What's wrong?"

"Wrong?" Felicity repeated, pushing the door open and letting the gentle breeze ruffle her hair. "It's the most beautiful thing I've ever seen."

She stepped onto the balcony, her eyes riveted to the scene before her. She understood now what Mrs. Winters had meant about exploring her suite. She had been given a room on the opposite side of the castle from the main entrance. And while the approach to the castle was all open countryside in that direction, Felicity's window looked north, toward the ocean. It wasn't quite close enough to hear the crashing of the waves, but she thought she could smell the salt on the breeze.

The castle clearly sat some distance back from a cliff that dropped into the water below, and most of the ground between the estate and the cliff's edge had been cleared, allowing an excellent view of the sea. The stretch of land between the castle itself and the estate's stone wall was filled with elegant gardens, and winding walkways marked by tall hedges, all looking a little overgrown. But Felicity's balcony gave her enough height to see over it all to the ocean beyond.

"Do you like the sea, then?" Viola asked, from the doorway behind her.

"I love it," said Felicity, lost in the gorgeous vista. "But I've rarely had the chance to actually visit."

"Yes, it's a shame we can't go to the swimming beach," Viola sighed. "We used to go quite often. But it's not actually on the estate, more's the pity, so we can't get there."

Felicity's eyes were drawn down to the garden below, and she stilled at the sight of a large figure skulking beside a fish pond.

Well, perhaps skulking was a little unfair. The prince seemed to just be sitting there, but given his size and general beastliness, there wasn't much difference to speak of between sitting and skulking. As she watched, he swept one paw-like hand idly through the water of the pond. Was he remembering the feel of the ocean? Wishing, like Viola, that he was still free to indulge in trips to the beach?

As if sensing her gaze, the prince looked up, his eyes latching on to hers. Even from a distance, their pale blue beam was piercing. His expression was inscrutable, but she could almost hear his words from the night before.

Do you like what you see?

She stepped back quickly, breaking the connection. She had done her best not to laugh at the question, but she was fairly certain the prince had seen her mirth. She knew her response had been a little harsh, but honestly. What kind of a question was that? Who would look at that monstrous form and *like* what they saw?

It was such a vain question, too. He almost reminded her of Kurt in that moment. If Kurt had been sulky and belligerent, rather than arrogant and self-satisfied, that was. And unlike Kurt, the prince hadn't seemed to expect a favorable reply. So why ask such a question at all?

She pushed the matter from her mind, turning instead to Viola. "Ready?"

Viola led Felicity out of the suite and down the corridor, describing everything they passed in enthusiastic terms. She seemed to do everything with an energy that was pleasant enough as long as Felicity made no attempt to push against the irresistible tide of her personality. Felicity listened with half an ear, making her own observations. She made a mental promise to wander the same route again later, when she was alone. She liked Viola, but it was a little hard to hear herself think when she was with the bubbly girl.

The path Viola took her on was well maintained and pleasant in the autumn sunshine. Many of the rooms were covered, but everything was in good order. It certainly didn't feel like a haunted castle, although Felicity couldn't quite shake the feeling of being watched. She kept glancing over her shoulder, but there was never anyone there. She tried to ignore the shiver running up her spine, concluding that she was a little highly strung from recent events.

"What did you mean when you said one of the chamber-maids wishes she hadn't stayed?" she asked Viola, as they climbed a winding staircase leading into one of the castle's towers. "I thought you were all trapped here."

"We are now," said Viola cheerfully. "But that part of the

curse didn't take effect immediately for some reason. That's how most of the servants, and all of the guests, were able to run away. Most of them couldn't get out fast enough once they saw what had happened to Prince Justin. But some of us were willing to stick by him. It was hours later that we discovered we couldn't actually leave."

"Why would you be so loyal to him?" Felicity demanded, thinking of the prince's impersonal behavior toward his guards, and the way he had snapped at the man who'd served them dinner the night before. "He doesn't exactly seem like a warm master."

"Don't judge on appearances," said Viola, and Felicity was taken aback by the sharpness of her tone. The maid glanced at her, taking in her surprise. "Sorry," she said quietly. "It's just a lesson we've all learned."

"I meant no offense," said Felicity carefully. They had reached the top of the tower, and she paused a moment, to admire the small conservatory. It was a pleasant spot, and like so many of the castle's rooms, it had a stunning view.

She was thinking about how to explain to Viola, with a minimum of disrespect, that it was the prince's behavior rather than his appearance that had given her a bad opinion of him. But a sound from behind a trailing philodendron made her spin swiftly.

Viola sighed. "Come out, Phillip." Her long-suffering tone— like a scolding parent rather than the teenage girl she was— would have made Felicity smile if she hadn't been so discomposed by the sight of a tall, handsome young man appearing from behind the shrubbery.

"I beg your pardon," he said, looking uncomfortable as he gave Felicity a slight bow.

"What are you lurking in the shadows for, Phillip?" asked

Viola, her tone lofty. "If you want to meet Miss Felicity, you could have just asked. I can introduce you."

Felicity hid a smile at Viola's superior tone. Clearly the girl was making the most of her proximity to the exciting new arrival to get a boost in status among their little community.

The young man, who looked about Felicity's age, mumbled something unintelligible, looking at his feet.

"This is Phillip," Viola told Felicity. "He's one of the guards. We have three."

Felicity smiled warmly at the young man, as Viola rattled on, a teasing note in her voice.

"You should really work on your stealth, you know. I could tell you were following us from the moment we left Miss Felicity's suite. Don't you have duties to attend to?"

Phillip shot Viola a disgruntled look that told Felicity the two were familiar friends. Clearly the guard was part of the group of young people Viola had mentioned.

Wait. The guard.

Felicity suddenly remembered the feeling of being watched that had followed her throughout the castle, and she frowned.

"These are your duties, aren't they?" she said suddenly. "The prince ordered you to follow me around."

Phillip didn't answer, but his wary expression told her she had hit the mark. Felicity narrowed her eyes.

"The pompous, self-righteous, puffed-up royal," she muttered, her anger getting the better of her. Both of her companions looked unduly alarmed by her insults, but she ignored them. "What does he think, that I'm going to steal the silverware if not watched every minute?"

"No, miss, I'm sure he was just—"

"Just making sure I didn't try to leave, I imagine," Felicity finished for him, her tone scathing. "Of course he can't trust the word of a *peasant*, so he has to have me followed around."

"I'm sure he meant no offense, miss," Phillip said quickly, looking distressed.

"Yes," Viola agreed, her eyes wide. "He was probably thinking of your safety."

"My safety?" scoffed Felicity. "In this magically concealed, inaccessible fortress? I don't think so." She looked between the two of them, her eyes narrowing again as she took in their earnest expressions. "Stop trying to convince me that his intentions are noble. You two may have chosen to be trapped here out of loyalty to your master, but I did it for my father. The only reason I'm still here is because I gave my word, and that means something to me. The prince was petty and despotic to throw my father in the dungeon for picking a flower. He's my captor, not my protector."

"But, miss—" Phillip protested, sounding genuinely distressed by her outburst.

"He's really not so bad," Viola chimed in over the top of the guard. "If you just give him a chance—"

"I'd rather not," said Felicity flatly. She drew a deep breath, forcing down her anger. She wasn't sure why the prince's scornful dismissal of her word irritated her so much, and it certainly wasn't the fault of these two. Their blind loyalty frustrated her, but it was none of her business, really. She gave Phillip as natural a smile as she could manage. "But you're very welcome to join us. That way you're fulfilling your duties, and I'll stop feeling like I'm being followed."

Philip somehow managed to look both apologetic and grateful, and Viola beamed at the suggestion. Felicity's smile became more genuine. It was clear that her enthusiastic maid welcomed the company of the reserved, handsome young man.

"I think you were very brave, Miss," said Phillip quietly, as he followed them out of the conservatory. "Exchanging yourself for your father like that. We all think it was a real sign of..." he exchanged a glance with Viola, "character."

"We certainly do," Viola agreed brightly, leading the way toward a sculpture hall she had promised to show Felicity. "I don't know if I'd do the same for my father, to be honest."

"Of course you would," said Phillip, with a tolerant smile. "You're fond of him, for all his strictures."

"I suppose I am," admitted Viola with a chuckle, and Felicity's interest was piqued. She hadn't thought about it before, but the young people must miss their families. Probably their poor parents thought they were dead.

Before she could ask about either of their families, a firm tread made them all turn. Mrs. Winters was descending on them, her expression businesslike.

"Miss Felicity," she said. "I've just been informed that your father's belongings have been brought to your suite. I apologize for the delay. It seems they had been forgotten."

"Thank you," Felicity said, even as her forehead wrinkled in confusion. What belongings had her father had?

"And Viola, isn't it time to start preparing your mistress for dinner?" Mrs. Winters added, giving Viola a pointed look.

"Of course," Viola said, springing into action. "Come on, Miss Felicity."

Felicity couldn't quite hold in a groan as she was chivvied back toward her suite. "I have to eat dinner with the prince again?"

"Again?" Viola repeated, sounding scandalized. "It's only the second time."

"His Highness will, of course, be glad of your company at the evening meal every night," said Mrs. Winters, with dignity.

Felicity groaned again. "You know," she said sternly, "I've heard of enchanters who can detect when someone isn't telling the truth, and one of those would make short work of you lot."

She gave Viola a look. "The prince was *not* thinking of my safety when he set a guard to trail me around—no offense, Phillip."

She gave the guard, who had followed them rather than peeling off as she expected, a warm smile. Then she turned to Mrs. Winters, meeting the redoubtable housekeeper look for look.

"And he is *not* glad of my company. I can recognize the look of someone being forced into it, because it's the one thing he and I have in common."

"Well, something is better than nothing," said Viola cheerfully.

Mrs. Winters quelled her with a look. "Now, now, Miss Felicity," she said indulgently, "you'll feel better with some food in you. But I would advise you to hold off on your talk of enchanters. We're not overly fond of magic around here." They had reached the door of Felicity's suite, and she gave Phillip a stern look. "I know I don't need to remind you that it would be highly improper for you to enter the young lady's suite, Phillip."

The poor guard, who had shown no sign of trying to enter the suite, fell to attention to one side of the door, his face burning. Mrs. Winters ignored Viola's giggles, prodding the two girls through the doorway. She surveyed the room once, giving a satisfied nod before sweeping back out of the door.

Felicity smiled after her for a moment, then scanned the room herself. A small bundle had been left on top of a chest, and she made her way toward it as Viola fussed around with the chosen evening gown.

A prickle of emotion clawed at Felicity's throat as she lifted the tattered garment. It was her father's traveling cloak, worn and dirty from his trek. Was he all right? Was he beside himself with worry for her? Or had he sunk back into the listless dejection that had gripped him after her mother had died? Was Ambrose taking care of him? Was anyone taking care of

Ambrose? She hated to think of her brother falling further into the clutches of Kurt, and his set, but it was hard to imagine her father exerting any helpful influence there. Not that she'd had much success when she'd tried.

A lump in the cloak made her pause, and she felt her way into the bulging pocket. She let out a soft gasp as something sharp pricked her finger. Reaching more carefully, she lifted out a single red rose, slightly wilted now, but clearly a brilliant specimen. She sighed, breathing in the perfume it released at being freed from its prison while wincing from the throbbing of her finger.

Just like this place, she reflected ruefully. So beautiful, it was easy to forget the sting that lay underneath the glamour. At what a cost this rose had come.

But there was still something else in the pocket. Frowning, Felicity reached in and pulled out the artifact she'd given her father. She felt a stab of irritation. So much for the bauble being charmed to help her father find his way home. He'd never been more lost than when she'd found him locked in a dungeon. That merchant woman had cheated her out of her two silver coins after all. She was on the verge of discarding it, but a surge of sentiment made her hesitate. It was her only physical reminder of home.

"What's that?" Viola asked brightly, appearing at her shoulder.

After a moment's consideration, Felicity decided not to explain the whole story. As Mrs. Winters had said, they were a bit sensitive about magic here. They might not like knowing she'd intentionally bought what she thought was an artifact.

"It was my father's," she said softly. "He left it behind. I'd like to keep it on me."

"Of course," said Viola, with unusual gentleness. She went to the jewelry case she'd brought in, and rummaged around in it. "I think it will fit nicely on this chain." She wrinkled her nose at it. "It's not the most delicate of pendants, but we can always hide it beneath your dress if it doesn't suit what you're wearing."

Felicity nodded gratefully, stringing the trinket onto the chain and letting Viola drape it over her neck.

Much too soon, she found herself at the doorway of the dining hall, bracing herself for another uncomfortable meal. Mrs. Winters ushered her in, and the prince rose to his feet with obvious reluctance. He was punctual, she'd give him that.

She noticed he was wearing a simpler cloak this time, and the circlet was nowhere to be seen, but she tried to hide her smile. It was probably best not to offend him right from the start.

The same man from the evening before laid out the first course, directing an inquiring look toward the prince.

"Wine," said Prince Justin shortly, tilting an eyebrow at Felicity.

"Not for me, thank you," she said cheerfully. "I prefer to keep a clear head when imprisoned in a haunted castle. You never know when you might need your wits about you."

The prince's expression remained stony, evidently not appreciating her humor. "That will be all, Stewart," he said dismissively.

Felicity watched the man withdraw. There was something vaguely familiar about him, although she couldn't place it. She turned to Prince Justin with interest. "Is he your butler?"

"I have no butler," said her host shortly. "He is my steward, or at least he was. Now he serves a number of roles."

Felicity blinked. "Really?" She couldn't resist a small laugh. "Your steward is named Stewart?"

The prince's stare was cold. "Is something funny?"

Felicity sighed. "Never mind," she said, picking up her fork and scrutinizing the unfamiliar food.

"Was your day pleasant?" The beast-prince asked, his tone anything but encouraging.

Felicity put down her fork, irked by his manner. "Well, I guess you would know, Your Highness," she said tartly. "Since you're having me followed everywhere I go." Phillip, now that pretense was abandoned, had hovered outside her suite the whole time she got ready, and followed her to the dining hall. Clearly his instructions had been very specific.

Prince Justin shrugged one massive shoulder. "What did you expect? That I would just trust you, a total stranger? That I would let you roam around my castle unsupervised, doing who knows what damage?"

"If I'm such a danger," Felicity snapped, "why keep me here? Release me, and I'll be gone by morning."

The prince narrowed his disturbingly human eyes. "I'm not so easily manipulated," he growled.

"And I'm not so easily intimidated," Felicity countered hotly. "I'm not afraid of you."

The prince was silent, and Felicity got the sense that he was unsure whether to be pleased or offended by the comment. She turned to her food with stiff dignity. The sight of the rose that was apparently worth a man's life had brought back all her irritation about the prince's despotic ways. Of course he would want her to be intimidated. Important for her to know her place, peasant that she was.

The meal passed mainly in frigid silence, Felicity too angry to initiate conversation, and the prince apparently too proud. Only as she stood to leave, this time having unashamedly made the most of the dessert, did he rouse himself.

She was at the door, but she turned as the prince cleared his throat. She looked back, eyebrow raised, but he couldn't quite bring himself to meet her gaze as he spoke.

"Do you..." another clearing of the throat, "do you like what you see?"

She stared at him, wondering if the curse had affected his mind as well as his body after all. Did he truly expect her to compliment him after his treatment? His servants were clearly all blinded by a lifetime of enforced loyalty, and it would do this self-important prince good to have someone tell him the truth for once in his life.

"No," she said bluntly. "I don't."

She swept from the room, feeling shaken by the odd question, despite her bold front. The whole place was strange and unnerving, its master most of all. If she wasn't so stubbornly determined to prove the trustworthiness of her word, she'd be tempted to try to escape. The luxury wasn't worth the unsettling feeling that everyone was hiding something important from her.

But her thoughts flashed suddenly to the servants. Phillip's softly spoken politeness, Viola's obvious but unacknowledged attraction to the reserved guard, Mrs. Winters' brisk manner and hen-like mothering of the younger ones.

They didn't deserve to be cursed and trapped, any of them. A surge of determination filled her. It wasn't just her promise keeping her here, not anymore. Viola had said that it was possible for the curse to be broken. Felicity was going to find out how, and help them do it.

CHAPTER TEN

Justin

Justin paced his study, his hands folded behind his back. His tail kept twitching in his irritation, and it only fueled his anger. The afternoon was well advanced, and he was still feeling humiliated over the disastrous second dinner with Felicity. With any luck he wouldn't have to endure a third. He had overcome his moment of weakness, or loneliness, or whatever it had been. He needed to think strategically.

A sharp rap at the door made him turn, and he gestured for the most senior of his three guards to enter.

"Ah, good," he said briskly. "I wish to speak to you about our intruder."

"Felicity's father, you mean?" the middle aged man answered.

Justin's tail twitched again, and he drew a deep breath. "No, I'm talking about Felicity herself, obviously."

"Oh." The guard looked taken aback. "Would you call her an intruder, Your Highness?" Justin raised an eyebrow, and the older man shrugged. "Everyone's grown quite fond of her, from what I can see."

Justin squeezed the bridge of his nose between a thumb and a finger. The gesture was much more challenging than it had once been, at least if he didn't watch to scratch an eye out. "She's only been here for three days."

The guard shrugged again. "She has a way about her, Your Highness. Surely you've noticed. She sort of...brightens up the space."

Justin stared at the normally hard-headed and unexpressive guard. Had his entire staff gone mad?

"Never mind that," he said, feeling it was time to steer the conversation back on course. "I've considered the matter, and I think she should be sent away from the estate."

"What?" The guard was so startled, he dropped his usual rigid posture and stared openly at his prince. "You want her to leave? Surely not, Your Highness! She's getting on so well with everyone."

"The goal isn't for everyone to make friends," Justin snapped. "It's to get free of this nightmare we've all been banished to!"

The guard didn't immediately respond to the impassioned outburst, and Justin took another deep breath. He let it out slowly, running a hand over the tufts of fur on either side of his face.

"And to intervene before my kingdom reaches a state of full crisis," he said, speaking quietly now. He met the guard's eyes. "We know from what happened with her father that Felicity will be able to leave the estate. I plan to send her to the capital with a message for my uncle." His voice turned grim. "A detailed message."

He wondered how good her memory was. He would have liked to have written a long letter to Uncle Cameron, but previous experiments with messenger birds had suggested that the curse would prevent a written missive from leaving the property.

The guard was frowning thoughtfully, clearly thinking the matter over in his methodical way. "I'm not sure it would do us any good," he said at last.

"You don't think she'd do it?" Justin asked. "I know that once she's out of the estate, there's nothing we can do to make her follow through, but I think we need to at least try."

The guard shook his head. "It's not that. I think she would do it if asked." He gave a one-shouldered shrug. "A big part of my job is having a good read on people, and she's not the kind to refuse to give us her help. But what could she do?"

"Tell the rest of the kingdom we're still here!" Justin protested. "Bring back a platoon of soldiers to help free us!"

Before Justin even finished speaking, the guard was shaking his head again. "The first part, yes. Provided anyone believed her. The second part would be no use, Your Highness. Brute force can't undo a curse like this. And I'm not at all sure she could bring anyone back. How would they find us? How would they get in?"

"She did," Justin insisted.

"But we have no idea how," the guard countered. "I was there when her father left the estate, you know. We could see him standing outside the gates, wringing his hands. But it was clear from his behavior that the moment he passed over the border, he could no longer see us, or the castle, or anything. I would wager that he couldn't get back in here if he tried."

"Oh," said Justin. "I see." Somehow he'd missed that information in the previous briefing. "So you think if the intruder—" He rolled his eyes at the guard's expression. "All right, if Felicity were to leave..."

"She might never come back to us," the guard finished for him. "I don't think she'd be able to."

"Well, that does change things," Justin admitted. Was sending a message to his uncle—on the off chance that an unknown peasant girl was able to get an audience with the acting regent and convince him of her tale—worth the risk of losing the only possible lead they had found on getting around the curse in over two years?

It didn't matter how infuriating she was as a dinner companion—he didn't have to think about that for long to know the answer.

"I suppose I'm stuck with her for now," he sighed, turning away so as not to see whatever disapproving look the guard might be sending toward him. "I want you to question her thoroughly, at least. Find out for absolute certain whether she knows anything about whatever anomaly allowed her and her father to enter the estate."

"Yes, Your Highness," said the guard, standing to attention before turning to take his leave.

"Wait," Justin said, and the man turned back. "What did her father do?"

"Your Highness?"

"When he found himself outside the gate," Justin clarified, not entirely sure why he was even asking. "Did he try to get back in? How long did he stay there?"

"Not very long, Your Highness," the guard said, his expression tightening. "He called for Felicity a couple of times, but he looked as edgy as a hare in a fox's sights. He didn't make much of an attempt to find the castle again, and after only a few minutes, he got onto the horse Felicity had sent with him, and rode away." He gave a disapproving frown. "Very poor seat he had, too."

"I see," said Justin, wondering why this information irked him. "That is all."

When he was alone again, Justin walked to the window. The view was pleasant. His few remaining gardeners couldn't maintain the whole estate, but he knew they gave special attention to the area outside his study. He'd never expressed it to them, but he was grateful. He'd always loved the gardens. The days had begun to be brisk, and he could see some fallen leaves swirling in a steady gust of wind. But a nearby bed of dahlias had only just begun to bloom. Their striking color added a spot of vibrancy to the overcast day, some pink, some an orangey color not unlike Felicity's copper hair...

He shook his head. What was wrong with him? Was he comparing flowers to the girl's hair now? That was what came of not laying eyes on a single woman—other than his servants, most of whom he'd known all his life—for over two years.

His eyes were drawn inexorably toward the rose garden. He hated that his study looked out on it. He'd once thought it a beautiful part of the estate, but now it was his least favorite place in the world. When he felt the need for fresh air, he usually walked in a different part of the garden entirely, like the day before, when he'd visited the fountain on the estate's northern side. His thoughts were drawn back to Felicity again, standing on her balcony like a maiden out of a poem, holding him momentarily in thrall with the intensity of her focus.

He sighed. He hated to admit it to himself, but he did know what his guard meant. She had a presence. He wouldn't have said that she brightened the place, exactly. For him, it was the fact that she looked at him. Really looked.

The servants who knew him well had mostly gotten over their initial reaction, and even those who didn't often interact with him no longer cringed at sight of him. But they averted their eyes, and not in the way servants used to do, simply because he was royalty. It was difficult to define, but undeniably different. And Felicity's father had become incoherent with terror at the sight of him, as Justin expected any outsider to do.

But Felicity was made of sterner stuff, it seemed. She had certainly been afraid at their first meeting, but she quickly overcame it. He smiled dryly at the thought of how readily her anger had replaced her fear. And now, when they spoke, there was nothing in her demeanor to suggest she was speaking to a creature, not a man. It was ironic, because while she might speak to him as a human, she was much more comfortable than anyone else to openly refer to his beastly form.

The memory of the evening before intruded uncomfortably into his mind, making him cringe all over again at his humiliation. It was her demeanor that was to blame. The fact that she hadn't seemed to fear his form—even when angry with him— was what had prompted him to ask her the question again. How warmly did she have to respond to what she saw in order to break that part of the curse? Could common politeness be enough?

But her answer had been fairly conclusive.

He pushed the matter from his mind, trying to convince himself that he had more important things to focus on. Sometimes he thought the worst part of the curse was the inability to escape his own head. He pulled the mirror out of the drawer where he had hidden it. The servants knew about it, but he didn't like to flash it around.

"Show me my uncle," he said authoritatively, and at once the surface shimmered.

It took him a moment to place the scene, but when he did, an extra surge of frustration shot through him. His uncle was giving a public address outside the castle in Allenton, in front of a sizable crowd. It wasn't the occasion itself that made him feel so bitter—Uncle Cameron was probably just welcoming those who'd traveled from across the kingdom to take part in the upcoming Harvest Festival. It was just seeing his uncle in yet another kingly duty, and such a visible one.

Justin watched listlessly as Uncle Cameron finished his address and made his way back into the castle, stopping to exchange pleasantries with various nobles of Justin's court.

The acting regent must have been allowed a minute to himself, because he made his way to the study he had occupied since Justin was a child. But the older man had barely sat down behind his desk when the castle's steward bustled in, not bothering to knock.

"*Dobson,*" Uncle Cameron sighed. "*Can't I have one minute of peace?*"

"*I'm afraid not, Lord Regent,*" Dobson said, his lips pinched as if he thought the request unreasonable.

Uncle Cameron gave a soft groan, pulling the simple circlet off his head and dropping it onto the stack of papers in front of him. "*I'm still not convinced about this. Are you sure I need to wear it? It makes my head hurt.*"

"*Of course I'm sure, My Lord!*" Dobson said, sounding scandalized. "*The kingdom needs stability. The populace needs to be reassured that we have a ruler.*"

Uncle Cameron didn't argue further, but Justin could tell it wasn't because he agreed with the steward. Justin frowned to himself as he tried to decide whether he agreed. Uncle Cameron had been the acting regent since Justin's father died, over ten years ago, but Justin couldn't recall him ever wearing any kind of crown before.

"*You needed me?*" Uncle Cameron's voice pulled Justin from his reverie.

"*Yes, Lord Regent,*" said Dobson importantly. "*The architects working on the new development in the city's east are at loggerheads with the group redesigning the public infirmary. The dispute has become quite serious, from what I understand, and it requires your immediate attention.*"

"No, no, no, no, no," groaned Justin aloud. "Don't get involved! That's a matter for the Architects' Guild! It will just put up everyone's backs if the crown interferes."

But as he had expected, Uncle Cameron didn't question his instructions.

"*All right*," he sighed, giving the steward his full attention. "*What do I need to do?*"

Justin put the mirror down, unable to watch any longer. He curled one hand into a fist and pounded the table with it, the impact so great that the whole structure rattled. He glowered at the clawed fist, the injustice of it all washing over him yet again. Physically, he was stronger than he'd ever been before, but he had never felt so impotent. Would this nightmare ever end?

A gardener traipsed past his window, whistling a cheerful tune. The sound made Justin pause. When was the last time he'd heard someone whistling? He thought of the chambermaid he'd passed on his way to his study, and the serving man who'd brought him his breakfast. Not to mention the unusually soft manner of the guard he'd just spoken to. Everyone did seem to be more optimistic lately. Was the guard right? Was Felicity the cause of it?

Acting before he could think it through too carefully, Justin picked up the mirror again. "Show me Felicity," he said.

The image shifted, and her cheerful face came into sight. She was laughing, as usual, although for once not at him. She also seemed to be covered in flour.

"I did *not* suggest a competition! I'm under no illusions— mine will be woeful compared to a proper apprentice chef's. All I said was that I've baked a lot of bread in my life, so there was no reason I couldn't be helpful."

Her companion, a girl not much older than her, beamed. Her efforts with her own knot of dough intensified, and Justin squinted in an effort to remember her name. He had a feeling she was the younger of the two remaining kitchen maids. He didn't know much about such things, but he was pretty sure the girl was far from being a "proper apprentice chef", so it was no wonder she was pleased by the imaginary promotion. Someone else moved into the mirror's range, and to Justin's astonishment he saw that even the normally dour-faced cook was smiling benignly on Felicity's chatter.

"It looks wonderful to me," the cook said. "I'll be sure to serve yours to His Highness at dinner, Felicity, and I'm sure he'll enjoy it."

Felicity snorted, then coughed violently when the action caused flour to go up her nose. "Sorry," she gasped, when she could breathe again. The kitchen maid still looked concerned, but stopped whacking her back. "I was just trying to imagine the prince *enjoying* anything, and couldn't quite manage it."

"Nonsense," said the cook quickly. "The duties of a crown are heavy, but His Highness can be lighthearted as much as the next young person."

Justin winced at this clumsy, and completely mendacious, attempt to praise him to his guest. Felicity looked unconvinced. If Justin was any judge, she was yet again on the verge of laughing, but to her credit she managed to hold it in.

"At any rate, I'd prefer you give it to someone a little less exacting, and a little more deserving of my efforts," she said lightly.

"Don't say that," pleaded the kitchen maid. "Prince Justin isn't so bad. You just need to get to know him. He's a good master." Her face brightened. "And he's a prince, you know."

Felicity's lips had formed a thin line, her disapproval clear, and Justin cringed. She looked up suddenly, calling a greeting. Presumably someone new was entering the kitchen, but it had seemed unnervingly like she was looking back at him, and calling him out for spying on her.

He put down the mirror hastily. Not only had that interaction been even harder to watch than his uncle playing king, he suddenly realized just how ignoble it was to watch Felicity without her knowledge. He had shaken off Mrs. Winters' accusation the first time he'd done it, but she'd been right. It wasn't the action of a gentleman.

He wasn't an idiot. He realized what his servants were trying to do. He also realized what none of them seemed to—there was no possible way it would work. Prince or not, neither Felicity nor anyone else was ever going to look at him in his current form, and like what they saw.

But she didn't say a word about your form, an uncomfortable inner voice reminded him. *She was talking about* you.

The thought stirred something deep inside him, below his beastly exterior, below even his bitterness over the transformation he had been forced to undergo. The fact that this girl looked past not only his form, but also his status as prince, and found the man underneath wanting, created a discomfort that not even anger could drive away. He made a promise to himself that he would try a little harder at dinner that night, to treat her more like a guest than an intruder.

And to make no comment whatsoever on the bread.

CHAPTER ELEVEN

Felicity

F elicity closed her eyes, drawing in a deep breath and relishing the brisk air. There was nothing quite like the smell of fallen leaves just after a good rainfall. Autumn was advancing, and in the distance she could see the gardeners, the grooms, and even the serving man harvesting the estate's tiny wheat field. Even the chambermaids could sometimes be seen bringing in some of the estate's produce, and she knew the cook and her two kitchen maids were busy inside, preserving all kinds of goods to last through winter.

In fact, in spite of Mrs. Winters' airy assurance that they had too many servants for one resident, everyone at the castle seemed to be working very hard to meet the estate's demands.

Not that Felicity was allowed to help, of course. She'd been giving it her best effort, but even after three weeks, she was barely allowed to help with anything. The cook would occasionally let her help with baking, and she didn't usually get much resistance from the chambermaids when she insisted on helping them with the endless cycle of laundry created by the twenty person household. The under groom—the only person at the castle younger even than Viola—sometimes let her help with the horses. But the head groom didn't approve of her being put to work, so she could only get away with it when the older man was away from his domain.

"Phillip," she said abruptly, "have they tried making a hole in the stone wall, in case the enchantment that stops you all from leaving is on the gate itself?"

She turned, but it was clear that her ever-present guard hadn't heard her question. He'd fallen back a step, his attention claimed by Viola. Felicity wondered humorously what excuse the maid had given Mrs. Winters this time for why she needed to accompany her mistress on an aimless ramble. She didn't begrudge Viola her escape from her duties, and she made no attempt to break in on her companions' conversation. Her amusement grew as she saw the playful way Viola swatted at Phillip's arm. Felicity was still trying to figure out whether the young guard was exceptionally oblivious, or not interested. For Viola's sake, she hoped it wasn't the latter.

Leaving them to their moment, she wandered into a walkway lined with hedges, now a splotchy mix of green, yellow, and orange. It wasn't as though Phillip would have given her a straight answer, anyway. However little success she'd had in getting Mrs. Winters to put her to work, she'd had even less in her attempts to help break the curse. She'd expected all the servants to be eager to explore any possible avenue for lifting it, but they were all strangely reluctant to talk about it. And no one seemed to have much interest in her various suggestions for circumventing it. There was definitely something they weren't telling her, and whatever it was, they had closed ranks completely.

It made her edgy, and not just because they were hiding something. She thought of her father, wondering if he was coping without her. He'd never liked the cold weather, and the days were beginning to feel frosty. Snow would be upon them soon, and she wouldn't be there to make sure the fire didn't go out, or to identify any patches in the roof that needed fixing. Ambrose might step in to fill her place, but she wouldn't want to put a wager on it. And as much as he frustrated her, she worried about Ambrose as well. Was he missing her as much as her father must be? Was he getting himself into trouble, running with Kurt and his crew?

She sighed, perfectly aware that her concern for them was mixed with guilt. Prisoner though she might be, a part of her was loving the luxury of life at the castle. For some strange reason, she was being treated like an honored guest instead of an interloper, and she had never been so well cared for. But it wasn't reality, and a sensible part of her realized that the longer it went on, the harder it would be to return to her old life.

Truthfully, she'd never expected to be here so long. Even on that disastrous first meeting, she'd recognized the petulance in Prince Justin's voice. He was clearly still in control of his mind, and after the first shocked moments, she hadn't really feared that he would attack her. She'd figured he would keep her in the dungeon for a few days, then realize that the hassle of keeping her there wasn't worth the point he was making, and send her home.

She paused by a fish pond, drawing her costly cloak—courtesy of some departed noblewoman—more tightly around her. Thinking about Prince Justin was more perplexing and unsettling than all the rest. He'd been so infuriating at the start, which had made things simple for her. It was easy to know how to respond to his rudeness. But he no longer made disparaging comments about her trustworthiness, or lost his temper. He was still aloof, and a little haughty, but he was clearly making an effort to be at least passably polite. And she had no experience that would teach her how she should respond to either a prince or a beast-man, let alone someone who was both at once.

She thought back to the night before. They'd dined together, as they had done every single night since she'd arrived. The prince had even inquired quite amicably about her day, and listened with tolerable politeness to her account of a near-disaster in the laundry room. He'd seemed surprised to discover she'd been helping there, and she hadn't quite known what to make of his expression.

Of course, as always, any ground they had made was instantly lost when he ended the dinner the same way he always did, with his awkward question. Felicity dreaded the nightly ritual, still unable to figure out how to answer both honestly and politely. At first it had seemed so absurd it was laughable, but it no longer tickled her usually responsive sense of humor. Surely he knew how she would answer—how could anyone like his appearance? The whole thing made her uncomfortable, sad in a way she couldn't quite articulate.

"Getting a little cold for a stroll, isn't it?"

Felicity jumped at the throaty voice, a slight flush rising up her cheeks. She had to remind herself the prince couldn't read her mind, and had no way of knowing he'd just interrupted her thoughts about him.

"You're out here," she pointed out once she regained her composure. She paused, considering the matter. "But I suppose you're covered in fur, aren't you? Does it keep you warm?"

For a moment Prince Justin remained frozen, and Felicity gave an internal sigh as she braced herself for his inevitable offense. He was so absurdly sensitive.

But he surprised her, his tension draining away as he gave what was almost a chuckle.

"It does, actually. It's quite convenient come winter. Even snow doesn't really bother me."

"That's handy," said Felicity brightly. "I don't much like snow myself, although cold like this doesn't bother me." She gestured toward the overcast skies.

"I often walk in the gardens after a good rainfall," Prince Justin said, again surprising her. He rarely spoke to her outside their nightly dinners, and he never volunteered information about himself. "There's something fresh about the air."

"Yes," she agreed, a little taken aback. "I feel the same way." She pulled in a deep breath. "What is that heavenly smell? It's more than just the rain on the leaves."

Prince Justin smiled. "It's the saffron crocus," he said, pointing to a bed of purple flowers. "My mother had them planted here. They're not from Solstice—some trading caravan brought them from the other side of the desert."

"Really?" Felicity asked, impressed. She regarded the prince thoughtfully for a moment. "Do you remember your mother? She died when we were children, didn't she?"

"Yes," said Justin, his face inscrutable. "I remember her a little. I was seven."

"I'm sorry," said Felicity, feeling like it needed to be said, despite his apparent lack of emotion. "My mother died when I was young, too."

She was silent for a moment, doing the calculations. "If you were seven when the queen died, I would have been five." She nodded to herself. "So it was after we moved away from Allenton, then. No wonder I don't remember much about it. All I recall was hearing people say that Queen Racquel was gentle, and sweet. No one talks much about her, or why she died." She shot a glance at the prince. "It's been a decade since your father died, but people still speak of him."

Prince Justin snorted, the unprincelike sound startling Felicity. "Yes, my father certainly made sure he'd be remembered." His eyes narrowed slightly. "And he felt no particular compunction to honor my mother's memory. She wasn't strong enough to survive, and he despised her for that. Ironic, of course, since he only outlived her by three years in the end. But I suppose a hunting accident is a more acceptable way to die than a broken heart."

Felicity was silent, struggling to find a suitable response to the unexpected confidence. But the prince seemed to regret the words almost as soon as they were out of his mouth. He gave his shaggy head a slight shake, as if coming back to his surroundings, and stepped toward the purple flowers.

"At any rate, I've been told this was her favorite flower," he said, his tone once again aloof. He reached for one of the saffron crocus blooms, but Felicity hurried forward, stopping him with a hand on his furry arm.

"No, let me. You'll crush it with your claws."

Prince Justin blinked, apparently speechless as his eyes passed from her hand to her face.

"I still retain the ability to use my hands, you know," he said dryly.

Felicity removed her hand, noting that his fur was softer and less matted than she'd expected. "You manage impressively well," she agreed soothingly. "But flowers are a delicate matter."

She plucked a bloom, pulling her braid over her shoulder and tucking the flower into the end of it. When she saw the prince watching her blankly, she shrugged. "I like them, too," she said, picking another one and handing it to him. He took it mechanically, and she suddenly realized what she'd done.

"Oh no!" she cried. "I forgot how protective you are over your garden." She touched the flower in her hair. "Is picking this a dungeon-worthy offense?"

A strange look passed over his face. "No," he said, and she was surprised to again hear a hint of humor in his voice. "You can pick as many crocuses as you like."

She brightened. "Thank you! I wouldn't mind displaying

some in my suite. Maybe Phillip and Viola would be willing to fetch me a vase."

"Phillip?" the prince repeated, clearly recognizing the name. He turned in the direction Felicity was looking, his wolf-like brow furrowing. "What is a guard doing loitering in the gardens while the wheat is being harvested?"

Felicity raised an eyebrow at his disapproving tone. "He's following me around everywhere I go, presumably at your direction."

Prince Justin made no attempt to deny it. "He's still doing that?"

"Naturally," said Felicity dryly. "Having had to physically restrain me from making a run for it at least half a dozen times, he can't afford to let me out of his sight."

Justin scowled. He clearly knew Felicity wasn't serious, so she could only assume it was her tone that annoyed him. To her interest, she saw his tail twitch slightly. She couldn't help her eyes being drawn to the movement.

"Does it feel strange?" she asked, fascinated. "Having a tail?"

"No," the prince snapped. "Of course not. It feels completely normal to have a wolf's tail growing out of my body."

Felicity rolled her eyes. "No need to be sarcastic."

The prince opened his mouth, clearly intending to retort. But with what appeared to be a supreme effort, he closed it without speaking. "I'll speak to the guard," he said stiffly, after an awkward moment. "His efforts would be more useful elsewhere."

Felicity sighed as he stalked away. They'd been doing so well for once, and she knew she'd been as much to blame as he had for the descent back to animosity. She should probably try to be a bit more like everyone else and avoid mention of his non-human body, but it seemed so silly. It wasn't like if she didn't bring it up, he'd forget he'd been transformed into some kind of lion-wolf-man hybrid.

"Fair maiden! So the rumors are true!"

Felicity spun, gasping at the sight of an unfamiliar man at the end of the walkway.

"Who—who are you?" she stammered. She didn't need the man's chain mail to tell her he wasn't from the estate. There were only eighteen servants, and by now she knew every one of them by name and face.

The man gave a flourishing bow. "I am Sir Gourding of Listernia, and I have heard of your plight."

"My...plight?" Felicity repeated blankly. Her eyes passed from the knight to the horse standing placidly some paces behind him. "Sorry, *who* are you?"

"Sir Gourding of Listernia," the man repeated impatiently.

"Yes, I heard that," Felicity said cautiously. "But I'm afraid your name doesn't mean anything to me. Do I know you?"

"Not yet," the knight said, his eyes roaming appreciatively over her, taking in her costly gown. "But I hope in time—"

"Why are you here?" Felicity interrupted bluntly. The enormity of the situation suddenly hit her. "Wait—more to the point, *how* are you here?"

"I'm here to rescue you from your prison," the knight said simply. "Word of your fate has reached us even in Listernia." His voice turned slightly sulky. "As for how, I traveled during the day, of course."

"No, I didn't mean how did you get out of Listernia," said Felicity impatiently. "I meant how did you get into this estate? It's supposed to be magically hidden from the world!"

"I know," said the knight, giving a shrug that made his chain mail clink. "But I don't know what to say. I came looking, and here it was. I just rode through the gate."

Felicity stared. "But this is incredible," she said. "Let me get—"

"Who are you?" The deep voice of the prince reverberated through the chill air, making Felicity spin on the spot.

"Justin!" she said, excitement tinging her voice. "Someone else got in! This is," she gestured vaguely, "Sir, uh...Gourd, from Listernia."

"Gourding," the knight corrected, his gaze passing from her to the cursed prince. "Who are you talking to?"

Felicity blinked. In her excitement, she'd forgotten that Prince Justin's appearance would be a shock to the visitor, and she had to admit she was impressed by how coolly he was taking it.

"Oh," she said quickly. "I know he looks a little different, but I can assure you, this is Prince Justin."

The prince barely allowed her to finish before he took control of the situation.

"I am Crown Prince Justin," he said commandingly. "How did you enter my estate?"

Felicity frowned at the menacing edge to his words. Did he want to scare the man off before they got answers? Surely someone else finding the castle was a good thing. But the knight ignored Justin altogether, his wary gaze fixed on Felicity.

"Maybe I'm too late," he muttered.

"Too late for what?" Prince Justin's tail was once again twitching.

"Yes, why are you here?" Felicity pressed.

"I'm here to take you away from this place," the knight said slowly and clearly, as if speaking to a simpleton. "As I said, we've heard about your situation in Listernia."

Felicity blinked. "You've heard of me?"

The man nodded. "I don't know your name, I'm afraid, but we've heard a rumor that a beautiful maiden was being held captive by a hideous beast."

Prince Justin growled long and low, and Felicity cast an apprehensive glance at him. She didn't want him to lose his temper and throw the knight out before they could find out what he knew, but she could hardly blame him for being irritated. The Listernian wasn't exactly doing anything to endear himself.

Looking past the prince, she saw both Phillip and Viola standing a short way behind him, staring at the newcomer with wide eyes. Prince Justin had followed the trajectory of her gaze, and he barked out a terse command.

"Fetch the other guards."

Phillip nodded quickly and took off at a run.

"Hideous beast?" Felicity scolded, returning her attention to the knight. "That's very rude."

He looked more bemused than ever. "Are you defending the creature?" He gave his head a slight shake. "Clearly it has you in its grip. You'll thank me when you're away from this place."

Without warning, he reached forward, seizing Felicity firmly by the arm.

She yelped, attempting without success to pull free. "What are you doing?"

"I'm helping you escape," the knight said, exasperated.

"But...why?" Felicity asked, more confused than ever. "We're total strangers!"

"I can tell you why," said Prince Justin, a sneer in his words. "Like he said, news of your *plight* has spread across the land. He's hoping to win renown by being your rescuer."

The knight again ignored the prince's words, neither confirming nor denying his assessment. His eyes were fixed on Felicity, and his grip on her arm was unyielding.

"Come, maiden," he said authoritatively. "I must free you from the magic of this place, before your mind is lost."

"No thank you," said Felicity flatly, trying again to pull her arm away. "I don't need rescuing, and there's nothing wrong with my mind."

The knight shook his head sadly. "Don't need rescuing?" he repeated. "Alas, if you could only hear yourself!"

Felicity stared at him. "Did you just say 'alas'?"

Sir Gourding responded by raising his voice. "I must get you away from here," he almost shouted. "Before it's too late."

"I told you," said Felicity, growing impatient, both with Sir Goulding's denseness and the prince's passive behavior, "I don't need your help. I gave my word I would stay here until released." Her voice grew excited. "But you might be able to help the prince, and the rest of them!" She tried to tug her arm away, but the knight held fast. "Let go," she said crossly.

The knight shook his head stubbornly. "You clearly need to be rescued from yourself."

Felicity scowled, starting to grow genuinely angry. "Let go."

Still nothing.

She turned impatiently to the prince. "Justin? A little help?"

The prince met her eyes, something silent passing between them that she couldn't name. Then he stepped forward, his voice at its iciest.

"The lady asked you to remove your hand. I suggest you do so, unless you want me to remove it from your body."

His tone sent a chill down Felicity's spine, but Sir Gourding was unmoved. He continued to stare at Felicity, looking wary. "Who are you talking to?"

"What do you..." Sudden understanding made Felicity gasp, her eyes flying back to Justin's. "He can't see you," she whispered, and Justin froze. She turned quickly back to Sir Gourding. The irritating man still hadn't released her, but she swallowed her annoyance over that detail. "Listen," she said quickly. "You may not be able to see or hear him, but the prince is right here." She gestured awkwardly with her free hand. "He's trapped. Maybe you can help him."

The knight shook his head sadly. "So lovely, and so lost," he said dramatically. "There's no one here but us, fair lady. I can only hope that once I free you from this place, your mind will also be free."

"All right, enough of that," said Felicity, losing patience. "I'm not leaving with you. I gave my word I'd stay. Now *let go of me*."

The knight's face remained stubborn, and his grip didn't loosen. With a low growl, Justin seemed to throw off his shock at Felicity's revelation. He stepped forward, his wolf-like claws closing around the man's arm. Sir Gourding yelped with pain as Justin wrenched his arm from Felicity, none too gently.

"Thank you," said Felicity brightly, rubbing her abused arm. She gave the knight a calculating look, but continued to speak to Justin. "So he can feel you. Interesting."

"How did you do that?" Sir Gourding asked, gazing around him in alarm. "This place really is cursed."

"Yes, about that." Felicity's tone had turned businesslike. "Maybe you can help break the curse." She stepped forward, but the knight was already retreating.

"It's clear the curse has taken your mind," he said, shaking his head. "I won't stay to let it take mine, too." He held out a hand, but didn't touch her this time. "Come with me. It might not be too late."

"I'm not leaving until I'm released," said Felicity impatiently. "I told you, I gave my word. But if you'll just come inside—"

The knight took another step back, shooting a look of alarm toward the castle behind them. "I must go, while my mind is free. I see I am too late to save you." He paused, casting another admiring glance over her form. "Unless your curse can be broken by a kiss, perhaps?" His tone had become hopeful. "I've heard that sometimes—"

"I don't think so," Felicity interrupted him flatly. She folded her arms across her chest, and the knight shrugged.

"If you prefer to be trapped," he said, his tone a little sulky.

"I really do," said Felicity shortly.

The knight sniffed, but after one more apprehensive glance at the castle, he turned away, striding swiftly to his horse. With a clink of his chain mail, he swung himself up into the saddle.

"Wait," Felicity cried, feeling like she owed it to her fellow inmates to give it one more try. "If you'll just come inside—"

She was interrupted by the knight's sentimental sigh. "Poor child," he said condescendingly. "If only I could have come sooner."

Felicity scowled, but there was no time for a retort. Sir Gourding swung his horse around, riding straight for the gate.

For a prolonged moment, Felicity, the prince, and Viola all stared after him in a stunned silence. Felicity was the first to shake off her stupor.

"He was ridiculous," she said with feeling. "How did he get in?"

"You tell me," said the prince, his voice like ice. "Since he seems to be a friend of yours."

"What?" Felicity asked, turning to him in surprise.

Prince Justin waved a misshapen hand toward the gate. "He came for you, didn't he? Since your terrible fate of being held captive by a *hideous beast* has spread throughout the lands."

Felicity felt her mouth drop open. "You're blaming me for what he said? That's the most unreasonable—"

"As if I care what some idiot Listernian says," the prince scoffed, cutting her off. There was a nasty edge to his voice. "But it does seem like, since he came all this way to free you from my cursed clutches, the least you could have done was send him off with a kiss."

Felicity bristled. Angry words rose to her lips, but she swallowed them with an effort. "Save your insults," she snapped. "We have more important things to think about. Someone just entered your magically concealed castle for the first time in years. We need to figure out how."

"But it's not the first time, is it?" said the prince, his tone mockingly pleasant. "So perhaps you can tell us how your friend got in. I assume he used the same trick you did."

"Trick?" gasped Felicity, her anger flaring back to life. "You think I came here on purpose? You think I wanted to be stuck in a prison with an unmannered animal?"

The prince's beastly face was further marred by a sneer. The sound of running feet announced the approach of Phillip with the other guards, and they both looked up.

"Took you long enough," the prince snapped, and Felicity instantly jumped to the guards' defense.

"Don't take it out on them!"

Prince Justin ignored her, directing his attention to the senior guard. "It seems our guest has been holding out on us. Your previous interrogation must not have been rigorous enough. I want her questioned again."

Felicity could only stare, and even the guards just blinked back at their master in stupefaction.

"Well?" the prince demanded, gesturing toward her. "You have your orders."

The head guard's brow was slightly furrowed, but he moved toward Felicity. To her relief, he didn't seize her, just stood beside her. The prince didn't wait to watch his orders carried out, turning in a swirl of cloak to stride past a wide eyed Viola and back toward the castle.

Felicity watched him go, angry tears springing to her eyes. For a moment, she'd almost believed he was beginning to trust her.

What a fool she'd been.

CHAPTER TWELVE

Justin

J ustin prowled the length of the portrait hall, his clawed hands clasped behind him. This part of the castle was far from his suite, or his study, or any room with a lit fire. He could sense the chill that permeated the air, and he could see through the windows that there was frost on the garden. But as he had said to Felicity, his fur prevented him from experiencing any discomfort from the cold.

Felicity.

He felt one ear twitch in irritation, as if flicking off a fly. He didn't want to think about the girl. He came to a stop in front of a portrait, and a soft sigh escaped him.

If she'd seen me when I looked like that, she would have liked what she saw.

He shook his head, trying to dislodge the embarrassing thought. For no apparent reason, he suddenly thought of the open admiration on the Listernian knight's face as he'd all but ogled Felicity that day in the garden. The hairs stood up on the back of Justin's neck, and not just because women used to look at him that way. He knew he'd been considered handsome before he was cursed, but honestly, his appearance wasn't something he'd previously been vain about. Such things weren't important for a prince, who had much more effective means of gaining power.

He should stop asking the question every night, but his very embarrassment drove him on. If only she would say yes, he could send her home and stop enduring the nightly torment. All he needed was for her to like what she saw—he could surely find a way to break the rest of the curse without her help. Perhaps if he wore her down with constant repetition, she'd give him a different answer just to get him to stop asking.

So far that tactic hadn't worked.

He stared up at the image of his former self, dark hair swept back and topped with a circlet, blue eyes staring straight ahead. Hand resting on the hilt of a sword he'd never had to use outside training, stance suggesting a confidence that had been a little forced, even then. He noted dispassionately how successful the artist had been in capturing the haughty expression his father had taught him to wear.

He could still hear his father's words. *A king cannot afford a* moment *of vulnerability, Justin, not even one moment. It was only a dog. Stop being so weak.*

Justin scowled at a portrait hanging next to his own. "I wasn't a king," he muttered to the heavy-browed man. "I was a small child who missed his mother." But of course his father hadn't connected his tears over the loss of his dog with his deeper grief over his mother's death. And Justin had already known better than to bring up his mother. If the king thought his son's grief made him weak, it was nothing to the disdain he had felt toward his wife.

His mind turned to another memory, although this one was harder to place. A similar conversation had occurred far too many times to count, usually any time his father thought he was getting too friendly with those around his own age in the court.

A king must have absolute power, Justin, which means you cannot allow anyone to have power over you. If you give someone your trust, you give them power. They will abuse it every time.

Justin's eyes were still lingering on the portrait, and he turned away quickly. Even in image, it was hard to look his father in the eye. His skin crawled with the feeling of being measured, and found wanting. Justin had been only ten when his father had died, but already he'd been a disappointment. He could tell it in the way his father looked at him. He'd even chosen Justin a future wife, a girl a year younger than him, with excellent connections in the court. He hadn't trusted Justin to make any decisions for himself.

Justin's expression soured as he thought of the young woman in question. His father, of course, had cared only for her connections. Her personality was immaterial. But Justin had always found her abrasive. And the memory of her horrified face, standing out from the sea of guests and servants who witnessed his humiliating transformation, was seared into his mind. She had been the first out the door.

He wondered with grim amusement what his father would have thought of her cowardly behavior. But the thought brought little comfort. Justin's father would be much more disgusted by his own son, and not just because of his monstrous form. He knew what his father would say if he could have seen inside Justin's head that day in the garden. He would say that Justin was even weaker as an adult than he had been as a child.

Justin grimaced, acutely aware of his own weakness. Perhaps he could get out of dinner tonight. It wasn't as though Felicity wanted to dine with him any more than he wanted her there. He'd thought her initial impertinence was irritating, but her frostiness was even worse. As someone who'd been raised to it from the cradle, he watched her attempts to be haughty as a bird might watch a fish attempting to fly.

He groaned to himself, directing his steps back toward his suite. He knew he couldn't get out of dinner. Not unless he wanted to be guilted by Mrs. Winters for the next decade.

If he was honest with himself, Felicity's behavior was all the harder to take because he knew he'd treated her unfairly. He'd watched the head guard's second interrogation, via the mirror, but he was unsurprised by the result. He didn't really believe she knew anything, any more than the guard did. His accusation had been merely a deflection.

The truth was that his own reaction had scared him. He'd let his defenses down, chatting with her about flowers and such stupid things. She'd even touched him, willingly, and he'd been too astonished to pull away. He couldn't remember the last time he'd allowed someone to touch him, even before he was cursed.

And then that idiot knight had appeared, and looked at Felicity like she was his to claim simply for the asking...and she'd refused to go with him. She'd said she didn't need rescuing —she'd even turned to him for help when the man wouldn't let go of her. He wasn't sure she'd even noticed, but in her excitement she'd dropped his title, calling him by his name for the first time. She'd even defended him when the knight had insulted him.

He'd lost his head, to put it simply. It hadn't showed on the outside, of course. He was far too well trained for that. But inside he'd been hit by a cascade of jumbled emotions that he couldn't ever remember feeling before.

And it had terrified him. *She* had terrified him. She'd looked at him as if they were allies, as if they understood one another, and he'd been alarmed to realize how far in he seemed to have let her. Well, most of him had been alarmed. A small part of him had been exhilarated, further proving his own weakness.

He couldn't even remember deciding to get angry. It was an instinctive reaction, the only method he knew for both hiding and quashing the embarrassing display of emotion. The knight had left by then, so Felicity was the only target left to bear the brunt of his attack. And with the memory of the knight and his various insinuations so fresh, the anger was all too easy to find.

He knew he'd been unreasonable. He knew none of it had been Felicity's fault. And while he'd certainly achieved his goal of creating some distance between them, the weak, vulnerable part of him had regretted it ever since. Of course, he hadn't said any of this to her, which was probably why she hadn't spoken to him in the two weeks that had passed.

Well, that wasn't entirely true. She had spoken to him several times, to ask him snidely if he was ready to release her yet. He gave a grim smile. It was as though she thought her continued coldness would be more than he could handle, so that he would be forced to get rid of her. If she only knew the upbringing he'd had, she would realize her feeble attempts to freeze him out were child's play.

For a moment he entertained the thought of releasing her as requested. He couldn't quite hold back a snort. If he thought the servants were annoyed with him after his outburst toward Felicity—which they all unquestionably were, although Mrs. Winters had been the only one bold enough to actually chastise him—he could only imagine how angry they'd be if he let Felicity leave. Quite apart from the fact that they were all convinced she was going to break the curse, everyone had lost their minds over the girl. He'd even seen the head groom, as crusty a fellow as he'd ever met, smiling fondly at her when she visited the stables.

The sound of footsteps on the floor below made Justin's ears prick up. In his human form he wouldn't have been able to hear them from so far away, but he no longer noticed the enhanced hearing. His first assumption was that Stewart was coming to remind him to ready himself for dinner, but he realized a moment later that the gait was wrong for the steward. Too rhythmic, too powerful. He started to sniff at the air, and clamped down furiously on the instinct. He didn't need the extra sense, anyway. He was certain it was the head guard approaching.

Sure enough, the man's grizzled head appeared at the top of a nearby staircase, followed by the rest of him.

"Your Highness," he said smartly, dipping his head respectfully before falling into step beside his master.

"Don't tell me," Justin said, his tone weary. "Another one?"

"Yes, Your Highness," said the guard.

Justin growled quietly. Two weeks since Sir Melon, or whatever his name had been, and already there had been three more. One more knight, and two separate hunters, all of whom seemed to be under the impression that a reward was being offered to anyone who could rescue the damsel. And presumably slay her captor, Justin thought, with a twitch of his tail.

He hadn't seen any of them himself, but apparently none of them had stuck around as long as the Listernian knight. They'd all run for the gate when Felicity not only refused to come, but insisted that the castle was populated with people who only she could see and hear.

Although considering how mad she still was at him, Justin did have to wonder how hard Felicity had really tried to convince them to stay and help.

"How are they getting in?" he muttered aloud, to no one in particular. "If the castle is open again, why aren't more people coming? And why can't everyone leave? If Felicity can see us all, why can't they?" He turned his attention back to the guard. "I assume this one also disappeared before the guards could get there? I might have to assign someone to follow Felicity around again, just to be on hand when they find her." He dropped his voice back to a mutter. "As they inevitably seem to." It was enough to make him wonder if she really was hiding something after all.

"No, Your Highness," said the guard unexpectedly. "His Highness didn't leave. Miss Felicity invited him to stay for dinner, and he accepted."

"What?" Justin froze. "Did you say His Highness? Who's here?"

"Prince Bentleigh of Bansford," said the guard, his tone as calm as ever.

"WHAT?!" Justin took off down the corridor again, his loping gait a little too fast and smooth for a human. He was vaguely aware of the guard following, but all his thoughts were on this latest visitor.

He burst into the entranceway, and pulled up short at the sight of Prince Bentleigh, standing in the middle of the marble floor and peering cautiously around him.

"Ben," Justin called. The nickname slipped out in his excitement, although they'd never been close friends. "Ben, can you hear me?"

There was no change whatsoever to the other prince's expression, and Justin's heart sank. He moved forward more slowly, until he stood just in front of the Bansfordian. He raised a massive hand and waved it in front of Prince Bentleigh's eyes.

Nothing.

Justin felt so crushed by his disappointment, he could almost have sunk to the floor. But his head guard was behind him, and he knew better than to show his emotions so plainly.

"Blast," he muttered instead.

"It seems he cannot see or hear us, Your Highness," said the guard stoically. "Like the others."

A sarcastic retort was on the tip of Justin's tongue, but he held it in. This was no more his guard's fault than the incident with the first visitor had been Felicity's.

"So I gather," he said, his tone mild. He began to circle the visitor, examining him. They were the same age, and had been thrown together a number of times during their childhood. It had been some years since they'd seen one another, however, and Bentleigh had changed. Well, not as much as Justin, of course. But he was tall now, and strong...again, not as tall and strong as Justin was at present...

Justin shook his head. Why was he comparing himself to the other prince like they were in some kind of competition? As if his appearance could measure favorably against that of any other man in the continent.

Bentleigh wandered across the entranceway, peering into Justin's study before turning back to the center of the space. He looked wary, but not fearful.

"What's he waiting for?" Justin asked the guard, and the other man shrugged.

Prince Bentleigh, of course, had no reaction to their conversation. It was beyond strange to be invisible, almost worse than being screamed at in terror.

"Your Highness!" Two of the three men in the room turned at the call, Prince Bentleigh remaining oblivious. Mrs. Winters hurried into the entranceway. She cast an appraising glance at Prince Bentleigh, but she was obviously aware of the situation, because she didn't address him.

"Prince Justin," she said instead. "I've had an extra place laid for dinner, as Miss Felicity requested." The housekeeper looked as though she didn't entirely approve of the plan, and for once Justin was in complete agreement with her.

"Dinner? What's the point of inviting him to dinner?" He scowled. "Where's Felicity? I can't communicate with Prince Bentleigh without her."

"She's preparing herself for the evening meal," said Mrs.

Winters, her lips pressed into a thin line. "She seemed a little discomposed."

Justin's heart sank again, for some reason. "Well, hurry her along, will you?" he barked. "And show Prince Bentleigh to the —oh, blast it all, you can't do that, can you?" He grunted in irritation. "I suppose Felicity will have to do it."

He swept from the room without a backward glance, heading straight for the private dining hall. He paced the ornate rug for a good half an hour before he heard the telltale signs of Mrs. Winters' nightly approach.

The housekeeper swung the door wide, her face now set in disapproving lines.

"Your Highness," she said stiffly. "Your guests, Miss Felicity and Prince Bentleigh of Bansford."

Justin sighed, but didn't bother to comment on the pointlessness of introducing the prince. Bentleigh gallantly waved Felicity through before following, his eyes fixed in wonder on the doors which must have seemed to magically open for their entrance.

"Felicity," Justin growled, when she failed to greet him. She gave him a look that told him just how annoyed she still was with him, before turning to Bentleigh.

"Please," she gestured to the table, "sit down. The food is limited to what can be produced on the estate, but the quality of the cooking is excellent, I promise."

"Thank you," said Bentleigh politely.

"What are you playing at?" Justin demanded, but Felicity ignored him. He had remained standing, but he regretted it when Prince Bentleigh sat tentatively in Justin's own seat, staring at the empty plate before him.

Justin's growl was interrupted by Stewart, who chose that moment to appear with a tray. He did a quick survey of the room, his subsequent sniff every bit as disapproving as Mrs.

Winters' expression had been. Then he placed a steaming bowl of soup in front of the visiting prince.

Bentleigh gave a yelp, his eyes riveted on the bowl. Presumably his soup had seemed to appear magically in front of him.

"Is it safe?" he asked tentatively. He glanced up at Felicity, adding hastily, "I don't mean to offend. I'm just...a little wary of enchantments."

"It's perfectly safe," Felicity assured him, her smile a little too warm. Justin felt a strange flicker inside him, one that reminded him of his unanswered question as to why he had been comparing himself to Prince Bentleigh in the entranceway. He actively refused to engage with the thought, pushing it to one side. He also refused to sit in the seat that had been set for his uninvited guest, prowling around behind the other two instead.

"I'm sorry I was so flustered before," Felicity was saying, in her cheerful, candid way. "I was a little awestruck, to be perfectly honest." She took a sip of her soup. "I've never met an actual prince before, you see."

Justin gave a pointed growl, glaring at her from his current position behind Bentleigh's—or rather his own—chair.

Her eyes flickered briefly to his, one eyebrow raised challengingly. "You don't count, because of the..." She waved her hand vaguely over her face.

Justin's growl grew rapidly to a crescendo. Felicity was undaunted, meeting him look for look.

"I'm sorry, what?" Prince Bentleigh looked confused, and she returned her attention quickly to him.

"Never mind, what were you saying?"

Poor Bentleigh seemed more bemused than ever, but he managed a friendly smile. "Just that the honor is all mine. You may not have met any princes before, but I've never met any ladies hidden away in enchanted castles before."

Felicity gave a delighted chuckle, and Justin cursed the

charming, handsome Bansfordian under his breath. Of course Felicity would like his foolish banter.

"Enough," he said abruptly, using his most commanding voice. "Felicity, tell him that I wish him to take a message to my uncle in Allenton." She opened her mouth, but he cut her off. "No, first ask him what he's doing here, and how he found the castle."

Felicity paused, her expression stony as she waited for him to indicate that he was finished. He gave her a curt nod, and her gaze returned to Bentleigh.

"So, Your Highness," she said, with a pleasant smile. Her eyes flicked momentarily back to Justin's. "Tell me about yourself."

Justin stalked around to her chair, towering over her. "What are you doing? Ask him!"

Felicity ignored him completely, her full attention on Bentleigh. He kept his response brief, politely turning the conversation back to Felicity.

"Oh, my life story isn't terribly interesting," she said cheerfully. "I was born in Allenton, but my mother died when I was a small child, and my father wanted to move away from the sad memories. So we moved to a little village, to the west of here. I have a brother, only a year older than me," she shook her head indulgently, "who usually acts like he's younger than me." Her expression dropped slightly. "Honestly, I'm not sure if they'll be managing without me. Especially when winter sets in."

"I'm sorry," said Bentleigh, looking genuinely concerned. "Is there something I can do to help?"

"That's very kind of you," said Felicity. She turned her head boldly, her eyes boring into Justin for a moment. "Very princely behavior." She swiveled back to face the Bansfordian. "But they'll be fine as soon as I get out of here."

A myriad of emotions chased one another through Justin's

mind, but he didn't even attempt to stop and identify them. "Felicity," he said, his voice low and dangerous. "Ask Prince Bentleigh how he found the castle."

"Surely you don't want me to speak for you," she said sweetly, her voice so low he doubted Bentleigh could make out the words. "That would require you to *trust* me."

Justin stared at her, a shot of panic going through him. For an unreasoning moment he thought she could read his thoughts, and somehow knew his father's words about the dangers of trust, and could see the weakness that had gripped him in the garden. But at the memory of their encounter in the garden, he soon realized why she was angry. She was offended at his lack of trust—first in having Phillip follow her around, then in ordering the head guard to interrogate her.

After a moment of silent challenge, Felicity went back to ignoring him, listening instead to the other prince's response.

"Can I help you get home?" He sounded hesitant, clearing wondering what she'd been muttering about. "It doesn't seem like you're trapped here, but I know that appearances can be misleading..."

"Oh, I'm not trapped here by some kind of magic," Felicity clarified in a sunny voice. "But I gave my word I'd stay, so I'm stuck for the time being." She leaned back as Stewart removed her empty soup bowl and replaced it with a plate of roast chicken. Bentleigh was again staring at his plate in amazement. "Is that why you came?" Felicity asked, tilting her head to one side. "To 'rescue' me? I know it sounds self-important to ask, but you wouldn't be the first."

"Yes, I gathered that might be the case," Bentleigh said, poking his food with a fork. He was clearly still mistrustful of it. "I actually didn't come here from home. I was in Listernia, where the story is running rampant." He gave her another friendly smile. "That's not exactly why I came, although I would be glad to assist you if I could."

"I bet you would," Justin growled, and Felicity shot him a look of reproach. He gave her a challenging glare. "He'll be trying to kiss you 'to free you from the curse' next."

"Of course he won't," said Felicity dismissively. "No one said anything about kissing."

"What?" Prince Bentleigh looked startled, and Justin couldn't blame him.

"Sorry," Felicity said, calmly. "Your mention of coming here from Listernia made me think of my first visitor. He was a knight from there, and he was awful. He thought my mind was disordered, but he still wanted to kiss me, supposedly to undo an enchantment."

"Oh." Prince Bentleigh still looked taken aback. "Well, I don't think your mind is disordered, for what it's worth. And I certainly won't try to kiss you. No offense," he added hastily.

"Smooth, isn't he?" Justin commented dryly, and Felicity gave an appreciative grin.

"None taken," she laughed, speaking to Bentleigh. "Although there's no need to be quite so definite about it."

Bentleigh laughed in return. "That came out wrong. I didn't mean to insult you, it's just..."

"Just what?" Felicity prompted, when he fell silent.

Justin rolled his eyes. "Stop trying to get his life story," he grunted. "You've made your point, I'm dependent on you to communicate. Now ask him what he knows."

But Bentleigh was speaking again, all in a rush.

"It's just that I'm already very much in love, with the woman I've been betrothed to all my life."

Justin blinked in surprise at this sudden declaration, but Felicity brightened instantly.

"How romantic!" she declared. "And convenient, I must say."

"Actually, it's extremely *in*convenient," said Bentleigh, his voice dry. "Because she's been in an enchanted sleep for almost two years. And that's the real reason I came."

CHAPTER THIRTEEN

Felicity

F elicity sat back in her chair, staring at the Bansfordian
prince in surprise.

"You're engaged to the Crown Princess of Listernia?"
she said.

"Ah, of course," Justin muttered, but she ignored him, her
attention on Prince Bentleigh.

The Bansfordian nodded, his expression glum. "Princess
Azalea and I were betrothed almost as soon as she was born.
We...but that's a long story." He squinted at Felicity. "I guess
you've heard what's happened in Listernia?"

Felicity nodded. "Just the basics. The princess sleeps all the
time, the rest of the kingdom sleeps at night, whether they want
to or not."

He nodded. "That's the sum of it. I've been trying to figure
out how to break the curse for two years, but I've achieved absolutely nothing." The poor man looked miserable. "She
succumbed to the enchantment only a matter of months after
this place," he waved a hand at the room, "apparently disappeared, along with Prince Justin. So when I heard the rumor

that the Summer Castle had reappeared, and there was a girl living there..."

"You came looking for me in the hope of finding answers," Felicity finished for him. "Thinking that if I'd found a way to break this curse, I might have a clue as to how to break yours."

He nodded. "Exactly."

She sighed, sitting back in her chair. "I wish I did have answers for you, Your Highness. But none of us can figure out what's going on here. Why some people can find the castle, while it seems to still be invisible to others. Or why no one but me can see and hear all the rest of the inhabitants."

"The rest of the inhabitants?" the prince repeated, looking at her blankly.

"Oh, yes," she said, belatedly remembering her vindictive little charade. "I'm not alone here. There are almost twenty servants left, who stayed when the curse hit. And Prince Justin is right over there."

She waved a careless hand in his direction, and Prince Bentleigh spun in his chair, looking wildly into the shadows in the corner of the room.

"Thank you for that dignified introduction," Prince Justin grumbled, but she rolled her eyes at him.

"How can I introduce you when he can't see or hear you?" She looked at Prince Bentleigh. He looked disconcerted as he glanced around the room.

"He's really here?"

"He is," Felicity nodded. She glanced at Justin. "Tell me something only you would know."

He leaned his maned head to one side, thinking. To Felicity's amazement, a small smile curved his lips. "Remind him of the time we gave our minders the slip at that market bazaar in Bant. We bought flat cakes from the desert merchants."

Felicity dutifully relayed the message, and Prince Bentleigh's eyes widened. "I remember that," he said. "We can't have been more than eight or nine. It was the last royal visit we received from Albury, before..."

He left the words hanging in the air, unable to hear Justin's unemotional conclusion. "Before my father had the idiocy to fall off his horse and get himself killed, leaving a ten year old in charge of the kingdom."

Felicity decided not to pass that part on. But she cast a thoughtful glance at Justin. He always came across as so confident, to the point of arrogance. She'd never considered before how terrifying it must have been for him to be left with such a responsibility at that age.

"So you see, I'm not crazy," she said warmly, her attention back on Prince Bentleigh. "Despite all appearances to the contrary."

He smiled. "I didn't think you were crazy. I could tell something was going on, of course, but it's still hard to wrap my head around the idea that Justin is actually here in this room." He glanced around again, as if saying the prince's name might make him suddenly appear. "When did he come in?"

"Oh, he's been here the whole time, I've just been tormenting him to punish him for...well, never mind that. I was just..."

"Being childish," Justin supplied curtly.

Felicity shot him a disgruntled look. He looked so sulky that the humor of the situation hit her all at once, and a chuckle bubbled over.

"Well, yes, I suppose I was being childish." She flashed a grin at Prince Justin before turning back to the other prince. "But I can't say I'm sorry. I got him to admit that he's dependent on someone else, and you have no idea how huge an achievement that is."

"Actually, I have some idea," said Prince Bentleigh, his voice dry.

"Really?" Felicity looked at him with interest. "So he's always been like this, then?"

"Well, I don't know what he's like now, so that's hard to answer," said Prince Bentleigh.

"What he's like now..." Felicity repeated. Her eyes met Justin's, and she could have sworn she saw a flash of vulnerability. It was gone a second later, but it was enough to make her moderate her words. "He's hidden under an enchanted form," she said discreetly, "but I think on the inside he's much the same as he ever was."

She was still looking at Justin, and for a moment those intense blue eyes held her in thrall, their expression impossible to read. She pulled her gaze away with an effort.

"By which I mean, surly and unmanageable," she added, trying to lighten the mood.

Prince Bentleigh gave a snort of laughter which he tried to disguise as a cough, and Prince Justin sent her a withering glare.

"I am standing right here, you know," he complained.

"True," said Felicity solemnly. She turned to the foreign prince. "He's reminding me of my manners."

"Yes, sorry Justin," said Prince Bentleigh, glancing carefully around the room. "It must be maddening to be silenced."

"I can be his mouthpiece," said Felicity cheerfully. "He wants to know how you found the castle."

Prince Bentleigh shrugged. "I just rode here. I left Listernia —traveling by day, obviously—and followed the route to where the Summer Castle used to be. And here it was."

Felicity shook her head. "It makes no sense." She glanced at Justin. "Do you think the magic of the curse is failing? That it sometimes stops working, temporarily, and at random times?"

"Maybe." He sounded unconvinced. "But it's still working in

part, isn't it? Or Bentleigh would be screaming in terror and running from the room."

Felicity smiled at his snippy tone. "I don't think he'd scream if he saw you. He seems more like the stand and fight type to me." She looked back at their visitor, who was watching the apparently one sided conversation in fascination.

"I crossed paths with one of your other visitors, if it helps," he offered. "At an inn, in a village just south of here. The whole situation is getting a bit of attention, and the inn is doing a roaring trade."

"I'm sure your arrival caused quite a stir," smiled Felicity.

He returned her smile. "Actually, I wasn't even their first royal visitor. Apparently I just missed Princess Wren of Mistra."

Felicity frowned. "Is that the one who doesn't speak? I thought her kingdom was in the middle of a war. Why in the world does she want to find the missing castle?"

Prince Bentleigh grimaced. "She doesn't, from what I could see. She was being bossed around by some pompous minder. She just sat in the corner, looking miserable and hugging her swan."

"Swan?" Felicity repeated, staring.

"Yes, apparently she has a whole bevy of them that follow her around," Prince Bentleigh said, with a shrug. "Although only one was with her at the inn. If the gossip swirling around the tavern was correct," he squinted around the room, presumably trying to figure out where Justin was, "she was dragged here to attempt an alliance with you, Justin, now that rumor says you might have reappeared."

"A marriage alliance?" Justin said, sounding startled.

Felicity frowned, not liking the idea at all for some reason. Probably because someone as shy as Crown Princess Wren was rumored to be would never be able to cope with Prince Justin's forceful personality. Yes, that must be it.

"Isn't she a little young?" she asked, trying to remember what she'd heard about the reclusive princess.

"She's only fifteen," Prince Bentleigh acknowledged, and Justin made a strange noise in his throat.

"I would never be interested in a marriage alliance with Mistra," he said shortly. "They're a weak, pathetic kingdom with nothing better to do than pick a quarrel with their neighbors. And as for Princess Wren...I'd say she's just a girl, but even that's too generous. She's more mouse than girl. She has about as much personality as that broccoli."

Felicity shot him a frown, but he didn't look in the least repentant.

"Oh, he's behind me, is he?" Prince Bentleigh asked, shifting uncomfortably. "What did he say?"

Felicity held Justin's eyes for another moment as she began to answer. "He says that he's honored Mistra would consider entrusting their precious daughter to him, but while she's a kind and sweet girl, she's a bit too young for him to see her as a serious option."

Prince Bentleigh couldn't hear Justin's growl, but he could see the way Felicity's lips twitched, in spite of her best efforts. He gave a bellow of laughter.

"He said absolutely nothing of the kind, I'm guessing. Well, I was surprised myself. Albury may be having a difficult time these last few years, but it's still a much stronger kingdom than Mistra. They would have a lot to gain from the connection, especially with their kingdom still at war. As for the age, I guess they wouldn't be in a hurry to actually seal the alliance." He shrugged. "I imagine they rushed here in the hope that the prince might consider the proposal more favorably if word of his disfigurement is true. And because, if rumor is to be believed, there are those in Mistra who are keen to be rid of their mute princess."

"Poor thing," said Felicity, full of sympathy for the unknown Princess Wren. "Imagine your own kingdom wanting to marry you off to a monster just to get you out of the way."

"Charming," said Justin dryly.

Felicity realized that her comment hadn't exactly been complimentary. She opened her mouth to apologize, but Justin was still speaking, in the same cutting voice.

"Imagine your own family being willing to abandon you to a monster without even a token attempt to rescue you."

Felicity closed her mouth, her cheeks burning. She felt like she'd been slapped, and it was all she could do to keep tears from her eyes. The snide remark came as a shock, because she and the prince had barely spoken of her family. She'd certainly never shared with him her hurt over their apparent lack of response to her plight. She'd originally told herself they weren't to blame, since the curse wouldn't allow them to find her even if they tried. But in light of all the visitors she was now receiving, that argument was less convincing.

She could see in the corners of her eyes that Prince Justin had stilled, and she could feel his gaze on her. He was probably wondering why she didn't have a quick retort for once, but she couldn't bring herself to meet his eye.

"It doesn't matter," Prince Bentleigh said, blithely unaware of the drama going on around him. "They couldn't find the castle. They said there was just...nothing here."

Felicity blinked at him, taking a moment to realize he was still speaking of the Mistrans, not her father and Ambrose. "Huh," she said at last, hoping her voice sounded normal. "Prince Justin is already betrothed, anyway."

"Really?" Prince Bentleigh looked intrigued, but Justin spoke over him.

"What? No I'm not."

Now that she had regained her poise, she dared a glance at

him, eyebrow raised. "You said that your father chose you a bride, back before he died."

"He *wanted* me to marry her," Justin said. "That doesn't mean there was an official betrothal." He gave a small shudder. "Thankfully."

"I see," said Felicity. She felt strangely pleased, and her curiosity was piqued by his reaction. "My mistake."

Prince Bentleigh watched her curiously throughout this exchange, but made no comment. She turned back to him with a sigh.

"I wish I could help you, Prince Bentleigh. But I'm afraid I have no idea how to wake your princess from her sleep."

He sighed as well, sitting back in his chair. "It was always a long shot." He gave her a smile that was weary but kind. "I wish *I* could help *you*, but I have no insights to share, either. I'd like to offer you the might and resources of a kingdom to help solve the problem, but I can't even do that."

"Ah, of course, you're just a lowly younger prince, aren't you?" Felicity teased.

Prince Bentleigh smiled. "I am, but that's not why. I doubt my parents would agree to help even if Rian were the one to ask them." He grimaced. "To tell the truth, I'm not really supposed to be here. I heard the rumors while I was in Liss, visiting Azalea, and I came straight here. If I'd gone home, I'm sure my parents would have prevented me from coming. They don't even like me visiting Azalea anymore. They don't want us involved with any enchantments."

"How stupid of me." Felicity slapped a hand to her forehead. "I forgot that Bansford has outlawed magic."

"I wouldn't expect him to go against his kingdom to help me."

Felicity looked up at the interjection, surprised by Justin's consideration.

"But can you ask him if he'd be willing to travel to Allenton on his way home, to take a message to my uncle?"

"That I can easily do," Prince Bentleigh said brightly, once Felicity had passed on the request. "I would be glad to take a message, and I only wish I could do more."

It was a little bit tedious, being the middle man in the following exchange, as Justin meticulously communicated his instructions. But of course Felicity didn't complain. Justin promised to write a letter for his uncle as well, but he explained that he had reason to believe the curse would prevent the parchment from leaving the estate.

When at last Felicity was free to retire, she climbed the steps to her suite slowly, feeling strangely depleted by the evening. As soon as she was alone, Prince Justin's words about her family came rushing back, carried on a tide of emotion. She wasn't sure whether it was hurt or humiliation that made her throat suddenly tight, but she didn't want to dwell on either. What right did the prince have to criticize her family? She encouraged the defiant thought, welcoming irritation in place of more painful feelings. Prince Justin was the one who had put them in this situation, after all.

Prince Bentleigh took his leave early the next morning, full of amazement at the way his room had been prepared by unseen hands. Justin was there to see him off as well, although of course Prince Bentleigh had to take Felicity's word for it. The departing prince was cheerful as he bowed gallantly over Felicity's hand, but her good humor hadn't quite returned, and Justin was his usual surly self.

Justin intended to accompany Prince Bentleigh to the gate, to see if the letter made it through, but Felicity found she preferred to stay. Being at the gate would remind her of things she was trying not to think about, like the world beyond, and by extension her family.

"I'm glad to have met you, Felicity," said Prince Bentleigh, as he pulled on his riding gloves. He gave a sly grin. "I didn't think Justin would ever meet someone who could get the better of him, but I'm thrilled to be wrong."

She gave a wan smile. "You overestimate me, Your Highness."

"Ben." He waved a gloved hand. "Call me Ben."

Justin had been waiting impatiently—like he had so much else to do with his time—and he swept out of the castle in Prince Bentleigh's wake. Felicity wandered outside as well, heading toward the fountain, the surface of which was frosted over. She walked aimlessly through the gardens for some time, before the chill in the air drove her inside.

As she crossed the marble entranceway, she was surprised to be hailed from the direction of the prince's study. She paused, and Justin came out to meet her, with his loping gait.

"I thought you would wish to know," he said shortly, "that as I expected, the letter with my name and seal was not able to leave the estate." He waved a parchment in the air. "Bentleigh had to remove it from his jacket before the curse would allow him to ride through the gate."

"That's a shame," said Felicity sympathetically. "We'll have to hope your uncle believes his account."

Justin nodded, and there was a moment of awkward silence. Felicity waited, wondering if the prince was going to scold her for the way she had baited him the night before. But when he spoke, his words were formal, with no hint of either reproach or warmth on his face.

"I appreciate your assistance in communicating with Prince Bentleigh." He gave the shallowest of bows. "That is all."

He turned abruptly and re-entered his study, leaving Felicity feeling more listless than ever. For some ridiculous reason, she was almost disappointed he hadn't taken her to task.

Perhaps this place was affecting her mind after all.

CHAPTER FOURTEEN

Justin

By the time the first flakes of snow fell, Justin was feeling more like a caged animal than he had since the early days of the curse. No further visitors had arrived, perhaps deterred by the sudden change in the weather that had followed Prince Bentleigh's departure. The castle and its estate were once more completely cut off from the rest of the kingdom, and only then did Justin realize how much he had begun to hope.

Even his message to Uncle Cameron had so far yielded no results. He'd tried to watch for it in the mirror, but he hadn't managed to catch the exact time of Prince Bentleigh's audience. He had since eavesdropped on a number of discussions about the prince's strange tale, however, and what he'd heard was disappointing, to say the least. His uncle's advisors clearly mistrusted Prince Bentleigh's decision to believe the word of a strange peasant girl who had set herself up as a fine lady in the prince's abandoned summer residence. They had agreed to send a small delegation to search for the castle, but from what Justin could make out, the group had come to the area and returned to the capital, without finding anything.

"*I don't know, Dobson.*" Justin was watching his uncle in the mirror, his frustration at boiling point. "*The Bansfordian prince said that some people could see the castle while others can't, and they have no idea why that is.*"

Dobson's lips were pursed. "*Lord Regent, I would hesitate to place too much weight on what the prince said. In some form or another, he has been exposed to the enchantment that afflicts the Summer Castle. His word is surely compromised as a result.*"

There was something of a bite in Dobson's voice, and Justin frowned, wondering what was behind the steward's words.

Uncle Cameron wasn't convinced either. He shook his head, his brows furrowed. "*I still think we should send a larger delegation, or perhaps several more small ones. Perhaps we just sent the wrong people, and a different group would have better luck.*"

"*Perhaps,*" Dobson responded. He hesitated, an unusual sight from the confident steward. "*If that's what you think, why don't you send more delegations?*"

Uncle Cameron sighed. "*Most of the court seems to be against it. No one wants to volunteer for fear of being swallowed up by the curse.*"

"YOU are acting regent," Justin snapped at his uncle's unresponsive image. "*You* decide what must be done. The court doesn't have to agree with every decision you make!"

Dobson seemed to be in agreement with him. "*Lord Regent, you don't need their permission. This may be a good opportunity to remind them who is in charge.*"

Justin snorted. He didn't altogether disagree, but it was still an ironic observation coming from a man who, from all Justin had observed, seemed to have promoted himself from steward to chief advisor. Justin hadn't had much to do with Dobson himself, so he couldn't remember if the steward had always been so officious, or if he was just being opportunistic.

"*Perhaps you should send Lord Ladner, My Lord,*" Dobson was saying. "*Give him his instructions, and don't take no for an answer.*"

Justin frowned at the name of an extremely influential earl, and for once Uncle Cameron seemed to be thinking along the same lines.

"*Lord Ladner?*" Uncle Cameron protested. "*He's dead set against the idea, and already one of my biggest critics. He'd raise an outcry if I forced him to go on this errand.*"

"*Very well, My Lord,*" said Dobson, sensing defeat and backing down hastily. "*It was only a suggestion.*"

Justin lowered the mirror, something dark swirling along the edge of his thoughts. He had once been so sure his uncle was plotting against him, but the acting regent certainly seemed genuine in his desire to find his missing nephew. He'd been acting regent for years before Justin had been cursed, and he'd never tried to consolidate his power. Surely it would have been easier to do so when Justin was a child than when he was grown.

Justin sighed, looking out the window of his suite. The snow that had been falling through most of the night seemed to have stopped with the dawn several hours ago. Everything was still and quiet now, muffled under a blanket of white. The cold wouldn't bother him, of course. He'd take a turn around the garden, see if it cleared his head.

As he ambled past the private dining hall, his thoughts strayed to the previous evening's meal. He didn't think Felicity was still angry with him, but she was more subdued now than she used to be. It had been a while since he'd heard her sunny laughter. Perhaps it was the snowy weather.

Perhaps it was his icy behavior.

He flicked an ear in irritation, refusing to feel guilty. She was the one who'd pushed herself into his life. She was already living in luxury at his expense, instead of working for a living like all the castle's other residents. Wasn't that enough? Did she need his attention as well?

The truth was he had been avoiding any meaningful interaction with her since Prince Bentleigh's visit. He'd been shaken by her reaction to his barb about her family. It was clear he'd wounded her, and he'd immediately regretted the words. But that very regret had shown him just how much of a danger she posed to him. He already seemed to care more about her opinion than he should. He couldn't afford to start worrying about her feelings as well. He could hear his father's voice in his head, despite the ten years that had passed since the old king's death. Making decisions based on your own feelings was weak enough. Making them based on someone else's was pathetically so.

But for all his frustration at the complications Felicity had brought to his life, Justin shied away from being angry or cruel to her just to keep her at arm's length. So here he was, trying to inhabit a middle ground, where he was polite, but didn't engage with her. No longer accusatory, but never personal.

He had spent some of the most uncomfortable weeks of his life.

He'd left the castle by this time, his enormous paw-like feet leaving large imprints in the fresh snow. He hadn't expected to find anyone else braving the weather, but he was only halfway to the fountain when he heard a painfully familiar voice.

"I was a little disappointed when I realized it wasn't the whole garden."

Felicity sounded cheerful enough with someone other than him as her companion. Without conscious thought, Justin found his steps redirecting, like a plant trying to grow toward the sun.

"But even one section of garden that's magically impervious to weather is pretty amazing."

"Not just weather." Justin recognized the voice of the girl

who had taken on the role of Felicity's maid. "They're sort of impervious to time. The ones that are left have been blooming constantly since the curse. There used to be about fifty, but twenty of them have wilted. Still, that's not bad for two and a half years."

Justin hadn't been paying much attention to their words, but his heartbeat picked up as he realized where they were. The rose garden! He knew how Felicity liked to pick flowers. He found he was almost running, an unreasoning anger rising inside him. She had already stolen his peace—would she also steal what little time was left to him?

"STOP!" he roared, rounding a bend and emerging between the rose bushes. Both girls jumped, clearly startled. Felicity was frozen with her hand extended halfway to a rose—its soft pink a bloom of incongruous color against the white snow—and his wrath targeted on her.

"DON'T TOUCH IT!" he shouted. "Are all peasants such fools? I thought your father was just too cowardly to come after you, but perhaps he was glad to be rid of your idiocy!"

Felicity reeled back as if struck, the color draining from her face at his disproportionate attack. Justin's chest was heaving, and already he could feel the regret creeping in. But the sensation only enraged him further, as it demonstrated how futile his attempts had been all these weeks, and brought all his pent up emotions spilling out.

"You think you've won everyone over with your laughter and your jokes," he spat. "Always ready to help anyone with anything. But I see straight through you. You don't care about helping people. You just need to feel needed to convince yourself you're worth their attention."

For a moment the scene was suspended, the maid frozen in horror, Felicity staring at Justin with her heart in her eyes. He had expected her to respond with the anger she used to show whenever he disparaged her promise, but all he could see was hurt.

"You are a monster," she said, her voice strangled. Then she suddenly turned and fled, a sound suspiciously like a sob escaping her.

Justin stood rooted to the spot for several endless seconds.

"She knew not to pick the roses, Your Highness." The maid's head was lowered, but her soft words were still deafening in the suffocating silence. "We were just admiring them."

Justin didn't respond, turning his back on the rose garden and striding back toward the castle without a word. He heard Stewart hail him as he crossed the entranceway, but he ignored him. The steward must have read his face, because he didn't follow. Justin reached his own suite unhindered. He didn't even break stride as he entered the room, immediately beginning to pace back and forward across the space.

What had he done? Why had he unloaded on her like that? He hadn't even had to think through the strategy of his attack. Finding people's weak points was a skill he'd learned at a young age, and knowing how to exploit them was one of the main lessons his father had passed on. Felicity had showed him her area of vulnerability the night of Prince Bentleigh's visit, when she'd been so rattled by his jab about her family's neglect. Without even realizing he was doing it, he'd locked away the information as a weapon in his arsenal. In the heat of his anger, he'd wanted to lash out at her, and his mind had known exactly how to do it to greatest effect.

He stopped pacing, putting his wolf-like head in his giant, clawed hands. He could still see the look on Felicity's face. Everything she was feeling had been clearly on display—he couldn't even imagine how terrifying it would be to have your emotions so transparent to the world.

When the enchantress cursed him, she said that his outside

would reflect what was truly inside. But never until that moment
had Justin believed he'd deserved her accusation. Never until
Felicity, good-natured, always cheerful, beloved by everyone in
the castle, repeated it in a whisper that came from the core of
her wounded heart.

You are a monster.

A sharp rap at the door startled Justin out of his personal
prison of misery. The knocker didn't wait for an answer, and it
was all he could do to school his features back to their usual
impassive state before Phillip came tumbling through the doorway, Felicity's maid at his heels.

"Your Highness," gasped the young guard, straightening.
"Miss Felicity is gone."

"Gone?" he repeated, taking a step forward. "She's left the
estate?"

"Yes, Your Highness," the maid said quickly. "She—"

"I see," Justin cut her off. He hoped desperately that his
sneer was enough to cover the shards of ice shooting into his
heart. "There was a limit to her promise after all." His thoughts
were plenty bitter, and he allowed the emotion to creep into his
voice. "I suppose she stole one of my horses, did she?"

"No, Your Highness," said the maid, shaking her head frantically. "That's why we came straight to you. She's on foot, and
she's in danger."

"Danger?" Justin repeated, frowning. "The snow isn't very
deep yet. As long as she keeps to the roads—"

"No, Your Highness," Phillip insisted. "She didn't go out the
main gate. She went through the northern gate."

Justin's frown deepened. "Are you sure? Why would she do
that?"

"We're sure," the guard insisted. "Her tracks are clear."

"It's my fault, Your Highness," said the maid, wringing her
hands. "I was talking to her just this morning about how we

used to go to the ocean in the winter, to admire the snow on the sand. She's often commented how much she loves the sea, how it's the most calming place she knows."

"You think she's heading for the ocean?" Justin stilled. "But the path will be covered by the snow. She knows not to go due north, doesn't she? She knows about the lake on the other side of the grove?"

A sob escaped the maid, and she shook her head. "I don't think she does, Your Highness. You can't see it from the windows. I'm terrified that she—"

Justin had already wrenched open a drawer, and he cut off the maid's babbling with three forceful words.

"Show me Felicity."

The mirror shimmered, and a spot of copper appeared in a blank white landscape. Felicity's head was bowed against the wind, and her shoulders shook, whether from cold or emotion he couldn't tell. Justin squinted at her surroundings, and his heart seemed to skip a beat. He cursed under his breath. She was heading straight for the lake.

He dropped the mirror on a table, loping toward the door without a word to the two servants. He didn't need them to tell him why they had run straight to him. He was the only one capable of leaving the estate.

In his haste, he forgot to restrain himself to a human speed, and his companions were left behind long before he reached the north gate. He braced himself for what he knew was coming, but he didn't hesitate as he threw the gate open and stepped through.

Immediately, every inch of him was assaulted by lancing pain. The intensity brought him crashing to the ground, and for a moment all he could do was lie there, taking deep shuddering breaths. But he couldn't afford the time. Even now Felicity might be reaching the lake, and he knew it wouldn't be frozen this early in winter. At least, not fully frozen. Just enough to give the semblance of solid ground when covered with a soft layer of snow.

With agonizing effort, he pushed himself to his feet. Every step he took felt like walking on spear tips, but he forced himself to put one foot in front of the other, again and again. A roar burst from his lips, half fueled by searing pain, half by frustration. He was moving too slowly.

He gritted his teeth and abandoned his pride, dropping onto all fours in a lopsided, excruciating run. If possible, the pain became more intense the further he got from the gate. His eyes were clenched shut against the agony, leaving him blind. But it didn't matter. He had already picked up Felicity's scent, and his hearing would tell him long before he reached her.

He stopped thinking, stopped trying to overcome the pain. He just focused on enduring it, on continuing to exist alongside it as he covered the ground. He followed the trail of broken snow, and he could tell he was moving much more quickly than Felicity had done. He was gaining on her.

No sooner had he thought it than he heard a terrible sound. An ominous crack, and a sudden scream, abruptly cut off.

With a cry, Justin threw himself across the last distance, forcing his eyes open. A thrill of horror went over him at the sight of the gaping hole in what looked like snowy ground, the cavity filled by water so dark it looked black.

A faint thumping sound from further into the lake propelled him into motion. He ignored every rule of navigating frozen water and threw himself on the weakened ice, falling through like a stone.

His fur kept him warm even in the snow, but nothing could defend against the searing fire of the frozen lake. He hadn't thought his body could register more pain, but he'd been wrong. He bobbed back to the surface, gasping in fresh air before diving back under. Looking frantically around, he saw a spot of color and dove toward it. Felicity had stopped thumping on the underside of the ice, but she didn't seem to have completely succumbed to the icy water. Her eyes, wide with shock, found him as he approached.

Justin knew that if he'd been in his human body, his actions would have cost him his own life rather than saving hers. But he wasn't in his human body. He'd never explored the additional capabilities of his enchanted form, too full of hatred for what he'd become. Now, for the first time, he welcomed the extra senses and unnatural strength that allowed him not only to withstand the water's ice, but to drag Felicity's limp form back through the water.

They emerged into the frigid air at the lake's edge, both of them gasping for breath that only seared their lungs. Justin was in too much pain to form words, but he managed to communicate with gestures for Felicity to hold on to the edge of his open vest. He could only be grateful her hands retained the capacity to hold a grip as he clambered out of the water and then dragged her up after him. Without a word, he picked her up, cradling her against his chest and hoping that some vestige of warmth remained in his chilled body to help her hold on until they reached the castle. The pain from the curse was so intermingled with the agony of freezing that he could no longer tell them apart.

He pushed it all from his mind, focusing once again on forcing one foot in front of the other. His progress was slower with his burden, but he didn't falter. Felicity seemed to be conscious, but she said nothing, merely clinging to his clothing with surprising strength. The journey felt interminable, as though each step covered no ground at all, until suddenly, familiar stone walls rose up before them.

Justin's senses were swimming as the gate swung open. With

the greatest effort of his life, he forced himself to take one more step.

The moment he crossed the threshold, the pain of the enchantment ceased. But the agony of the icy water rose up to take its place. He could barely see, but he could hear frantic shouts on all sides. The last thing he was aware of was Felicity's weight being tugged from his grip as the ground rose up to meet him.

CHAPTER FIFTEEN

Felicity

F elicity became gradually aware of the feeling of something heavy on top of her, and the sound of a crackling fire. She inched her eyes open, a lingering sense of danger making her fearful of what she would find. But only her own innocuous suite greeted her, the sight more familiar and comforting than she would have believed possible a few short months ago.

"You're awake!"

The delighted exclamation was followed by the sight of Viola's face bobbing into view.

"We've been so worried for you."

"We certainly have," confirmed a second voice. Felicity smiled wearily at the housekeeper who appeared alongside Viola. Mrs. Winters' scolding tone was belied by the warmth of relief in her eyes.

"How long have I been sleeping?"

"Only a few hours," Viola assured her. "It's almost dinnertime."

Felicity struggled to sit up, several heavy blankets shifting down the bed. The warmth radiating from near her feet suggested that a warming pan had been left between the covers. "It's a little hazy, but I was very foolish, wasn't I?"

"It was my fault," Viola gushed, her voice a little teary. "I shouldn't have been complaining about not being able to walk to the ocean anymore. It didn't occur to me that you might try it, so I didn't even think to mention the lake."

"Don't be silly," Felicity protested, as images flashed through her mind. A blanket of snow. A silent, shrouded world that cared nothing for the tears rolling down her cheeks. A sudden crack and a short fall, followed by instant, unbearable pain. She winced as her muscles tightened at the memory of the pain. "How could you guess I'd go running out into the snow like a fool?"

"Don't blame yourself, Miss Felicity," Mrs. Winters cut in. Her expression was unimpressed. "From all I hear you had reason to be upset, and I daresay you weren't thinking clearly."

For a moment Felicity frowned in confusion, trying to remember what had sent her out across the fields. Memory came flooding back, and she winced again as a different type of cold rushed over her body. She'd been admiring the rose garden, and Justin had said those terrible things. His words had touched her deepest discomfort, and instead of calling him to task for his rudeness, she'd run away like a frightened child. She gave an audible groan.

"What is it?" Viola asked anxiously. "Does it hurt some-where? We did our best to warm you up, but we don't have a physician here anymore. You didn't seem to have any injuries, but maybe we missed something."

"No, I'm fine," Felicity said, flopping back against the cush-ions. "I mean, I feel exhausted, and embarrassingly weak. But that's not it. I was just remembering what an absolute fool I made of myself."

"Nonsense," said Mrs. Winters sternly. "It's His Highness

who should be embarrassed, not you, Miss Felicity. And so I shall tell him when he comes to."

"Comes to?" Felicity repeated.

She tried to sit up again, but her efforts brought instant protests from her companions. She gave up, since her limbs didn't seem to want to obey anyway. Her question went unanswered as Mrs. Winters fetched her some sweetened tea, and Viola helped her prop herself against the cushions so she could drink it.

Felicity's thoughts were still sluggish, and for a moment she just sipped the tea, not even trying to figure out what Mrs. Winters had meant. Then, quite suddenly, her mind filled in the gaps. She gave an involuntary gasp as she recalled the moment when her panicked mind, unable to comprehend anything but her approaching death, saw an inhuman form swimming toward her through the frigid water. She felt the ghost of his iron grip as he dragged her from the lake. An extra shot of heat passed through her as she remembered the way he had held her against his misshapen body, carrying her easily in his arms for a much greater distance than a normal man ever could.

"Oh good, she's getting some of her color back," said Viola brightly.

Felicity's gaze latched on to the maid, and the housekeeper nodding wisely beside her. "Where's Justin?"

The other two exchanged looks at the abrupt question. There was a strange gleam in both pairs of eyes, although Mrs. Winters answered calmly enough. "Last I heard he was still unconscious. Stewart is with him, of course, and his manservant."

"It took five of them to carry him up to his suite!" said Viola, her eyes wide. "Phillip helped, naturally, and the other guards. But they needed the head groom and one of the gardeners, too!"

She sat on the edge of Felicity's bed. "What happened? I assume you fell in? Did he have to jump in after you?"

Felicity nodded, struggling to find her voice. "Surely his body is stronger than mine. Why is he still unconscious?"

"Well..." Viola hesitated, exchanging another glance with the housekeeper. "I'm sure he'll be fine. He just looked very weak. I expect he'll be more exhausted than you because of the..."

She trailed off, and Felicity was about to prompt her to finish when a thought suddenly occurred to her. "Wait a minute!" She pushed herself upright, managing it this time, and almost spilling her tea. "How was he able to come after me? I thought the curse wouldn't let any of you leave the estate! Maybe it really is weakening!"

"I don't think so," said Viola, with a sad smile. "I think the curse is as strong as ever."

"What do you mean?"

Viola glanced again at Mrs. Winters, and the older woman took over. "The curse never physically prevented His Highness from leaving, at least not in the way it does the rest of us."

"Then...I don't understand," said Felicity stupidly. "Why has he stayed here if he doesn't have to?"

"He does have to," Mrs. Winters said shortly. "He is physically able to walk through the gate, but it's not without cost. The roses in the rose garden start dying as soon as he's gone, for one thing."

"The magical roses?" Felicity asked, confused. "What do they have to do with it?"

The two women looked at one another yet again, and Mrs. Winters gave a tight nod.

Viola sighed, turning back to Felicity. "I didn't explain it to you properly, because we don't like to talk about the details of the curse. But the enchantress told Justin that if he couldn't..."

break the curse...by the time the last rose in the rose garden dies, he'll stay the way he is forever. At first we were all terrified, thinking he had only a couple of weeks. But I guess she always intended to at least give him a chance, because there's some kind of magic on the roses that keeps them alive. They're wilting, but very very slowly."

"Unless he leaves," Mrs. Winters added. "In which case they begin to die rapidly."

Felicity looked between them, her mind reeling. "That's why he was so angry when he thought I was going to pick one," she said softly. A sudden, larger realization hit. "That's why he was angry enough to lock my father up just for cutting one."

Viola nodded. "I know he didn't mean to, but your father stole a chunk of whatever time we have left to figure out a way to break the curse."

Several emotions chased each other through Felicity's jumbled thoughts. She thought of her accusations against Justin regarding his treatment of her father, and she raised her hands in a frustrated gesture. "Why didn't he just tell me that?"

"My guess is he didn't trust you," said Mrs. Winters simply. "He was most likely concerned that if he gave you that information, you might vindictively destroy the garden."

"I would never—" Felicity began hotly, but Viola cut off her with a sad smile.

"*We* know that, Felicity."

Felicity fell silent, thinking over their words. "He didn't have much of a role model when it comes to trust, did he?" she asked at last, directing the question to Mrs. Winters.

"No, I'm afraid not," the older woman answered softly. She sighed. "I know he's wronged you, Miss Felicity, more than once. Heaven knows he's not perfect. But if it seems like we make excuses for him, just remember we're comparing him to what his father was, and what Prince Justin could so easily have become."

"That's why you all stayed, isn't it?" Felicity asked gently. "When the curse hit. You stayed because you have faith in him. You care about him, and you believe he can be a good king."

Mrs. Winters nodded, and Felicity could have sworn she saw moisture in the normally stoic woman's eyes.

"Of course he'll be a good king," Viola declared. "He just needs to learn not to take himself so seriously." Her expression turned sly. "And to find the right queen, of course."

Felicity nodded absently, her thoughts elsewhere. "Was there another cost?" She pinned Mrs. Winters with her stare, and the older woman looked confused.

"Another cost?"

"You said that if Justin leaves the estate, the roses start to die. But you made it sound like there was something else."

The housekeeper hesitated, and Felicity's eyes narrowed.

"Tell me," she insisted.

Mrs. Winters met her eyes. "He suffers extreme pain every second he's outside the walls. He tried to downplay it the first time he attempted to leave, to find help. I'm not sure he realized we could see him through the gates, in spite of the curse. He was clearly in agony, and it seemed to get worse with every step he took. He lasted only a matter of minutes before he had no choice but to turn back, or risk the pain incapacitating him completely."

Felicity's eyes were wide by the end of this unflinching account. Memories once again swirled around her, seen in a new light. Justin's sure strokes as he approached her in the water. The strength of his grip as he tugged her free of the ice. The tension in his muscles as he carried her, never faltering. She would never have guessed he'd been in agony that whole time, but she didn't doubt Mrs. Winters' words.

"Take me to him," she demanded.

"To the prince?" Viola asked, startled. "But he's in his suite. And you're still too weak to move."

"I don't care, and no I'm not," said Felicity. "I want to see him."

She had expected Mrs. Winters to protest, but to her surprise the housekeeper said nothing. The two women helped her to rise, and Viola slid a simple dress over the dry shift Felicity had been changed into. She and the housekeeper supported Felicity on either side as she made her slow way through the castle. She actually felt a little better for the exercise, and it wasn't long before she no longer needed to lean on their arms.

She'd never been to the prince's suite before, of course, and she was surprised to find that it was only one wing away from her own. The door to the suite stood open, and Mrs. Winters led the way into a richly furnished receiving room. Another door stood ajar, and seeing a glimpse of a massive four poster bed, Felicity pushed her way forward without waiting for permission.

The castle's one serving man jumped to his feet in astonishment at her arrival, and even Stewart looked so startled that he almost dropped the cushion he was fluffing.

"Miss Felicity," he protested, his disapproval clear in every line of his frame. "This is His Highness's private chamber!"

"I don't think he minds, do you?" Felicity asked dryly, her eyes on the enormous figure stretched out on the bed. The prince was indeed still unconscious, although Felicity was pleased to see that his breathing was steady. Still, everything about him seemed limp and depleted.

His disfigured face was peaceful, no sign of the lowered brows that so often marred it. For a long moment she just stared at him, trying to understand what had driven the surly prince to put himself through more than one kind of agony to pull her from the frozen water.

"Will he be all right?" she asked softly.

"I believe so, Miss Felicity," said Stewart, his voice more gentle. "He seems to be properly warm again. The challenge now will be convincing him to take it easy for a few days."

Felicity gave a snort of laughter. "Good luck with that." A small smile curved her lips. She didn't envy the steward the task of trying to make Justin follow instructions.

Satisfied that the prince was in one large, unharmed, furry piece, she made her slow way back out to the corridor.

"Viola," Felicity said thoughtfully, seeing that Mrs. Winters had lingered behind to speak with Stewart. "You mentioned a portrait gallery once. Can you take me there?"

"If you're really strong enough," Viola said anxiously.

"I am," Felicity assured her. "I promise after that, I'll go straight back to bed."

Viola nodded, offering her arm. Felicity's weariness had returned once her immediate concern about Justin had been removed, so she took the arm willingly. They moved slowly, neither of them attempting conversation. The portrait gallery was further away than Felicity had expected, and she was on the point of asking to postpone the visit when Viola pointed to a doorway.

"Through there."

Felicity let go of the maid's arm, moving forward. "I assume there's one in there of King Justus?"

"Of course," said Viola, surprised. "Why do you want to see his portrait?"

Felicity shrugged, following Viola down the gallery. "I can't explain why, exactly. I just want to see the beast's true form."

Viola gave her a strange look, but didn't comment, just gesturing toward a floor to ceiling painting of a dark haired, dark eyed man on a white charger. Felicity gazed thoughtfully up at Justin's father, taking in the imperious posture, and the cold expression. She could only assume he'd had the final say in the details of the painting, so presumably he wanted to project a proud and uncaring image. She scowled. What was it her father had said?

Don't be deceived by the glamour of castles...King Justus never cared about his people.

Not even about his own son, it seemed. She turned away with a sigh, her eyes captured by the next painting along, a considerably smaller portrait of a young man.

"Is that Prince Justin?" she asked.

"That's right," said Viola, stepping up next to her. "That was painted no more than a year before he was cursed, maybe less. I told you he was handsome, didn't I?"

"You were right," said Felicity thoughtfully, her eyes dwelling on the face of the painting-Justin.

His expression was almost as cold as his father's, but his eyes were the same clear blue as they were in his beast form. It made a striking combination with his dark hair. The hair was closely cropped, the color the only similarity to the wild tufts that covered his body now. The style didn't suit him, in Felicity's opinion, but his face was certainly handsome, and his form was strong and lean. Her gaze rested on one strong, well-formed hand, resting on the hilt of a sword in a stance that reminded her unpleasantly of Kurt's signature pose.

"I like him better now," she said frankly.

"What?" Viola's squeak made Felicity chuckle, but the maid's next words sobered her up. "What are you saying, exactly?"

Felicity turned to Viola with a frown, trying to identify the edge in the other girl's voice. "Nothing. I mean, obviously I don't like what he looks like now." She gestured at the painting. "I just get the sense that this version of him was more handsome, but less likable."

Viola was silent, and Felicity couldn't read her expression.

She knew the servants were fiercely loyal to the prince, and wondered if she'd offended the other girl. She started to wander toward the door, her exhaustion washing over her now that she was no longer distracted. But her eyes were caught by another painting, hung just below Justin's. It showed a family, a dark haired father with his hand on the shoulder of a young boy, and a fair haired mother with an infant on her lap.

She frowned, her eyes on the father. Surely that was King Justus. Before she could ask, Mrs. Winters' horrified voice cut across the silence.

"What are you doing out of bed still, Miss Felicity? And all the way out here! You need rest, child! Straight back to your suite!"

Felicity obeyed, locking her questions away for later. Truthfully, she probably had pushed herself too much. Reaching her suite again took a supreme effort, and by the time she got there, every inch of her ached. She collapsed gladly onto her bed, barely able to make it through the simple meal one of the kitchen maids had delivered. Her last thought as she drifted into sleep was that it was the first night since her arrival that she hadn't dined with Prince Justin.

She woke with the dawn, feeling anything but refreshed. Perhaps she had been a little feverish from her misadventure, because her sleep had been plagued by vivid dreams. She had been wandering the castle, searching for the handsome version of Prince Justin, the one from the portrait. She had glimpsed him occasionally, but never been able to catch up to him. And every time he'd disappeared from her sight, she'd been haunted by a terrible fear that he was ill, perhaps even dying.

She dressed quickly, her limbs still weak and her head sluggish. It was foolish, but she wanted to see the prince, to assure herself he was still all right. It was the first morning she'd left her suite before Viola had arrived, and she felt tentative as she walked through the corridors. Was she allowed to be about so early? Phillip had stopped following her after the visit from the Listernian knight, but it was still rare for her to be alone.

She wasn't quite bold enough to go to the prince's suite just after dawn, so she made for the servants' hall, intending to ask for news of him. She never reached it, however. Her path took her toward the entranceway, and she was surprised to see two familiar figures crossing the marble floors, the prince's hulking form shadowed by Phillip's lithe one.

"Felicity." Prince Justin came to a stop, seeming as surprised as she was. He looked up at her, standing at the top of the staircase, and their eyes met across the distance. Something intense but silent passed between them, and she felt heat rising up her neck at the memory of their last meeting.

"Should you be up and about?" The prince spoke curtly, but she was surprised by the concern in his eyes. She was even more stunned when he stepped toward her, one arm raised, as if to offer assistance.

"Allow me, Your Highness," said Phillip hastily. "You aren't at your full strength yourself." He hurried up the stairs, offering Felicity his arm with a gentle smile. "We can't have you tumbling down the stairs, miss."

"Thank you." Felicity returned the smile warmly. She didn't think she needed the help, but she appreciated the gesture.

Justin, however, didn't seem pleased by Phillip's intervention. A hint of his habitual scowl had returned, and his eyes lingered on the young guard. Phillip seemed to notice it, because once he had deposited Felicity safely on the marble floor, he bowed himself out of the entranceway altogether.

"You shouldn't glare at him," Felicity said, frowning. "He was just concerned for you." Justin's scowl didn't disappear, and Felicity gave a huff of annoyance. "They're all like that, far too protective of you. It still makes me want to knock their heads together sometimes, their blind loyalty despite how you treat them."

Justin raised an eyebrow. "You don't think my servants should be loyal to me?"

Felicity's frown deepened at the chill in his tone. "I think you have a responsibility to them, and they would have reason to be angry with you after you landed them in this fix."

The words tumbled out, but she regretted them instantly. She hadn't sought Justin out to argue with him. But her emotions were in a tangled mess, unsure where to land after the confrontation in the garden, the intensity of the rescue, and her unsettling dreams. He would respond in kind now, they would both lose their tempers, and they would be back where they started.

She braced herself, but Justin surprised her, not responding at all to her accusations against him.

"Really?" he asked, his tone challenging, but not aggressive. "You say they've made excuses for me, served me faithfully even when I failed in my responsibilities to them. Made sacrifices I didn't deserve. You have no sympathy with their attitude?"

Felicity frowned, confused. Then all of a sudden the truth of his words crashed over her, and her breath caught in her throat.

CHAPTER SIXTEEN

Justin

Justin waited, his eyes on Felicity's flushed face. He was certain she'd taken his meaning, but he wasn't sure if she would acknowledge it.

"You're...you're talking about my family," she said, her voice small. "You're saying I'm angry with your servants for doing precisely what I've done myself."

He remained silent, judging it was unnecessary to speak the confirmation aloud. He'd caused her enough pain on this topic already. There was no need to remind her of what she clearly knew—that her father had a responsibility for her that should have brought him back for her much sooner than this. Or to go back a step further, it should have stopped him from abandoning her to Justin so easily in the first place.

"I know my father might seem...weak," Felicity said defensively. "But there are reasons. He used to be a successful merchant, but his fleet went down, and he lost everything. I think he could have coped with that if he had my mother at his side, but she died so soon after. And he never recovered from losing her. And Ambrose isn't really to blame for his selfishness. He's been too much indulged, and..."

She trailed off, fidgeting uncomfortably under Justin's continued silence.

"I'm doing exactly what you accused me of, aren't I?" she asked, with a weak attempt at a smile. "Making excuses." She gave him a searching look. "I suppose your servants have their reasons as well."

Justin deemed it time to reenter the conversation—the last thing he wanted was to direct her thoughts toward whatever pathetic aspects of his history might have the servants making excuses for him.

"I wasn't trying to accuse you of anything," he said. "You're not the one who should feel ashamed."

She flushed, but made no further attempt to defend her father.

"In any event," she said in a rallying tone, "Phillip was just trying to help. I'm sure he didn't mean any slight on your capabilities." Her expression softened. "He cares about you, you know. They all do. That's why they stayed, when everyone else ran away and abandoned you."

It took Justin a moment to catch up with her thoughts, and when he did, a wave of discomfort washed over him. She had misunderstood the reason for his irritation when Phillip raced forward to help her. He preferred not to explore his reaction even internally, so he pushed the thought aside.

"I'm glad to see you recovered."

Felicity nodded, her eyes on her feet. "You as well." She cleared her throat. "About yesterday...I'm sorry I overreacted in the garden. And I'm sorry I left the estate. I didn't mean to break my word—I never intended to actually leave. I just wanted to clear my head. And..." She looked up at him at last. "Thank you. For coming to my rescue."

He stared at her, completely taken aback by the heartfelt words. Knowing what he did of her, he had expected she would probably thank him for saving her life. But since he also knew, deep down, that he had been in the wrong, he hadn't for a moment imagined she would apologize. She was willingly making herself vulnerable, and in all honesty, he didn't trust himself with the power that gave him.

"I do take my responsibility to those on this estate seriously," he said gruffly. "Whatever you might think. You are a guest here, and I would be greatly in the wrong to leave you in harm's way."

She nodded, the warmth gone from her eyes at his formal response. All of a sudden Justin was unsatisfied by it himself.

"I was wrong," he said quickly, before he could change his mind. "To attack you in the garden. I know now that you weren't intending to pick a rose. And I shouldn't have said what I did in any event."

She looked up, and he winced internally at her astonishment on hearing him apologize. She didn't comment on it, however.

"Thank you," she said. "And I know now why you're protective of the roses." She hesitated. "They told me what happens when you leave the estate." She shot him a quick glance, but didn't refer to the physical pain he'd experienced when coming after her. He was glad—he would have no idea how to respond. "I hope the damage to the roses wasn't too significant."

"I've just been inspecting them," he said, trying to sound nonchalant. "The garden still stands."

She looked at him apprehensively. "How many wilted yesterday?"

Justin hesitated, but he supposed he couldn't hide it from her. "Ten."

Felicity gasped. "Ten! That's a third of what was left!"

Her eyes were wide and horrified, and it suddenly hit Justin that she was genuine. She really cared, even though she—alone of all the castle's residents—had nothing to fear from the curse.

He was overwhelmed by a sudden desire to wipe the guilt from her face.

"Don't let it trouble you," he said softly. "I was wrong to suggest that a rose, however enchanted, was worth your father's life. *Your* life is certainly worth more than ten roses."

He didn't wait to see her response, making for the staircase with a slightly uneven gait. He was full of a strange mix of discomfort and exhilaration. This girl had come out of nowhere and turned his life upside down. So many of the rules he'd always lived by were crumbling away one by one. He was starting to think that if the experience didn't kill him, it just might save him.

JUSTIN SQUINTED INTO THE MIRROR, irritated at how thick his head still felt. It had been two days since his venture out of the estate. When would he be back to his full strength?

Uncle Cameron sat in a meeting with some of the influential members of Justin's court, and the fool couldn't seem to keep his attention on the conversation. He kept rubbing his head, where he wore the circlet he'd argued about with Dobson.

"*Don't you agree, Lord Regent?*" Lord Ladner was speaking, his eyes narrowed as they rested on the acting regent.

"*I'm sorry, My Lord, what did you ask?*"

Justin winced at the display of weakness from Uncle Cameron. His role seemed to have aged him. It was true he'd never had the sharp mind necessary in a successful monarch, but he'd always been sensible enough. Now he came across as a confused old man.

"*I suggested that preparations be made for soldiers to be dispatched to the border towns once the snow melts. We would be wise to preempt the increased bandit attacks we saw last spring.*"

"*Ah yes, the bandit attacks,*" said Uncle Cameron, straightening. "*I appreciate the suggestion, My Lord, but I have been reliably informed that a military presence would be more likely to cause ill will than to reassure the villagers.*"

Justin frowned. Reliably informed by whom? That advice made no sense. He couldn't count the number of times he'd heard representatives from the border villages seeking additional protection against bandits. Even Justin's father, who cared little for the plight of the villagers, would usually provide the requested aid. Keeping order within the kingdom was essential.

A knock at the door of his receiving room interrupted his thoughts. He stowed the mirror safely in a drawer before responding, his face still turned from the doorway.

"Come in."

The door swung open, but no one entered. Justin looked around, expecting to see Stewart or his serving man, and started in surprise at the slim form of Felicity hovering in the doorway.

"I'm sorry to interrupt you." She gave him a disarming smile. "And I have a feeling Stewart would upbraid me for coming to your suite uninvited."

"Not at all," Justin said with slightly stiff politeness, wondering what she was about to ask for. "Is something amiss?"

"No, nothing," said Felicity brightly. "It's just that Viola is helping wash laundry, and I've been banned from doing anything useful on pain of dismemberment."

Justin raised an eyebrow at the dramatic comment, and Felicity chuckled. "Well, perhaps I'm putting words in her mouth, but that was the general idea. I suppose she doesn't do it to you, but Mrs. Winters can be terrifying when she chooses to be."

"On the contrary," Justin said dryly, pushing himself to his feet, "she does it to me all the time."

Felicity chuckled again. "Well, she seems to think I'm still recovering, and she won't let me help. I'm not even allowed to go outside. It's as if they're afraid I'll freeze instantly if exposed to snow."

"Yes, I'm under the same prohibition," Justin admitted, still waiting for her to come to the point.

"I thought you might be." Felicity's smile was a little hesitant. "And I wondered if you might like to, you know, walk with me. Inside, of course."

Justin blinked, trying to hide his astonishment. She'd sought him out just for his company? She'd been at a loose end, perhaps feeling lonely, and she'd come to him?

He tried to think of a time anyone had ever done that before, and he came up blank. His heart did a strange kind of flop, but he kept his voice level.

"If you like." He took a step toward the doorway. "Where do you want to go?"

"Take me to the place with the best view this time of year," Felicity said, seeming pleased at his response.

He thought about it for a moment. "The north tower," he said decisively. He started walking, and she fell into step beside him. "It will be cold at the top, though," he warned her. "Almost as cold as outside, probably."

"Noted," she said solemnly. "We need to exercise subterfuge. I won't tell our jailers if you don't."

He laughed in spite of himself. They walked in companionable silence for some time, Felicity seeming content with her own thoughts. Justin was amazed at how comfortable it was.

"You looked concerned when I interrupted you," Felicity said abruptly, as they strolled down a broad corridor flanked with suits of armor. "Are you worried about the roses?"

"No," said Justin, hoping she hadn't been blaming herself for the loss of the blooms. "I was thinking of my uncle, actually."

"The one who's acting regent?" Felicity asked curiously. Her foot slipped on a rug, and she reached out instinctively, steadying herself on Justin's arm. A tingle went through him from the touch, but Felicity barely seemed to notice she'd done it. Incredibly, she seemed genuinely unconcerned by Justin's fur-covered form.

"Yes," he said, drawing his thoughts back to the conversation with an effort. "The truth is he's not cut out for this role."

"But if he's your uncle, wasn't he raised a royal?" Felicity pressed. "Shouldn't he know how it all works?"

Justin shook his head. "He's not a prince. He's my mother's brother, not my father's. If my father had a brother, Uncle Cameron would never have been appointed acting regent when my father died." *If my father had a brother, that brother would probably have killed me off in a fake accident when I was still a child, and taken my crown permanently*, he thought wryly, remembering what his father had been like.

"Oh, I see," said Felicity. "But hasn't he been the regent for ten years?"

Justin sighed. "Yes, in theory." He saw that Felicity looked confused. "You said once that the acting regent has *continued* making decisions since I've been gone. But the truth is, he never exercised much power until I was cursed. The law prevented me from becoming king until I was eighteen, and required the court to appoint an acting regent. But no one ever expected Uncle Cameron to take on the role of monarch. My father's key advisors ran things, always building toward the day when I could take over."

He paused. "My training had always been intense for a child, but after my father's death, it became doubly so. Uncle Cameron filled any gaps, mainly ceremonial ones, in readiness for me to take the crown—and full authority—the moment I turned eighteen."

"Except then you were cursed before your birthday," Felicity finished softly.

Justin nodded. "That's right. My uncle has retained the role of regent, but from what I can tell, no one's quite sure who should really be exercising power, him or my advisors."

He thought Felicity would ask the obvious question, about how he knew all this, but her thoughts seemed to be going in a different direction.

"I looked at your portrait," she said abruptly. "The day you pulled me out of the lake."

Justin looked at her, startled. "What did you think?" he asked.

She shot him a quick look, and he winced internally. He had meant the question to be sardonic, but it had come out too curious. He wondered uncomfortably if the same thought was flashing through both their minds. The question was a little too close to the one he'd asked her every night up until their misadventure on the lake.

"I think you looked cold," she said, with her usual candor. "I'm not altogether sorry that I didn't know you back then."

Justin was silent, entirely unsure how to respond. They had reached an upper floor of the castle now, and he suddenly realized she was shivering.

"I did tell you it would be cold."

"I suppose you don't feel it." Felicity cast an envious glance at his thick fur, and Justin's lips twitched in amusement. Was she jealous of his deformation now?

"It does have its benefits, doesn't it?" she said blithely, as if reading his thoughts.

He raised an eyebrow. "I don't really think being impervious to cold is worth being no longer human."

"You're still human," Felicity scolded. She broke the effect with a cheeky grin. "Mostly. But I wasn't just talking about the cold. The way you carried me back from the lake was incredible.

Surely you wouldn't have been able to do that when you were the stripling from that portrait."

Justin gave her a look at this unflattering description of his normal form, but on the inside he was astonished yet again. She showed no awkwardness in talking either about his beastliness, or the fact that he'd carried her in his arms.

"Speaking of the portraits," said Felicity. "Was the one underneath yours a picture of your family?"

"Such as it was, yes," said Justin wryly.

"But..." Felicity hesitated. "There was another child. A baby."

"Yes, that's right," said Justin unemotionally. "I had a younger sister who died as an infant. Aurelia."

"How awful," said Felicity, her voice hushed. "I'm sorry."

Justin shrugged. "I don't remember her very well, to be honest. I was only a young child myself. But it destroyed my mother. She died less than a year later."

"That's terrible," Felicity said, with feeling. "I knew your mother had died when we were children, but I'd never even heard about your sister."

"Yes, Father didn't like it talked about."

Felicity hesitated, clearly trying to be delicate. "It must have been very distressing for him."

Justin snorted. "Not in the way you mean. Aurelia was a spare, and it's not like he really knew her. He certainly didn't spend time with us when we were babies. And he wasn't exactly warm toward my mother. He was more angry than upset. Angry with the physicians for failing to figure out what was wrong with Mother, angry with her for dying from no other cause than grief." His eyes were unfocused, looking back over the years. "Angry with me for taking so long to get over it."

"Justin," said Felicity, her use of his name startling him as much as her touch on his arm. "I'm so sorry."

He came back to the present, looking down at her. Their eyes locked for a moment, then he shook off his reminiscent mood. This was no time to dwell on the flicker of sentiment that always tugged at him when he thought of his mother, or his baby sister.

"It was a long time ago."

They began to climb a spiral staircase, forcing them to go in single file.

"It's the sort of thing people think doesn't happen to royals, just to ordinary people," Felicity said sadly from behind him. "How did Aurelia die?"

"A fall." He gave a mirthless smile. "So it's the servants who really deserve your pity."

"Servants?" Felicity asked, sounding confused.

"She was being carried by her nursemaid at the time. They both fell into a ravine. What the woman was doing over there in the first place..." He broke off with a sigh. "My father agreed with you, that such things aren't supposed to happen to royals. He wasn't the gentlest of masters before, and he became an absolute ogre to his servants after that. Thought the whole lot of them were useless and stupid, and didn't hesitate to tell them so."

Felicity was silent, and Justin wondered uncomfortably if she was thinking that his description applied also to his own treatment of his servants. They'd reached the top of the spiral staircase, and he hastened to change the subject.

"What do you think?" He gestured to a small window.

Felicity hurried over to it, her skirts swooshing with each step, and her cloak pulled tightly around her.

"It's gorgeous," she breathed, looking out at the frozen landscape. "Like a wonderland."

"Tormenting me with its nearness, and its inaccessibility," Justin said, glancing down at his companion.

She gave him an inquiring look, her cheeks appealingly tinged from the cold, and their eyes locked.

He gave a tight smile. "I used to walk in the woods outside the estate whenever I could get the chance."

"Your Highness, Miss Felicity?" The faint voice wafted up from the base of the spiral staircase, and they both turned.

"Yes, we're up here."

Justin heard the sound of hurrying feet, and a minute later Phillip appeared.

"What is it?" Justin asked, frowning as he tried to read the look on Phillip's face.

"There's a man—a young man—wandering around the castle," Phillip said, breathless from his sprint. His eyes flashed to Justin's companion. "And he's calling for Miss Felicity by name."

CHAPTER SEVENTEEN

Felicity

Felicity started at the guard's words, and a shot of excitement coursed through her.

"Ambrose!" she exclaimed aloud.

It had taken her brother long enough, the dolt, but he'd finally come looking for her. He'd even braved the snow to do so, and she knew how he hated the cold. She hurried to the stair-well, glancing back when there was silence behind her.

"Aren't you coming?" she asked, and Justin unfroze. Felicity turned away again, a warmth growing in her chest. Justin had been wrong—her family did care about her. Ambrose had come to take her home.

Not that she would go with him, of course. Her word was still her word, and she wouldn't leave until Justin released her. But it would make her feel better to be able to reassure her family that she was well and unharmed.

She followed Phillip down a seemingly endless series of corridors, aware that Justin was coming more slowly behind them. She had expected Ambrose to be in the entranceway, so she was thrown completely off kilter when, halfway down the corridor where her suite was located, she encountered a tall figure glancing into a room.

She had already opened her mouth to call out to him when he turned. She skidded to a stop as the greeting died on her lips.

"Kurt," she gasped. Waves of disappointment crashed over her, making her even less enthusiastic to see him than usual. "What are you doing here?"

His head shot up at her voice, and for a moment he just looked stunned. Then his eyes raked up and down her form, and his face settled into its usual smirk.

"Felicity, my dear girl. So the rumors of the fine lady in the abandoned castle are true." He cast another amused look at her finery. "Or at least, I can see why they thought you were a fine lady."

Felicity heard a firm tread behind her, and she felt bolstered. Kurt didn't know it, but she wasn't alone this time. She didn't look at Justin, but she could feel his disapproval, and she didn't blame him. Kurt's obnoxiousness oozed out of him, as always.

"What are you doing here?" she asked again, her eyes narrowing.

"I've come to take you home, you silly girl," Kurt said lazily. Again his eyes flicked to her costly gown. "I'm sure you've enjoyed yourself playing courtiers, but it's time to return to reality."

He stepped forward, and Felicity stepped back. She was reluctant to let him know how uncomfortable he made her, but she was even more reluctant to let him touch her.

"I'm not going anywhere with you," she said bluntly, as Justin stepped past her. Disdain dripped off him as he circled Kurt in a way the villager would have found highly disconcerting if he could see or hear it.

"No need to be coy, Felicity," said Kurt, a hint of irritation in his voice. Felicity thought she heard a growl from Justin, but it was so faint she might have imagined it. "Don't let all your fancy visitors go to your head." He shook his head indulgently. "I hear you've even been entertaining princes here in your lonely castle. I don't know what you've fooled them into believing, but I thought I'd better remind you that you're a simple peasant girl."

"Who is this clown?" Justin demanded. "Is this his idea of courting you?"

Felicity's lips twitched. "Not a clown," she muttered. "They're funny on purpose."

Kurt's expression became uneasy as he glanced around. "Are you talking to yourself?"

"No, just chatting with the spirits that haunt this place," Felicity said cheerfully. "I must say, Kurt, I'm touched you were willing to brave a haunted castle to find me."

Kurt snorted. "I'm not a fool like your brother, to believe such stories."

Felicity narrowed her eyes, Kurt's mention of Ambrose bringing back the sting of her disappointment. "How did you find the castle?"

"It wasn't hard," shrugged Kurt. "The Summer Castle is on every map."

"I thought you said Ambrose was a dunce for thinking he'd found the Summer Castle."

"Yes." Kurt struck his signature pose, weight back on his heels, hand on the hilt of his hunting knife. Justin, who had circled back to Felicity, gave an audible snort. "I was as surprised as you to discover that Ambrose had been right for once in his life."

Felicity scowled. "Where is Ambrose?"

Kurt regarded her in silence for a moment, his expression somewhere between indulgent and mocking. "They're not coming to look for you any time soon, Felicity. It seems you're dispensable to them."

A cold rush passed over Felicity at his words, and her vision spun. She tried to keep her face impassive, but she could feel the moisture in her eyes. She'd never thought of herself as sensitive before, but this constant prodding at her weakest point was getting hard to take.

"I don't like him." Justin's deep rumble broke her from her thoughts.

"He's not saying anything you haven't already said," Felicity snapped, without looking at him.

She knew she'd been unfair, and she expected Justin to retort. But he just fell silent.

Kurt frowned at her, clearly trying to make sense of her words. After a moment he seemed to decide to disregard them, continuing instead with what was probably a rehearsed speech.

"But *I* missed you." He took a step forward. Felicity stood her ground this time, on principle, with the result that he towered uncomfortably close to her. "You're not dispensable to me." He smirked. "Replaceable perhaps, but I hope it won't come to that."

"You're as charming as ever, Kurt," Felicity said, her skin crawling unpleasantly at the way Kurt was looking at her.

"I am, aren't I?" Kurt agreed, choosing to miss the sarcasm. "It's time to leave fantasy behind, Felicity. You can't survive here," he glanced around at the apparently deserted castle, and shifted even closer, "all alone."

Felicity's discomfort heightened, and she struggled to find one of her usual quick retorts. Justin's growl was now a constant rumble, and even Phillip was making disapproving noises. Their presence should have comforted Felicity, but it didn't. She was back in her cottage, suffering another of Kurt's unwanted advances, knowing that the proximity of her brother, even her father, was no protection at all.

"She's not alone," Justin growled, although he must know it was pointless. "And if you don't back up, you'll regret it."

"This place is a fantasy, Felicity," Kurt was purring, his eyes on her fancy clothes, and the pearls Viola had woven through her hair. "I know you like your little games, but I'm tired of them. It's time to acknowledge that your real future is with me."

"No," Felicity said, her voice unsteady. "You have no part in my future, Kurt. You never have."

Kurt chuckled, maddeningly unconcerned by her words. He raised his hand, and Justin's growl became so menacing even Felicity felt a chill go down her spine.

"Don't touch her," Justin snarled.

Kurt, of course, didn't respond, reaching up to touch the hair that was cascading freely over Felicity's shoulder. The smell of leather enveloped her, and she gave an involuntary shudder. A flash of anger went through her, but it was as much with herself as with Kurt. She knew he was ridiculous—why did his presence paralyze her? Why was it so hard to think of the words to say to put him in his place?

"Don't touch me, Kurt," she snapped, hoping her anger masked her illogical fear.

Kurt gave as little heed to her words as he had to Justin's. He twirled a strand of copper hair around his fingers.

Felicity was still struggling with herself when a sudden roar filled the space. Kurt was ripped away from her, and it took her a moment to realize that Justin had him by the throat. Felicity's gasp was frozen in her mouth as Justin flung the broad-shouldered villager down the length of the corridor.

Kurt crumpled to the floor, unmoving, and for a horrifying moment Felicity thought he was dead. She took a step toward him, reluctant to get too close, and was relieved to see that his eyes were open, his expression dazed.

Slowly, painfully, he pushed himself to his knees.

"What *was* that?" he rasped, gripping his throat. His eyes darted around the corridor in terror, although of course they failed to latch on to the monstrous form of Justin, stalking toward him.

"GET OUT," Justin roared.

Felicity knew Kurt couldn't hear the words, but it almost seemed like he could, the way he scrambled to his feet.

"This place really is haunted," he whispered, staring at Felicity out of wide eyes.

"You're not welcome here," she said, her expression hard.

A flash of anger lanced through the fear on Kurt's face. "You're not worth it," he scoffed, his attempt at nonchalance undermined by the trembling passing over him. "It's no wonder your father and brother left you and never looked back."

Felicity drew a shuddering breath, but before she could retort, Justin once again stepped in.

"You don't take a hint, do you?" he growled. He extended one enormous leg, tripping Kurt so that the other man crashed to the floor. Then he bent, seizing Kurt by one ankle, and began to drag him down the corridor.

Kurt's terrified cry gave Felicity no satisfaction. His parting words filled her with fear. What did he mean about her father and Ambrose leaving? She was the one who had left them, wasn't she? Was he just talking about the fact that they hadn't come looking for her? Or was there something more sinister in his words?

There was no opportunity to ask, however. The moment Justin's grip on Kurt loosened, the uninvited visitor leaped to his feet, and this time he didn't pause. He ran for the entranceway like a frightened rabbit.

For a moment there was silence, except for the pattering of Kurt's footsteps out of sight. Then Justin turned, striding back to Felicity with barely restrained energy.

"Are you all right?" he asked, his intense blue eyes boring into hers.

She nodded, swallowing hard. "Of course I am," she said, attempting to speak casually. "He barely touched me."

Justin didn't respond, just stood silent, continuing to stare expectantly at her. She noticed that his breaths were coming rapidly, although she doubted his attack on Kurt had been any great strain on his strength.

"All right," she admitted, hugging herself uncomfortably. "He frightens me a little. I know it's absurd," she hastened to add. "He's just a foolish peacock. I could always shrug it off in the village. But for some reason it was harder all those times I came home to find him waiting for me, constantly hovering—"

"That sniveling snake went into your home?" Justin demanded, his tone dangerous.

Felicity shrugged, her arms still wrapped around her torso. "Only because he's a friend of my brother's. I asked Ambrose not to bring him over, but...well, Ambrose is..." She glanced up at Justin, and her tone became defensive. "My father would have told him he wasn't welcome if he understood these things, but... well...my father doesn't understand these things."

Justin was silent for so long it began to feel awkward. When he spoke, his voice was level, and his face impassive.

"Well, as I've said before, I take responsibility for those on this estate. While you're here, you're under my protection. And I can promise you he won't bother you again."

Felicity wasn't sure she could speak around the lump in her throat, but she didn't need to. Justin turned abruptly and strode toward a stairwell, his cloak billowing behind him.

～

IT WAS in a subdued frame of mind that Felicity made her way to dinner that night. She felt almost as weary as she had after Justin pulled her from the lake, and she wished she could hide away in her room with a tray. Not that dinners with Justin were unpleasant lately. Quite the reverse. He'd even stopped asking his old nightly question, so she had no awkwardness to dread.

But the confrontation with Kurt had shaken her in more ways than one, and she wasn't entirely sure how to face Justin. She was grateful to him for his intervention, but at the same time humiliated that it had been necessary. She'd been dealing with unwanted attention for years. Why did Kurt get under her skin so much?

But she knew why. It was for the reason she'd told Justin. Being accosted out on the street was one thing. Being pursued into your home, where you were supposed to feel safe, was something else altogether. She'd always hated Kurt being allowed into the cottage. She'd felt just as uncomfortable about his presence in the castle, only a stone's throw from the door of her suite. Her own reaction had made her realize how much Justin's castle had begun to feel like home. And she wasn't sure how to feel about that revelation, on top of everything else.

Fortunately, Justin not only refrained from mentioning Kurt, but made considerably more effort than usual to initiate trivial conversation. Felicity was just starting to feel relaxed again, when the sound of raised voices made both of them pause.

Felicity glanced apprehensively at Justin's face. He looked disapproving, and she wasn't surprised. In all her time at the castle, she'd never heard any servants argue like that. Before either of them could take any action, the door opened and a wide eyed chamber maid hurried in.

"Your Highness," she said breathlessly, although her eyes flicked to Felicity. "There are three more visitors looking for Miss Felicity, although I don't think they all know each other."

"Three?" Felicity leaned her head back, willing herself to remain patient. She was too weary for this. "This is getting ridiculous."

"I think one is another prince," said the chambermaid, sounding torn between nervousness and excitement.

"Another prince?" It was Justin who repeated her words this time, and a glance at his face showed that he looked as irritated as Felicity felt. He met her eyes, his expression difficult to read. "You're making quite a name for yourself with the royalty of Solstice, it seems."

Felicity groaned. "Not by my choice, believe me." She cast a long-suffering look at the maid. "Do I need to come and fetch them? I suppose no one can direct them to me."

The maid glanced behind her. "Well, they seemed to be coming this way. If I leave the door open so they can see the light from the fire..."

It was obvious why she had trailed off. The arguing could still be heard outside, and it was definitely getting closer. Felicity gave her hair a cursory pat, unable to hold in a sigh. She glanced at Justin to find him watching her with a hint of humor in his eyes.

"I see it's an arduous chore for you, entertaining princes."

She chuckled reluctantly. "I should be flattered, I suppose, but truth be told, it's starting to feel like a nuisance. If I thought any of them would actually help break the curse, it would be different. But no matter how many of them come and go, nothing seems to change."

Justin's massive brow furrowed. "It is strange," he agreed. "But it can't be a coincidence that before your father arrived, no one had found us for over two years, and since then, we've had a steady trickle. We must be missing something obvious."

There was no time for Felicity to respond, because the voices outside cut off abruptly, and hurried footsteps sounded in the hall.

"Look, there's a door open! Is that a fire?"

A moment later the chambermaid leaped hastily out of the way, and a fresh faced young man appeared in the doorway.

"Aha!" he cried, just as if he was playing hide and seek, and he'd caught Felicity out at last. Then his face fell comically. "Well this is a bit of a letdown. You don't look oppressed at all!"

CHAPTER EIGHTEEN

Justin

Justin almost laughed aloud at the look of blank astonishment on Felicity's face, but he held it in heroically. The boy looked vaguely familiar, but he couldn't immediately remember who he was.

"Well," Felicity said, her stunned expression slowly giving way to the look that indicated laughter was bubbling just below the surface. "I apologize for disappointing you."

"Your Highness," muttered a long-suffering voice from behind the intruder, and the boy grinned.

"Whoops. *I* should be apologizing, I suppose. That wasn't very polite, was it?" He gave a courtly bow, momentarily exposing a broad-shouldered man of about Justin's age standing behind him. "I'm Prince Amell, at your service."

Ah, Justin thought, Amell. He'd been a mere child the last time Justin had seen him, so it was no wonder he hadn't recognized him at first.

Felicity rose to her feet, curtsying clumsily but with good humor. "Honored to meet you, Prince Amell of..."

"Fernedell," Justin supplied, when she glanced at him for assistance. He hadn't bothered standing, given that it was clear no one but Felicity and the hovering chambermaid could see him.

"Of Fernedell," Felicity parroted. "I'm Felicity."

"The honor is mine, My Lady," said Prince Amell, sweeping another bow. The man behind him sighed.

"Oh, this is my personal guard," said the prince, gesturing behind him. He gave another grin. "His name is Sir Very Patient Man, or at least that's what my parents seem to call him."

The guard shot the prince a look that caused Felicity to stifle a giggle, and even Justin's lips twitched. He didn't envy the unfortunate guard his post.

"I am Sir Furnis, My Lady," the guard said politely, bowing to Felicity.

"Well, I'm very pleased to meet you," said Felicity warmly, "but I'm not a lady, you know."

"I do know," interrupted a new voice, as another man pushed his way through the crowded doorway. "And it seems to me that you have a great deal of explaining to do, young woman."

Justin suddenly got a good look at the newcomer, and stood up quickly, energy coursing through him. Finally, someone useful had come!

"That's one of my advisors!" he gasped, and Felicity's eyes widened in excitement. Justin cast his mind around for a moment, trying to remember the man's name. "Lord Brooker," he said, with satisfaction.

Prince Amell obviously couldn't hear Justin's words, so he responded merely to Felicity's accuser.

"That's not very polite." He scowled at the other man. "I may not get to defend the lady from monsters after all, but I can still defend her from rudeness."

A stifled sound drew Justin's attention to Felicity. She was clearly trying very hard not to laugh at the heroics of her youthful champion, and again Justin felt humor tug at him. But the advisor's acid reply quickly sobered him.

"With respect, Your Highness," Lord Brooker snapped, in a tone that was anything but respectful, "this matter is none of your affair."

Justin frowned. The hostility crackling between the pair told him instantly who had been arguing in the corridor earlier. He'd always found the middle aged advisor abrasive, but Lord Brooker should still know better than to argue with a foreign prince, however young.

"You're very gallant to come to my rescue, Your Highness," Felicity said to the prince, in a rallying tone. "Most wouldn't be willing to brave a cursed castle at such a young age." Her words hung hopefully in the air.

"It's my pleasure," the prince said with dignity, refusing to take the bait.

Felicity again glanced appealingly at Justin, who pulled to mind his detailed coaching on the royal families of the other kingdoms of Solstice. Fernedell's crown prince was five years younger than him, so...

"He's fifteen," he said briefly.

Felicity took a moment, her expression flickering in a way that told Justin how desperately she was trying not to laugh. When she had regained her composure, she continued.

"But I'm afraid our companion is right. I do have some explaining to do." Her gaze flicked to the advisor from Allenton. "You must be wondering how I come to be here, making myself at home in Prince Justin's castle, sir."

There was a prolonged silence, during which Justin's eyes narrowed as he watched Lord Brooker. The advisor was staring at Felicity with an expression Justin didn't like. It was nothing like the hungry gleam in that villager's eye earlier, the one that had made Justin want to rip the man limb from limb like the animal he tried not to be.

No, Lord Brooker was watching Felicity with a cold fury that seemed to grow with every passing moment. His unspoken aggression triggered a protective instinct that was still on alert from the previous visitor. Without consciously deciding to do it, Justin found himself striding around the table to hover protectively at Felicity's side. She seemed to sense the advisor's animosity as well, and she drew back, her shoulders hunching inward slightly.

"I *was* wondering," Lord Brooker said at last. "I thought you were some brazen peasant girl, making the most of the opportunity presented by an abandoned castle full of discarded finery." His eyes narrowed. "But now I know better. I see I was more right than I realized, to ignore all the nonsense about invisible people, and focus on the young woman who had set herself up like a fine lady at the absent prince's expense." Anger flashed across his face. "I even thought it worth battling my way through the snow to expel you, but I little expected what I would find."

He took a menacing step forward. "How did you enchant the prince, you vixen? Where is he?"

Felicity stumbled back a step at the advisor's approach, and Justin heard a low growl rumble around the room. It took him a moment to realize it had come from his own throat.

"Step back!" demanded Prince Amell, giving voice to the words Justin wished he could audibly say. "How dare you threaten her?"

"What are you talking about?" Felicity asked, her face draining of color as she stared back at Lord Brooker. "I didn't enchant this place! And Prince Justin is here, like I told Prince Bentleigh!" She looked to Justin for help. "Tell me something to convince him, Justin!"

Justin searched his mind for a suitable piece of information, but the advisor interrupted his thoughts with a brittle laugh.

"Don't try your tricks on me, wench. It's very cute, using his name, pretending intimacy with an invented prince. Do you think that impresses me?" His eyes narrowed. "You'll find I'm not so easily convinced as Prince Bentleigh." He drew his cloak close. "I don't know if you enchanted him as well, or if he's just gullible by nature. But I won't be so neatly ensnared. If you think I'll spend the night here, to let you pull me into whatever dark magic you've called upon for your revenge, you're mistaken."

"Revenge?" Felicity repeated, still ashen-faced. "What are you talking about?"

"You think I don't know what you're up to?" He gave a harsh laugh. "You're out of luck, because I never forget a face." His eyes narrowed again. "I'll be back, and your little game will be over. I'll see you hang."

With that dramatic utterance, Lord Brooker turned and disappeared back through the doorway, his traveling cloak pulled tightly around him.

Justin stared after him, too astonished to even attempt to stop the man. He'd been so excited by the advisor's appearance, sure that here was someone who would finally be of use. But it didn't seem likely that Lord Brooker would have accepted any communication coming through Felicity. And Justin found he didn't even want to try, not when the advisor was making death threats against her.

He turned to Felicity, to see her frozen to the spot, her eyes riveted on the empty doorway. She seemed to feel his gaze, and her eyes swung slowly to his. He could read her fear, and his heart did a painful kind of flip. He'd been able to tell the moment she entered the room that she was still fragile from her earlier encounter, and this latest attack was the last thing she needed.

"I don't know what that was about," she whispered, her eyes pleading with Justin. "I swear I had no hand in the enchantment."

Justin started, realizing all at once that he had misread her fear. She wasn't afraid about Lord Brooker's threats against her. She was afraid that Justin would believe his accusations. The earlier tug at his heart was nothing to the way this realization made it somersault.

His eyes searched hers for a long moment before he responded.

"I believe you," he said softly, feeling the truth of the words down to his core.

Felicity obviously felt it too, because she visibly relaxed. Prince Amell, on the other hand, was still a little worked up.

"Of course you're not behind the enchantment," he said indignantly, apparently under the impression that Felicity had been speaking to him. "You're the damsel in distress, everyone knows that." He gave a good natured sigh. "Or at least, you're supposed to be."

Felicity turned to him with a valiant attempt at a smile. "I'm sorry to have disappointed you with my lack of distress, Your Highness."

He gave her a wheedling look. "Are you sure you don't need help of any kind? No dragons to slay, or quests to be completed?"

Felicity's smile appeared more genuine this time. "I thought dragons were unslayable."

"Yes, they are, from all I hear," sighed Prince Amell, sounding personally disappointed.

"As for quests..." Felicity glanced at Justin inquiringly.

It took only a moment of thought before he shook his head. "Let's not bring him into this. I'm sure the kid means well, but if Bentleigh couldn't help, Amell won't be able to. I'm much more interested in figuring out what Lord Brooker meant."

Felicity nodded. If he was reading her correctly, she looked relieved not to have to be his mouthpiece again.

"I won't trouble you with any quests, either," she said apologetically. "I'm afraid I'm quite safe here, and I'm not even here against my will." She glanced at Justin. "And although it's a little hard to explain, I am actually allowed to be here."

"We are, of course, most relieved to hear that you're not in danger, miss," said Sir Furnis quickly, before his young charge could speak. "And you have no need to explain your situation to us. On the contrary, we apologize for intruding on your privacy." He threw the fifteen-year-old prince a dark look. "We were, perhaps, a little impulsive in pursuing the rumor of your capture."

Felicity's lips worked in an unnatural way. Justin could only assume that, like him, she interpreted Sir Furnis's words to mean that Prince Amell had run away in order to chase adventure, with only his long-suffering guard for protection. But Justin couldn't bring himself to be very interested in the young prince's escapades. His eyes were still riveted on the way Felicity was biting one lip in an attempt to keep laughter in.

"Oh, you're no fun, Furn," Prince Amell scolded his guard, without malice. He gave a wistful sigh. "Ah well. I suppose I'll just have to keep my ear to the ground. Considering I'm a prince, it's an absolute crime how hard adventure is to come by."

A choke of laughter escaped Felicity at last, and Amell gave her a self-deprecating grin.

"I know, I know," he said. He brightened. "So you had Prince Bentleigh of Bansford here, did you? He came a long way."

Felicity smiled. "Actually, he came from Listernia, and he wasn't the only one. Even the princess from Mistra tried to come."

"Bansford, Listernia, Mistra, now Fernedell." Prince Amell counted them off on his fingers. "That's almost every kingdom represented." His face fell slightly. "I doubt you'll get anyone coming from Entolia. Prince Basil and I used to be good friends, but he doesn't have time for anything like that now. These days he's too serious, and too occupied by the war with Mistra."

"Plus trying to keep eleven younger sisters in line," Justin muttered, shuddering at just the thought.

"Prince Basil has eleven younger sisters?" Felicity repeated, startled.

"Twelve actually," said Amell, looking confused at her tone. "They just had another one."

Justin shuddered again. King Thorn and Queen Lucille really needed to stop trying for a spare. Prince Amell was prattling cheerfully on, but Justin tuned him out. His eyes were drawn again to Felicity, and he saw that she looked weary underneath her friendly smile. She probably had no idea how to extricate herself from the situation politely. He knew exactly how to handle such situations, and he wished he could take the lead. When Bentleigh had come, he had been infuriated at having to rely on Felicity to speak on his behalf. This was the first time he'd wished for his voice so that he could speak on hers.

"We've intruded too long, Your Highness." Sir Furnis cut in on the young prince's chatter, and Justin felt a surge of gratitude to the man. "We should be on our way."

Felicity made the appropriate protestations, convincing the pair to stay the night rather than venturing back into the snow. She promised them food and lodgings, and although they looked bewildered, they didn't press for an explanation as to how she would cater for them.

When Felicity finally managed to retire from the dining hall, Justin followed immediately. He had no interest in eavesdropping on the conversation of the pair from Fernedell. He was confident he wouldn't hear anything useful.

"Felicity," he called softly, once she was out of hearing from the dining hall. She turned, her expression uncertain.

"I'm sorry we didn't find out anything useful from your advisor," she said uncomfortably.

"Never mind that," said Justin. "Why did he recognize you?"

Felicity shrugged. "I have no idea. I think he must have been mistaken. I haven't left the general area of my boring little village since I arrived there, when I was four."

Justin frowned at her, deep in thought. She must have misunderstood the expression, though, because her voice became pleading again.

"It's the truth, Justin. I'm not hiding anything from you."

He searched her eyes silently. He wanted to trust her. It was almost frightening how much he wanted it. But he retained enough sense not to say the words aloud.

"Are you all right?" he asked instead. He didn't explain the question. She knew as well as he did that she'd sustained visits from two hostile men that day. His thoughts flew back to the villager, and another surge of hot anger passed over him.

"Of course," Felicity said, her calm cheerfulness not altogether convincing. She bid him good night and hurried down the corridor, but Justin stood staring thoughtfully after her for some time.

He had more questions than ever, and still no explanation for the erratic behavior of the curse. He reached a sudden decision—he would start setting the guards to watch the gates again. He hadn't bothered since the early months of the curse, but two things had changed since then. For one, their hidden fortress was no longer reliably inaccessible.

And, more importantly, the castle now held something to protect. Something of great value.

CHAPTER NINETEEN

Felicity

There he was, just ahead. Felicity hurried, tripping over the foolishly fancy gown Viola had laced her into. Why did she need a train?

Prince Justin's cloak swirled behind him, the flash of movement all that was visible of him as he rounded a corner. She reached the doorway, and paused, frowning. A long corridor stretched out in front of her, but it was empty. Moonlight slanted through the broken windows that lined one side of it, and a bitter wind swept flakes of snow through the gaps in the glass. She pulled her own cloak more tightly around her shoulders as she forced herself forward.

She peered into the first room, but it was swathed in covers. The second was the same, and the third. She had begun to despair of ever finding him when she reached the last door. It was ajar, and she pushed it open tentatively.

At once she recognized Prince Justin's bedchamber, although she'd only been there once. As on that occasion, he was stretched out on the bed, unmoving. It was an even more alarming sight in his human form, since it showed the pallor of his face.

"Justin?"

Her soft voice brought his head around, and he opened his eyes.

Their piercing blue was unnervingly familiar, set in a face she still didn't really know.

"Felicity," he whispered, an anguished sound. "I tried to be good enough. But it was too late."

He looked down, and following his gaze, she saw that there was a rose in her hands, and dozens more littered the ground at her feet. What had she done?

The distinctive sound of a curtain being ripped open cut across the room, and both Felicity's and Justin's eyes snapped to the windows.

FELICITY WOKE WITH A START, a gasp escaping her as she sat upright in her bed.

"Miss Felicity!" Viola hurried over from where she'd clearly just pulled open Felicity's brocaded curtains. "Are you all right? I didn't mean to startle you."

Felicity stared at the maid out of wide eyes, her breath still coming quickly. Seeing Viola's increasing alarm, she made an effort to master herself.

"I'm fine." A shudder ran over her. "I just had an unnerving dream."

"Do you...do you want to tell me about it?" Viola asked.

Felicity gave a decisive shake of her head, her waking mind asserting itself and taking over. "Definitely not."

Viola asked no more questions, bustling about the room with her usual morning preparations.

"There was a heavy snowfall last night," she said. "It's a good thing that prince from Fernedell took himself off promptly yesterday. If they'd stayed a second night, they might have been stuck here."

"Yes," said Felicity, amused. "Imagine the horror of being stuck here."

Viola rolled her eyes at Felicity's teasing. "You know what I mean. Something tells me there'd be trouble for Albury if the crown prince of a neighboring kingdom disappeared into our missing Summer Castle."

"True," Felicity agreed. "Now the trouble will be limited to Prince Amell himself, I suppose." She considered it. "And probably Sir Furnis too, poor man."

"What would you like to do today, then?" Viola pushed on.

Felicity smiled to herself at the maid's refusal to show any interest in the fate of the pair from Fernedell. It was entertaining, if a little strange, how determined all the servants were to be unimpressed by the foreign royals who had visited the castle. Felicity considered herself loyal to Albury, but her fervor didn't drive her to sniff at the mention of any other prince.

"I don't think even you will want to walk in the gardens today," Viola was saying. "It's not fit for man or beast out there."

Felicity had taken a sip of hot tea, but she spat it out in a choke of laughter at the unfortunate choice of words.

"Whoops," said Viola, grinning as she realized her mistake. "Force of habit."

"Don't let Justin hear you saying that," Felicity said, with a watery cough.

"I won't," Viola assured her, a smug smile stretching across her face for some inscrutable reason. Felicity gave her an odd look, and she hastened on. "I was going to suggest you might like to spend the morning in the library. I'm sure I could convince the cook to send us hot cocoa there."

"That sounds heavenly," said Felicity brightly. She pushed herself out of bed and picked up a couple of books from where they sat on a chest at the foot of her bed. "I've finished these, so it's about time for another visit. I'm not sure how I've spent so little time there."

"I am," said Viola dryly. "It's because you insist on doing our work for us. If you weren't so stubborn, you could have spent every day reading in the library."

Felicity made a noise of protest. "I hardly do any chores!"

Viola shook her head indulgently. "Trust me, compared to any other guest who's ever stayed at this castle, you do a great many chores."

Felicity shrugged into the gown Viola was holding out, and submitted to having her laces tied. It was a particularly elegant dress, covered with delicate embroidered flowers, but thankfully it was missing the impractical train from her dream.

"Well, I'm not exactly a guest, am I? I mean, I was never supposed to be. All those previous guests were probably lords and ladies."

"Mostly," Viola agreed dismissively. "And none of them were ever half as nice or friendly as you."

Felicity smiled at the girl's loyal tone. She was aware that the servants had taken her as some kind of champion. She was a bit bemused by it, but she appreciated the support all the same.

"I can afford to be friendly," she said cheerfully. "I think coldness comes with rank, so the higher your station, the less friendly you can be."

There was silence while Viola finished her task, and when Felicity turned around, she saw that the maid looked downcast.

"What's wrong?" she asked.

Viola met her eyes. "Do you really think His Highness is so cold and unfriendly?"

For a moment Felicity was confused, then her thoughts caught up. "Oh Viola, I didn't mean any offense! I wasn't talking about Justin specifically." Viola's face didn't brighten, and Felicity realized she hadn't answered the question. She took a moment to think about it, to be sure her answer would be honest. "I don't think he's unfriendly, no. And he's not as cold as he used to be, either. I'm not sure if he's changed, or if I'm just giving him more of a chance."

Viola's ready smile was back, and Felicity watched her shrewdly.

"It's really important to you that I think well of him, isn't it?" she said. "Why?"

Viola let out a long breath, and her words came out hesitant. "I know we don't exactly seem unhappy, and we do get on well enough. But we are still trapped you know, Prince Justin most of all. We don't want to be stuck like this forever."

"Of course you don't," said Felicity quickly. She took the other girl's hands and held her gaze for a searching moment. "Believe me, I want to do all I can to break this curse. Is there something I can do? I would do anything to help."

Viola gave a tremulous smile, returning the pressure of Felicity's hands. "I know you would, Miss Felicity." She dropped her hold, and her voice turned rueful. "That's just the problem."

Felicity frowned, confused by this answer, but Viola had already changed focus.

"You're all ready, and you look absolutely lovely, if I say so myself." She tucked a stray strand of hair back into the loose braid she'd threaded around Felicity's head.

"I'm not sure why I need to be dressed up to read in the library," Felicity grumbled. But she knew her protest fell flat when she realized Viola had caught her admiring the effect of the deep blue gown in the looking glass that stood by the dresser. The maid's reflected smirk made Felicity roll her eyes, and she hurried from the room with what dignity she could.

Viola trailed after her, but to Felicity's surprise, the maid melted away once they reached the library, rather than accompanying her in. Felicity blinked at Viola's retreating back, confused. Perhaps she had gone to wheedle the cook into providing the requested cocoa. Felicity hummed cheerfully to herself as she replaced the books she had been reading in her room. She didn't mind being alone.

"Good morning."

The voice startled her so much that she actually dropped a book on her foot, and for a moment all she could do was hop awkwardly as the pain subsided. Once her eyes stopped watering, she blinked quickly in an effort to bring her companion into view. So much for being alone.

"Good morning," she returned, wincing slightly at her graceless entrance. The realization made her pause. She'd never been self conscious around Justin before. "I didn't realize you were here," she added.

"I often sit in here in the colder weather," Justin said, reaching down to pick up the book she'd dropped.

Felicity watched in some surprise as he deftly returned it to the correct place on the shelf. Clearly he was familiar with the library.

"The outside view from my study is more pleasant in the other months, but once we get snowed in, it's all much the same," Justin continued. "And the inside view here is much better."

Felicity followed his gaze, nodding her agreement. It was a truly beautiful room, two levels of shelves crammed full of books lining each wall of the large space, and lots of cozy corners hidden between the freestanding shelves.

"Yes, I love this room," she said, smiling at the memory of when Viola had showed it to her. She'd squealed aloud like a delighted child, and Viola hadn't been able to help laughing.

Justin reached out an inquiring hand, and Felicity placed her last book into it. Justin raised a wolf-like brow as he read the title.

"*Waterfowl: Habits and Habitats*. You're reading a book about birds?"

Felicity laughed. "Well, I didn't read the whole thing," she admitted. "Just the bit about swans. I was curious after what Prince Bentleigh said, about the Mistran princess having a whole bevy of them, and even bringing one traveling. I'd never heard of someone having a swan as a pet before." She nodded at the book. "And from what I read, it's not very common."

"I didn't realize you had such an inquiring mind," Justin said, a hint of amusement in his voice. Felicity followed him cheerfully as he strolled to the other end of the library and returned the book to the shelf where she'd originally found it. He turned back to her. "Any more?"

Felicity shook her head, smiling as she held out her empty hands. "Surely the crown prince is too glorified a person for a job like re-shelving," she teased.

Justin shook his own head, a smile playing around his lips. "Haven't you heard? I'm a little short on staff at present. We all have to take on extra roles."

Felicity grinned, delighted that he was joining in her banter in such a human way. "And yet you were extravagant enough to hire out to fill the role of damsel in distress," she scolded. "You would have been much more sensible to bring in an extra servant."

"If you recall, I did try," Justin responded dryly.

Felicity laughed aloud. "Of course, how silly of me." She'd been following him absently, and she now realized he'd led her back to where he must have been sitting when she entered. It was a pleasant little nook, containing a settle and a couple of stuffed armchairs next to a small fireplace. Justin took up the entire settle, and at a wave of his hand she sank into one of the armchairs.

"Admit it," she said, watching him humorously. "You were furious when Mrs. Winters set me up like a guest instead of putting me to work."

A brief smile passed over Justin's face. "I was." All of a sudden, the smile fell away, and his eyes drilled into hers with that unnerving intensity. "But not anymore. I'm glad she did. And I'm glad you stayed."

Felicity was silent, her heart picking up speed. There was an unusual flash of emotion in Justin's blue eyes, and it reminded her of her dream, and the way the human prince had looked at her with such anguish. Felicity's mind seemed incapable of forming any words, and the silence stretched out, broken only by the quiet crackling of the fire.

A squeaking sounded near the door, and to Felicity's relief, the moment was broken. She looked up to see Stewart wheeling a trolley through a gap in the shelves, his expression placid. Again that sense that he was familiar tugged at her mind, but before she could place it, she noticed Viola hovering behind the steward, looking a little too pleased with herself.

Felicity blinked at the two mugs of steaming cocoa on the trolley, and narrowed her eyes at her maid. She hadn't questioned the girl's innocent suggestion of the library before now, but suddenly Justin's presence there seemed a little too coincidental. Her heart sank as a longstanding suspicion crept toward certainty. If Viola was trying to do what Felicity thought she was, it could only end badly. She glanced at Justin. He looked surprised by the appearance of the cocoa, but he accepted a mug with a soft word of thanks to Stewart. The simple courtesy made Felicity realize how long it had been since she'd heard the prince barking curt orders at his servants.

A strange pang went through her heart. Justin was a much more complex person than she had at first assumed. The more she saw of him, the more she found to like. She would never forget the heroic way he'd come after her in the frozen lake. But truthfully, his intervention with Kurt was a rescue for which she was equally grateful. She'd put up with Kurt's overtures more times than she could count, and it had been the first time anyone else had even acknowledged they were a problem, let alone backed her up.

But she couldn't afford to get carried away by her changing emotions toward Justin. He was disfigured and isolated now, but they would figure out a way to break the curse. They had to. And then he would go back to being the powerful crown prince of Albury. Or rather, the king, she realized with a start. At least as soon as a coronation could be carried out.

"Felicity?"

She came back to the present to find Justin looking at her inquiringly, his head tilted toward the other mug of cocoa.

"Sorry," she said. "I was somewhere else."

She'd spoken lightly, but Justin gave her a long, searching look. She heard a squeaking, and saw that Stewart and Viola were withdrawing, taking the trolley with them. Viola's expression was still smug, and Felicity had to fight a trickle of annoyance at the girl. Viola was presumably trying to help, but she should realize without needing to be told that Felicity was the one likely to get hurt in this situation. It was absurd of her to allow her heart to be in any danger. She would never have even considered such a thing only a short time ago. But her recurring dreams about the Justin from the portrait had reminded her on some unconscious level that Justin was not only human underneath his beastlike exterior, but a young and unattached man.

"This really is a gorgeous library," she said, trying to encourage her thoughts toward less personal channels. She took a sip of the steaming cocoa as she glanced around her. "It must be incredible to have access to a collection like this. Before I came here I could only dream of such a luxury."

"It's a luxury I've taken a little for granted, I'm afraid," said Justin, following her gaze. "But I am fond of this library." He wrinkled his feline nose slightly. "The one in the castle in

Allenton will always be a little too connected with memories of my tutor. He was a slave driver."

Felicity gave a soft chuckle. "Count your blessings," she scolded him. "I wish I could have had a tutor."

"No library in your village, I take it?" Justin asked, and Felicity gave an unashamed snort.

"Not quite." She shook her head. "We brought a few books when we came from Allenton, and my father would occasionally bring me one from a market." She reached out to run a hand along the spines of the books on the nearest shelf. "But I haven't seen an actual library since I was a small child." Her eyes glazed over for a moment. "I have a memory of my mother reading to me in a library. It's one of the few memories I have of her, and it's beautiful."

"How old were you when she died?" Justin asked softly.

Felicity looked at him, surprised. He didn't generally ask her about her own life. But his expression suggested he was genuinely interested, not asking out of mere politeness, so she didn't deflect the question.

"I was four."

"So young." Justin's deep, throaty voice was as even as ever, but Felicity thought she could detect sympathy in his eyes. The thought melted something in her a little, but she sternly told herself to stop being sentimental. This was Viola's fault, for planting foolish ideas in her mind.

"I don't remember it at all," she said, trying to speak matter-of-factly. "Her death, I mean. Father doesn't like to talk about it, and I think I must have blocked it out a bit. I remember moving to the village, and only snatches of life from before. Like the library." She smiled, brightening. "Maybe I can find it again, if I make it to Allenton one day."

"Of course you'll make it to Allenton," said Justin unexpectedly. "If that's what you want, I'll make sure of it."

"Thank you," said Felicity, not quite meeting his eyes. She was frustrated by her own sudden shyness, but she couldn't seem to shake it.

"And perhaps I can help you find the library," Justin continued. "I'm pretty familiar with the capital. Can you remember anything about what it looked like?"

Felicity wrinkled up her face in concentration. "There were lots of books," she said.

"Helpful," said Justin dryly.

Felicity chuckled. Justin had made the comment with good humor, but the flash of his usual surliness made her feel more natural.

"I'm just building a picture in my mind," she said with mock dignity. She frowned again in concentration. "I think there was a garden outside the window, with a big fountain surrounded by hedges. And the library itself had an archway for the entrance, with these huge marble pillars inside."

Justin stared at her, and she raised an eyebrow.

"What?"

"That's the royal library," he said. "Inside the castle." He leaned back in his chair, his eyes still fixed on her. "So the good news is that it won't be difficult to find."

Felicity blinked back at him in surprise. "Are you sure?" She frowned. "How would I have been in the royal library?"

Justin shrugged. "They open it for public days from time to time. Your mother must have come along to one of those, and brought you with her."

Felicity's frown deepened. It was a long time ago, so she couldn't be sure of her memory, but she had thought her mother had taken her there lots of times, not just once. She hesitated, but decided not to say anything. Justin was still looking at her strangely.

"What is it?" she asked, and he shrugged.

"It's just a strange thought, to picture you in my castle."

Felicity rolled her eyes. "I *live* in your castle."

Justin gave a perfunctory smile. "Now, yes. But I'm still trying to get my head around the idea of us being in the same place at the same time, back when we were children."

"It is a funny thought, isn't it?" Felicity agreed. "Would we have been friends, do you think, if we'd met?"

Justin's harsh bark of laughter was instant. "No."

Felicity felt her face flushing, and instantly regretted the foolish question.

"Of course not," she said, trying to speak lightly. She downed the rest of her cocoa and stood. "Well, I know how irritating it is to have someone hanging about when you're trying to read. Thank you for sharing your sanctuary with me."

"Of course," said Justin. He hesitated. "You're welcome to join me here anytime you like."

Felicity paused, trying to read his face. His words were friendly, but she could see the shadow of their awkward moment in his eyes.

"Thank you," she said noncommittally. "That's very kind."

She bobbed her head quickly, and hurried from the room. Those clear eyes were a little too piercing, and she had an illogical fear that Justin could read her thoughts. That was the last thing she wanted.

She was humiliated enough just acknowledging the true cause of her awkwardness to herself. If Justin scorned the very idea of friendship between them in their normal state, she shuddered to think how he'd react if he knew she'd begun to harbor involuntary thoughts about something more.

CHAPTER TWENTY

Justin

J ustin flicked his riding whip against his leg in a compulsive rhythm. He was staring out the window of his suite, his eyes glazed over, taking nothing in. As they had for the last few days, his thoughts were circling endlessly around the conversation in the library.

He wanted to kick himself for his idiocy. They'd been having such a pleasant interaction, the coziness of his reading corner making the moment feel intimate. And then, once again, he'd managed to drive her away.

Ever since Justin had told Felicity—truthfully—that he believed her over the advisor from Allenton, he'd stopped trying to deny the change in himself. The truth was she'd become important to him. He didn't quite know how to put it into words, but he cared more about her safety and well-being than he had ever cared about anyone before. His instincts had come to the realization first—he could still feel his hackles rise anytime he thought about the villager's brazen touch on her hair, or even Lord Brooker's threatening manner—but his thoughts had finally caught up.

And instead of communicating any of this to Felicity, he'd sneered at the very suggestion of them being friends.

He grimaced at no one in particular. She had tried to gloss over the moment, but it had been clear at the time that he'd hurt her. And even if it hadn't been immediately obvious, he would be a fool not to notice her careful distance since then. Her sudden discomfort around him seemed like an overreaction to his rude words, but he'd learned that despite her general resilience, Felicity had some areas where she was particularly sensitive. He thought of his explosion when he'd found her in the rose garden and grimaced again. She wasn't the only one.

He sighed. She'd misunderstood his response to her question, but of course he hadn't explained it to her. He was no better at explaining himself than he was at apologies. Neither had played any part in his life before the curse.

He gave his leg one final slap with the riding whip, making up his mind. It was beyond stupid to mope around wishing she knew what he was thinking. He would approach her and explain himself. He could hear his father's voice yet again, but he flicked it away. He had nothing to fear from making himself vulnerable to Felicity. He was *almost* sure of it.

He glanced toward the drawer where he'd placed the mirror, but didn't linger. He knew from previous inquiries that Lord Brooker had been snowed in at a small town by the heavy fall, and still hadn't made it back to the capital. The chances of him saying anything revealing before he reached Allenton seemed slim.

Justin strode down the corridor, feeling oddly nervous. He knew where Felicity's suite was, of course, but he'd never actually approached it since her arrival. His keen ears picked up the sound of cheerful conversation, even through the closed door. He hesitated for only a moment before knocking with an enormous fist.

"Come in!" Felicity called brightly.

Justin hesitated again, and after a moment, he heard pattering footsteps. The door was pulled open and Felicity's maid appeared, her smile turning instantly into a look of astonishment.

"Your Highness!" she exclaimed, and behind her Felicity turned hastily.

She was in the act of threading a ribbon through her own hair, to match the deep green of the elegant gown she wore. She looked extremely pretty, and Justin was uncomfortably aware of his own attire. It had once belonged to one of the castle's caretakers, an enormous man who had fled when the curse struck. The fabric hung limply on Justin in some places, while in others his transfigured limbs bulged against it.

Justin cleared his throat, realizing that neither young woman was going to break the stunned silence.

"Good morning," he said, his eyes on Felicity. "I wondered if you'd like to go riding with me."

Felicity blinked. "Riding? With you? On a horse?"

Justin's lips twitched slightly. "Well, separate horses, preferably," he said gravely. "There are only a couple of horses in the stable who can carry me these days, and only for short periods. I think a second rider would be too much."

"Oh, no, I know. I mean, I wasn't saying that..." Felicity trailed off into incoherence, and the maid took over.

"Of course she'd like to, Your Highness," she said briskly. "Give us ten minutes, and she'll be with you."

With that, she shut the door unceremoniously in Justin's face. For a moment he stood there, stunned at being so casually dismissed by a teenage servant girl, but he shook the thought off. He could hear their cheerful bickering on the other side of the door, and he felt it would be more polite to move further down the hallway.

It was more than ten minutes until Felicity reappeared, although Justin couldn't imagine what she'd been doing. The only difference he could see was that she was now wearing riding gloves, and carrying a whip similar to his.

"It was kind of you to ask me to ride with you," said Felicity, as they began to walk toward the entranceway. "But..." she spoke in a rush, "I think I should tell you that I don't know how to ride very well."

Justin looked at her in surprise. "How did you get from your village to the castle?"

"I rode," Felicity assured him. She flashed him a grin. "Just not very well."

He shook his head, amused, but Felicity was still explaining herself.

"I can stay on pretty reliably so long as the horse is only walking."

"Pretty reliably?" Justin repeated, alarmed. "Maybe this is a bad idea."

"I'd love to learn," said Felicity. Looking down into her hopeful eyes, Justin knew he stood no chance.

"I'll teach you, if you like," he said gruffly. "Or at least, I can try."

Felicity's smile grew. "That would be wonderful."

There had been no fresh snowfall since the one that had driven them into the library, and the path to the stables had long since been cleared. Justin breathed in the fresh cold air, trying to clear his thoughts for what he needed to say. He waited until a groom had saddled two horses for them, and it was time to mount up.

"Here, let me help you," he said. Without waiting for a response, he lifted Felicity by the waist, depositing her on the back of the sedate mare he had selected for her.

She gave a little gasp which made him think he should have

given her more warning, but he didn't stop to ask. With her on a horse, he was no longer towering over her, and that made it easier for some reason.

"I'm sorry for what I said in the library," he said quickly, his eyes on the strap he was adjusting on her saddle.

There was a moment of silence, and he dared a look up at her. Her eyes were pinned on him, their expression startled.

"You don't need to—"

"I want to," he cut her off. "I should have explained myself better. I didn't mean that I wouldn't have wished to be your friend. The truth is, I didn't really have friends, even at that age. My father discouraged it, and if I got too close to anyone, he had his methods for ending the connection." He cleared his throat. "I laughed because it was, well, laughable to imagine that I would have been allowed to befriend you back then."

"I see." Felicity's voice was soft, and her expression was impossible to read. "Thank you for explaining that. And..." Her face grew as soft as her words. "And I'm sorry your childhood was like that."

Justin shrugged, feeling strangely carefree now his apology was out. He sprang onto his horse with a suddenness that made the poor animal stagger.

"Come on," he said, his voice almost sounding cheerful in his ears. "Let's start by seeing how you walk."

The morning passed pleasantly, Felicity proving to be a quick learner. Justin was pleased to see that after his apology, she had become more cheerful, and it took no persuasion for her to agree to another lesson the following morning. But she still seemed cautious in a way she hadn't before, and he couldn't help but wonder if he'd wounded her more deeply with his careless words than he'd realized.

"If the curse was broken, and you were free to go anywhere, where would you go?"

Justin raised his eyes at the cheerful question. It was their second morning of lessons, and they were riding along the track that had been cleared just inside the perimeter of the estate's wall. Felicity was traveling at a passable attempt at a trot, and Justin had been watching her form with a critical eye.

"To Allenton, of course. I have a kingdom's worth of mess to untangle once I'm free."

Felicity pouted. "Boring and responsible. I'm not asking what you *should* do. I'm asking where you would go if you could travel anywhere."

Justin shook his head, amused. "I would go to Allenton," he insisted. "I've been to every kingdom in Solstice, and however arrogant it sounds, the truth is I like mine best."

"Well, that's nice, I suppose," Felicity conceded.

"Where would you go?" Justin asked curiously.

Felicity thought about it for a moment. "Well, unlike you, I've never really been anywhere. As much as I like your kingdom, Your Majesty," she put a teasing emphasis on the words, "I'd still like to visit them all. But if I had to choose just one place, I'd want to see the dragon colony." She fell silent, appearing to be lost in recollection. A rueful smile spread across her face.

But Justin stiffened, feeling no inclination to smile. "The dragon colony? Why would you want to go there?"

Felicity looked surprised at his tone. "It would be fascinating, don't you think? I've only ever seen a dragon up close once, and I'd love to know more about them. Wouldn't you?"

Justin shrugged one hunched shoulder. "Not really." Felicity raised an eyebrow, but Justin made no apologies for his sudden coldness. "I have my reasons for not being overly fond of magic, remember?"

Felicity frowned. "But you were cursed by a human enchantress, not a dragon."

"But magic comes from dragons," Justin said. "They say that before dragons came to Solstice, there were no enchanters or enchantresses."

"But that was centuries ago," said Felicity dismissively. "Besides, the dragons can't help shedding their magic, any more than they can help the way some humans imbibe it and pass it on down the generations." Her frown deepened. "Even those humans can't help that."

Justin just shrugged again. "I still disapprove. I'm beginning to wonder if Bansford has the right approach."

"Surely you wouldn't outlaw magic!" Felicity protested. "I can understand you being angry at the enchantress who cursed you, but are you truly against magic altogether?"

"I don't think it's right, or safe, for some people to have an innate power that others don't," said Justin seriously. "Doesn't it bother you, knowing there are humans out there with a power you can never match?"

Felicity gave an incredulous laugh. "Do you hear what you're saying, Justin? *You* have a power I can never match. Being born with magic isn't so different from having royal blood."

Justin made a dismissive noise. "Royal blood doesn't give you that level of power."

Felicity shook her head. "You only say that because you've never experienced what it's like for the rest of the kingdom, who don't have it. Royals *do* have a power no one else does, whether you want to admit it or not. Does that mean a crown is an evil thing?" She pierced him with an uncomfortably challenging look. "Your father abused his royal status, and did evil things with his power. Does that mean the status of royalty should cease to exist? Surely magic is the same: not good or bad in itself, but as good or bad as the way it's used."

Justin fell silent, thinking over her words. He had never thought about it in quite those terms, but he could see her point.

He didn't say as much, but Felicity seemed to take his silence for what it was, a willingness to take her words seriously. She looked pleased, and Justin felt his own spirits lift. It was a little disconcerting to realize how much he valued her approval.

They rode in silence for a few minutes, following the line of the wall. Felicity seemed sobered by the talk of power, and Justin found himself missing her cheerful chatter. He cast a glance at her face, and saw that she looked troubled.

"What's wrong?" he asked quietly.

Felicity didn't immediately answer, and when she did, she didn't look at him. "Nothing's wrong. Your responsible answer just got me thinking."

Justin frowned, trying to remember what he'd said. "You mean about going to Allenton when I'm free?"

Felicity nodded. "Seeing the dragons wasn't a serious answer, of course. If I was..." her eyes flicked to him then quickly away, "free to go anywhere, of course I would return home. To check on my father and brother."

A sick surge of discomfort shot through Justin at her words. Her company had become so important to him, it was easy to forget she was a prisoner rather than a guest. He was prevented from leaving by the magic of the curse. She was only kept there by his selfish refusal to release her. But his thoughts also flashed to the villager, Kurt. He felt a flicker of resentment at the idea of sending her back to the family who had failed to protect her from the wolf, even within her own home.

"To check on them?" he repeated gruffly, eager to shift the topic from Felicity's enforced presence in his castle. "Aren't they both grown men?"

Felicity sighed. "Of course they are. But...well, I'm the one who usually takes care of things. Plus what Kurt said worried me."

"I would think so," Justin growled, but Felicity shook her

head. "Not all the rude things. I mean his comment about my father and brother leaving me and not looking back."

Justin raised an eyebrow. "That wasn't rude?"

Felicity gave a half-hearted smile. "It was, of course, but that's not why I'm concerned." She met his eyes. "Do you think they would have actually left? They had nowhere else to go, and now that winter has set in..."

Justin was silent, unsure what to say, and a flush rose to Felicity's cheeks. She fidgeted with the reins, her eyes on her hands.

"I know you don't have a very high opinion of my father, and no reason to care what becomes of him or Ambrose, but—"

"Felicity." Justin was riding close to her, and without thinking it through, he reached over and placed one enormous hand on top of her gloved ones. "If they're important to you, that's reason enough for me to care."

Felicity looked up at him, her eyes wide with something he couldn't name, but he knew wasn't fear.

But she had no chance to respond. Justin had chosen Felicity a placid mare, wanting an easy ride for a beginner. What he hadn't considered, though, was that the gentler horse was kept on the other side of the stables from his spirited charger, and so wasn't used to his beastly self. The horse had been quiet enough with Justin's horse alongside it, but when Justin actually reached across the space, it had flattened its ears in alarm. Justin had been too distracted by his conversation with Felicity to notice the mare's unease, and so was taken completely by surprise when the horse bolted.

Felicity's gasp was lost in an instant as the horse took off down the path. Justin gave a shout and spurred his horse after hers. The mare hadn't completely lost her head—she was cantering rather than galloping wildly, but even that was more than her inexperienced rider was ready for. Alarm swept over

Justin at the way Felicity was lurching in the saddle. He had almost caught up to her when her horse plunged into a narrow pathway between two hedges. The creature reared in alarm at finding itself in a tight space, and Felicity was clearly struggling to cling on.

Justin's horse—always edgy under him now, in a way it had never been when he had the form of a man—refused to enter the narrow walkway. Justin slid from the saddle with a curse, loping into the gap and trying to avoid the other horse's flailing front legs. Felicity was clinging onto the reins with impressive success, but at Justin's approach, the horse gave one last wild plunge and threw her off at last.

Justin darted forward with his arms outstretched, and she fell straight into them. He pulled her against him, turning his back on the still-panicking horse and curving his form protectively around her. The horse pushed its way past the hedge and took off in the general direction of the stables. Justin dismissed it from his mind entirely, trusting in his grooms to locate and restrain it. His whole focus was on the girl in his arms, who was clinging to him as tenaciously as she'd been gripping the reins.

"That was terrifying," she said. Her face was still pressed into his enormous furry chest, and her words came out muffled. "I've changed my mind about wanting to learn how to ride a horse."

Justin gave a deep chuckle that reverberated around his chest, and his tension drained away at the realization that she was unharmed. But when she made no move to get out of his arms, his muscles tightened again with a different kind of tension. He'd never been so aware of her slender form, and he wished desperately that he could read her thoughts. Was she still frightened from her fall, or did she actually want to be near him?

"You're so soft," she said, her voice still muffled but her tone bright. "It's a very comfortable way to break a fall."

Justin gave an involuntary choke of laughter, and loosened his hold at last. He set her gently on her feet, but she didn't step back. She raised her head slowly, her expression almost shy.

"Thank you for catching me," she said softly. "That's twice now."

Justin didn't respond, still a little dazed by her nearness. She was so close they were almost touching. His eyes roamed over her face, taking in the flush that still stained her cheeks, and the way her lips sat slightly apart.

"You're really not afraid of me, are you?" The thought slipped out as words before he realized he'd decided to speak.

A look of surprise flitted across Felicity's face. "Of course not." She hesitated for a moment, then laid a hand on his arm, as if to prove her words. "I trust you. I don't believe you'd ever hurt me."

Justin's heart seemed to have swollen to twice its normal size, causing it to beat uncomfortably against his ribs. He couldn't pull his gaze from her face, and heat seemed to bloom from the place where her hand touched his arm. For a brief moment, he allowed himself to imagine what he would do if he wasn't cursed. He'd reach toward her with a normal, human hand. He'd lay it on her cheek, feel the warmth of her blush against his skin. Maybe he'd tangle his fingers through her hair. He'd lean in, and—

He ripped his eyes from her lips, bitterness coursing through him. He wasn't going to do any of those things, because he *was* cursed. He couldn't thread his fingers through her hair—his claws would shred her skin to ribbons. He certainly couldn't think about kissing her—his own lips were no longer even human.

Besides, said an uncomfortably honest voice in his head, *you wouldn't do those things even if you weren't cursed. You still wouldn't*

*let her see what you're feeling, because if you let her in that far, you'd
be too vulnerable.*

His father's cold face rose up in front of Justin's sight, and all
at once, some dam within him broke, releasing a torrent of
emotion. His bitterness was driven away by an intense longing to
be human. Not just in form but at heart. To have the kind of
warmth that radiated from Felicity. To show his true self to the
people around him without the constant fear that letting them
in would give them power he couldn't afford for them to have.

"I trust you as well," he said, and the truth of his words
crashed over him with liberating and terrifying force. He
thought of how much he valued her opinion, and how deeply he
cared what she was feeling. He thought of his unselfish need for
her to be safe, and his thoroughly selfish desire to keep her
near him.

He no longer had the option of deciding not to let her in too
far. It was too late for that. She was already past his defenses.
She already had his trust, and he could see with blinding clarity
how right his father had been. In giving her his trust, he had
given her enormous power over him. She could destroy him if
she chose, and he would be powerless to stop it.

The thought terrified him, but he refused to dwell on it,
because his father had been wrong about everything else.
Felicity wouldn't abuse his trust. And surely the risk was worth
it, to feel what he was feeling now, with Felicity's hand still on
his arm, and her eyes still locked with his as his world silently
overturned.

"There's a way," he said abruptly.

Felicity dropped her hand, her forehead creasing in confusion at the change in tone. Justin's heart twisted, his muscles
aching to pull her back, to hold on to the moment he had
broken. But he knew that it was well past time for him to stop
being selfish.

"A way to do what?" Felicity asked cautiously.

"To find out where your father and brother are."

CHAPTER TWENTY-ONE

Felicity

"In there?"

Felicity stood in the doorway, blinking stupidly into Justin's suite. Her mind was still trying to catch up with what exactly had happened out by the hedge. Something had changed in Justin, something significant. But she still didn't really know what he was trying to say.

Justin gave an amused smile. "I won't tell Stewart if you don't."

Felicity chuckled at that, coming into the receiving room at last. "Mrs. Winters is the one you need to worry about, if you ask me."

"Wait here," Justin said, as he disappeared into his bedchamber. Felicity looked curiously around the room. She hadn't paid much attention to the furnishings on her one previous visit, but she saw that it was decorated in a rich mahogany. A book sat at an angle on a small table by the window, an armchair alongside it. She smiled, remembering their morning in the library. She was guessing it wasn't a book about waterfowl.

Justin reappeared suddenly, something glittering in his

hand. Felicity stepped forward curiously, and Justin held the object out.

"A mirror?" she said, doubtfully.

"It's enchanted," Justin explained. "That cursed enchantress gave it to me."

Felicity couldn't help shooting him a glance of amusement. "I think she was the curser, actually, not the cursed."

Justin shot her a long-suffering look, but made no attempt to dampen her humor.

"It allows me to see what's happening elsewhere," he said simply, handing it to Felicity. "I use it mainly to see what my uncle's doing in Allenton."

"Mainly?" Felicity raised an eyebrow, and he shrugged. "Do the people you're watching know you can see them?"

"No," said Justin shortly, with a slight edge of discomfort which instantly raised Felicity's suspicions. "It's a one-way image. Obviously I can't communicate back and forth, or I wouldn't have been isolated here all this time."

Felicity transferred her gaze from the mirror to Justin, waiting until he reluctantly met her eyes.

"Have you ever used it on me?" For a long moment there was silence, and she narrowed her eyes. "Justin?"

He sighed. "Yes. Four times. Once when you first arrived, and you were having tea with Mrs. Winters. Once when my head guard was interrogating you. Once when you left the estate, to check if you were heading for the lake." He paused, and Felicity was amazed to see him fidget. "And once when you were baking in the kitchens."

She frowned, wondering which of her many baking sessions he had witnessed, and why he'd been reluctant to mention it.

"Well, that's unnerving," she said frankly. "I suppose I can't complain when it saved my life one of those times. But I'm glad it wasn't more. I was having this horrifying image of being watched constantly."

"Of course not," said Justin quickly. "I don't normally use it on anyone in the castle. It is useful to be able to follow some of what's happening in the kingdom, though."

Felicity nodded, deciding to let it go and focus on the matter at hand. "I can understand that." She returned her attention to the mirror itself, excitement rising. "So you think it can show us what my father and brother have been doing?"

"It can show what they're doing now," Justin corrected. "It doesn't show the past, only what's happening this moment."

"That's better than nothing," said Felicity eagerly. "How does it work?"

"Like this." Justin lifted the mirror, but angled it so Felicity could still see. "Show me Felicity's father and brother."

Felicity watched in amazement as the surface of the mirror shifted, the reflection of Justin's receiving room disappearing. She leaned in, her heart racing at the idea of seeing her family. But no familiar faces appeared. The mirror just went blank, losing its reflective quality for a moment, then returning to its normal state. For a moment she blinked at her own disappointed face, then panic started to rise.

"Why didn't it work? What does that mean? Surely it doesn't mean that they're..."

She couldn't quite say the word, but Justin clearly understood.

"It doesn't mean they're dead," he said reassuringly. "If they were, it would show their faces as they last were, but the whole surface would be shrouded in this thick gray fog, not just blank like that."

Felicity raised an eyebrow, and Justin looked away quickly, staring unseeingly at the mirror for a moment. "I tried asking it to show me my mother once."

Felicity nodded, her heart aching for him. She knew what it was to grow up without a mother. "So what does it mean?" she asked.

He frowned. "The enchantress didn't explain the mirror's limitations, but from what I can discover, it's connected to me, and my position as the kingdom's ruler. So it only shows things happening within Albury. The only other times I've seen this result are when I've tried to look at something or someone outside the kingdom."

Felicity stared at him. "But surely they haven't left Albury. Why would they do that? And where would they go?"

Justin shrugged, watching her silently. Of course he wouldn't have those answers. Felicity's forehead creased as she tried to solve the puzzle. She suddenly realized she was playing with her father's trinket, still on its chain around her neck, and she dropped her hand.

"You want to go, don't you?"

Justin's quiet question startled Felicity so much that for a moment she could just stare at him. His face was hard to read, but she could see the struggle of some kind of strong emotion in his eyes.

"You want to go looking for them."

"I..." Felicity hesitated. Why was it so difficult to force herself to say the words? "Of course I do," she finally managed. "I want to be sure they're all right. But I won't break my word."

"You don't have to," said Justin evenly. "I release you."

Felicity froze, overwhelmed by a strange mixture of excitement and disappointment.

"I'm...I'm free?"

"That's right," said Justin calmly. "I should never have made you stay in the first place. You were right—your father's actions didn't deserve imprisonment or servitude. I was wrong." His voice was still calm, but the turmoil in his eyes was stronger than ever.

"I don't know what to say," Felicity whispered.

"And I'm sorry that I insulted your word," Justin said, as if she hadn't spoken. "You've put me to shame by how faithfully you've kept your promise. You've proved that you're a person of worth."

His voice actually got a little choked on the last word, and Felicity was more speechless than ever. Her feet seemed rooted to the spot, and her mind was spinning. She couldn't comprehend her sudden release.

Not one hour before, she'd said that if she was free to go anywhere, she'd go home. Well, here was her chance. But if she was honest with herself, the idea of returning to the cottage on the outskirts of her village held absolutely no appeal. And the suppressed emotion in Justin's eyes seemed to steal the breath from her throat.

"I can send you with a horse, and supplies," Justin continued, his deep voice level once again. "I wish I could do more, but since none of us can leave..." He cleared his throat. "Even with a horse, if you want to reach your village before dark, you'd better leave at once."

Felicity's mind whirled with confusion. Was she being released, or kicked out?

"Thank you," she said, her lips dry.

Justin gave a curt nod. Watching him, Felicity had no doubt his impassive expression was a mask for whatever was happening inside him. She pulled herself together. Something was going on with him, but it wasn't something she could solve right now.

"I will go," she said, more decisively. "I have to find out what's become of them. But I'll come back."

Justin's smile was unconvincing, and she stepped forward,

reaching up to place a hand against his fur-covered cheek. He stilled instantly.

"I will," she said firmly. "I promise. I'll come back, and I'll help you break the curse."

Slowly, Justin raised his hand and placed it over hers, so gently she didn't even feel the claws.

"I don't think even you can break this curse, Felicity," he said. She could feel her heart crack at the sadness in his eyes.

"Justin—" she started, but he was clearly done with sentiment.

He cut across her with a practical comment, striding to a bell pull on the wall, and setting the castle's remaining servants in a fluster.

Within an unbelievably short time, Felicity found herself at the gate, dressed in the warmest of her borrowed gowns, clutching the reins of a fresh horse, and confronting a host of crestfallen servants.

"Don't look at me like that," Felicity said, trying to speak cheerfully. "I'm not leaving forever."

"Never mind us," said Mrs. Winters briskly. "You have a life to live out there."

"But what about the curse?"

It was Viola who spoke, and Felicity's heart was wrung to see actual tears standing in the girl's eyes.

She stepped forward and took the other girl's hands. "I'll come back and help you break the curse, Viola, I promise."

"Our problems aren't yours to solve, my dear," said Mrs. Winters, shaking her head. "You find your family and make sure they're all right."

"You've become family as well," Felicity declared, her hands still gripping Viola's, and tears in her own eyes now.

"One of us should really be going with you," said Phillip. He stepped up beside Viola, anxiety on his face. "I don't like the thought of you out there all alone."

"That's very kind," Felicity told the guard. "But I'll be all right."

There was a rustling from the back of the assembled group, and a moment later Justin's tall form appeared in their midst. Viola dropped Felicity's hands and stepped away hastily. The maid wiped her eyes on a sleeve, and in the corner of her vision Felicity saw Phillip reach a tentative hand out in comfort. They were all taking her departure much harder than she'd expected.

But Justin had reached her now, and even the servants' distress couldn't hold her attention. She looked up at him, still not sure where they stood after the various events of the day. They were standing not far from the place where her horse had thrown her, and he'd caught her in his arms. He'd certainly seemed to want her close in that moment. But mere minutes later, he was all but expelling her from the castle.

"I hope you find your answers," he said, his voice a low rumble.

Felicity just nodded, unable to find words. To her surprise, he stepped forward, standing so close she had to lean back to look up at his face.

"I'll miss you." The words were too soft for the servants to hear, so soft that Felicity could almost believe she imagined them.

"I won't be gone for long," she whispered.

"You're under no obligation to return, Felicity," he said.

"I wasn't talking about obligation," she responded stubbornly.

Justin's face was inscrutable, and Felicity's thoughts chased one another in a hopeless jumble. Was it that he didn't believe her that she'd return? Or was it that he didn't want her to return? She didn't know what to make of his talk of obligation. It suddenly struck her that now she wasn't required to be there, it would be unreasonable to expect to be put up in the luxury of the castle without any formal role. *Could* she even return? Emotion clogged her throat as she realized that even if she did come back, things would never be the same as they had been these past months.

She swallowed, pulling herself together. If Justin didn't want her to come back, there wasn't much she could do about that. But if he didn't believe her, there at least she could reassure him.

"I'll just have to leave something with you," she said cheerfully. "So you know I'll come back for it." She crinkled her nose. "Unfortunately, everything I have is borrowed from your runaway guests..."

She cast her mind around, and it suddenly hit her. "I know!" She struggled with the front of her high-necked woolen dress and pulled out the chain. "Here." She tugged it over her head and removed the pendant. "The chain isn't mine, but this is. My father left it in the dungeon, and I've kept it on me the whole time I've been here."

Justin stared at it for a long moment, saying nothing. Felicity jiggled it impatiently, and he reached out a hand, allowing Felicity to place the trinket into it. A spark seemed to jump between them at the touch, and she withdrew her hand quickly. Justin's fingers closed mechanically over the item, and he stared at his fist.

"I'll come back for it," Felicity promised. Their eyes met, the piercing blue of his holding her in thrall. She could see the warmth that she hadn't even realized she'd come to expect in their depths. But she could also see it was at war with something else, something more intense.

"Goodbye, Felicity," he said. He turned on his heel and strode for the castle, the pendant clutched in his hand.

FELICITY RAISED HER HEAD, squinting in front of her. The day, although cold, had at least been clear. But now the wind was picking up, and she was eager to be out of the weather. She didn't much relish the prospect of riding in the dark, and the sun had begun to set.

She glimpsed a pointed roof ahead, and her spirits lifted. The village! She was almost there. She pushed the tired horse forward, feeling a surge of gratitude that her cottage was on the outskirts of the little town. Within minutes, she was swinging down from the saddle outside her own home.

Pushing open the door of the little cottage was the most surreal experience of her life. The place looked the same, but everything about her life had changed. She felt a surge of foreboding when the door opened without resistance. The smokeless chimney had already told her that no one was home, but if Father and Ambrose were just in the village, they would have locked the door.

A chill passed over her as she stepped into the silent, empty cottage, and not just because of the unlit hearth. It was obvious that the place had been empty for some time. The roof was leaking in one spot, and there was a thin layer of dust on every surface. The main room looked a little disordered, but not as though there had been any kind of struggle.

She bit her lip anxiously as she checked the other rooms, with the same result. Where had they gone? Why would they flee their home?

She made her way back to her horse with heavy steps. She had no means for stabling a horse, so she had little choice but to seek assistance from the closest neighbor with a barn. She remounted, wincing as her sore behind made contact with the saddle again. Within twenty minutes, she was plodding up the drive to a small farm. Her heart was heavy, but she took some small comfort from the smoke curling from the chimney. She tried to keep her thoughts positive as she knocked at the door. At least she would have more success here.

"Good evening, Martha," she said, summoning a faint smile for the stout woman who opened the door.

"Felicity!" Martha looked as astonished as if Felicity had been an apparition. "We thought you was dead!"

"Dead?" Felicity repeated, startled.

Martha nodded. "Are you sure you're not?"

Despite how trying the day had been, Felicity couldn't help feeling a trickle of amusement. "I'm fairly sure," she said gravely, holding out her hand. "Do you want to check?"

Martha hesitated, then gave Felicity's arm a tentative pat.

"Well, that's a relief," she said, letting out a breath.

"My horse is alive, too," Felicity said hopefully. "Do you think...?"

"Of course." Martha nodded, then hollered over her shoulder. "Oi! Take Felicity's horse to the stables, and quickish! It's biting out there!"

"What?" Martha's son ambled into sight, stopping dead when he saw their guest. "Felicity!"

Felicity held in a sigh, trying to ignore the way his eyes passed up and down her form, growing wider as he took in her costly dress.

"So Kurt was full of manure," he breathed, his eyes lighting with excitement. "I'm glad you're back, Felicity! Where will you live now your father and Ambrose are gone? You could stay with us!"

"That's enough, now," said Martha sternly, throwing her son a quelling glance. "See to the horse."

He shuffled out the door, looking like a sulky child, and Felicity turned to Martha. "So they are gone. Where are they?"

Martha waved her into a chair, and fetched her a bowl of hot soup. "Aye, they're gone all right. As to where, I couldn't tell you. Your father just said they had to get out of Albury, and quick-like. They went south. My guess is they were going to Fernedell."

Felicity frowned. "He didn't say why?"

Martha snorted, taking a seat across the scrubbed wooden table. "Not in any ways we could understand, he didn't."

Felicity's frown deepened. "Why did you think I was dead?"

Martha gave her a shrewd look, her eyes also assessing Felicity's gown. "What else were we to think? Your father came back with a tale about a haunted castle and a monster who could talk like a man. He said it was the prince's curse, and it had taken you away from him. He said if the curse hadn't killed you, the prince had for sure." She was silent for a moment, watching Felicity's face. "Real cut up he was about it, too. I've never seen a man so stricken. Crying like a child, he was."

Felicity felt a tug of concern for her father, but another feeling pushed back against it. "Not cut up enough to do anything about it," she said quietly.

Martha raised her eyebrows. "I never thought to hear you stick up for yourself like that, Felicity. Not but what you're right, of course." She narrowed her eyes. "Then we started hearing rumors about this fine lady who lures royals and nobles into her haunted castle and enchants them while they sleep."

Felicity snorted at this dramatic version of her role at the castle, and Martha gave a grim smile.

"Well, that's what I thought, too. But some of the village boys," she jerked her head toward the door where her son had gone, "got it in their heads this fine lady might be you. That fool Kurt went looking."

Felicity felt a surge of warmth for the older woman. "And what tale did *he* come back with?" she asked dryly.

"He said he'd found the castle, but that he'd been too late to save you from being tragically killed by the monster." She gave Felicity a look. "He reassured us that we have nothing to fear, because he heroically avenged you by slaying the monster."

Felicity rolled her eyes. "Of course he did. Well, he did come to the castle. The rest is total nonsense, of course."

Martha raised her eyebrows. "You really were at a castle?"

"Never mind that," said Felicity quickly. "How long ago did Father leave? You said Ambrose went with him?"

"It's been weeks." Both women turned to the doorway, where Martha's son had reappeared. "And Ambrose didn't want to go. But your father didn't give him a choice. Said the prince would be coming after them next."

Felicity frowned. Why would her father think that? She couldn't think of anything Justin had said in the dungeon that would suggest he knew or cared where Felicity's father lived, or would seek further retribution against him.

Her frown deepened as she remembered her father's incoherent panic when he'd been dragged from the dungeon, and all the bitter things he'd ever said about the royals. She'd always assumed it was just a general dislike, but had he actually been afraid of them? When Martha said her father was devastated by her death, she'd begun to think he must have left Albury in an attempt to flee his grief, like he'd done after losing his wife. But perhaps there was something more behind it.

"So what are you going to do now?" Martha's son asked. His voice turned smug. "Kurt will be livid when he hears you've come back, and that you came here instead of to him."

"It's none of Kurt's business where I go," said Felicity sharply. "I don't answer to him."

"You don't answer to me either," said Martha, unperturbed, "but I'm still curious what you plan to do. Seems to me you can't really go chasing your father into Fernedell, at least not in the middle of winter."

"No, that would be foolish, wouldn't it?" Felicity sighed. "To tell you the truth," she gazed unseeingly out the window, at the darkness beyond, "I haven't the faintest clue what to do."

CHAPTER TWENTY-TWO

Justin

Justin sank back into his armchair, abandoning all pretense of reading the book in his lap. He turned Felicity's pendant over in his hand, glad of the privacy of his library nook. It was a strange object for a woman to wear around her neck, but he didn't care about that. All he cared about was that it was hers, and she'd left it with him.

I'll come back for it.

But hard on the heels of the ghostly voice came another, that of his head guard in a conversation months ago, speculating on what would happen if Felicity were to leave.

She might never come back to us. I don't think she'd be able to.

A pang of pure anguish went through Justin at the thought that he might never see Felicity again. His life had been cold and hard before she'd arrived. Felicity had somehow managed to melt that ice, and now he felt exposed, vulnerable to the pain of her loss.

She only left because I sent her away.

Justin shook off the thought. He refused to regret what had probably been the only genuinely unselfish act of his life. Even when he rescued her from the frozen lake, he'd been driven by his own guilt, his own fear of suffering the regret he'd feel if he let her die. But setting Felicity free, knowing there was nothing now binding her to him, had been all about her. He had nothing to gain from it, and everything to lose. But she had committed no crime—she shouldn't be a prisoner.

"Prince Justin."

Justin looked up, closing his fist over the pendant guiltily. He hadn't even heard Stewart approach. The steward held out a steaming mug of cocoa, and Justin almost groaned aloud. Did his servants really think he needed reminding of Felicity? As if he was going to forget what he'd lost.

He didn't complain, however, just took the mug. He expected Stewart to disappear, but the middle aged servant lingered, something clearly on his mind. Justin was pretty sure he knew what. He looked up and met the steward's eye, releasing his breath in a sigh of resignation.

"Why release her so suddenly, Your Highness?" Stewart asked, needing no more opening. "After all this time, why so abrupt?"

Justin stared into his cocoa. "So I didn't have time to change my mind," he said simply.

"You didn't believe she might be able to break the curse?" Stewart asked delicately.

"No."

The servant's disbelief radiated from him. "But, Your Highness..." He was obviously struggling for the best way to put it. "We all thought that she seemed to be warming to you. That she might come to...to care for you."

"She does care for me," said Justin quietly. "Little as I deserve it." He didn't speak out of arrogance. He could still remember Felicity's face, so open and genuine, as she said the words that had rocked him.

I trust you.

If there was any greater sign of caring for someone, Justin didn't know it. He had no doubt that Felicity saw beneath his beastly form, and valued him. More, perhaps, than anyone ever had when he was attractive to look at.

"Then why send her away?" Stewart demanded. "When you were so close?"

Justin looked up at last. "Don't you understand, Stewart?" he said wearily. "She cares about me, the real me, because she has the worth, the character to see beyond this." He waved a hand over his visage. "But that's not what the curse requires. Someone has to look at me and like what they *see*. Even Felicity, with a heart of gold, valuing me much higher than I deserve, can't like this."

He shook his head sadly. "I'm sorry, Stewart. I know I've failed you, and your family. The curse is unbreakable. I can never be what I was. How can I condemn her to this prison if this is all I could ever offer her?"

Stewart looked troubled. "But it must be possible. The enchantress must have meant for you to succeed, or why enchant the rose garden to continue blooming all this time?"

Justin turned his face away. "A cruel trick, I suppose. Felicity will find her father and her brother, and they'll prevent her from ever returning, if they have any integrity. We might be trapped here, but she can be free." He gave a weak smile. "We must just be grateful the estate is self sufficient. I know it's lonely here, and I wouldn't blame you if you regret your decision to stay. But we'll survive."

"I don't regret it, Prince Justin," said Stewart softly. "None of us do. If I may speak freely, you are a better man than your father ever was. And I still believe you will be a better king."

Justin was unable to speak around the lump in his throat, so he just nodded, hoping it conveyed his gratitude.

"Your Highness!"

Both men looked up quickly. Justin could tell from the way Stewart stiffened that he had also detected the note of urgency in the serving man's voice. The man appeared around a bookcase, out of breath, as if he'd run from the entranceway.

"What is it?"

"Your Highness, someone's here!"

Justin found himself on his feet, hope rising against his better judgment. Felicity had only left yesterday. She couldn't possibly be back already.

"Who?"

"It's that advisor from Allenton," the serving man puffed. "He's back."

"Lord Brooker?" Justin frowned. He had been distracted, and hadn't followed the man's progress in the mirror. Had he gone to the capital and returned? "He's wasted a trip," he said listlessly. "Without Felicity, we can't communicate with him."

The serving man was shaking his head frantically. "No, Your Highness, you don't understand. He can see us! He's speaking with Mrs. Winters now!"

Justin froze. Was he wrong? Was the curse broken? Had Felicity's warmth toward him been enough? Had his selflessness in sending her away satisfied the curse's other requirement?

One glance down at his still beastly form was enough to correct that thought. The curse was most definitely still in place. But something significant had changed, and excitement coursed through him, bringing him to life for the first time since he'd said goodbye to Felicity.

"I'll speak with him at once," he said, putting down his cocoa and slipping Felicity's gift into his pocket. "Show me the way."

He followed the servant through the castle, Stewart close behind. His blood was pounding in his ears. Was the curse weakening? Perhaps he would be able to leave the estate without pain, even if he remained in this form. He could go after Felicity, brave the reaction of his subjects to his appearance. He shook off the foolish idea. What was he thinking? If he was free to leave, he had to go to Allenton immediately, to set right his uncle's mistakes, put Albury back on track.

But still, his thoughts strayed to Felicity. What would she think of this new development?

The servant led him to a parlor regularly used by the senior servants. Justin had time only to take in Mrs. Winters' admirably calm countenance and the visitor's look of astonishment before a high-pitched, nasal scream caused everyone in the room to jump.

Everyone except Lord Brooker, of course, whose mouth remained open in a silent scream of terror even once the sound ran out.

Justin stood in irritated impatience, waiting for the advisor to pull himself together.

"That's quite enough of that, sir," said Mrs. Winters, as though scolding one of the kitchen maids. "I did warn you that the changes to His Highness's appearance might be a bit of a shock."

"A bit of a shock?" Lord Brooker echoed faintly. "I thought you meant he would have some scars. He's an animal!"

"This *animal* can understand speech, My Lord," Justin cut in dryly, "so I suggest you watch your words."

Lord Brooker's mouth fell open again in astonishment. "I—I beg your pardon, Your Highness." He executed a shaky bow. "I didn't realize..." He fell silent, his gaze passing over Justin's form. Justin saw the moment when his eyes widened in renewed horror.

"Yes, I have a tail," Justin said in a long-suffering tone. "If you must laugh, get it all out now."

"Laugh?" The advisor's eyes were bulging. "I can't imagine what would be funny about this situation, Your Highness."

Justin eyed him unfavorably. "No, I daresay you can't. You should try for a little more imagination."

Lord Brooker blinked at him in abject astonishment. "Y-yes, Your Highness."

"Now, I'd very much like to know why you can see us this time, when you couldn't last time," said Justin.

Lord Brooker shook his head helplessly. "That I can't explain, Your Highness. Your housekeeper has just been telling me the details..." He shook his head again. "It's the most astonishing tale I've ever heard. I wouldn't believe it if I wasn't seeing it with my own eyes." Those same eyes narrowed. "I was delayed on my journey home after my last visit, and it gave me time to clear my head. I realized it had been foolish of me to leave without making a proper search for you at the castle. I sent a message on to Allenton and came back, looking for you, in the hope of revealing the lies of that scheming wench who had installed herself—"

He broke off, alarmed at the low growl issuing from Justin's throat.

"Watch what you say," Justin snarled, and the advisor's eyes widened.

"Your Highness, don't let her deceive you," he insisted, swallowing nervously. "She has a hold on you with her magic."

Somehow, impossibly, Justin felt his lips twitch humorously. The man was both incredibly wrong, and more right than he could know.

"Felicity is no enchantress," he said, trying to speak calmly. "And she is no longer here, in any event." He kept his face impassive, ignoring the stab of pain that went through him at the words.

The man watched him carefully, seeming to measure his words. "I'm glad to hear that she's no longer here, Your Highness. It may be true that she isn't an enchantress. She may have used an artifact that she acquired from such a person. But that she is your enemy, there can be no doubt."

"Nonsense," said Justin dismissively. "She is the last person I would count an enemy." He suddenly remembered Lord Brooker's previous behavior, and his eyes narrowed dangerously. "You have some explaining to do for the way you spoke to her, My Lord. You may not have been able to see me, but I was present. And I don't tolerate death threats against guests under my protection."

The advisor made an angry noise in his throat. "She understood my words, Your Highness, even if you did not. Do you truly not know who she is?"

Justin blinked. "Of course I know who she is. Her name is Felicity, and she comes from a village to the west of here."

Lord Brooker was shaking his head long before Justin finished speaking. "She may live in some village, but she doesn't come from there. As I told her, Your Highness, I never forget a face, and I recognize hers. She comes from the capital."

Justin's frown was deepening by the second. "It's true that she was born in Allenton," he said. "She told me as much herself. But she left as a small child, and hasn't been back. There's no way you could know her face."

The man gave a brittle laugh. "Yes, I realize that the whole family fled. I didn't mean to say that I'd met her, Your Highness. I'd never seen her before in my life. But I still knew her on sight. She bears her mother's face—the resemblance is uncanny. Once I saw it, I knew at once she was your enemy."

For a long moment, Justin was speechless, trying to make sense of the unexpected turn the conversation had taken.

"Her mother?" he repeated slowly. "What does she have to do with anything? She died when Felicity was a small child. Or at least..." he hesitated, his certainty wavering, "that's what she told me."

Lord Brooker nodded wisely. "I'm sure she did. The most convincing lies are always surrounded by truths. I remember her mother's death well. The whole kingdom knew of it, after all."

Justin stared. "The whole kingdom knew of a peasant woman's death?" He glanced at Stewart and Mrs. Winters, but they both looked as lost as he felt.

The advisor made an impatient noise. "She wasn't just a peasant woman. And it wasn't her death that was significant, of course. It was Princess Aurelia's."

"My sister?" Justin's mind swam with confusion, and he leaned on the back of a chair for support. "Are you saying...are you saying that the nursemaid who fell into the ravine while carrying Aurelia was Felicity's mother?"

Lord Brooker nodded vigorously. "Without a doubt. Like I said, Your Highness, I never forget a face." He frowned. "And although I'm not surprised His Majesty spoke of her in such terms, she wasn't exactly a nursemaid. She was one of your mother's closest friends, from Allenton's most influential merchant family. She was in place to be Princess Aurelia's lady-in-waiting."

"I don't understand," Justin said stupidly. "You speak like there's some conspiracy. Why would she want to kill Aurelia?"

"Oh, I'm sure she didn't intend to fall," the advisor said in surprise. "Her negligence cost her own life as well, after all."

"Then...why do you say Felicity is my enemy?" Justin asked. The words tasted bitter in his mouth, and his stomach churned.

Lord Brooker hesitated. "I do not in any sense condone her petty revenge," he said carefully. "But I can acknowledge the girl has some reason to resent the royal family. Perhaps to wish you harm."

Justin frowned, more confused than ever, and the advisor hurried on.

"After the regrettable incident, His Majesty King Justus was..."

"Livid," Justin supplied dully, vividly picturing his father's response.

"Well, yes," Lord Brooker agreed. "His first intention was to have the woman's entire family executed in retribution for her negligence." He shook his head slightly. "As you know, I was his advisor even then. We managed, through unanimous agreement," his voice turned dry, "unprecedented, I assure you, to talk him down from that course of action. After all," the advisor gave Justin an appealing look, "the woman had young children. A son as well as a daughter, I believe."

Justin nodded numbly, his mind overwhelmed with conflicting reactions. The thought of Felicity being executed as a small child in punishment for an accident which had already taken away her mother was horrifying. But the protective instinct which rebelled against the image belonged to the part of his heart that had let Felicity in, and he was no longer sure he wanted to trust that decision.

"King Justus banished them from the capital," Lord Brooker continued. "He decreed that they were never to return. Neither the circumstances of the deaths, nor the punishment were ever publicly announced—he didn't want to draw attention to the fact that the princess had been killed through such a foolish act of carelessness. But he made it very clear to the woman's husband that he was not to show his face in Allenton again. I personally witnessed him telling the man that if he ever caught sight of any member of the family, they would be killed immediately."

The advisor hesitated, taking in Justin's continued paralysis. "So, you see..."

"Felicity has ample reason to wish me harm," Justin finished in a hollow voice.

"That's right, Your Highness," Lord Brooker said, clearly relieved that Justin had understood. "It seems too great a coincidence that she of all people could have just stumbled in here, when no one else could even find the castle."

Justin sat heavily into a chair, causing it to creak under his bulk. He thought of Felicity's repeated mention of how she wished her family had never had to leave the capital, how she wanted to go back there. Had all those comments hidden accusations, contained threats for revenge? Had he missed the constant undertones?

He tried to shake off the thought. Surely not. Felicity wasn't like that. She was genuine, she was kind. She'd never attack him, either subtly or outright.

But he thought of the way she'd baited him when Prince Bentleigh came, of the anger in her eyes when she'd first encountered him. How well did he really know her?

If you give someone your trust, you give them power. They will abuse it every time.

Justin winced at the return of his father's voice in his head. He had been so sure his father had been wrong about this. But there was no justification for Felicity keeping such a thing secret from him. She must have had a hidden agenda. Like Lord Brooker had said, it was too great a coincidence.

He thought of the gentle way he'd touched her hand when she'd placed it against his cheek, of his foolish, humiliating words. *I trust you as well*, he'd told her. *I'll miss you.* He had to give her some credit. She had planned a more crushing revenge than even he could have dreamed up.

He gave a bitter laugh that made everyone in the room look at him in alarm. What a fool he'd been. The moment he'd let down his guard, a viper had struck. He resisted the urge to bury his head in his hands, clinging to whatever shreds of dignity he had left. If only he could just harden his heart again, undo the damage. But it didn't work that way. He'd let Felicity in, and he'd given her power over him. As he'd known it could, her betrayal had struck him in a place so deep he couldn't defend against it. He had no choice but to endure the pain.

"So you think Felicity is behind the curse," Justin said, pulling himself together. Both Mrs. Winters and Stewart made sounds of protest, but he ignored them. "To what end? Just for revenge? Or for some larger purpose?"

Lord Brooker shook his head slowly. "I don't pretend to understand all that's happening here." He gave another apprehensive glance at Justin's tail. "And it's clear that you remain cursed, Your Highness. But I am relieved to see that with the departure of that *woman*," his scathing emphasis on the word made Justin flinch as if physically struck, "the magic that has kept you concealed from the rest of the kingdom has at least lifted."

"Yes," said Justin, his voice sounding dead in his ears. "That is a blessing, at least." He was still running back over all his conversations with Felicity, and he almost growled at the memory of how determinedly she had defended the use of magic. He narrowed his eyes in sudden thought. "Was Aurelia's nursemaid—Felicity's mother, I mean—was she an enchantress?"

Lord Brooker shook his head. Justin frowned, remembering Felicity's father as he cowered in the dungeon. Surely that man had no magic in his blood.

"So it's unlikely that she is," he muttered. Perhaps she'd been using an artifact, like the advisor had said.

He looked up in sudden realization. The pendant she'd given him! She admitted she'd worn it the whole time she was at the castle. And then she'd made some flimsy excuse to leave it behind when she left. His first instinct was to rip it from his pocket and fling it straight through the glass of the parlor's window. But he quelled the impulse, trying to think strategically. What was its purpose? Could he turn it to good account somehow? He would have to consider the matter further.

"Thank you for your assistance," he said abruptly, looking at the advisor. "Mrs. Winters will see to it that a room is prepared for you. We will speak more tomorrow."

Lord Brooker bowed. "Yes, Your Highness."

Justin swept from the room, irritated to find that Stewart was following him.

"Your Highness." The steward hurried to overtake Justin, forcing the prince to stop and look at him.

"What?" Justin snapped, then closed his eyes. He pulled in a deep breath, reminding himself that none of this was Stewart's fault. The man had been as deceived as Justin had, and he didn't deserve to be the target of Justin's wrath. "I'm sorry," he tried again. "What is it?"

A look of surprise flitted across Stewart's face, but he hurried to state his piece. "Your Highness, I know we've all had a bit of a shock, but I don't believe Miss Felicity was deceiving you, or that she had some ulterior purpose in being here."

Justin's forehead creased in a frown. "Do you doubt the accuracy, or the honesty, of Lord Brooker's account?"

Stewart shook his head reluctantly. "No, I believe he's telling the truth about what happened when the princess died. But I still think he's wrong about Miss Felicity. He didn't spend time with her like we did."

Justin shook his head pityingly. "The kingdom is full of people who wish to manipulate whoever wears the crown, Stewart. And they are generally very good at playing a part." He gave the steward a searching look. "She didn't look familiar to you?"

"Not at all," Stewart said. "I've spent my whole life at the Summer Castle. Like most of us here, I've only been to Allenton a handful of times. I heard the whispers about the circumstances of Princess Aurelia's death, the same as everyone else. But I never laid eyes on her myself, let alone on her lady-in-waiting."

Justin nodded, weary down to his bones. "None of us could have known. It was a well-planned attack."

"I don't believe there was any attack, Your Highness," Stewart insisted stubbornly.

Justin just shook his head, no fight left in him to argue with his steward. He extricated himself and made for his own suite, desperate for privacy. When he was at last behind a closed door, he collapsed on his bed, overcome with agony. He had been wounded in a place he'd never been wounded before, not even when his mother had died. And the pain was more than he could bear.

CHAPTER TWENTY-THREE

"**Y**ou don't have to leave, you know. You could stay with me."

Felicity's hand stilled on the saddle girths, and she closed her eyes, willing herself to be patient. She turned around, letting out a breath as she took in the hopeful look in her admirer's eyes.

"It's kind of you to say that, but I don't want to stay."

He hesitated, then leaned in, putting one arm on the wooden door of the stall, and raising an eyebrow suggestively.

"I could make it worth your while."

"That's more than close enough," said Felicity sharply, and she saw his cocky expression falter.

She sighed, her own expression softening as she looked him over. Advances like this somehow seemed less intimidating now she'd stopped waiting for protection from a source that was never going to provide it. She remembered playing with Martha's son as children—he'd been a fun playmate, almost a friend. It was only since Kurt had started leading him and all the others into mischief that he'd begun behaving so foolishly. Her heart suddenly went out to the shy and good-natured boy still hiding underneath.

"I'm not the girl for you," she said, as cheerfully as she could manage, "but I'm sure you'll find her. And I hope you'll be very happy. I'm even sure you can make her happy, if you go about it right."

He looked a little taken aback, but not altogether displeased. And he stepped away enough to allow her to negotiate her horse free of the stall, which was all the outcome she wanted.

"Please thank your mother again for her hospitality," she said, as she used a mounting block to clamber into the saddle. "And if we don't meet again, I wish you all the best."

He stood back, acknowledging her words with a nod, and Felicity prodded the horse forward. They cleared the stable, and within minutes were riding away from the town. She headed north, although she knew the castle was to the east. The truth was that she felt unaccountably nervous about returning to Justin. She still wasn't sure if he'd pushed her to leave because he no longer wanted her there, or if he was only trying to help her. Either way, it was a little humiliating to have left with such determination to find her family, and then to return so soon with no idea where they were and no way to find them.

As little as her sore rump would welcome the additional time in the saddle, she decided it was worth taking a longer route in order to travel along the coast. Riding beside the sea would be sure to clear her head, and would give her extra time to work out her conflicting emotions regarding her beastlike host.

No, not host. The thought made her deflate. She no longer had any right to claim a place in Justin's castle, and she had no idea what to expect if she returned there. Perhaps going back was a foolish idea after all.

But where else would she go? She realized with a flash of

panic that with her father and Ambrose gone to an unknown new home, she had nowhere else to turn. She didn't relish the idea of throwing herself on Justin's generosity, but it was better than asking to move in with Martha and her admiring son.

Besides, she'd promised to return. If Justin asked her to leave again, she would do so. But she would at least have kept her promise.

She rode steadily, the air biting on her cheeks. She was grateful there had been no fresh snow, and the drifts weren't deep. She was following a small track that led from the village to the cliffs that overlooked the ocean. She heard the calling of seabirds a few minutes before she saw the sight she'd been waiting for.

The sea. She breathed deeply, relishing the smell of salt. Knowing the ground was treacherous under the snow, she kept well back from the cliff's edge, gazing out at the choppy surface of the water. The ground seemed stable, and she rode on at a steady pace, following the line of the cliff.

The morning dragged on into afternoon, and she stopped periodically to rest the horse, and to eat the food Martha had kindly sent with her. But she didn't linger over it. She might have mixed emotions about returning to the castle, but she had only one reaction to the idea of spending the night outside in the middle of winter.

When she still hadn't reached the castle by mid-afternoon, she was beginning to be seriously concerned that she would have no choice. She hadn't realized the route along the coast was so much longer. She was just debating whether to keep going or start looking for shelter, when a sudden movement in front of her startled both her and her horse. The animal reared up in alarm, and Felicity, caught by surprise, was thrown instantly from the saddle.

There was no Justin to catch her this time, but she fell into a soft drift, and had the wits to roll swiftly away to avoid the horse's hooves. She struggled to her feet, and for a moment all she could see was the panicked form of the plunging horse in front of her.

Then the creature stilled, and all at once she saw what had startled it. Her mouth fell open in a soundless exclamation as her eyes lit with recognition.

It was a dragon. And not just any dragon, but *the* dragon. Rekavidur, if she remembered correctly.

Felicity, still stunned into silence, watched in astonishment as the scaled beast snaked his long neck forward. Rekavidur brought his head down to the level of her still-panicking horse, and opened his mouth. For a horrified moment, Felicity thought he was about to eat her horse, or roast it with legendary dragon fire. But there was no noticeable warmth in the breath that the dragon released over the mare, and instead of showing fear, the horse stilled at once. It pawed the ground a couple of times before trotting forward, stopping when it was fully in Rekavidur's shadow.

Felicity blinked, her eyes traveling from the horse back up to the dragon's mighty head.

"Greetings once again, Felicity," Rekavidur said placidly. "I trust you remember me?"

"I do indeed," she said hastily. "Greetings, Rekavidur."

The dragon seemed satisfied, and gave a deep nod.

"How...how did you find me?" Felicity stammered.

The dragon made a noise of amusement. "I have not been looking for you, young human. Since we last met, I have traveled across this continent extensively. I returned to this area because when I first passed over it—the day you and I met, in fact—I sensed a source of magic here that I wished to know more of. I have been in the area for some time now, observing. When I heard your approach, I recognized you, and I wished to have speech with you." He fixed her with a penetrating look. "Are you heading for the large dwelling located a short distance to the east of here?"

Felicity blinked in surprise. "How did you know?"

The dragon's tone again sounded impatient. "I didn't know. Was that not evident from the fact that I asked?"

"Uh..." Felicity stammered, taken aback. "I suppose it was. What I meant was, how did you guess?"

The dragon sighed. "If that's what you meant, that's what you should have said. I guessed because there doesn't seem to be any other human habitation out here. As I have already said, my purpose in this area is to explore a strong source of magic nearby. The dwelling I mentioned is that source—that much I have ascertained."

Felicity drew in a breath. "Of course," she muttered. "The curse must leave some kind of magical signature." She looked up at the dragon. "If it's not rude to ask, why are you particularly interested in the type of magic around that dwelling?"

The dragon considered her in silence for a long moment, and she had the sense he was himself deciding whether or not the inquiry was rude. Apparently he decided not, since he unbent slightly and spoke.

"Before I answer your question, let me ask one of my own. Do you know much about dragons?"

Felicity shook her head. "Not much. I see them fly over occasionally, of course. They're not as common in this part of Solstice, but in the kingdoms surrounding their home, I believe they're often seen. I only really know the things that everyone knows about dragons—like how you get bigger the older you get, and don't grow frail with age like humans. And how dragonlings are born bright, but their scales darken over time."

She cast a surreptitious look at the dragon's yellow scales, tinged with purple. Another clue as to his youth. Rekavidur was still watching her with an air of expectation, so she cast around for a further answer to his question.

"From what I understand, the dragons of this land speak reasonably often with royalty, and some of the more powerful enchanters and enchantresses. But an ordinary person, such as myself, would be unlikely to ever interact personally with one." She smiled. "So I'll be telling my grandchildren of our meetings for certain."

"Interesting," he mused, and she was fairly certain he wasn't talking about her grandchildren. "Have you ever heard of farsight?"

Felicity shook her head, nonplussed.

"Interesting," he repeated, his gravelly voice a murmur. "But not decisive, given you know little about the dragon colony."

He met her gaze. "Do you remember that I told you I come from a different land, a different dragon colony?"

Felicity nodded.

"In that land, it is only a few short generations of human life since the first power-wielders—or enchanters—appeared." Rekavidur frowned. "But here it seems that magic has spread more freely through the human population, although perhaps not with the same potency."

He lowered his reptilian head slowly, and passed it across her form. "I have sensed small flares of magic all over this land, including on you. It is why I approached you that first day. But I could tell you were not lying to me when you told me you were no enchantress. To be frank, I wasn't sure what to make of you."

"You sensed magic on me?" Felicity asked in surprise.

"I did," Rekavidur assented. "And I still do. Although it is not as strong as before." He inhaled once again. "I see what you mean, though," he added wisely, "about not being an enchantress. The magic does not emanate from your core. It hangs around you like a garment." He frowned. "Powerful, however, for an enchantment separated from its source."

Without warning, he leaned back in, giving her another long whiff that centered between her collarbones. "It lingers especially there. Do you carry some power-saturated object?"

Felicity patted her front, feeling nothing but the empty chain. She pulled it out from under her dress and gave a soft gasp as she realized what the dragon must be talking about. The trinket must have been an artifact after all!

"I did have an object on this chain," she said. "And I had just acquired it the day you first approached me! But it's gone now." She wondered if Justin had kept it on him, or whether he'd been uninterested in such a sentimental token.

"It must have contained great power to leave behind such a clear signature," the dragon said simply.

Felicity's mind was reeling. What did "great power" mean? If the artifact was what the merchant woman had claimed, was it powerful enough to help Justin find what he was looking for? A way to break the curse? It seemed unlikely, given the potency of the curse, but it was worth consideration. If only she'd given it to him the moment she found it! She was suddenly more eager to return, to discover if any progress had been made in her absence.

Her thoughts were pulled abruptly back to the present by a snuffling near her ear. Rekavidur was giving her another examination, and it was hard to concentrate on anything else with the dragon's snout nosing around through her hair.

"Whatever it was, it isn't the only source of power on you," he said unexpectedly. "Some other magic has been cast over your person, and lingers still."

Felicity blinked rapidly, not at all sure what to make of this information. "Is it a good enchantment?" she asked anxiously. "Or a bad one?"

The dragon frowned. "I don't know what this means, good or bad enchantment. Magic is a tool, like a sword in the hand of a human warrior. It is neither good nor bad. The magic seems intact, if that's what you're asking. It has not been warped or twisted from its original purpose."

"Do you know what that purpose is?" Felicity pressed. It suddenly struck her that she was not only speaking to a dragon, but demanding that he give her answers to her own puzzles. Part of her admired her own daring. The rest of her was worried about getting eaten.

Rekavidur sat back on his haunches, giving his tail a little flick along the ground. It left a deep groove in the snow. The horse, which had been displaced by the dragon's movements, settled back into his shadow.

"The flavor of the magic in this land is still unfamiliar to me," Rekavidur said, sounding frustrated. "I do not know the purpose of the magic currently hanging about you. But I do recognize the magic surrounding the dwelling near here, at least to some extent."

"You do?" Felicity demanded.

Rekavidur nodded. "It is an enchantment designed to conceal. That type of magic is key in the life of my own colony. We have a similar, although not identical, enchantment constantly in place around our realm, to keep humans from wandering in." He frowned. "I have visited the dragon colony in the south, and they also employ concealment magic. But..." He trailed off, casting his eyes over her. After a moment, he spoke again, seeming to modify what he'd been saying.

"The enchantment over the nearby dwelling is not the same as that surrounding the dragon colony. I cannot tell which of them, if indeed it is either, is the source of the lingering concealment magic that seems to cover this whole land."

Felicity started. "What do you mean, concealment magic covers the whole land?"

The dragon tilted his head to one side, his expression bemused. "I mean that concealment magic covers the whole land," he said blandly.

He fell silent, and Felicity waited, feeling it would be rude to prompt him. The silence stretched out for an uncomfortably long time, although the dragon didn't seem to feel any awkwardness. His eyes were narrowed as if in great concentration, and the longer he looked, the more his body seemed to lean in the direction of his gaze.

At last he sat back on his haunches, a look of frustration passing over his face. He released his breath in a huff that felt unnaturally warm in the frigid air, then turned back to Felicity.

"Yes, there is certainly some magical concealment in play. My farsight doesn't work, and from what I can discover, the other dragons don't even..." He trailed off again, giving his head a little shake. "But that is none of your affair. All you need to know is that I have an interest in concealment magic. It is possible that the enchantment emanating from the dwelling nearby might be the source of the magic affecting the land. Given that, I wish to know more about it. The enchantment is so strong that even I cannot see the structure."

Felicity had no idea what farsight was, but she was too daunted to ask. And she was distracted by Rekavidur's other revelations. It was alarming to think how powerful the enchantress must be if her magic could affect even a dragon.

"The dwelling is the Summer Castle of this kingdom's royal family," she explained. "The prince lives there. He's bound there because of a curse placed on him by an enchantress two and a half years ago. It transformed him to look like a beast, although the change is only outward. It also prevents anyone from finding him or the castle."

"Hm." Rekavidur's expression was shrewd. "Then how do you know about it?"

Felicity hesitated. "I don't exactly know how. It's a long story."

The dragon gave a huff of amusement. "I doubt it is long by dragon estimation."

Felicity laughed in spite of herself. As briefly as she could, she explained the circumstances of her time at the Summer Castle, including her reasons for leaving to search for her father and brother. Rekavidur listened in silence. When she finished speaking, he shook himself off with a flick that passed from his head, down his back, and all the way to the tip of his tail.

"Your tale raises many questions," he said. "I think I will accompany you to this Summer Castle. Perhaps it will be among humans, not dragons, that I will find my answers." He let out a small huff of air. "How humorous," he added, his voice and expression remaining even, with no hint of mirth.

"Is it?" Felicity asked blankly.

Rekavidur nodded wisely. "Your kind are always seeking answers from us. It's entertaining to think of you providing some for a change."

"I see," said Felicity, untruthfully. "So you...you want to come with me to the Summer Castle?"

The dragon tilted his head to one side. "You are reluctant for my company?"

"Of course not!" Felicity protested. She cracked a smile. "Speaking with a dragon is incredibly exciting, you know." She crinkled her forehead curiously. "Is it exciting for you? Talking to a human?"

The dragon looked faintly amused this time. "Not really, no." He gave a tolerant smile. "But I have spoken with more humans than most dragons." He settled his wings back against his sides, continuing with a noticeable drop in his formal manner.

"The truth is that most of the dragons in my colony still don't have a great deal of time for humans. But I find that surprisingly often humans make discoveries that elude even our kind."

Felicity felt a surge of amusement at the dragon's lofty tone as he spoke of "our kind". Perhaps it was a result of his relative youth, but underneath his initial formality, Rekavidur wasn't quite what she'd expected a dragon to be.

"So," she ventured, "are you saying that you'd like to lift the concealment enchantment affecting the Summer Castle, in the hope that it will remove the lingering magic over the land, and give you back your...farsight?"

"I am saying I wish to know more," said the dragon unencouragingly.

Felicity hesitated, not wanting to press him, but feeling that she would be mad not to make the most of this opportunity.

"If you were able to counteract it," she said, "I'm sure the prince would be forever grateful." She thought of Justin's disparaging words about dragons and magic, but shook the thought off. Surely if it came to lifting his curse, he would welcome any help he could get.

The dragon looked amused again. "If by 'forever', you mean for the remainder of his incredibly short lifespan..." He shook his head. "I don't need anything from your prince. I'm not as impressed by royalty as most dragons."

Felicity deflated slightly, and the dragon's eyes seemed to soften as they rested on her.

"But that does not mean I do not wish to help."

Felicity smiled warmly. "Thank you." She glanced at the sun, now disappearing below the horizon. "I don't think I can get there before dark, though. I'll have to try to make camp."

Rekavidur cocked his head slightly. "I can get you there before dark," he offered. "I can carry you there in a matter of minutes." He glanced down at the horse, standing placidly by his side. "Although I've never carried a horse before."

"Heavens, no, let's not put the poor thing through that," said Felicity, silently panicking at the idea of being carried by a dragon herself. "If you don't mind the delay, I think I'd better ride as planned."

The dragon made a guttural noise deep in its throat. Felicity froze in momentary alarm, before realizing it was laughter.

"Delay," the dragon muttered to himself, still chuckling. "As if a few hours might be more time than I could spare."

"It's not the time I'm worried about," Felicity said, pulling her cloak tighter, "so much as the cold." She gave the dragon a hopeful look. "I don't suppose you have some magic way to keep a fire going, even in the midst of this snow?"

The dragon smiled, showing an alarming number of teeth. "My fire is always going, young Felicity." As if in proof, he turned his head away from her and let out a jet of bright orange flame, tinged with purple. Felicity gave an involuntary shout, but the dragon continued to spew fire, unconcerned. He blasted the ground for long enough that when he stopped, the snow had not only melted, but the ground beneath it was dry.

He curled up on the large patch of dry earth, and the horse ambled over unconcernedly to settle itself against his flank. Felicity stood staring at the pair, wondering what she was supposed to do.

"Come, young human," the dragon said placidly, as if answering her thoughts. "I didn't clear the ground for myself. Snow makes no difference to me."

Hesitantly, Felicity moved forward, stepping from the snow onto the dry, packed earth. The air was bitterly cold now that darkness had begun to fall, but she could feel the warmth emanating from the dragon. She could see what he meant—his fire really was always going.

She stretched out on the hard ground, her mind vacillating between wistfulness at the thought of her luxurious suite at the castle, and absolute incredulity at the fact that she was camping the night with a dragon.

Rekavidur kept her warm, but even his presence couldn't keep the dreams away. It felt like the moment Felicity closed her eyes, she was submerged into her usual nighttime wandering of the castle, searching everywhere for the human prince. Only this time, when she finally found him, he wasn't dying from the loss of the roses. He was lying, near death, with blood pouring from a wound in his side. And above him, with knife still raised, crouched the massive form of the beast she knew. Only his eyes were no longer human and piercingly blue—they were red and savage.

Felicity woke with a gasp, disoriented by the gray light of dawn. She felt as if she'd been asleep for mere minutes, but morning was upon her. If Rekavidur noticed her distress, he made no comment, either when she woke, or while she ate her simple breakfast and readied herself for departure.

Felicity felt sluggish, like she was submerged in water. It was hard to decide which of the two realities was the dream, everything felt so surreal. But whether dreaming or awake, within minutes, she was once again mounted on her horse, riding in the direction of the Summer Castle, with a dragon wheeling in large, unhurried circles overhead.

CHAPTER TWENTY-FOUR

Justin

Justin let out a growl, slamming the mirror down onto his dresser. Was there anyone who wasn't lying to him?

On second thought, he snatched the mirror back up, gripping it in one hand as he strode out of the room. It was still early, but if Lord Brooker wasn't up yet, he was about to be.

"Your Highness!" The surprised serving man intercepted Justin just outside his suite. "I was coming to let you know that breakfast is being brought to Lord Brooker in the private dining hall."

Justin grunted in acknowledgment. He redirected his steps, feeling aggrieved that he was to be denied the satisfaction of dragging the advisor rudely from sleep. He swept into the dining hall, trying not to think of all the meals he'd eaten there with Felicity. Lord Brooker jumped to his feet, his initial fear once again spreading across his face as he took in Justin's furious demeanor.

"What is the meaning of this?" Justin demanded, shoving the mirror in the man's face.

"The...the mirror, Your Highness?" the advisor asked, his eyes wide and confused.

Justin let out a grunt of impatience. "Show me my uncle," he snapped at the mirror, and its surface shimmered, solidifying into the image of a room full of men, engaged in a heated argument.

"I...I don't understand what I'm seeing," Lord Brooker said.

"The mirror shows me what's happening in Allenton," Justin said curtly. "And it's currently showing an emergency council called by my uncle, to discuss the contents of your message, which he received late last night."

"I see," said the advisor, although his tone made it clear that he didn't.

"I've just been listening to my uncle explain to his senior advisors that he has received word that I have been killed by an enchantress of especial infamy. Apparently the woman has set herself up in my summer residence, and begun to exert her magical influence to win the countryside over to her cause, namely claiming rulership of the kingdom."

Lord Brooker's eyes were round with horror by the end of this speech, and as soon as Justin gave him a chance, he protested.

"My message said nothing of the kind, Your Highness! I never said that you were dead, merely that there was no sign of you! I did, of course, explain that a woman had set herself up here, and that she—"

"Enough," Justin cut him off curtly. "Which is it? Is Felicity the daughter of Aurelia's dead lady-in-waiting out for petty revenge, or is she an *infamous* enchantress looking to take control of my kingdom? You can't have it both ways!"

"I said nothing of her being an enchantress," the advisor cried. "I said that I feared she may have been behind the curse, that she may be using magic against you, but nothing about her trying to claim the kingdom!"

A particularly loud shout from the mirror made them both pause, and Justin transferred his attention to the reflected scene.

"*We must act decisively, Lord Regent!*"

It was Lord Ladner speaking, and his eyes were narrowed as they rested on Uncle Cameron.

"*If this enchantress is powerful enough to cast the curse that has been in place these last two years, we cannot give her an opportunity to cast her magic over the whole kingdom. Think what's happened in Listernia!*"

"*No one wants to see the kingdom fall under a curse,*" said Uncle Cameron, holding his hands up placatingly. "*I just don't wish to be hasty. You're suggesting an attack against our own castle. The Bansfordian prince claimed that Prince Justin was still present, just invisible to the eye. If we bring catapults against the castle, as you propose, we could kill him!*"

"*We cannot afford to delay, Lord Regent!*" another nobleman shouted, standing up. "*The prince from Bansford only believed Prince Justin was present because this woman told him so! She clearly cast her magic over him as well!*"

"*I am not willing to rule out the possibility that my nephew is alive and simply unable to communicate,*" Uncle Cameron said stubbornly. "*I will not order an attack against the Summer Castle.*"

Lord Ladner stood. "*You are not the king, My Lord. If the entire council is in agreement, we can order that attack without your approval.*"

Justin tensed, and he could see the shock on Uncle Cameron's face. To his credit, the acting regent spoke evenly. "*That can only occur if the council unanimously rules that I have shown myself unfit for my role. Is that what you claim, My Lord?*"

"*It is,*" said Lord Ladner, his face hard. Justin gripped the mirror compulsively, ignoring the startled gasp from the advisor beside him in the dining hall.

Lord Ladner made a gesture with his hand, and a nervous-looking page boy came trotting up to him.

"*I have received a warning,*" Lord Ladner said, his voice carrying around the silent room. He took a parchment from the page, and waved it in the air. "*My source claims that the acting regent is plotting to take the crown permanently, through the use of magic. I do not know whether he wishes to grant leniency to this enchantress merely because he is sympathetic to magic-users, or whether she is his accomplice.*"

A gasp went around the room back in Allenton. Even Justin was frozen in shock at the turn of events, his accusation against the advisor forgotten.

"*Either way,*" Lord Ladner continued, "*I claim that he is unfit to make this, or any, decision.*"

The room erupted, and Uncle Cameron succeeded in making his voice heard only with great difficulty.

"*This is preposterous!*" he cried. "*Who is this source? What proof did he offer?*"

"*I'm glad you asked, My Lord,*" said Lord Ladner smoothly. He nodded at the page boy, who ran quickly from the room. "*According to this warning, you are using an artifact designed to place others under your influence.*" The nobleman pointed dramatically. "*Your crown!*"

Uncle Cameron reached up a hand to touch the circlet, his expression utterly confused. "*My crown?*"

Justin narrowed his eyes at his uncle's countenance. Uncle Cameron was either innocent or a much better actor than Justin had ever given him credit for. He thought of the way Felicity had played him for a fool, and his scowl deepened. It was entirely possible.

"*I have invited three senior members of the Enchanters' Guild to attend today,*" Lord Ladner declared. "*They have agreed to examine the item.*"

Uncle Cameron didn't even protest when two men and a woman, all in the robes of guild members, entered the meeting hall. The acting regent still looked completely floored, and Justin felt a flicker of sympathy for him. He quelled it ruthlessly.

"*Meaning no disrespect, My Lord,*" one of the enchanters said gruffly, holding out a hand.

Uncle Cameron hesitated for only a moment before handing over the crown, and Justin was torn between relief and frustration. He wanted to know the outcome—the senior enchanters were well known to him, and he did not believe they had been bought—but it was also hard to watch his uncle behaving so meekly, when he was the acting monarch of the kingdom.

The three visitors bent over the crown, a faint glow surrounding them as they presumably cast enchantments over the item. After several painful minutes, they straightened. Justin couldn't hear their whispered conversation, but the room stilled when the most senior enchanter turned to the assembled noblemen.

He cleared his throat. "*It is undoubtedly an artifact,*" he said, sounding reluctant. "*Further examination would be necessary to understand the full extent of the enchantment, but preliminary observations suggest that it does indeed relate to the exertion of influence over others.*"

The room was once again overtaken by uproar, and for a few minutes it was impossible to make sense of what was happening. Justin glanced at Lord Brooker next to him, and saw that the advisor was as astonished as he was.

He tried to think dispassionately about the allegations. Did he believe that his uncle was plotting against him, and using magic to do it? He stared at the reflection of Uncle Cameron, trying to read him.

No. He shook his head. He didn't believe it. A few months ago, he might have, but that was because he was so determined to be suspicious of everyone that he saw enemies when they weren't there. This wasn't like the way he'd been deceived in Felicity. He'd known Uncle Cameron all his life, and the man had never given Justin reason not to trust him.

So what was the truth? It was conceivable that Uncle Cameron might have used an artifact to try to increase his influence with the court, simply to help things run. Justin had seen his struggles to gain their respect and cooperation. But if so, his uncle was doing a good job of looking utterly stunned.

Justin's rumination was cut short as the scene in the mirror quietened. He tuned out Lord Brooker's muttered protests and exclamations, trying to focus on what was happening. He listened in alarm as Lord Ladner called for a vote, and the gathered noblemen unanimously agreed to remove Uncle Cameron from his position, pending further inquiry. Justin watched mutely as his uncle was led from the room, in the wake of the three departing enchanters. The mirror's image followed his uncle, and Justin quickly gave it a new command.

"Show me Lord Ladner."

The mirror shimmered and cleared, and it was instantly obvious that Justin had been accurate in his assessment of the new center of the action. Lord Ladner wasted no time in taking control of the meeting.

"*This is a serious situation, My Lords,*" he said gravely. "*And now that the guild members have left, I do not hesitate to speak freely.*" He paused, casting a glance around the room. "*It is clear that our first course of action must be to eliminate the threat of this enchantress at the Summer Castle.*" A chorus of agreement met his words, and he nodded in acknowledgment. "*But once that danger has been removed,*" he continued, "*we should consider whether it is truly safe to allow magic a place in our kingdom at all.*"

Justin drew in a sharp breath. He was talking about outlawing magic, like Bansford had done. Justin's mind was in turmoil as he tried to decide how he felt about the idea. He had been considering it himself for some time now. But somehow hearing Lord Ladner say it caused alarm bells to go off inside him.

Justin thought of Felicity, and her argument that the power of magic was neither good nor bad in itself, and no more to be feared than the power of a crown. But thinking of Felicity made him narrow his eyes. If she truly had been able to use magic to reach into his heart and crush him in his most vulnerable place, then maybe Lord Ladner was right.

But had she? *Was* she working against him, or was Stewart right that she wasn't to blame? Justin's heart ached with the question that had kept him awake most of the night.

"*It's decided, then.*" Lord Ladner's heavy voice broke into Justin's reverie. What had they decided? A quick glance at the face of Lord Brooker beside him gave him a clue.

"*There's no time to waste,*" another lord piped up. "*If we are to destroy the Summer Castle, we must do so immediately, before word reaches this enchantress, and she has time to create defenses.*"

Lord Ladner nodded. "*The closest garrison has been on high alert since Prince Bentleigh's visit. A runner will be dispatched immediately, and I expect them to be ready to attack tomorrow.*"

Tomorrow? Justin froze, as Lord Brooker gave a sharp gasp.

"*The garrison is stocked with the last of the enchanted projectiles,*" Lord Ladner said. Justin felt a chill pass over him as he remembered himself approving the creation of those stones, intended for use by the catapults. It had been back when the war between Mistra and Entolia commenced, and Albury feared being drawn into it. He had been only sixteen, and yet so sure of himself. Far too sure.

"*I propose we give the order that they be used to destroy the*

Summer Castle," Lord Ladner was saying. "*Wipe out the scourge of this enchantment once and for all.*"

Justin gave a soft snort as the other lords hastened to agree. So the man was happy to use magic for his own ends. He just wanted to ban anyone else from doing so.

"I—I think I had best make haste, Your Highness," stammered Lord Brooker. "Perhaps I can intercept the army, try to explain the mistake."

Justin's lip curled. The advisor may as well save his breath. It was clear why he wanted to be out of the castle.

"By all means," he said, making no attempt to hide his scorn. "You are not a prisoner here."

Lord Brooker had the decency to look a little ashamed at the reminder that the rest of the castle's inhabitants had no means of escaping the magical destruction about to be unleashed.

But not ashamed enough to prevent him from making a hasty departure, less than an hour later. Justin watched him go without regret. He was unlikely to be any help, and his panic would only distress everyone else.

Justin had already sent the guards to check the gate after the advisor's arrival the day before, but he sent them again. There was no improvement. Whatever change had allowed Lord Brooker to find them, it hadn't removed the magic keeping the estate's inhabitants from leaving. There was a small army coming to destroy the castle, and they were all trapped inside it.

He wasn't sure what was more painful—seeing the panic in the eyes of the servants when he told them what he'd witnessed, or seeing their heroic attempts to conceal it. Mrs. Winters snapped instantly into her most practical mode, setting the servants to work clearing out the castle's underground storage cellars. Justin made no comment on the plan. Against ordinary catapults, the cellars would probably protect them all. But against enchanted projectiles...well, he supposed it wasn't impossible, but his hopes weren't high.

He spent the next two hours pacing the frozen gardens, trying desperately to untangle the hopeless mess everything had become. He had to assume there was foul play at work in the circumstances that had led his nobles to order this attack. But he had no idea who was behind it. It was possible Lord Ladner was the instigator, of course, but it was equally possible that someone had deceived him.

And always, against his will, his thoughts circled back to Felicity. What was her part in it all? He couldn't bear to think that she had any hand in this attack. Even if she hated him for what her family had suffered, surely she wouldn't want to see all the servants killed? But if everything had been an act all along...

He suddenly realized he was holding her token and scowled, putting it back in his pocket. He had considered attempting to destroy it, in case doing so broke the curse. But he'd quickly realized that couldn't be the case. They'd been cursed for more than two years before she showed up. And while those in the capital may not have the full story, Justin knew perfectly well who had cast the actual curse, and it wasn't Felicity.

A sudden shout from the guard on duty at the gate pulled Justin's attention away from his inner turmoil. He loped quickly toward the sound, trying to decide whether the guard had sounded excited or afraid. There was no way any troops could have reached them yet, he reasoned.

When he rounded the bend of a hedge and saw who was at the gate, he froze in his tracks.

Felicity.

What was she doing here? She'd been greeting the guard, but she looked up suddenly, locking eyes with Justin. A shy smile spread across her face, and she hurried toward him.

"You see?" she said, by way of greeting. "I told you I'd come back."

For a prolonged moment Justin just stared at her. In all that had happened since, he'd forgotten about her promise to return to the castle. He struggled to comprehend the fact that she didn't even know what he'd discovered about her.

"Justin?" she said, looking uncertain. "Are you all right?"

Justin didn't answer, still wrestling with himself. A maelstrom of emotion had descended on him at sight of her, and he felt his face harden to cold disdain in an instinctive method of protection.

"I'm sorry if I'm intruding," Felicity said at his continued silence. Her face was now flushing to match her hair, bright spots of color in the wintry landscape. "I realize I have no reason to live here at your expense now, but I wanted to keep my word..." She snuck a glance at him, but dropped her eyes again quickly. "I didn't find my father and brother. They've left the kingdom, from all I can tell."

"How convenient," said Justin smoothly, and Felicity's eyes darted to him.

"Maybe to you," she said, with a flash of anger. "But I don't especially enjoy not knowing where my family are, or if they're even alive."

Justin narrowed his eyes at her. She was incredibly convincing. He had seriously underestimated her all these months. *Or,* prodded a voice in his head, *she truly isn't your enemy.*

Justin's thoughts writhed uncomfortably, desperate to know the truth. It scared him how much she'd gotten under his skin. With death speeding toward him and all his household, he still couldn't focus on anything but the brightness in her eyes, and the emotions she unleashed within him every time she was near. Even in spite of everything, his heart had leaped at the sight of her, and his own powerlessness made him feel angry.

"Tell me again about your mother," he said abruptly.

Felicity blinked at him. "My mother? She...I hardly remember her. Why do you want to know about my mother?"

"I received another visitor while you were gone," Justin said, ignoring her question. "Or rather, the same visitor back again. Lord Brooker, the advisor from Allenton, returned." He raised an eyebrow. "Care to explain how, as soon as you were gone, he was able to both see and hear me?"

Felicity gasped, and her eyes widened. "The artifact!" she cried. "The pendant I left with you! It must be!"

A growl escaped Justin before he was even aware of it. "So you admit you've been using magic against me!"

"What?" Felicity was looking at him like he'd lost his wits. "Of course I haven't been using magic against you! I bought that artifact for my father, because it was supposed to help him find his way home. But when he got so lost after the markets that he ended up in a dungeon, I figured it was a fake. Except then—"

"You conveniently forgot to mention to me that you had an artifact on your person the entire time you were living in my castle," Justin growled.

Felicity raised her hands in frustration. "I told you, I didn't think it was genuine. And," she hesitated, "I didn't know if I should tell you that I'd tried to buy an artifact. I know you're a little...edgy about magic."

"So you intentionally concealed it from me," said Justin, his anger rising. "I thought you told me, after Lord Brooker accused you, that you weren't hiding anything from me."

Felicity made an impatient noise in her throat. "I honestly didn't think it was important. I'd forgotten all about it by then. I didn't hide anything else from you, Justin."

"Oh, you didn't hide anything *else*. How reassuring," Justin said mockingly.

Felicity narrowed her eyes. "What's your problem? What is

this really about? Surely it's a good thing that my pendant is an artifact, if it's helped someone find you!"

"Oh, Lord Brooker did more than just find me," Justin said smoothly. "He had a great deal to say, about you in particular."

"Me?" Felicity fell back a step, looking unnerved. "What did he say about me?"

Justin narrowed his eyes at her reaction. "More about your mother than you," he said, and Felicity froze. "It seems there are some quite incredible details you never mentioned to me. Like the fact that you look so very much like her."

"Yes, so I've been told," Felicity said slowly. Her face was almost as pale as the snow around her. "But what does my mother have to do with anything? She's been dead for more than twelve years."

"The same length of time since my sister died," Justin said conversationally. "How remarkable."

Felicity frowned, a spark of frustration giving life to her features. She stepped forward again, seizing the lapels of Justin's coat. "What are you saying, Justin? I don't understand you!"

Justin froze at the touch, his eyes locked on hers. For a moment he was almost overwhelmed by the urge to pull her close, to keep her near him. But this reminder of the hold she had over him only inflamed his anger.

"Lord Brooker recognized you as your mother's daughter," he snapped. "I know the truth now—that your mother was the servant who was carrying Aurelia when she fell into the ravine. I know you have reason to want to see me hurt, maybe even dead."

Felicity dropped her grip like his clothes had burned her. She fell back again, her eyes wide and her remaining color draining away. "That's not possible," she whispered.

"Really?" Justin pressed. "How *did* your mother die? I'm not sure how I missed it—we talked all about my parents' deaths, even my sister's. But you never told me what happened to your mother."

"I...I don't know the details," Felicity said, her voice still a whisper. "Just that there was an accident. Father would never say more. He hated talking about it."

"I can imagine," Justin said acidly. "If I'd been banished from the capital on pain of death, I probably wouldn't want to talk about it either."

"Banished on pain of..." Felicity echoed, her voice fainter than ever. "Is that why he was so afraid?"

Her eyes were unfocused, and Justin watched as she slowly pulled herself together, transferring her gaze to him.

"If this is true, Justin, I swear I didn't know it."

"Just like you didn't know your pendant was a powerful artifact?" Justin sneered. Her distress tugged at his heart, and he felt torn apart as his desire to pull her close and reassure her battled with his fury at himself for being so easily taken in. "Am I supposed to believe that it's pure coincidence that you and your father were the ones to suddenly find my castle, after two years of isolation?"

Felicity shook her head helplessly. "I know it seems unlikely, but I have no explanation." She stared pleadingly up at him, and it took all his willpower to keep his face impassive.

"And I suppose you have no explanation for the information my uncle has received, that the woman who has set herself up in my castle is a powerful enchantress seeking to wrest control of my kingdom?"

"What?" Felicity looked outraged. "That's absurd! None of that is true, Justin, and you know it. The only reason I even stayed here in the first place is because you made me!"

"So I thought," said Justin coldly. "And yet who knows what magic might have been involved in that sequence of events?

Ordinary people don't usually wander around carrying artifacts, after all."

Felicity was beginning to look impatient. "This is ridiculous, Justin. Don't let your prejudice against magic blind you. You surely can't believe such a foolish story?"

"I know how strong an advocate you are for magic, after all," Justin snapped.

Felicity stared at him, her expression difficult to read. Then all of a sudden, a look of determination swept over her face.

"I can't make you believe me, Justin, but you're wrong if you think I want to see you hurt. I never wanted that. I want to help you," she gestured toward the castle, "all of you. And I might have found a way to do it."

"If you're talking about your so-called artifact," Justin started, but she cut him off.

"Not that, although we should definitely explore its role in all this. No, I'm talking about...well, about someone I met while I was gone. He might be able to help. I asked him to hang back a bit until I had the chance to talk to you, but he's not far away."

Justin frowned, his suspicions well and truly raised. "Who is this person?"

"Well, that's just it."

Felicity was fidgeting, and Justin raised an eyebrow. What was she hiding?

"He's not so much a person as a...well, a dragon."

CHAPTER TWENTY-FIVE

Felicity

F elicity braced herself for Justin's reaction, and he didn't disappoint.

"A dragon?" he repeated, his voice deadly calm. "You asked a *dragon* for help? Knowing how I feel about magic, you brought the creature here?"

"Well, he wanted to come," she reasoned, exasperated by his hostility. "I couldn't really stop him, could I? I mean, he's a dragon. But he said he wants to help. Or at least," she considered the point, "he said he doesn't *not* want to help, and I think we should take what we can get, don't you?"

She peered up at him hopefully, but his face was still impassive stone. She sighed.

"He has a particular interest in concealment magic, and he indicated he'd be willing to try to remove the enchantment that hides the castle from the rest of the kingdom."

Justin clearly wasn't listening. "No dragon is going to help with this curse. Don't you know anything? Don't you realize how dangerous it would be for me to go to the dragons? You think this nonsense will make me more likely to believe that you're not using magic against me? I don't know what your plan is, but do you really think I trust you enough to let you set a dragon loose on my home?"

Felicity felt a flush rising up her face, and it was suddenly hard to meet Justin's eye. "You said once that you trusted me," she said quietly.

There was a moment of silence. "I was a fool," Justin said at last.

Felicity flinched at the expressionless tone. He was acting like he had when she'd first arrived, but worse. So much worse. He'd never seemed less human, and after everything they'd been through, with everything she'd begun to feel, it was almost more than she could bear.

"Justin..." she started, but she had no idea what to say, how to break through to him. And he obviously didn't intend to give her the chance.

"There's no place for you here," he said tonelessly. "And while I still live, I will not allow you to unleash a dragon on my servants."

"Justin," Felicity protested, frustration rising up inside her. "Don't be stubborn about this. I'm just trying to help."

"You've done more than enough," Justin said coldly. "You need to leave."

"But—"

"You need to leave NOW."

Felicity flinched at the growl that accompanied the last word. Anger and hurt battled for position within her, but she forced back her tears. She was far from finished, but she could see she wasn't going to be able to reach him in this mood.

She turned without another word, her steps agitated as she headed for the gate. She couldn't even summon a goodbye for the guard on duty, just claiming her horse and leading the animal from the grounds.

The moment she left the estate, she felt something collapse

inside her. She'd been nervous about returning, but she'd never imagined anything as awful as the confrontation she'd just endured. Justin's cold anger was so much worse than the awkwardness she'd feared.

Could it be true, about her mother? A well of emotion rose up within her, but she fought against it. It would have to wait. The accusation, following so close on the confirmation that her father and brother were gone far from her reach, made her feel like she'd been uprooted, and was adrift. But she tried to remove herself from the picture, to imagine what Justin must be thinking and feeling. He had been cruel in his wrath, but she knew him well enough by now to realize that he often hid behind anger. And he had a point—it was all staggeringly coincidental. It wasn't completely outrageous for him to suspect her of some ulterior motive.

But it had to be coincidence. Didn't it? The idea of her father intentionally seeking out the Summer Castle all those months ago, intent on causing mischief, was utterly absurd.

Felicity plodded on for some minutes, heading for the grove where she had arranged to meet Rekavidur. She had asked the dragon to stay out of sight until she could explain his presence to the residents of the castle, and he'd seemed quite happy to hang back and observe.

"Felicity."

The gravelly voice made her jump, although her horse showed no sign of being startled. She looked up to see the astonishing sight of Rekavidur, perching halfway up a large spruce. How the tree was holding his weight—not to mention how he'd fit into the enclosed space—she couldn't say.

"You really are in a hurry," the dragon said placidly. "Even for a human."

"Actually," said Felicity dryly, craning her neck up. "He kicked me out."

In a surprisingly fluid motion, Rekavidur descended from the tree, barely making a noise. Felicity wouldn't have thought there was room for him on the forest floor, but somehow he was there, his form woven around the trunks.

"So he does not want our assistance, then?"

Felicity sighed, looking back over her shoulder, although the trees now hid the castle from sight.

"He's angry with me, and hurt, I think. He's not thinking clearly." She scowled. "Besides, even if he doesn't want your help to break his curse, he should think about what the rest of them would want. None of them deserve to be trapped like this."

"Hm." The dragon looked thoughtful. "If this enchantment that has affected his form is a curse directed against him personally, I doubt I would be able to undo it without his cooperation, even should I wish to." He swiveled his enormous head, squinting through the trees. "But during your absence, I have been once again examining the magic that encases the dwelling. It is certainly concealment magic. But I was right when I told you it is not quite like the similar enchantment around the dragon colony. There is a crucial difference." He turned to face her again. "Nevertheless, it must help that I have seen such enchantments before. I have even broken one, a much stronger one."

Felicity felt a surge of hope. If Rekavidur could free the castle's inhabitants, it would be worth Justin's anger at her disobeying his instructions. "What's the crucial difference?" she asked curiously.

Rekavidur's voice was heavy with meaning. "Ordinarily such enchantments keep people out. It is not common for them to also keep them in."

Felicity frowned. "So, does that mean this enchantment is... what did you say before? Twisted from its original purpose?"

The dragon shook his head slowly, weaving it back and forth

like a snake. "That is harder to say. It is not quite like any magic I have encountered before. One minute I think it has been warped, but the next its purpose seems too clear to be so." A strange rippling shrug passed over his whole body. "I have never seen a concealment enchantment quite like this one, as I said. But perhaps the branch of magic that keeps the residents of the dwelling contained is part of the concealment. After all, if they were to leave, they would be able to reveal their presence to others, thus making the concealment incomplete."

"Well, let's not worry about the details now," said Felicity. "If you think you can break it, and you're willing to try, then I don't see any reason to delay."

The dragon gave a deep, guttural chuckle. "Always in such a hurry."

But in spite of his words, he dropped instantly into a crouch, launching himself upward. Felicity couldn't quite see how he did it, but he shot straight up through the branches and into the sky, dislodging some snow but leaving the trees unharmed. After a moment's hesitation, she made her way to the edge of the grove, clambering halfway up a fir tree for a better vantage point.

Rekavidur was wheeling through the air, in the direction of the castle. As she watched, he banked, passing in a wide circle over the top of the structure. She was too far away to hear anything, but her imagination conjured a shout of alarm from the guard on the gate. Justin would be furious with her when he saw the dragon. He might even see it as proof that she was plotting against him. But surely he would forgive her if it broke the enchantment.

She watched eagerly as Rekavidur opened his jaws wide. It looked like he was about to spew fire mid-flight, but nothing visible came from his mouth. He started to weave back and forth, breathing on the castle all the while. A buzz of pure excitement went through Felicity. Never did she imagine she would get to see a dragon working its magic right in front of her.

By the time the afternoon began to slide toward evening, she'd changed her mind. She never wanted to watch dragon magic again. She'd assumed the process would take minutes at most. It had never occurred to her that it would be hours. As far as she knew, Rekavidur was still circling the castle, although she couldn't see him from where she currently sat.

She had long since descended from the tree, and was huddled in a makeshift shelter of branches, attempting to escape the wind. She'd eaten more of the cold food Martha had sent, but it wasn't much, and her stomach was rumbling. She felt incredibly deflated. She'd hoped to spend tonight in her suite at the castle, not alone in a frozen grove. She got up, performing one of her periodic circuits of the grove, trying to warm herself up.

She began to feel nervous as the sun slipped below the horizon. She had no idea if there were predators out here, let alone the cold.

As utterly exhausted as she was, she was sure she wouldn't sleep, not when she felt chilled to the bone. But she must have drifted, because all of a sudden she found herself blinking in the sunlight of a new day. She lay perfectly still for a moment, trying to make sense of the radiating warmth at her back. All of a sudden she caught sight of a scaled tail curling around in front of her, and she sat up quickly. Rekavidur was asleep behind her, the horse once again nestled against him.

Felicity pushed herself to her feet, every inch of her aching from a second night on the hard ground. How long had the dragon been there? She was torn between gratitude for his warmth, and irritation that he hadn't woken her to tell her he was finished.

She picked her way through the trees to relieve herself, and when she came back, the dragon was stirring. He opened one catlike eye and stared at her with unnerving clarity for a creature just roused from sleep.

"Good morning, Felicity."

"Good morning," she said, an eager note creeping into her voice. "Did it work? Did you succeed in lifting the magic of concealment, and removing the constraint keeping people inside?"

"I believe so," the dragon said, opening his mouth in the most terrifying yawn Felicity had ever seen. Abruptly, he rolled onto his back, dislodging the horse and rolling into a patch of snow. It sizzled on contact from his scales, and melted instantly into slush. Rekavidur stood up, shook himself off in a motion that showered both Felicity and the horse with warm, dirty water, and stretched his wings, causing several large branches to snap off their trunks.

"I suppose I should be on my way," he said placidly.

"What?" Felicity had been watching the dragon's waking routine speechlessly, but that got her attention. "Aren't you going to tell me about the enchantment?"

Rekavidur frowned. "No, I don't think I will. It is enough to know that it is lifted now, and that it was strong."

"And did lifting it remove the lingering magic that you mentioned, that's covering the whole land?"

The dragon was silent for so long that she didn't think he was going to answer.

"No," Rekavidur said at last. "But that doesn't mean I learned nothing."

"It took so long to remove it," Felicity said.

The dragon blinked at her in evident surprise. "What do you mean? It took mere hours. I thought I was efficient, given the strength of the enchantment, and its many layers."

Felicity got the sense from the dragon's tone that she had offended him, and she hastened to apologize.

"Did everyone leave the estate?" she asked curiously, once he seemed mollified.

The dragon looked faintly surprised once again. "I don't know. I didn't see anyone leave."

Felicity frowned, realizing that they probably didn't even know they could leave.

"I saw very few people within the estate," Rekavidur added. "Not nearly as many as those outside it."

Felicity's frown deepened. "People outside the estate? What do you mean? There's no one else living near here."

"These people weren't in their homes," Rekavidur said patiently. "They were gathered in a group, approaching the castle at a glacial, human speed."

Felicity felt a spike of alarm. "What did they look like?"

"Like an army," Rekavidur said, unconcerned. "They had weapons of a type I've seen before." He paused for a moment, thinking. "Catapults, I believe you call them." His tone betrayed some interest. "They smelled of magic, though, and I have never witnessed such a thing before. It was most intriguing."

Felicity's eyes widened in horror. There was an army marching on the castle, with enchanted weapons? She thought of Viola and Mrs. Winters, of Phillip and Stewart. And Justin. She had to warn them, tell them to get out. Tell them that they *could* get out.

"How far away do you think they are?" she asked urgently.

The dragon squinted, as if he could see through the trees, then let out a huff of frustration. "I keep forgetting I can't see."

Felicity blinked, confused by the strange comment, but Rekavidur had already shot up into the air with a powerful gust of wind. Before she had time to wonder what he was doing, he had landed beside her, the movement surprisingly silent, despite the wind that still whipped around her.

"They're to the south of the castle," he said calmly. "But

they've stopped moving. I suspect their catapults can now reach its walls."

Felicity groaned. "There's no time to waste." She felt a surge of irritation at the fact that they'd just been sleeping the morning away. "I'll go to the castle, warn them what's coming. Are you willing to stall the army?" She paused, thinking rapidly. "No, that's a bad idea. It could be seen as an act of war by the dragons against Albury, and who knows what chaos that would unleash?"

She bit her lip, anxiety making it hard to think. "I'd better go to the army, try to convince them not to attack. I have no idea what kind of damage magically enhanced catapults can do, but I don't want to find out." She looked up at Rekavidur hopefully. "Do you think you could take a message to Justin, and the others in the castle?"

"Of course I could," he said flatly, his tone making her realize that she had erred in politeness somehow.

"I'm sorry," she said carefully, hiding her frustration at the delay. "What I should have said was, would you please be so kind as to take a message to them?"

The dragon inclined his head in a stately gesture, and for all his fearsomeness, Felicity wanted to roll her eyes. Perhaps it was something about being a talking beast, but his haughty expression reminded her of Justin when he was up on his high horse about something.

The thought of Justin sent a pang through her heart. If she was too late...She shook off the pessimistic thought. She wouldn't be too late. She couldn't be.

They made their way to the edge of the trees, Felicity mounting the horse as soon as they were clear of the grove. She paused to watch Rekavidur fly in a leisurely way in the direction of the castle. Then she turned her back on the familiar estate and urged the horse southward, toward the army.

When she caught the first faint sounds of the camp, she couldn't help the ripple of apprehension that ran over her. Perhaps this wasn't her smartest idea. How was she going to convince an army to ignore its orders and hold back an attack? What was the penalty for a peasant trying to interfere with the king's army?

Her steps slowed, and she paused beside an enormous boulder, taller than her. She wasn't sure exactly how far from the army she still was, but she had a feeling that she would be visible from the camp once she climbed the next rise. She placed a hand on the rock, closing her eyes and steadying herself with a deep breath. She had to do this, for Justin and the others.

But she had no chance to prove her mettle. Her eyes were still closed when rough hands grabbed her from behind, pinning her arms to her sides and dragging her backward through the snow.

"Felicity," drawled an unpleasantly familiar voice. "This is a nice surprise. How considerate of you to come out of your lair, and save us the trouble of smoking you out."

Felicity twisted fruitlessly against the iron hold of the soldier who had grabbed her. She glared at the handsome, ash-blond man who had just emerged from the other side of the boulder.

"Kurt," she spat. "What are you doing here?"

"You see?" Kurt's voice had turned businesslike, and his gaze was no longer on her. He locked eyes with the soldier who still held her arms in a death grip. "She knows me. Like I told you, this is her. This is the enchantress you're looking for."

CHAPTER TWENTY-SIX

Justin

"Your Highness."

The grim voice of his head guard told Justin he wasn't bringing good news. Not that the news could get much worse than it already was. He turned slowly, keeping his face impassive, and nodding for the guard to go on.

The man hesitated before doing so. "Did you sleep at all, Your Highness?" he asked gruffly.

Justin sighed. "It's a little hard to drift off when an army is marching toward us, bent on destroying the castle with everyone in it."

What he didn't say, of course, was that the memory of his confrontation with Felicity had kept him awake as much as the impending attack. He had told her to leave, in no uncertain terms, but if he was honest, he hadn't expected her to comply so readily. And now he would never see her again.

He tried to shake the thought off, aware that the guard was still watching him. "What's the situation?"

The guard straightened. "I think Phillip already reported to you that the dragon flew away shortly after dark. The purpose of its surveillance is still unclear."

Justin nodded curtly.

"And I've just returned from the south tower," the guard said, his voice once again grim. "The army is now within sight. They seem to have set up camp."

"Catapults?" Justin asked sharply.

The guard nodded. "It's difficult to be sure from this distance, Your Highness. But it looks like it."

Justin nodded slowly. "It's time to get everyone below ground."

He could see from the guard's face that he was as skeptical about the cellars' protection as Justin was, but neither of them said it in so many words.

"You could leave, you know, Prince Justin."

The guard's quiet comment made Justin whip his head around in surprise. "What?"

"You could leave the estate, endure the pain for the duration of the attack, then come back to whatever's left."

Justin's brow lowered. "While a single member of this household remains on the estate, so will I."

The guard gave a slow nod, something in his eyes softening.

"Your Highness!"

The breathless shout made both men spin toward the doorway of Justin's suite, the head guard's hand going to the hilt of his sword in an instinctive gesture. But it was only Phillip who came tumbling into the room.

"The dragon is back!" he gasped. "It's sitting on the carriageway, as though it wants to speak to us!"

Justin's brow furrowed. "Is Felicity with it?"

Phillip shook his head. "No, Your Highness. It's alone."

Justin felt a stab of disappointment, but he shook it off. He was still conflicted about Felicity, but even in the tug of war going on inside his heart, both sides agreed with his decision to send Felicity away. If she was somehow involved in all this, her presence would only put everyone in further danger. If she wasn't...well, that made the idea of her being at the castle even worse. He didn't want her anywhere near the place when magical catapult fire began to rain down on it, and the Felicity he'd thought he knew would never agree to leave while the others were stuck there, and in danger.

"I will speak with it," he said curtly, sweeping from the room. He had no idea what fresh attack this might be, but he didn't have a great deal to lose.

The guards fell into step, flanking him as he strode through the corridors. He emerged into the brightness of a clear day, the sun reflecting blindingly off the snow. As Phillip had said, a dragon was waiting on the carriageway, its front legs between its haunches, and its long tail wrapped loosely around itself.

Justin came to a stop about twenty paces away, casting a shrewd glance over the beast. He had seen dragons a handful of times, but this one was unknown to him. The first impression, as always, was of immense size and strength. But on closer inspection, he realized that this dragon was not especially large. And its yellow scales, with their purple tint, were still quite bright. A young dragon, then.

"Greetings, Mighty Beast," he said in the traditional manner. "I am Crown Prince Justin of Albury."

The dragon inclined its head regally.

"Greetings, Crown Prince Justin," it said, its gravelly voice placid.

Justin felt an unexpected surge of warmth toward the creature. It was hard not to appreciate the dragon's total lack of response to Justin's cursed form.

"I am Rekavidur," the dragon continued. "Of a land far distant from here."

Justin blinked in surprise. He had never heard such a

greeting from a dragon before. But he knew better than to press for details of the dragon's identity.

"I must say," the dragon's voice was a little brighter now that the formalities were over, and he glanced around him as he spoke, "I am pleased to get a proper look at your castle. It is a very pleasant dwelling, for something made by human hands."

A tiny twinge of amusement broke through Justin's grim mood as he took in the inquisitive look on the dragon's face. He would have thought the beast had gotten a fairly good look during his hours of silent surveillance the night before, but he didn't say so.

"Thank you," he said instead, speaking politely. For all his complaints to Felicity about magic, he wasn't such a fool as to antagonize an actual dragon. "I am honored to receive you, Rekavidur. For what purpose have you come?"

"I bring a warning," the dragon said matter-of-factly. "From Felicity."

Justin felt rather than saw the startled reactions of his two companions.

"She wishes you to know that an army approaches your dwelling," Rekavidur continued. "And they carry magic weapons."

"Does she?" Justin asked, his voice dry. "How kind of her."

The dragon pulled his eyes from contemplation of the castle, snaking his long neck down so that his head hovered before Justin's. He gave a sudden, exaggerated sniff, then sat back again.

"Your words and your tone are at war," he observed. "How curious."

Justin made no attempt to explain himself. "We are already aware of the presence of the army," he said shortly. "So the message is unnecessary. I anticipate that the army will soon attack this estate, so if you wish to avoid the inconvenience, I suggest you leave now."

"Yes, I think I will," the dragon said gravely. "And you would be wise to do the same."

Justin ground his teeth together, trying to maintain his polite tone. "Unfortunately that is not possible," he said. "We are bound here by an enchantment."

"Ah yes, that is the other part of the message," Rekavidur said, his voice still placid. "The enchantment of concealment is now broken. I removed it yesterday. There is still strong magic in this place," he leaned forward again and gave Justin another small whiff, "especially around you. But the magic preventing people from either entering or leaving this place is present no longer. From what I could tell, it was a part of the concealment magic, designed to prevent the residents of this dwelling from revealing your presence to those outside."

For an endless second, Justin stood frozen, staring blankly at the dragon. He could hardly comprehend the words. This Rekavidur had removed the magic that had kept them all trapped on the estate for more than two and a half years? It was impossible. The most basic principle of dragon and human interaction was that the beasts did not use their magic directly on humans, either to help or hinder. It was the foundation of the peace that existed between the two kinds. As a royal, Justin was well versed in dragon lore. He would no sooner ask a dragon to help with a curse cast by a human enchantress than he would declare war on their colony.

"Why would you do that?" he asked numbly.

The dragon did a strange rippling shrug. "I had my reasons. One of them is that Felicity asked me to. And I've taken a bit of a liking to her."

"She has that effect," chipped in the head guard, sounding as dazed as Justin felt.

Justin's mind was whirling. There was something very strange going on here, that much was certain. Felicity had sent a dragon to help them? How had she achieved that? And what did it mean? In spite of his fears as to the implications of the dragon's actions, his heart lifted slightly. Perhaps Felicity didn't want any of them to get hurt. Perhaps he hadn't been totally wrong about her. He turned to the two guards.

"We must test this at once."

At a nod from the head guard, Phillip took off, sprinting toward the gate. Justin watched, breathless, as the young guard reached the wrought-iron structure. Phillip paused, then pushed the small side gate open. Justin's breath caught in his throat as Phillip disappeared through the portal.

He turned to stare at the other guard. "Gather everyone," he said. "Immediately. Tell them to leave all their belongings, just get out as quickly as possible."

The guard nodded again, disappearing toward the castle. A moment later Phillip, who had reentered the estate, jogged past Justin to assist. His excitement seemed to bubble out from him as he went by.

Justin turned back to the dragon, who had watched these proceedings with a detached air.

"Did you really not believe me?" he asked curiously.

Justin gave a humorless smile. "It's not exactly that I didn't believe you," he explained. "But humans aren't good at learning from others. We need to discover things for ourselves, often painfully."

Rekavidur nodded sagely. "Yes, I've observed this."

"You have my deepest gratitude," said Justin, bowing low to the dragon. "If there is some way I can repay your deed, I hope you will tell me."

"Nothing at present," the dragon said cheerfully. "But I'll let you know."

And with those ominous words, he dropped into a crouch and shot straight up into the air. The wind from his wings temporarily flattened the trees lining the carriageway. As soon as the dragon was gone, the trees straightened, flinging their burdens of snow across the drive. Justin received a faceful of flying snow from two directions, and could only be grateful that his guards had already disappeared from sight.

He contemplated going back for some of his more treasured belongings, but he thought he'd better set a good example and follow the instructions he'd given. Hopefully it wouldn't matter. He only needed to reach the army and convince whoever was in charge of his identity, and he could stop the attack altogether.

In a few short minutes, figures began to appear from the direction of the castle, their excited chatter reaching him well before they did. Mrs. Winters had naturally taken charge of the evacuation, and Justin had nothing to do but watch as they trickled past, bowing distractedly with their eyes on the open gate. He was sure Mrs. Winters would have everything in hand, but he counted the heads nevertheless.

He frowned when the last servant—the crusty head groom —passed him. Nineteen, including himself. They were one short. He looked back toward the castle in concern before the truth suddenly hit him. He'd been counting Felicity.

He turned resolutely back toward the gate, following the group at a sedate pace. Two of the guards were once again flanking him, and Stewart was only a few steps ahead, regularly glancing back at Justin. He became distracted when the first servants passed through the gate, however, and Justin didn't blame him.

In spite of the tangled mess they were still in, he couldn't help but smile at the shouts of delight that cut through the still air when his servants stepped off the estate for the first time in years. From what he could see through the gate's iron bars, the girl who had appointed herself as Felicity's maid even threw herself down on the ground, making a snow angel in a fresh drift.

Justin saw Phillip, the youngest of the guards, laughing at the girl's antics and reaching out a hand to help her up. They all looked so carefree and happy, it made something ache deep within Justin. He'd become used to their demeanor, and hadn't realized until this moment how heavily they'd all been carrying the uncertainty of their future. And they'd endured it so uncomplainingly, even though they were in no way to blame.

When Justin reached the gate, he realized that his guards were hanging back, waiting for him to leave first. He shook his head at the head guard, repeating his words from earlier.

"While a single member of this household remains on the estate, so will I."

The guard let out a breath, his forehead knitted. Then, with a curt nod, he stepped through the gate, the other guard following close behind him.

Justin glanced back at the castle, his prison of more than two years. The memories it contained were so bittersweet, he couldn't bear to dwell on them. He faced forward, taking the final step that would carry him over the boundary of the estate.

Instantly, searing pain pierced every inch of him. He fell heavily to the ground, his mind struggling to grasp the implications of his sudden agony. With a supreme effort, he rolled himself back over the threshold.

At once the pain disappeared, and he was able to take in the astonished shouts of his servants. Several of them were rushing back toward the gate, but he scrambled to his feet, holding out a commanding hand.

"No! No one enters."

"But Your Highness!" the head guard and Stewart protested in unison.

Justin shook his shaggy head. "Who knows what will

happen? Obviously the magic is still in place in some form. If you come back in, you may not be able to leave. And the attack could begin at any moment."

"That's a chance I'll take," the head guard said grimly, taking a purposeful step forward.

Justin growled, shedding the careful restraint he always exercised in an attempt to seem—and feel—human. The sound was so ferocious, the guard stopped in his tracks.

"No one enters," Justin snarled. He locked eyes with the man. "If you do, I'll throw you bodily from the grounds." He stretched out his powerful arms meaningfully. "You know I'm capable."

The guard hesitated, looking torn.

"You're no use to me in here," said Justin bluntly. "Go to the camp, explain the true situation. Stop the attack, then we can figure out what's happening with the curse."

The guard wavered for a moment longer, then gave a curt nod. With a quick gesture to the other two guards, he turned and took off at a jog, both of his subordinates following in his wake.

"The rest of you, get well clear of the estate," Justin ordered, still speaking through the open side gate. He pinned his housekeeper with a glare. "Mrs. Winters, I'm counting on you to make sure everyone is at a safe distance."

On that order, he swept down the carriageway, eager to get away from his audience in order to sort the chaos erupting in his mind. He had never even considered the possibility that the servants would be able to leave, and he would still be trapped. Even if the guards managed to stop the attack, the prospect of true isolation didn't bear thinking about. He realized in a flash of clarity how much he had undervalued the loyalty and sacrifice of the servants in staying with him. He would have been lost without them.

He hadn't been paying attention to where he was going, but he found himself in the rose garden. A low growl rumbled through him. This was the last place he wanted to be. The sight of a fallen rose, red as blood against the snow, barely even made him pause. It was presumably the result of his brief moment outside the estate, but it hardly mattered now.

He directed his steps toward the castle, his thoughts still swirling wildly. Felicity had gotten the dragon to lift the enchantment affecting everyone but him. So her resentment against the royal family didn't extend to wishing to see all his servants die with him. There was some comfort in that, at least.

A horrible thought flashed across his mind. Unless the purpose of lifting the concealment was only to allow the army to see their target. But no, Lord Brooker had found them before the dragon did anything, hadn't he? Justin set his face grimly. Whether it was intended or not, the action had allowed his servants to escape, and for that he was glad.

His feet carried him to his suite. His servants probably assumed he would shelter in the emptied cellars, but he had no intention of doing that. He paced up and down his suite three times before striding to the dresser with convulsive steps.

He yanked open a drawer and pulled out the mirror.

"Show me the army outside the castle," he ordered curtly. The mirror shimmered and solidified, showing a dire scene. It looked like half the garrison had come, and they were already loading the enchanted projectiles into the catapults. It was clear that they could see the castle.

"Show me the officer in charge," he specified, and the image zoomed across the snowy ground to settle on a grim-faced man with grizzled hair.

"*Well, the castle's there, right enough,*" he was saying to the soldier next to him.

"*Do you think this enchantress is still in there, sir?*" the man responded, his eyes wide as they looked ahead. *"It feels strange to attack our own castle, doesn't it?"*

The commander nodded. *"It certainly does. But unless we can draw the enchantress out somehow, I don't think we have much choice."*

"Sir!" The urgent voice made both men turn, to see a soldier approaching at a run. The man gave a smart salute, his eyes on the commander. *"Sir, I've been on a scouting patrol. My partner and I came across a peasant from a nearby village, wandering around near the castle. He claims to know something about the enchantress. Given our orders not to allow any strangers to approach the camp, the other scout stayed with the peasant, while I returned to inform you."*

The commander frowned. *"Is that so? Stay with me. Once I have seen all the catapults made ready, you can lead me to this peasant."*

Justin frowned into the mirror. Who was the peasant wandering through the snow? Did the man really know something about the real enchantress who had cursed him? Or was this all part of the misapprehension that seemed to have spread throughout the kingdom, that Felicity was the one behind the curse? An ominous feeling swept over him.

"Show me Felicity," he said, staring hungrily at the mirror as he at last allowed his thoughts to go in the direction they'd been pulling him for days.

The mirror shifted once again, and Justin froze at the sight of Felicity, her arms gripped by a dour-faced soldier in the uniform of Albury. She was speaking, her voice urgent and her eyes panicked.

"You don't understand! You have to call off the attack! The prince is still in there, and eighteen servants!"

A band Justin hadn't even realized was around his chest suddenly loosened. Whatever Felicity's part in the various enchantments, it seemed she wasn't behind the army's attack.

"*That's quite enough talk,*" said a smug voice from outside the range of the mirror.

A rush of anger passed over Justin at the way the restraining soldier shook Felicity's slim form.

"*You have to listen!*" she cried, undeterred. A familiar fire was in her eyes, and it woke an answering flame within Justin. "*Let me speak to whoever's in charge!*"

"*Oh, we'll take you to who's in charge, all right,*" said the soldier who was holding her. "*But you won't be doing any speaking.*"

Justin watched helplessly as the man whipped out a gag, tying it efficiently on a struggling Felicity. For a moment he couldn't understand their harsh treatment of her, but then Lord Ladner's overheard words flashed through his mind.

...our first course of action must be to eliminate the threat of this enchantress at the Summer Castle...wipe out the scourge of this enchantment once and for all...

Justin's breath caught in his throat as he realized what would happen if these men figured out that Felicity wasn't just another wandering peasant. He had told her himself that she'd been accused of being an enchantress, and seeking to take over the kingdom. Surely she wouldn't be foolish enough to identify herself to the army as the woman who'd been living at the castle all this time?

Justin cast his mind around, trying to think who else might be able to identify her. He knew from previous use of the mirror that Lord Brooker wasn't with the army. The idiot advisor had headed straight for the capital, either not knowing or not caring that the garrison was stationed in a different direction, south of the Summer Castle. Perhaps, if she kept her head, she wouldn't be at any great risk.

"*Or were you hoping to enchant us as well, witch?*" The malicious voice was accompanied by a tall figure, who strolled into

Justin's view with a smirk on his face. *"Your game is up—you won't be ensnaring anyone else."*

Justin's vision swam with red as he recognized the villager who had pursued Felicity to the castle. The image in the mirror wobbled as if there was a tremor, and it took Justin a moment to realize it was because his hand was shaking with fury.

The villager leaned close to Felicity's face, his whisper carrying through the mirror which was still targeted on Felicity.

"Thought you could make a fool of me, didn't you, Felicity? Well, who has the last laugh?"

A roar of pure fury burst from Justin, starting in his core and exploding out through his fanged mouth. He wasn't aware of dropping the mirror, or even of leaving the room. But the next thing he knew, he was charging for the gate, disregarding all thought of the pain that awaited him on the other side. There wasn't room for himself, only for Felicity, and the fact that she was about to be killed for something she hadn't done.

Because of course she hadn't. How could he have doubted her? He knew her, knew her heart. He pictured her face of shock when he'd told her about her mother the morning before. He'd been utterly absurd to believe, even for a moment, that she was part of a sinister plot. She had never pretended with him, never been dishonest.

He burst through the gate, his steps barely faltering as pain assailed him. His thoughts were on Felicity, and he poured his anger, his determination, even the slashing pain into a bellowing roar as he pushed himself forward. An indefinable urge tugged at him, directing his steps over the frozen ground. Without warning, like a taut bowstring suddenly released, some invisible band snapped, and the pain disappeared as suddenly as it came.

Justin didn't hesitate, his labored steps gaining strength and momentum as he surged southward.

CHAPTER TWENTY-SEVEN

Felicity

F elicity stilled for a moment at Kurt's whispered taunt. She had thought he was just being interfering, but the full reality of his vindictiveness suddenly crashed in on her. She remembered Justin's words, about the information his uncle had received, claiming that there was an enchantress trying to take over the kingdom from the Summer Castle.

The soldier who was still restraining her thought she was an enchantress, one who had attacked the crown prince, and who was plotting to seize his kingdom. The gag suddenly made sense —she had a very hazy idea about how magic worked, but she'd heard of enchantresses who could cast a spell simply with the sound of their voice, without use of their hands.

Panic washed over her. Would she be able to convince them of her innocence? Would they even give her a chance? She suddenly remembered her mission, to stop the attack on the castle. Would everyone on the estate die because of Kurt's malice?

Anger rose up within her, and she struggled furiously against the soldier's grip. Her glare drew an obnoxious chuckle from Kurt.

"Yes, I'm sure you'd like to bury me, wouldn't you?" He turned to the soldier. "She knows I'm the only one who can identify her."

"So can I, now," said the man gruffly.

Felicity struggled harder, trying to speak through her gag, to protest her innocence. The soldier narrowed his eyes.

"She's fiery, isn't she?" He cast Kurt a doubtful glance. "Do you think you can keep her here while I fetch the chief?"

Kurt's eyes lingered maliciously on Felicity's angry face. "Oh yes, I can handle her."

The soldier still seemed unconvinced. "I'll bind her, to be on the safe side."

At his direction, Kurt stepped up and seized Felicity's arms. His touch set off a blaze of defiance in her, and she struggled so fiercely that it took both men to subdue her enough for the soldier to bind her hands and feet. Then the man left at a swift jog, leaving Felicity on the ground, with the last man in the kingdom she wanted to be alone with.

"Felicity, Felicity, Felicity," Kurt drawled, shaking his head at her.

She just glowered. She had a lot of things she would like to say to him, but the gag prevented her from giving vent to her fury.

"*Are* you an enchantress?" Kurt leaned close, examining her face. "Honestly, at this point, I don't really care." A hardness entered his eyes, making him seem almost inhuman. Felicity drew back involuntarily. "Very amusing, your little performance to that oaf neighbor of yours. Making me out to be some kind of fool."

Felicity made a scoffing noise through her gag. Kurt *was* a fool, and all she'd done was tell Martha's son the bare truth. If Kurt had been humiliated, it was by the exposure of his own lies.

"Well naturally I wasn't going to leave it there," Kurt said

loftily. "I came after you, and imagine my surprise to run into
that scout back there," he jerked his head in the direction of the
departed soldier, "and discover that I wasn't the only one
looking for you." His eyes gleamed. "Apparently there's a
dangerous enchantress living in that castle, and these soldiers
have orders to kill her on sight."

His smile was ugly, marring his handsome features. "So
convenient for them that I came along, since I'm able to identify
you." He reached up and ran a finger slowly, tauntingly, down
her cheek. "I could never forget this lovely face now, could I?"

A cold rush went over Felicity, but she kept her face impassive, unwilling to let him see her fear.

"It all makes sense now," Kurt said nastily. "I should have
realized you had access to some kind of magic, the way you
ensnared everyone."

Felicity made a derisive noise, pouring every bit of her scorn
into her eyes as she glared back at him. He was pathetic. Of
course he found it easier to believe that she'd cast an enchantment over him than that she was just a regular woman who was
uninterested in his attention.

She may not have been able to speak, but Kurt clearly took
her meaning. His eyes narrowed to slits, and he stepped up to
her. Seizing her elbow, he yanked her painfully to her feet,
glaring menacingly down into her face.

"You think you can laugh at me, even now, do you? Maybe I
should save the soldiers a job, silence your magic once and for
all."

Something sharp jabbed at Felicity. She glanced down, and
her eyes widened as she realized that Kurt had produced a small
knife, and was pressing it against her side. He was angry, but
surely he wouldn't actually stab her. Would he?

She tried to pull away, but she was hampered by her bind-
ings, and Kurt held her in a painfully tight grip. If not for the

gag, she would have ground her teeth in frustration at her own powerlessness.

Before she could give in to despair, a terrifying and beautiful sound ripped across the muffled landscape. Kurt started, his grip on Felicity tightening as he turned to look for the source of the enraged, inhuman roar.

Felicity saw his eyes widen with terror, as a strangled scream died in his throat. Her eyes slid past him to see Justin, tearing toward them with impossible speed.

Tears of relief sprang to Felicity's eyes as she took in his beastly form, fury evident in every line of it.

It was the most beautiful sight she had ever seen.

The thought had barely flashed through her mind when a blinding light erupted from the ground at Justin's feet, swallowing him completely. Felicity's cry of horror was held prisoner by her gag, and her eyes were momentarily seared by the brightness. She blinked away the stars in her vision, as the light receded and Justin's limp form came into view. Felicity tried to step toward him, but her bound feet wouldn't obey, and Kurt still gripped her arm tightly.

She watched in astonishment as Justin's fur began to fall off in enormous clumps, and his whole body seemed to shrink. His claws retracted and disappeared, and the skin on his hands became clear and smooth. One final blink revealed a very attractive, very human man lying stunned in the snow, in clothes so baggy they hung off him.

Felicity's eyes felt like they would fall out of her head, and she struggled again to be free of Kurt. Her movement drew Justin's attention, and he leaped to his feet with impressive agility.

For a moment he just stood there, breathing hard as he flexed his hands in front of his face. Then his gaze snapped to hers, their silent communication overwhelming her completely.

"Who...who are you?" Kurt demanded, stunned.

Felicity wanted to roll her eyes at the stupid question. It was Justin, her Justin, obviously. She'd know him anywhere, and not just because she'd seen his portrait. Everything about him was so familiar, and so very dear.

At Kurt's words, Justin's attention had flicked to him. His gaze passed to Kurt's hand, still gripping Felicity, then to the knife in his other hand. A storm grew on his clear, handsome face. Without a word, he strode forward, only the slightest wobble betraying how unfamiliar his own legs must feel. Despite his human form, a low growl escaped him as he reached out and seized Kurt by the throat, just as he had done in the corridor of the castle.

He ripped Kurt away, and Felicity struggled to stay on her bound feet as Kurt's grip abruptly disappeared. Justin flung Kurt to the ground at his feet, pulling free the sword that hung off an absurdly loose belt. He held the tip to Kurt's throat, murder in his eyes.

"How dare you touch her?"

Kurt's face was white with terror. He tried to speak, but only a squeak came out. Justin's blade was unwavering at his neck, and Felicity felt a trickle of fear. She shifted, trying to shuffle toward the pair.

Again Justin's eyes were drawn to her, and as they rested on her face, some of the fire seemed to die out of them. He turned his gaze back to Kurt, sniveling on the ground.

"Go," he said, his voice more menacing than Felicity had ever heard it. "If you ever so much as look at Felicity again, I will run you through."

Kurt didn't need to be told twice. He pushed himself to his feet, whimpering, and threw himself away from them so clumsily he fell into the snow. He quickly righted himself, his undignified form disappearing rapidly over the nearest rise. Felicity wondered what tale he would tell in the village this time, to make himself sound heroic. She found she didn't much care.

Justin reached Felicity in two steps, slicing through the ropes around her hands, then stooping to unbind her feet. As soon as her hands were free, Felicity ripped the gag from her mouth.

"Justin!" she gasped, and he looked up, pushing himself quickly to his feet.

"Felicity," he started, sounding endearingly uncertain.

She stared at him for a frozen moment. His dark hair was long and matted, but his eyes were as piercingly blue and intense as ever. Even with the ill-fitting clothes, his posture was unconsciously proud, powerful with the strength of a well formed, well trained man. He was even more handsome than his portrait, even more captivating than the dream Justin she'd been chasing.

"Felicity," he tried again, reaching a tentative hand toward her. "I—"

Felicity wasn't quite sure what came over her. She just knew that he was going to say something foolish and apologetic, and she didn't want to waste time on such nonsense. She flung herself at him, throwing her arms around his neck—which was now within her reach—and pressing her lips to his for one glorious moment.

He froze at the contact, and she pulled back, overcome with a strange mix of humor and embarrassment. Perhaps she was becoming unhinged from the chaos of the last hour.

"I'm sorry," she said breathlessly. "I probably shouldn't do that now that you're a prince again."

"I was always a prince," Justin reminded her. His voice was still deep and rumbly, sending a thrill down her spine, and his arms were strong as they trapped her in place, refusing to let her back away. "And in no form could I ever deserve you," he added, his eyes searching hers. "But I love you. And I'm so sorry I ever doubted you."

The world seemed to spin around Felicity, but Justin's strong arms kept her upright. She could hardly breathe, and she felt like she was drowning in the intensity of his gaze.

"I love you too," she whispered, and his grip on her tightened. "When I saw you coming, I knew. I'd never seen anything so wonderful."

Justin let out a sudden, rumbling laugh. He was holding her so close that she felt the vibrations in his chest, and a thrill raced over her.

"You liked what you saw," Justin said, his eyes warm as they rested on her face.

Felicity gave a gasp as sudden realization hit. "That's all it took? That's why you kept asking me every night?"

"All?" Justin repeated dryly. "It was an impossible feat, to like what I had become." His voice softened. "Only you could manage such a thing."

"Well," said Felicity frankly, her eyes roaming over his face. "I hope it won't reignite the curse if I admit that I like this *much* better." She reached up to run a hand along the line of his brow, trailing it down his cheek.

Justin had let out another rumble of laughter at her words, but her touch on his cheek made him still completely. His gaze was suddenly more intense than she could handle, then all at once he was lowering his head, and Felicity found herself leaning in without conscious thought.

His lips claimed hers, and for a moment she lost all sense of time and place. All she was aware of was the feel of his fingers threading through her hair, the warmth of his lips on hers, and the frantic rhythm of his heart under the hand she had pressed against his chest. If she'd had any lingering doubt about his true transformation, the utter vulnerability of his declaration, along with his apology, swept it away.

She pushed herself onto her toes, far from finished with the kiss, and Justin showed no sign of wanting to pull away either.

Someone else had other ideas, unfortunately. A shout from behind Felicity made them break away from each other, both turning quickly. The soldier who had bound Felicity had returned, with what looked like a whole squadron at his back.

"Well," Felicity muttered, her breathing still uneven from the kiss. "I guess it's kind of flattering how big a threat they think I am."

She thought she saw a twitch in Justin's lips—very human lips which she could barely keep her eyes off, even now they had company—but his voice was so commanding, she must have imagined it.

"Stop. Don't come any further."

The soldier leading the group, someone senior judging by his uniform, came to an abrupt halt.

"Who are—" His eyes narrowed as he studied Justin, and he let out a sudden gasp. "Your Highness?" His gaze darted from Justin to Felicity and back again. "How—? Where did you—?"

"Yes, it's me," Justin said imperiously. "You will call off this ill advised attack against my castle immediately."

The soldier's gaze transferred to Felicity again, and the man who had bound her stepped up beside his commanding officer, speaking in an urgent—and carrying—whisper.

"Sir, that's her! That's the enchantress!"

Justin gave a low growl that caused a nervous ripple to go through the squadron. Felicity couldn't help but be impressed. Even in human form, with unkempt hair, and clad in loosely hanging clothes, Justin's presence was commanding.

"Be careful what you say," he said, fixing the unfortunate soldier with a stare.

"Sire," the commanding officer said, stepping forward bravely. "This woman is dangerous, and she has you under her spell. Our orders are—"

"I know what your orders are," Justin interrupted grimly. "And I'm giving you new orders." As he spoke, he swept Felicity behind him with one arm, drawing himself up to his full height. Felicity didn't feel even the smallest flicker of fear. This was Justin's army—Justin's kingdom. He would protect her.

"But Your Highness, she's an enchantress, and she's—"

"Felicity is not to blame for any of this," Justin cut him off. "You've been misinformed. She was caught up in the curse only a few months ago, through no fault of her own. She is not an enchantress, and she certainly wasn't the one to cast the curse on me."

"No," interjected a new voice. "I did that."

Everyone present turned in surprise, and Felicity blinked at the unexpected sight of a woman stepping out from behind the ranks of soldiers. She let out a sharp gasp as recognition hit her.

"You're the—"

"The merchant who sold you that artifact, yes," the woman said, with a tight smile. "It certainly seems to have been effective!" She tilted her head to the side in a gesture that reminded Felicity of Rekavidur. "I think I can feel it. Do you still have it?"

Before Felicity could answer, Justin stepped forward, letting go of her. "You," he growled, and Felicity saw his hand ball into a fist.

"Yes, it's me," said the woman matter-of-factly. "And you have every right to be furious with me." She bowed her head, her voice sounding ashamed. "I lost my temper, and behaved inexcusably."

Justin paused, and Felicity could see that he was taken aback by this meek response. But his expression hardened again quickly.

"An enchantress as powerful as you cannot afford to lose her temper."

"But I'm not that powerful, Your Highness," she said quickly, straightening. "I cannot explain what happened with my enchantment." She shook her head. "The magic I used shouldn't have lasted more than a few weeks, and I even enchanted the rose garden to make sure the blooms couldn't all die too soon..." Her voice trailed off, then she squared her shoulders. "I did intend to teach you a lesson, I admit it. I wanted you to have to humble yourself and admit you needed help from someone else, and to know what it was like for no one to be inclined to help you."

Justin's face was still stony. "It was a little hard for me to experience needing someone's help when I was magically prevented from communicating with anyone who could help me."

"But that wasn't part of it, Your Highness," the woman said hastily. "My enchantment affected your appearance, but I never intended for it to prevent you, or anyone else, from leaving the castle. Or to prevent others from finding you."

Justin's eyebrow was raised, his expression almost as cold as when Felicity had first met him. The sight made her uncomfortable.

"And yet it did just that," he said icily. "For two and a half years."

The woman shook her head helplessly. "I can't explain it, Your Highness. I'm simply not that powerful."

Felicity stepped forward, slipping her hand into Justin's. The gesture seemed to startle him out of himself, and he looked down at her with a slightly softened expression.

"I think she's telling the truth, Justin," she said quietly. "She didn't have to come and confess like this. And I think she sent me the artifact to help."

"That's right," said the enchantress, stepping forward eagerly. "Did it work?"

"I don't know," said Felicity. "What was it supposed to do?"

The woman made an impatient noise. "Exactly what I told you. To help you find and be found. It's an extremely powerful object, acquired from someone with much more magic than I have. Its first act was to help me find you, a person of enough worth that you could break the curse. I scoured the whole kingdom for you, my dear."

Felicity stared at her. "But you said it would help my father find his way home! And he ended up not only lost, but locked in a dungeon!"

The woman shook her head. "That may have been the purpose you wanted it for, but I certainly never said that. So you gave it to your father, did you?" She eyed Felicity with disfavor. "It was intended for you." She frowned. "It's true that it was intended specifically to reveal the castle and its inhabitants, so it would have had the same effect on your father once he reached the estate. But if it led him to the castle in the first place, he must have been looking for it."

Felicity opened her mouth to contradict, then closed it, feeling stupid. Of course it had led him to what he'd been looking for. The roses.

"It helps the bearer to find *and* to be found," she said softly. "That's why I was able to find him, wasn't it?"

The enchantress nodded wisely, but Justin wasn't as impressed.

"Why could some visitors find us and not others, then?" he challenged. "And why couldn't they see me and the servants, even though they could see Felicity?"

"Well, I don't have all the information," said the enchantress matter-of-factly. "Because I wasn't in the castle with you. But my best guess is that it was because Felicity had the artifact." She pinned her with a stare. "Did you keep it on you?"

Felicity nodded numbly. "Not at first," she said. "But once I found it, I wore it on a chain. And," she realized suddenly, "it was only after that we started getting visitors."

The enchantress gave a brisk nod. "By then the story of a damsel being held captive had spread. I suspect those visitors who were able to find the castle found it because they were looking for *you*, the holder of the artifact. If they'd been looking for the prince, the artifact would have done nothing to counteract the powerful enchantment concealing him and his castle."

Felicity looked up at Justin in amazement. "Like how Prince Bentleigh was looking for me, but the Mistran princess was looking for you." Her excitement grew. "And that's why Lord Brooker was able to see you when he came back! He must have been looking for you that time, and you had the artifact!"

"But he couldn't just see me," said Justin, his forehead creased. "He could see everyone."

"I'm not surprised," the enchantress cut in. "The rest of the castle's inhabitants didn't have a curse of their own. They were just captured in yours, so to speak. If you had the artifact on you, you would have been findable to someone searching for you. And the others caught by your curse would have been visible along with you."

Justin frowned down at Felicity. "But *you* were able to see me from the beginning, even when your father still had this." He pulled the artifact from his pocket, and a shot of warmth went through Felicity at the realization that he'd kept it on him, even when in doubt as to her trustworthiness.

"I can explain that, too," said the enchantress. "Once the artifact identified Felicity for me, I cast an enchantment of my own over her, one specifically designed to reveal the castle to her. The artifact was supposed to lead her to the estate, but she never actually needed it to be immune to the concealment enchant-ment." She gave a rueful grimace. "It took everything I had. I was basically in hibernation for the next month." She glanced appre-hensively at Justin. "But I'd been trying for two years to help you out of the mess I'd created. I wasn't going to let her slip through my fingers."

"That's the other enchantment Rekavidur could detect on me," Felicity said softly.

The enchantress looked confused. "Who?"

But Justin's mind was evidently on other things. "And the pain when I left the estate, that was what? Petty cruelty?"

"Pain?" the enchantress asked. "What do you mean? I thought you couldn't leave."

Felicity shook her head, wrapping her arm around Justin's and leaning against him sympathetically. "He could leave, but it was agonizingly painful every moment he was outside the gate."

The enchantress's eyes were wide. She almost looked impressed. "It sounds like someone's attempt to get around it," she muttered. "But that would take a great deal of power."

"Get around what?" Justin demanded.

She brought her eyes back into focus. "The ancient magic of your kingdom," she said matter-of-factly. "I was astonished when I got wind of the fact that you couldn't leave. I'd realized before then that the enchantment had been twisted somehow, but that was my first inkling of how much power it seemed to carry." She met Justin's eyes. "Your royal blood has a power of its own, you know."

Felicity couldn't help but throw Justin a smug look, and he rolled his eyes.

"The magic that ties you—Albury's rightful ruler—to your kingdom, is older, subtler, and more powerful even than dragon magic. For an enchantment to actually be able to prevent you from freely moving around your own land...I'm not sure any power could actually do that. But debilitating pain..." She grimaced. "Well, unfortunately that's a type of power some people have made careful study of."

"Why are you telling me any of this?" Justin demanded suddenly. "Why turn yourself in?"

The enchantress shook her head. "I should have turned myself in long ago. I was running scared, if I'm honest, afraid of what I'd done. I thought that by sending Felicity to break the curse, I could atone for it." She turned pleading eyes on Felicity. "But I never intended for you to get caught up in danger. When I heard the rumor that the enchantress who cursed the prince was living in his castle, plotting to take over the kingdom, and that an army was being sent to kill her, I knew I had to come forward, and fast. I couldn't let you pay for my crimes." She squared her shoulders, looking resolutely back at Justin. "I'm ready to face the consequences of what I did."

Felicity looked from the enchantress to Justin. He was looking down at her, his heart in his eyes, and she saw the moment he gave in. The enchantress had been motivated by a desire to protect Felicity, and Justin simply couldn't resist that.

"What you did was outrageous," he said sternly. As he said the words, he extricated his arm from Felicity's grip, draping it around her shoulder instead. "But I did have a lesson I needed to learn. And by sending Felicity into my life, you did more for me than you'll ever know."

His voice turned grave. "I believe you that the enchantment went beyond what you intended. I am willing to offer you a pardon. Although I must insist you accompany me to Allenton, as there is a great deal more I need to ask you."

Felicity squeezed Justin's side, more proud of him than she could say. He was not the man who had ignited the enchantress's wrath. He had grown so far beyond the cold, inhuman ruler his father had molded him to be.

Justin turned his attention to the head soldier. "Send some of your men to search the area surrounding the estate. There are eighteen people out in the weather, who—"

"Actually, Your Highness," cut in a familiar voice. "We're here."

Felicity and Justin both turned, to see Mrs. Winters standing a stone's throw away, with all the rest of the servants ranged behind her. Felicity's eyes searched the group, locking on Viola. She saw that the girl was leaning against Phillip's side, much the way Felicity had been leaning into Justin, and she raised her eyebrows. Viola grinned, tilting her head pointedly toward the prince, and the arm he still had around Felicity. Felicity sent back a smug grin of her own, and Viola's face positively beamed. Felicity shook her head at the silent exchange. Viola had been more perceptive than Felicity had given her credit for.

"May I say, Your Highness," Stewart piped up, "on behalf of my family, and all of us," he gestured behind him, "we are delighted to see you returned to your true form."

"Yes, the curse has been broken, thanks to Felicity," said Justin, with a smile. "We are all free."

Felicity was only half listening, distracted by Stewart's mention of family. He was looking back at the other servants with an uncharacteristically fond expression. Following his gaze, she let out a surprised laugh. So that was why he had seemed familiar. She never would have guessed that bubbly Viola was the daughter of the staid and serious steward. She shook her head. It just went to show that one should never be deceived by appearances.

"And I'm pleased," Mrs. Winters chipped in, "to see that you've come to your senses, Your Highness, and have stopped with all this nonsense about blaming Miss Felicity for things out of her control."

Justin looked down at Felicity, his eyes apologetic. "I am

more sorry than I can say about that," he said softly. "I lost my head, and I took it out on you, yet again." He reached up, tucking a strand of hair behind her ear. A pleasant tingle went through Felicity at the touch. "Your mother's accident was not your fault, and that tragedy had already caused you enough pain."

Felicity raised her own hand, covering his with it and trapping it against her cheek. "We both lost someone dear to us that day. But it doesn't have to pull us apart. I hope it will bring us together."

"Close together," Justin murmured, once again taking her in his arms. His eyes searched hers. "I know I'm a bit of a beast," he said, an edge of anxiety in his voice. "But you seem to be able to put up with me astonishingly well. You will marry me, won't you?"

Felicity's mind whirled at the realization that he was asking her to be queen. But locked in the beam of his intense—and achingly familiar—blue eyes, she didn't hesitate.

"Of course I will."

Justin barely waited for the words to be out before he pressed his lips down on hers again. The kiss was brief, interrupted by sudden cheers from the watching servants, but it was still enough to send a thrill all the way to Felicity's toes.

"I guess I'll finally get to go back to Allenton," she said brightly, unable to help grinning at the way Viola was dancing on the spot.

"Yes," said Justin, his voice suddenly grim. "And as soon as possible. I'm afraid there's still one knot left to untangle in this mess." He glanced down at himself. "But first I need to change into proper clothes."

"Yes," Felicity agreed, trying not to laugh as she took in his unflattering attire. "It must be uncomfortable wearing clothes that fit so badly."

"It's not that," said Justin, completely destroying her attempts to keep her mirth at bay. "It's blasted cold out here!"

CHAPTER TWENTY-EIGHT

Justin

Justin looked up at the walls of Allenton, his heart swelling. He was home at last, and in his right form. It was so surreal that he was still expecting to wake at any minute from the beautiful dream.

He glanced sideways at the woman riding stiffly on a mare, alongside his charger. Speaking of beautiful dreams...

"You should have ridden in the carriage, like I offered," he scolded, taking in her attempts to hide a wince every time the horse went over an uneven patch of road.

"Nonsense," said Felicity brightly. "I want to be up front with you, where the action is." She gazed excitedly at the enormous gate, which stood wide. "I've been wanting to return to Allenton for fourteen years, remember?"

Justin leaned over to give her hand a quick squeeze. "And now it will be your home."

Felicity sent him an unusually shy smile, and warmth roared through him. The idea of making a home and a future with Felicity was more surreal than all the rest. He knew he didn't deserve such a reward, but he fully intended to claim it anyway.

A shout went up from the guards on duty, and Justin

straightened in his saddle. It had been well worth the extra time it took to go back to the estate and change his clothes, not to mention let Stewart cut his hair. He gave an imperious wave as he passed under the portcullis, adopting his most regal posture, and setting his face in an expression of calm command.

"Wow," said Felicity, her voice impressed. "That's quite a transformation! Can you do that at will, or is it some kind of enchantment on the gates?"

Justin struggled to hold his expression steady, refusing to be baited into an undignified snort of laughter when he was being watched by so many eyes.

"It's in the royal blood," he said calmly, barely moving his lips.

Felicity narrowed her eyes at his statue-like expression. "Hm." She lowered her voice to a whisper that sent a pleasant thrill down his spine. "I'll crack you yet, Your Highness. And when you least expect it."

Justin's lips twitched despite his best efforts, and he shook his head slowly. Heaven help him, he had no doubt she was right. He glanced sideways at her cheeky grin, and couldn't keep an answering smile from spreading slowly across his face. Life with Felicity at his side was going to be unrecognizably different from his life before the curse.

But for all her jokes, Felicity was perfectly serious and appropriate when she, along with the others from the estate, followed Justin into the entranceway of his castle. A messenger had been sent on ahead, and they were greeted by a delegation of nobles, led by Lord Ladner.

"Your Highness," the nobleman said, bowing deeply. "You have returned to us. May I say how delighted I am to see you restored to your—"

"I'm sure you have a great deal you wish to say," Justin interrupted him. "As do I." He glanced around commandingly, as if he didn't know the answer to his own question. "Where is my uncle?"

Lord Ladner's expression grew dark. "Your Highness, the acting regent has been placed under arrest in his rooms. He is believed to have been exercising—"

"I want him released at once," Justin said, again cutting the nobleman off. He still wasn't sure whether Ladner was behind the foul play, but either way he had no intention of giving the man a platform in front of the sizable crowd that had now gathered. "I will hold an audience with him immediately. I expect you to be there, My Lord, as well as the three most senior members of the Enchanters' Guild."

Lord Ladner blinked at the curt command, but offered no argument. "Of course, Prince Justin," he said, bowing again. "As you wish."

Justin nodded in acknowledgment, then turned to survey the group behind him. Felicity was looking a little overwhelmed, but when he gave her the hint of a smile, she returned it. He addressed his comment to all the residents of the Summer Castle.

"I wish you all to attend as well."

"Certainly, Your Highness," said Stewart, with dignity.

Justin nodded curtly, and was about to sweep toward the audience hall when a voice rang across the space.

"Prince Justin!"

Justin turned slowly, recognizing the voice all too well. Distaste washed over him at the fawning expression on the face of the beautiful young woman. It was a stark contrast to the last time he'd seen that same face. He knew a moment of gratitude that the laws of Albury didn't allow formal betrothals before the age of sixteen, and Justin's father had been dead by then, and unable to force his son into an unpleasant marriage.

"You've come back to us," the young noblewoman simpered, her eyes roving over his very human form.

"My Lady," Justin said stonily, inclining his head. "I regret that your visit to my Summer Castle was cut short. I trust you were able to entertain yourself in some other way."

The lady's demeanor drooped slightly at his icy tone, but it didn't stop her from sashaying toward him. Ever aware of Felicity, Justin saw her shift in the corner of his eyes. Glancing at her, he almost laughed again at the uncharitable look she was casting over the other woman. Felicity's eyes suddenly slid to his, and her expression warmed when she saw that he was looking at her. The noblewoman followed his gaze, and her eyes narrowed as they fell on Felicity.

"Is that my dress?" she asked, sounding outraged.

Justin had begun walking again, and was already halfway across the entranceway, but he still heard Felicity's cheerful response.

"I don't believe so. It had been abandoned—quite heartlessly, really—and I claimed it."

Justin couldn't help glancing back, amazed and a little delighted at the hint of steel that entered Felicity's voice on the last two words. Who knew his gentle girl had claws of her own? He indulged in a momentary grin at her subtle declaration of war. If she could protect him from the unwanted attention of the noble girls, he was more than happy to let her.

His thoughts sobered again as he entered the audience hall, striding to the raised platform on one end. He was tempted to actually sit on the throne—his people needed to be reassured that they had a ruler—but he refrained. He hadn't actually been crowned yet, and it would be best to do things properly.

He had made no order for the audience to be private, and curious people were already gathering in the public gallery. It wasn't long before Uncle Cameron appeared in the doorway of the antechamber, his eyes wide. Justin fixed him with a steady look, searching his countenance for several long seconds. Then he relaxed slightly, holding out a hand. It was time for Justin to trust his instincts, and there was no mistaking the relief on the older man's face at his nephew's arrival.

Uncle Cameron hurried forward, bowing low before taking the offered hand.

"Justin," he said softly. "Thank heavens."

Justin gave a tight smile. "Thought you'd gotten stuck with the crown, didn't you?" He frowned, his gaze traveling across the room. Felicity and the Summer Castle's residents had followed him in, and were watching him unwaveringly. He could even see his spurned admirer hovering near one of the doors, looking sulky. And there was Lord Ladner, with a group of other senior noblemen, and the three prominent members of the Enchanters' Guild. Excellent.

"And speaking of the crown," Justin muttered.

He stepped to the front of the platform, and the room instantly stilled. "I am glad to be back among you all," he said in his most carrying voice. "I am aware there has been a great deal of speculation—most of it incorrect—about the circumstances of my absence. I intend to set the record straight. But first, I wish for an explanation as to the extraordinary situation I find upon my return. Not only was my acting regent under house arrest, but my own army was preparing to attack the castle where I was being held captive."

"Your Highness." Lord Ladner hurried forward, bowing again. "I can explain both of those decisions." He proceeded to give a summary of the council Justin had witnessed in the mirror. Justin noted with approval that Lord Ladner did not embellish, or exaggerate either the allegations or the proof. He was, in fact, impressively succinct.

"And where is this crown?" Justin asked evenly.

One of the guild members came forward, and Justin saw that he had a bundle in his arms. "Your Highness," he said quickly. "Here it is. We've examined it in some detail, and it has been enchanted to make the target more susceptible to influence. But the thing is..."

"Yes?" Justin prompted.

"So far it seems to be a standard type of third class enchantment," the man went on. "Which is to say, it is effective only through physical contact, meaning..."

"Meaning the acting regent was likely the target of the enchantment, not the perpetrator," Justin said grimly.

A murmuring swept the room as Justin glanced at his uncle. Uncle Cameron looked taken aback, but he met Justin's eyes squarely. "I couldn't feel anything magical about it," he said.

"You wouldn't, My Lord," said the enchanter from the guild. "Only those with magic can sense magic."

Justin nodded slowly. The artifact that Felicity had brought to the castle was an excellent example of this principle. Justin turned to his uncle again. "Where did you get the crown, Uncle?"

Uncle Cameron shrugged. "It came from the royal treasury, I believe. I didn't personally retrieve it."

Justin nodded slowly. "The steward, Dobson, brought it to you, didn't he?"

Uncle Cameron looked taken aback by his knowledge, but he confirmed it.

Justin's eyes sought Lord Ladner in the crowd. "My Lord, who was the informant who made the accusation against the acting regent?"

Lord Ladner lifted his hands helplessly. "It was anonymous, Your Highness," he said. "I must confess it tallied with my suspicions, but I wasn't sure whether it was credible until I arranged for these enchanters to examine the crown."

Justin frowned. Whoever had sent that accusation must have known it was a half-truth, convincing enough to make Uncle Cameron seem guilty, but not strong enough to withstand full scrutiny. It was almost as though they were trying to buy time. But for what?

"The message you received from Lord Brooker," he said to his uncle. "The one that prompted the attack on the Summer Castle. Can you produce it for me?"

There was a scurry of movement as a page was dispatched on this errand, and whispers broke out as the wait stretched on. Justin locked eyes with Felicity, bolstered by her smile of encouragement. He didn't like seeing her standing among the massed crowd, like just another subject. He wanted her up there beside him. But all in good time.

It wasn't the page who returned, but Dobson himself. The steward bowed to Justin as he handed over the missive. Justin spread it out, distracted for the briefest of moments by how delightfully easy it was to handle the fragile parchment with his human hands.

As he scanned the message his uncle had received, his frown grew. "This bears little resemblance to Lord Brooker's account of the message he sent to Allenton," he said curtly.

Someone had tampered with it, he had no doubt. Perhaps the same someone who had sent an anonymous message to Lord Ladner, accusing Uncle Cameron of treason? Someone who, for some inscrutable reason, wanted the court to believe that his uncle was using magic against them, and to turn on him. And who also wanted the court to believe that Justin had been killed by magic.

The kingdom had suffered enough through the enchantment that really had been cast over Justin. Why was someone trying to make it seem like more, and even worse, magic was at work when it wasn't?

He glanced up at his uncle. "How was this received?"

"Through the usual channels," Uncle Cameron said help-lessly. "Dobson always delivers such messages to me. I don't know the details of the process."

Justin's eyes narrowed as they passed to Dobson, who had stepped back into the crowd. Through the mirror, Justin had formed the impression that the man was officious and eager to put himself forward. Not at this moment, apparently.

"Dobson," he said imperiously, and the steward straight-ened. "Did this message go directly from the courier to the acting regent, without any opportunity for tampering?"

"Yes, Your Highness," Dobson said, bowing.

A cleared throat drew Justin's attention back to the three members from the Enchanters' Guild. The one enchantress of the trio was looking at him apologetically, and he gave her an encouraging nod.

"I beg your pardon, Your Highness," she said. "But part of my gift is the ability to detect when someone is lying. And that was not the unvarnished truth."

"How dare you?" protested Dobson, and Justin was surprised by the malice in his eyes. "You are all alike. You think you can use your parlor tricks in place of real evidence, to put innocent men behind bars!"

"You say it was Dobson who brought you the crown, Uncle?" Justin asked, his eyes still fixed on the steward. The man's face suddenly paled, and Justin's suspicions hardened into certainty.

"That's right," said Uncle Cameron slowly, staring at the steward. "He insisted that I should wear it, even though I'd never worn a crown before." He scowled, his voice dropping to a mutter. "And like a fool, I let him persuade me."

"Your Highness." Someone cleared her throat to one side of him, and Justin turned to see the enchantress who had cursed him. "I recognize that man. I've seen him in Myst." Justin raised an eyebrow at her mention of Mistra's capital. He'd forgotten that she came from the neighboring kingdom. She'd been pleading the case of the Mistran enchanters when she cursed him.

"There's an organization there that's always causing us trouble," she went on. "They believe magic should be outlawed everywhere, like it is in Bansford. I've seen your steward," she pointed at Dobson, "at their rallies, up the front."

At her words, Dobson's face turned ashen, and he started to edge toward the door.

"Guards," Justin said curtly. Several guards hastened forward to prevent Dobson from leaving. "Detain him in the dungeons," Justin ordered. "I believe we'll find that he has the answers to this mess." He fixed his gaze on Dobson. "I do not know why you wished to cause Albury harm, but—"

"Harm?" interrupted Dobson fiercely. "I'm trying to help Albury. I'm trying to do for our kingdom what everyone else is too blind to do. I wanted the whole kingdom to see the truth that I learned the hard way—that no one is safe if people like them," he spat the word as he glared at the enchanters from the guild, "are allowed to run wild, using their unnatural power with impunity." There was pure hatred in his eyes as he glared at the enchantress who had accused him. "They claim they can tell someone is lying just by looking at them, and who's to challenge them? My father died behind bars thanks to the likes of you, but I tell you, he was innocent!"

The enchantress looked shaken, and Justin felt taken aback himself. But none of that showed on his face as he cut across Dobson's furious words.

"That's enough," he said sharply. "You will have your chance to state your case." At a nod from Justin, the guards pulled Dobson from the room.

There was a moment of stunned silence, and Justin tried to

put the steward from his mind for the moment. He cast his eyes over the assembled crowd, allowing his stern expression to soften a little.

"I need to set some rumors straight," he said. "And I'll need some help from the woman who broke my curse at last." He held out his hand to Felicity, as rustles moved through the watchers. "Felicity," he added in a quiet voice that nevertheless carried around the room. "Soon to be my queen."

The room erupted at this matter-of-fact announcement, and Felicity blushed furiously as she made her way forward. Justin forgot all about the crowd for a moment as their eyes met. She was looking at him in the same way she had always looked at him, whether he was beast or man or prince. As if she really saw him.

When she gave him her hand, the warmth of her skin on his melted the last of the ice from his expression, and he couldn't hold in his smile. The noise in the room was deafening at this display of affection from the cold Prince Justin, but he didn't care. Felicity was at his side now, and together they could face anything.

"REALLY?" Justin couldn't keep the dry note out of his voice as he caught up to Felicity. "This is where you're spending your free time?"

She turned, her face lighting up at sight of him. "What?" she laughed, gesturing at the bare bushes around her. "This rose garden isn't enchanted."

"It's also not much to look at in winter," Justin said, glancing around at the unadorned spikes.

"I know," said Felicity. "But it grounds me, somehow." She

gave him an apologetic look. "It's all a little overwhelming, you know."

"I do know," said Justin repentantly. "And I wish I was able to support you more."

"You support me plenty." Felicity waved a dismissive hand. "You have a lot of responsibilities to catch up on."

Justin sighed in acknowledgment, grateful for how well she seemed to be managing. "Dobson has just received his sentence," he said heavily. Felicity cocked an eyebrow. "He's been exiled," Justin said. "I don't believe he's a further threat. And he named some others, which, frustrating as it is, gets him better treatment."

Felicity nodded slowly. "So it's true that he was working with that Mistran group?"

"Yes," said Justin, frowning. "And from all we can tell, they truly are against magic. The use of the crown was an anomaly—Dobson's idea, apparently, and it hasn't won him favor with the rest of them."

"So they had no hand in strengthening the curse against you?" Felicity pressed.

"None whatsoever," Justin sighed. "We still have no idea who was behind that." For a moment he was silent, mulling uneasily over the fact that he still had an unknown enemy out there, and a powerful one at that. "They were simply opportunistic," he continued at last, "seeing an opening to be exploited for their cause. Dobson was in Uncle Cameron's ear for some time, pushing him to alienate his advisors, and using the crown to influence him in the wrong direction. He was canny—he knew just how much to push, and in what areas. He always intended to use the crown as false evidence that Uncle Cameron was using magic, and to turn the people against him. We just forced his hand too soon, by breaking the curse so that I emerged once again."

"Most inconsiderate of us," said Felicity brightly, and Justin smiled. Even heavy matters of state seemed less depressing with her sunny attitude.

"The group figured that if the crown prince had been removed by a curse, and the acting regent was using magic to drive the kingdom into the ground, there would be great sympathy for a proposal to outlaw magic altogether."

Felicity frowned. "But why did a Mistran group care whether Albury outlaws magic?"

"Oh, they've been working for the same end in their kingdom, of course," Justin said. He scowled. "No one's said as much, but I suspect that some among the Mistrans were scheming about what might happen to Albury if I never reappeared. I think these players must have been behind Princess Wren's visit in search of me."

Felicity raised her eyebrows. "So their preference was for you not to reappear, but if you did, they hoped to marry Princess Wren off to you and...what? Merge the kingdoms?"

Justin shrugged. "Who knew what they deluded themselves into thinking? But it certainly didn't serve their purposes for me to emerge, especially if I was unscathed by the curse. Dobson not only intercepted and rewrote Lord Brooker's message to my uncle about what he'd found at the Summer Castle, he also sent the anonymous warning to Lord Ladner."

"So Lord Ladner acted in good faith," Felicity said. A flash of anger crossed her face. "But Dobson and the others were willing to kill you to prevent you from ruining their plans."

Justin sighed. "I don't think they particularly wanted my blood on their hands. They were just happy for me to be killed by magic, so everyone could see its danger. As you heard when he was arrested, Dobson had more personal reasons to turn the kingdom against magic. His father was accused of treason, and sent to prison, back before I was ever born. Apparently some of the evidence against him came from an enchanter asserting that he was lying."

"Do you think he was actually innocent?" Felicity pressed.

Justin shrugged. "Who can say now?" He grimaced. "I'm afraid it's entirely possible that my father didn't give him a just hearing if he thought the man was his enemy. But if he sent someone to prison unfairly, you can be sure he was the one pulling the strings, not an enchanter. Dobson's bitterness is directed at the wrong target."

"Your Highness?" The voice made Justin sigh, but he tried not to show his frustration as he turned toward the approaching page.

"Yes, here. I'm needed?"

"Well, Your Highness, I was told you wished to be informed immediately if..."

Justin shifted, revealing Felicity behind him, and the page faltered. Justin's frown of confusion gave way as he realized the order the page boy was referring to. He looked between the messenger and Felicity.

"Felicity's father?" he asked quietly, and the page nodded.

"And her brother, Sire."

Felicity gasped sharply. "Father and Ambrose are here?"

Her eyes met Justin's for one heart wrenching moment, then she took off running. Pushing his grim thoughts down, Justin hurried after her.

The pair were waiting in the entranceway, and their evident fear softened Justin in spite of himself. He suddenly remembered that Felicity's father had been told never to return if he wished for his family to live.

"Felicity," gasped the man, as soon as she came into sight. Felicity's brother took a compulsive step toward her, but his eyes flicked to Justin, and he fell back, swallowing.

"Father!" Felicity cried. "Ambrose!" There were tears

standing in her eyes, but she didn't throw herself on the two men, as Justin had expected. She hung back, waiting for them to speak first.

"Felicity," her father tried again, his voice choked. "You're alive. And you're..." His gaze shifted to Justin, and he trailed off, apparently unable to say the words "betrothed to the king". He drew a shaky breath. "I thought you were lost forever when the castle disappeared. I thought you were..."

"I'm sorry, Fliss." Ambrose cut through his father's struggles. "We should never have left without you."

Felicity swallowed audibly. "Why didn't you try to find me?" she asked, her voice small.

"We did try!" Ambrose said hurriedly. "After you left, I was ashamed that I'd been too cowardly to even look for Father when he disappeared. I just ran for home like a frightened rabbit." He met her eyes miserably. "Then Father came home, and told me what had happened..." There was a pleading note to his voice. "I won't deny I was still afraid, but I insisted we go back to look for you. But there was nothing. No castle, no beast, no you."

Felicity glanced at Justin, and he frowned down at her in confusion.

"The artifact must still have been in the dungeons," she said softly. "I didn't have it on me yet."

Ambrose was still speaking in an unsteady voice, oblivious to their quiet conversation. "Then Father told me the truth about what happened when Mother died..." He cast a fearful glance at Justin. "And, well, I thought he was right that there was no hope for you."

"I'm sorry as well," said Gustav softly, a pained look in his eyes. "Your mother was the strong one, not me, but I've been making excuses for too many years." He drew a deep breath. "I hope you can forgive me for leaving you behind."

Justin felt a flicker of unexpected sympathy for the old man. His admission of weakness reminded Justin of his own parents. His father had disdained his mother for not being strong enough to survive the loss of her daughter. Justin had never blamed her for it—was it unfair of him to blame Felicity's father?

He looked at Felicity, whose tears were starting to well over. He didn't have a moment of doubt as to the outcome. Her heart was far too warm to stay closed.

"Of course I forgive you," she choked out, throwing herself forward and embracing them both in turn. "I've been so worried about you, and I had no way to tell you I was all right. But everything is going to be fine now." She leaned back against Justin, swiping her eyes with a sleeve. He instinctively put an arm around her, although his eyes were still on Gustav.

"Were you truly in Fernedell?" Felicity asked. "Did you come back because you heard what had happened here? News must have traveled quickly."

"Yes, we were in Fernedell," Ambrose answered. "And it certainly did travel quickly." He exchanged a look with his father, and Justin raised an eyebrow at their dazed expressions.

"What is it?" Felicity asked.

"Well, I can hardly believe it myself," said Ambrose. "But we heard the news from a dragon. An actual dragon, Fliss!"

Felicity gasped. "Rekavidur!"

Her father nodded eagerly. "Yes, that was his name. An incredible beast."

"He said he'd been looking for us," Ambrose cut in. "He sort of smelled us!"

Felicity gave an incredulous laugh. "He must be able to recognize you as my kin." She shook her head wonderingly. "I did tell him about our situation, but I had no idea he was going to do that."

She shot Justin a look of delight, and he smiled tightly. This Rekavidur was certainly a different kind of dragon from anything he'd encountered before. He wasn't entirely sure what they were dealing with, and that made him uneasy. He still had a lingering fear that the dragons would bear some ill will toward Albury for benefiting from this dragon's intervention. Every royal in Solstice understood how dangerous it would be to ask the dragons for help with magical issues. It went against the unwritten code that had allowed dragons and humans to coexist peacefully for centuries.

Not that Justin had asked for help, of course. But would the other dragons see it that way? Rekavidur's actions were certainly in contravention of the agreement, and Justin had been the one to benefit. And even though Felicity hadn't been of any importance to the dragons when she met Rekavidur, she was about to be queen. Her actions—arising from well-meaning ignorance—could well have unintended consequences. But he couldn't bring himself to dampen Felicity's happiness with such ominous reflections.

"I'm so glad you're here," Felicity was saying, her expression radiant. "You'll have to stay in Allenton, of course."

Ambrose brightened at her words. "I'm glad, because I don't really want to go back to the village. Did you know that several others from the village are here? We ran into them on our way to the castle. They've come to be nosy of course. No one can quite believe you're going to be queen."

Justin didn't miss the shadow that passed over Felicity's face. "Anyone I know?"

"You mean Kurt?" Ambrose asked frankly.

Justin stiffened in anger at mention of the repulsive villager. Surely he wouldn't dare to show his face in the capital?

"That's another thing I should apologize for, isn't it?" Ambrose continued, shamefaced. "But I don't think you need to worry about him following you here. I have no idea why, but from what the others said, it sounds like he's changed. Apparently he's a bit of a wreck, barely leaves his house."

Justin felt a stab of vicious satisfaction. Part of him would always want the man's blood, but he knew he should rise above the gruesome desire. He would have to be satisfied with the villager's humiliation.

Gustav didn't seem especially interested in discussion of Kurt. "It's a kind thought, Felicity," he said, his apprehensive gaze on Justin, "but I'm not sure it will work for us to live in Allenton."

Felicity, clearly picking up on his uncertainty, hastened to reassure him.

"You don't have anything to fear from Justin, Father." She turned to him. "Do they, Justin?"

Justin didn't answer at once, weighing the older man with his eyes. "My father was wrong to banish you," he said at last, his voice even. "What happened was not your fault, and you should not have been punished for it. I don't hold my sister's death against you." His voice hardened. "What I do find hard to forgive is your failure to perform the most basic role of a father and protect your daughter from the dangers around her."

Gustav looked stricken, making no attempt to deny it. Justin saw that Felicity was watching him with a myriad of emotions in her eyes, and he let out a long breath.

"But I realize the irony of me saying that, when *I* was one of the chief dangers you failed to protect her from. And I also realize that what happened between you before I met Felicity is none of my business. If she can forgive you, I could have no good reason not to." He felt Felicity slip her hand into his, and returned the pressure. "But I want you to know that Felicity's well-being *is* my business now. I will do whatever it takes to protect her."

Looking into Gustav's eyes, he saw the pain of a man who knew his own failures. Justin was all too familiar with the feeling, and he judged that he'd said enough. Knowing that he had allowed his fear to leave his daughter vulnerable must be bitter punishment in itself.

"Well, I'm planning to stay out of trouble from now on," Felicity chipped in, clearly trying to lift the mood. "So you might all be out of a job."

Justin relaxed, letting the tension drain out of him as he turned to her with a wry smile. "Why do I find that hard to believe? If it's not artifacts and enchantments, it's dragons and armies with you." He shook his head. "You think adding a crown will make your life *less* troublesome?"

Gustav and Ambrose looked a little taken aback at their banter, but Felicity laughed merrily.

"Well, you wouldn't want things to get too boring, Justin. You might be at risk of turning back into an icicle." She grinned. "I promise to keep your life interesting, at least."

Justin groaned, although the twinkle in Felicity's eyes told him she wasn't fooled. "My fate is sealed," he said solemnly. "Because we all know you never break your word."

Felicity

F elicity sat bolt upright with a gasp, a book falling heavily from her lap.

"What is it?" Justin's muffled protest suggested that he, too, had become drowsy in the warmth of the fire that burned in the royal library's massive fireplace. She didn't blame him. It turned out that royal life was exhausting with its endless demands. Most days she began to feel sleepy before the sun had even set.

So, naturally, Felicity had made no comment when, at least half an hour before, Justin had abandoned all pretense of reading his reports. It had been around the time when Felicity had finally given in to the relentless tug of gravity, and had lain down across the settle, with her head on his lap. With his hand absently running through her hair, it was no wonder she'd started to drift.

She turned to him now, excitement cutting through her sleepiness. "Prince Bentleigh! Why didn't I think of it before?"

Justin raised an eyebrow. "I don't know, but it's a little late to think of it now," he said, with an endearing mix of humor and anxiety. "You're supposed to be marrying me and being crowned queen in three days, in case you've forgotten."

Felicity chuckled. "Oh dear."

That got Justin's attention, and he sat up straight at last, looking faintly alarmed.

Felicity grinned. "I'm teasing you," she reassured him. She sighed. "I mean, I'm a little terrified about being queen, it's true. But," she leaned in to give him a quick peck on the cheek, "marrying you I could never forget, or regret."

Justin glanced quickly around the quiet library before trapping Felicity in his arms, pulling her in for a more substantial kiss.

Felicity broke it off, chuckling. "Did I just hear Stewart's signature throat clearing, or is it my guilty conscience?"

Justin scowled pointlessly at the absent steward. "Why is he still in Allenton? I thought I sent him back to the Summer Castle weeks ago."

Felicity nestled against him, letting out a contented sigh. "Officially, he's finishing the interviews for extra staff at the Summer Castle, since we declared our intention to spend time there every year. Unofficially, though, I think he just wants to see Viola properly settled in here." She smiled fondly. "He would never admit it, but he's bursting with pride at his daughter being appointed lady's maid to the future queen."

She sat up, shaking her head in bemusement. "Speaking of Viola, I asked her the other day why they didn't just tell me what was needed to break the curse. I could have tried harder much earlier. But she said that was exactly what they were afraid of. Apparently, I was too nice."

Justin must have caught the note of outrage in her voice, because he smiled sympathetically as he tucked a strand of copper hair behind her ear. "What an insult," he said gravely.

Felicity chuckled reluctantly. "I know they didn't mean it as an insult. But still...apparently they all agreed not to tell me what I would have to do to help break the curse. They were sure I would fake it out of a desire to help them, and it would confuse the issue. They thought that if I forced it when it wasn't sincere, it might be impossible for it to grow naturally."

"Maybe they were right," said Justin, shrugging. He fixed her with a look. "Now. Why are you talking about marrying Bentleigh?"

Felicity couldn't help the giggle that escaped. "You're doing your beast scowl," she informed him, smoothing his brow with a finger. "And I wasn't talking about marrying Prince Bentleigh. I was talking about helping him marry Princess Azalea. Or at least, wake her up, which is a necessary first step, don't you think?"

"How can we do that?" Justin asked, relaxing visibly.

"Well, it's just a theory," said Felicity, warming to her theme. "But I wondered if Rekavidur could help."

"The dragon?" Justin asked, sitting up straight.

Felicity nodded eagerly. "I know the curse over Listernia is much bigger than our curse was, but it's surely worth him taking a look."

Justin didn't answer immediately, and Felicity wondered what was behind his hesitant expression. "Felicity," he said at last, "dragons don't usually help humans with...magical problems. In fact, they *never* do. It's an unwritten agreement between our kinds that dragons don't use magic against humans, or humans against dragons."

"That seems foolish," said Felicity. "They're so much more powerful than enchanters—surely it's easy for them to help."

Justin shrugged. "And equally easy for them to do us harm. Personally, I'm grateful that they keep their end of the agreement. Not having their assistance is a small price to pay for knowing they won't use their magic to attack us." His expression became more serious. "It would be a great offense for a royal to ask the dragons for help. And every royal in Solstice knows better than to offend the dragons. They could wipe us all out in a heartbeat if they chose."

"But they would never do that," said Felicity, thinking this over, "would they?"

Justin's expression was still solemn. "Let's hope not, since there would be little we could do to defend against it." He sighed. "I imagine you wouldn't know much about the history of the dragons, but it's a standard part of the education of a royal. Do you know that they came to Solstice centuries ago, and that our ancestors were already living here?"

Felicity nodded. "We spoke about it once, remember? About how there were no enchanters before dragons came and started shedding magic all over the land, to be unconsciously picked up by those few humans who have that aptitude."

"That's right," said Justin gravely. "What you may not know is that relations weren't always as smooth between humans and dragons as they are now. At least," he shrugged one shoulder, "that's the story. It's so long ago that the true details aren't really known."

Felicity could feel how wide her eyes were. "You mean they were aggressive at first?"

Justin shook his head. "On the contrary. They must have been friendly enough. Because the basic story is that before humans had any magic of their own, they used to pester the dragons for magical aid. So much so that they became a nuisance, and some of the dragons began to think better of the idea of peacefully coexisting with the human population."

"You mean they were going to leave?" Felicity pressed.

Justin gave her an expressive look. "That would be one solution. Another—probably easier for the dragons than seeking a new land to start fresh—would be to simply wipe us out and claim the continent."

"But they couldn't!" Felicity gasped.

"Actually, they could," said Justin ruefully. "Quite easily. And I don't know if it was just my tutor trying to scare me, but he would certainly have me believe some would've liked to. Fortunately for us, most of them seem to have disagreed, because that's not what happened."

"What did happen?" Felicity asked impatiently.

"An agreement was reached," said Justin calmly. "A basic principle of human dragon relations. We don't use magic for or against them, and they don't use magic for or against us. The thing is, by the time tensions had risen to breaking point, magic had begun to appear in humans. We had our own access to magical aid, even if it was nothing like as powerful as the dragons' magic."

"I suppose the reciprocation was just for our dignity," said Felicity. "They surely weren't actually worried about us using magic against them."

Justin looked thoughtful. "I don't know. Dragons are wise, and have long memories and long foresight. They couldn't have known—still can't know—how powerful human magic might grow to be."

Felicity was silent for a long moment. "Well," she said at last. "I understand now why you weren't exactly excited about Rekavidur's involvement. But he helped so readily. He was probably as ignorant of this agreement between the dragon colony and the royal families as I was. Surely they can't be offended with us that he helped."

Justin shrugged. "Maybe. But I doubt the royal family of either Listernia or Bansford would be willing to take that chance." He met her eyes frankly. "I doubt I would have been willing to risk it if you hadn't taken the decision out of my hands."

Felicity frowned. "I'd apologize, but..."

"No, don't," Justin said quickly. "I'm not sorry for what happened, not with the way it all turned out. But that doesn't mean I'd recommend it to Bentleigh."

"Well, I still think he should be given the option," Felicity said stubbornly.

Justin raised an eyebrow. "Do you know how to contact the dragon?"

"No," Felicity admitted, deflating. "I haven't seen him since we split up, when he went to tell you all the castle was unsealed, and I went to try to stop the army."

Justin's arm tightened around her, and his voice dropped to the rumbling growl she secretly loved. "Have I mentioned how very dangerous that was?"

"Several times," said Felicity cheerfully. She shot him a cheeky look. "And since I know you would *never* risk your own safety for my sake, I take your scolding very seriously."

Justin grunted, unimpressed, but she knew he wasn't really annoyed with her. He struggled to stay cross with her for five minutes at a time, a situation she found extremely humorous when she thought of how grumpy he'd been when she first met him.

"What are you thinking about?" he asked softly.

Felicity smiled. "You. The way you were when we met, the way you are now." She laid her hand over his, lacing their fingers. "The wonderful king I know you'll be."

Justin's blue eyes blazed with intensity as he met her gaze. "From the moment we met, you always seemed to see me," he said.

"Even under all that fur, you mean?" Felicity asked, unable to help herself.

He gave her a look. "I'm trying to be sentimental."

"Sorry," Felicity said demurely. "Please continue."

Justin watched her for a moment, a slight curve to his lips. "I never learned how to laugh at myself, you know. I don't think I ever would have learned, if you hadn't come along and mercilessly laughed for me."

Felicity chuckled. "It was a little heartless," she acknowledged. "But I couldn't help myself."

"Thankfully," Justin said, as he turned his hand under hers so their palms were touching. He tightened his clasp. "My point is, I had been turning into a beast long before I ever met that enchantress. I'll be forever grateful that you could somehow see something of worth beneath all that mess."

Felicity lifted her free hand, running the backs of her fingers along the strong line of his jaw. "I see you, Justin," she said softly.

He closed his eyes momentarily at her touch, and she tried to imagine how it would feel to be back in a human body after two and a half years of beastliness. When his eyes sprang open, a spark of humor showed in their blue depths.

"And do you like what you see?"

Felicity let out an un-queenly snort of laughter. "Yes, Justin," she said innocently. "I like it very much."

NOTE FROM THE AUTHOR

Thank you for reading *Kingdom of Beauty*. I hope you enjoyed this first venture into the continent of Solstice! I would be so grateful if you would consider leaving a review on Amazon—it would really make a difference!

Join up to my mailing list at deborahgracewhite.com to receive an exclusive bonus chapter for *Kingdom of Beauty*. In addition to being kept up to date on new releases, specials, and giveaways, you will also receive some great freebies, including *An Expectation of Magic*, a novella which is a prequel to my YA fantasy series *The Vazula Chronicles* (and which features the dragon Rekavidur).

Plus, you'll receive *Dragon's Sight*, an 8,000 word prequel to *The Kyona Chronicles*, told from the perspective of the dragon Elddreki (Rekavidur's father).

If you want to get lost in Bentleigh and Azalea's story, check out *Kingdom of Slumber*, the next installment of the series. As always, more adventure, fantasy, mystery, and romance await.

For more, if you want to discover the unknown land across the ocean, and follow the story of Rekavidur's ancestors, check out the completed series of *The Kyona Chronicles*. Grab your copy of the first book, *Heir of the Curse*, today!

Again, thanks for entering the world of *The Kingdom Tales*! I hope to see you back again.

ALSO BY DEBORAH GRACE WHITE

The Kyona Chronicles: YA Fantasy

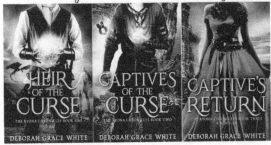

The Kyona Legacy: YA Fantasy

The Vazula Chronicles: YA Fantasy

The Kingdom Tales: Fairy Tale Retellings

The Singer Tales: Fairy Tale Retellings
(releasing throughout 2023)

ACKNOWLEDGMENTS

Like so many fairy tale lovers, I first discovered the delightful world of retellings as a young girl, when I read *Ella Enchanted* by Gail Carson Levine. It was funny, it was sweet, it was clever. I was lost in a heartbeat.

In more recent years, I've enjoyed many of the fairy tale retellings being released by indie authors, and I'm not sure why it took me so long to start writing my own. I thought it would be fun, and boy was I right! I had a blast writing *Kingdom of Beauty*.

An even more heartfelt thanks than usual must go to my husband Ray, who has been truly heroic in entering into a genre not entirely up his alley. Ray, you're the best. Your dedication is inspirational, and your feedback was fantastic.

A huge thank you also to my beta readers: Tamara, Andrew, Mel W, Mum, Dad, and Steph. Your feedback has been encouraging and has made the story much better.

Extra thanks to Dad for very on-point developmental and copy editing, and assistance with publication and release.

Karri, I still can hardly believe we got this cover on the very first try, but how do you improve on perfection? And Becca, you once again nailed it with the beautiful map.

To you, the reader, thank you for giving me the privilege of being an author.

And most importantly, to God, who is the source of beauty, and who is never deceived by what's on the outside.

ABOUT THE AUTHOR

I've been a reader since I can remember, growing up on a wide range of books, from classic literature to light-hearted romps. The love of reading has traveled with me unchanged across multiple continents, and carried me from my own childhood all the way to having children of my own.

But if reading is like looking through a window into a magical and beautiful world, beginning to write my own stories was like discovering that I could open that window and climb right out into fantasyland.

I cannot believe how privileged I am to actually be living that childhood dream and publishing my own novels. I do so from my hometown of Adelaide, Australia, where I live with my husband and our three little ones.

I've never outgrown my love of young adult stories, so the genre of young adult fantasy was always going to be my niche. Feel free to email me at deborah@deborahgracewhite.com and introduce yourself! Or subscribe to my mailing list at deborahgracewhite.com for free giveaways, sales, and updates.

Made in the USA
Monee, IL
15 October 2023

44641667R00215